THE
DUKE'S
RULES OF
ENGAGEMENT

USA TODAY BESTSELLING AUTHOR
JENNIFER HAYMORE

Entangled Publishing, LLC
644 Shrewsbury Commons Ave., STE 181
Shrewsbury, PA 17361
Visit our website at www.entangledpublishing.com.

Amara is an imprint of Entangled Publishing, LLC.

Edited by Heather Howland
Cover art and design by Bree Archer
Author font design by Elizabeth Turner Stokes
Cover images by VJ Dunraven/PeriodImages and
FairytaleDesign/Depositphotos
Interior design by Toni Kerr

Print ISBN 978-1-64937-275-8
ebook ISBN 978-1-64937-291-8

Manufactured in the United States of America

First Edition October 2022

AMARA

THE
DUKE'S
RULES OF
ENGAGEMENT

For Lawrence

CHAPTER ONE

SPRING 1817

Joanna Porter *loved* love.

She believed in love. In the air rushing from a person's lungs when they laid eyes on their beloved. In how lovers' hearts pounded in unison when they felt each other's touch. In the way two souls could come together to create something unique, brand-new, and absolutely complete.

Jo dedicated herself to ensuring her clients were not only happy, but floating on that cloud of bliss. She made people believe in everlasting love. After her work with them, they became romantics, poets, lovers.

And she adored every second of it.

Of course, as a spinster firmly tucked high upon the shelf, *she'd* never experienced any of those things. Nor, most likely, would she ever. But her faith in happily ever afters was renewed again and again by the happy couples who walked out of her office.

Jo's newest client, Flavio Pellegrini, grinned widely, his hand clapped to his chest as he gushed, "You are a genius, Mrs. Porter! An absolute genius! You travel straight to the heart of the matter."

"I try to," she told him as the heat of a flush crept over her cheeks. "Finding a perfect match does involve one's heart, after all, not only one's attractive physical characteristics—"

"Quite true, quite true!"

Smiling, she looked down at the pages strewn across her desk, each of them covered with writing—his answers to her in-depth questions. He'd been effusive, long-winded, and thorough, which had given her an excellent mental picture of the woman who would be his perfect bride.

She couldn't wait to find him his match.

"I think those are all the questions I have for you today, Mr. Pellegrini. I shall compose a list of potentials for you in the next few days. Shall we meet again on, say, Tuesday?"

"Brilliant!" he said. "I cannot wait to lay my eyes on the name of my future bride."

She showed him out of her tiny office, then hurried upstairs a few minutes late.

"Sorry, sorry!" she exclaimed to the small group of ladies assembled in the parlor. "Did I miss anything?"

"Of course not," her dearest friend, Lillian Appleby, said. "We were waiting for you."

"Thank you, but you didn't have to wait." Lowering herself beside her mother, Jo poured some tea from the fancy china teapot Mrs. Ferguson had brought out for the occasion. Sitting on the sofa across from Jo and Mama, Mrs. Ferguson was a petite woman with gray-streaked auburn hair and boundless energy. She poured love into everything she did, and over the years, she'd become far more than a servant to Jo and her mother.

As Jo stirred some milk into her tea, Mrs. Ferguson patted the hand of the petite, pink-cheeked and freckled young woman who sat beside her. "I cannot believe you are twenty, Bessie. My dear little lass—all grown up."

"That's how I have felt each and every day since Jo turned twenty," Mama said. "It all happened so quickly. It is as if I woke up one day and my sweet little girl turned into a lovely young woman." Her smile was radiant.

Her mother was being very kind—or blind—because "lovely" wasn't a word people used to describe Jo. She wasn't pretty like her mother. She was tall and thick-boned rather than petite, gray-eyed rather than blue, curvy rather than slight, her hair neither blond nor brown, and skin that instantly tanned golden brown in the sun.

"I turned twenty ages ago, Mama," Jo reminded her. Seven years ago, in fact.

"Yet it feels like yesterday." Mama turned her smile on Lilly. "And I watched our dear Lilly become a woman, too, and now she is about to become a lovely bride."

Lilly had lived with Jo and her mother since they'd moved to London from Nottingham, after Jo's father's sudden and tragic death. They had lived here for nearly nine years now, subsisting for the past handful of those years solely on the income Jo made from her matchmaking.

Lilly *would* be a lovely bride, Jo thought. She was willowy and radiant, with silky black hair and long, dark lashes over changeable hazel eyes. But what would really make her lovely was how happy she would be to proclaim her devotion to her beau, Charles Cherrington.

Lilly clasped her hands under her chin. "I cannot

wait to become a bride."

Hopefully Mr. Cherrington would propose soon. He'd been courting Lilly for half a year now, and they had all but promised themselves to each other. All that was missing was a formal agreement.

All five women sipped their tea in silence, and Jo was certain all of them were conjuring the same image she was: Lilly looking lovely at the altar, Mr. Cherrington standing beside her as they repeated their vows, love shining on both their faces. It was going to be perfect.

Lilly set down her tea. "Back to your special day, Bess." She bent down and tugged out a bulky package wrapped in tissue paper and a red ribbon from beneath her chair. She handed it to the younger woman. "A little something Jo and I made for you to celebrate this happy occasion."

"Happy birthday, dear Bess," Jo said. It was generous for Lilly to say Jo had a hand in making the gift, since it had mostly been Lilly who'd secretly labored on the embroidery while Jo had been downstairs working in her office. Though, Jo supposed, her income was what had paid for the fabric and thread.

Bess untied the ribbon and tore open the paper. "Oh!" she breathed, gazing down at the identical green silk pillows embroidered with bursts of yellow daisies.

"Do you like them?" Lilly asked.

Bess clutched one to her chest. "I love them. Thank you so much."

They all drank their tea and munched on the poppyseed cakes Mrs. Ferguson had made, while

Bess stroked her fingertips over the pillows. They were bright and sunny, a perfect match to Bess's cheerful disposition.

Then Mama said, "Jo, dear, tell us about your new client."

"Mr. Pellegrini is wonderful," Jo said. "I can't wait to find him his match."

"What is he like?" Bess asked, dabbing her lips with her napkin.

"He's very pleasant—like a bottle of champagne that has just been uncorked," she said with a grin. "Exuberant and bubbly."

He'd easily charm his potential brides, but she'd need to find someone to balance him, Jo thought, to ground him when he started to lose his footing. Names began filtering through her mind, but a knock on the door jolted her from her thoughts.

Mrs. Ferguson popped up and went to see who it was. A moment later, she returned, bearing a letter. "For you, Miss Lilly."

"It must be from Charles," Lilly murmured. She rose, her smile beatific, and took it from the older woman before unfolding it and beginning to read. As she did so, her face changed. The smile slipped away, and her lips turned downward. Her shoulders hunched, her breaths began to come out in short gasps, and tears filled her eyes.

"What is it, dear?" Mama asked.

Lilly looked up, blinking around the room as if she was surprised at where she was, that other people surrounded her.

"I—" Lilly gasped. "Please...excuse me." She spun around and rushed from the room.

Jo, Bess, Mama, and Mrs. Ferguson looked at one another, stunned, then Jo put her cup down and stood. "I'll talk to her."

Mrs. Ferguson rose, too. "I believe it is time we switch to a pot of my cheer-me-up tea." Mrs. Ferguson's special tea was heavily milked and contained a "secret" ingredient all the women in their household pretended not to recognize. They all knew what the ingredient was, though—a healthy splash of spiced rum.

As the older woman headed to the kitchen, Jo hurried up the narrow stairs and was just stepping onto the landing when Lilly slammed the door to her bedroom. Jo stopped outside it. "Lil, may I come in?"

No answer. Just the sound of muffled sobs.

Jo sighed. "I'm coming in."

She pushed into the room, where Lilly lay curled on her bed with her knees tucked into her chest.

Jo rushed forward. "What happened?" Kicking off her shoes, she climbed onto the bed and lay facing her friend.

Lilly squeezed her eyes shut. She reached toward Jo with a closed fist and opened her fingers. The crumpled letter dropped onto the counterpane between them.

Jo took a moment to unfold the tightly wrinkled-up ball, and then she read.

Lilly, My Dearest,
This is my eighth attempt to pen this, each attempt more painful, my pen growing heavier until I doubt my ability to heft it if I am forced to try one more time.

How to say what I must? How to say it without breaking us, destroying us both?

But I must say it. I must, as much as I would choose any other path offered to me. But there is none, no other path but one, and this is how it must be.

I shall not call upon you anymore. I will see you in town, certainly, and I do hope that we shall maintain a friendship, of sorts, but I must terminate our courtship at once.

Forgive me, ~~my love~~. I would shower reasons upon you, but there is no point. Reasons, as powerful as they might be, will do naught to sew the pieces of our broken hearts back together.

Suffice it to say, I must marry another. Though whether I shall be able to offer the broken shards of my heart to that other lady remains doubtful. No, not doubtful. Impossible. *There will never, in my life, be a love as pure as the one I have experienced with you.*

My sincerest affection will remain with you. Always.

-C

By the time she finished the letter, Jo's heartbeat was a dull thud against her chest. She couldn't believe it. Charles Cherrington had been utterly devoted to Lilly. What on earth could have caused him to withdraw his affection like this?

Dropping the letter slowly, she gazed at her friend. Poor Lilly's eyes were still squeezed shut, but tears were finding their way through, dampening her lashes in clumps against her cheeks, and sobs wracked her body.

"Oh, Lilly." Jo drew her friend close. "Shh," she murmured into Lilly's silky hair as she rocked her. "Hush now…"

They remained there for a long while as Lilly spent her tears, but all the while, Jo's mind churned. *Why?* How could Charles Cherrington do this to Lilly? To himself?

She needed to talk to him. Trap him alone somewhere, drag the truth from him, and discover a way—any way—she could change his mind and save Lilly from experiencing this kind of pain.

"What am I going to do?" Lilly sobbed in her arms. "I cannot go on, Jo."

"Of course you can," she murmured soothingly.

"I cannot. I cannot live without him."

"I know it feels that way right now, but you can, Lil. You will."

But she wouldn't have to if Jo had anything to say about it. She had absolutely no inkling as to what she could possibly do, but she did know how happy Lilly had been with Mr. Cherrington. How deep her feelings ran for the man. How excited she'd been about their future together.

And it had all been shattered in the few lines of a letter. What a cad.

Jo closed her eyes, her mind whirling. How could she find him? How could she manage to speak with him alone?

And then, all of a sudden, she knew. She opened her eyes and gritted her teeth, determination tightening her arms around her sweet friend.

Next Thursday, at Mr. and Mrs. Dickerson's soiree.

CHAPTER TWO

The days leading up to the soiree progressed as if Jo were pushing through a vat of honey, slow and sticky. Lilly kept to her room, the rest of them heard her weeping into her pillow late at night, and all of them were heartbroken for her.

Jo just wanted to pin Charles Cherrington down, understand what had made him write that awful letter, and mend it. She was a matchmaker. Surely there was something she'd be able to do.

After sharing her list of potential brides with Mr. Pellegrini on Tuesday afternoon, Jo sat at her desk rubbing her fingertip over the names "Mr. and Mrs. Jeffery Worthington." She tucked her thumb under the seal of the letter she'd just received from them and broke it open.

Dear Miss Porter,
Words cannot describe how ecstatic we are, now that we have wrapped ourselves fully within the heavenly bonds of matrimony. We have just spent a most *exquisite honeymoon on the delightful banks of Lake Windermere, and it was the most wonderful and joyous month of our lives. All of this is due to you, dear, kind Miss Porter, and we will never be able to thank you enough for bringing us together and ensuring our lifelong happi—*

Jo's attention snapped up as a sharp knock

sounded on the door. *Who on earth?* She hadn't scheduled any more appointments today. Rising, she smoothed her skirts, crossed her tiny office, and opened the door. A man stood on the threshold, his impressive height made more pronounced by a tall hat.

She looked up…and then up some more. Past the elegant black-gloved fingers wrapped around the glossy knob at the top of his walking stick, the deep blue tailored coat of the finest wool, a row of five cloth-covered buttons, broad shoulders, the crisp white of a cravat under the points of a starched collar. The clean-shaven, strong chin and square jaw, the slope of a proud nose bisecting chiseled cheekbones. Her gaze finally came to a stop at the narrowed, light brown eyes that gazed coolly down upon her.

Not just a man. A gentleman of the aristocracy who not only dressed in the height of fashion but whose clothes fit his form so cleanly, she was fairly certain they'd been sewn onto him.

A beat of silence passed, then Jo cleared her throat. "May I help you, sir?"

"You may." The words came out clipped and brisk, like the spring air.

Another beat, during which she observed the imperious expression on his face. And his dark hair, most of it hidden under that fashionable hat, though the ends curled softly at his shoulders, perhaps the only thing that might be considered "soft" about this man.

She cocked a brow at him. Waited. Then finally said, "And *how* might I help you today?"

"I should like to speak with Mrs. Porter."

Would he, now? So this stern, stiff man wanted to find a bride. He certainly didn't appear to be excited about the prospect—rather, he looked as if being here was a repulsive chore that might result in permanent damage to his person. She stepped back and gestured politely into the tiny space. "Please, come in."

He entered, and she closed the door behind him. "May I inquire who referred you to Mrs. Porter?"

"You may."

She waited once more. Did he really expect her to ask *again*?

The seconds ticked by. Evidently, he did.

"Who referred you to Mrs. Porter?"

"Sir Harry Acheson."

Ah, Sir Harry. Jo's heart softened. He had been one of her first clients, so eager to find a wife—any wife—that it had been as much work to keep him from proposing to every lady that crossed his path as it had been to find him that special woman who was just right for him. He and his wife, Mary Anne, had been blissfully married for four years now and had become her good friends.

"I am Joanna Porter."

He stared blankly at her. "I require *Mrs.* Porter."

"That is I."

"Of course it is not," he informed her. "Mrs. Porter is a married lady of middle age. You," he said with a scowl, "are hardly out of the schoolroom."

Jo's smile broadened. "I am, in fact, several years out of the schoolroom." A decade, if you wanted to be exact about it. "But you are correct that I am not married."

"There must have been some confusion. Forgive me." He turned as if to leave, but Jo lunged between him and the door. This close, he smelled of bergamot and citrus, sweet and tart and cool, and she couldn't help inhaling as she looked up into his handsome face.

"You see," she said, somewhat breathless, "discretion requires I use the professional name of *Mrs.* An older, married lady in my profession tends to be better received than an unmarried younger woman."

He merely shook his head, his posture radiating distrust, and she tried again. "Trust me, sir, I am quite skilled at what I do. My clients are exceedingly satisfied—as I am certain Sir Harry has attested."

He stared at her for a moment, his lips flattening as her own spread into a smile. He had rather nice lips, despite his insistence on setting them in such a thin, stern line.

"I am not certain this is entirely—"

"Proper?" She didn't wait for him to answer before saying, "Oh, I assure you, it is quite proper. I am here solely to assist my clients in a most upright and professional manner. I am conscientious of discretion, and if we happen to meet outside of this office, we will strictly adhere to all social protocols. My clients are often in the public eye, and I assist them in avoiding rumor, innuendo, and gossip at all costs. What happens in this office remains in this office." She pressed her fingertips to her heart. "You have my word."

Well, that had been more than Jo had intended to say. *"What happens in this office"*—ugh! Hopefully he didn't take that as an implication that something would be *happening* here, besides their in-depth interviews so she could determine exactly what kind of woman would be his perfect match.

Heat prickled over her cheeks, but she kept her smile firmly in place and her eyes locked on his. They were the most extraordinary color—a complex caramel brown with the slightest hint of amber—

"Well," he finally grumbled, "I suppose it is acceptable."

It was suddenly glaringly obvious that he hadn't given her a name. She had no idea who this man was, nor how to ask him. Usually, when it was men who entered her office, they introduced themselves to her post-haste, like Mr. Pellegrini: "Mrs. Porter? *Eccellente!* I am Flavio Pellegrini! And I wish to find a bride!"

Mr. Pellegrini made everything so easy.

Mr. Tall, Dark, and Nameless here was no Mr. Pellegrini.

"Please," she said, gesturing to the green armchair in front of her desk, "do sit down."

After studying her warily for another moment, he sat rigidly, which was a feat—the chair was so soft and comfortable, most of her clients sank into it and instantly relaxed with a sigh of pleasure.

Releasing a measured breath, Jo moved behind her desk and settled into her seat across from him. "All right, then. What can I do for you, Mr…" *Tall, Dark, and Nameless.* Fortunately, she let the salutation hang rather than blurting *that* out.

He stiffened—if that was even possible. He had already been stiff as a board. Now he looked brittle, like he might crack straight down the middle. "I am

Matthew Leighton…"

"Mr. Leighton—" she began when he hesitated, but he interrupted her.

"The Duke of Crestmont."

The words whacked into her like a jab to the sternum, and she struggled to hide the resulting cringe. She knew *of* the Duke of Crestmont, of course, like she knew the names of the princes of England, but she didn't know anything *about* him. People like him were so far out of her realm of existence, she hardly paid any attention.

She had been extremely forward with him, and impolite, given his position on the ladder of prominence—one tiny step down from royalty.

Oh, dear.

Well. Maybe it had been for the best he hadn't told her right away. She'd already presented her true self, free of the nervous, polite facade she surely would have borne if she'd known of his title. She must continue to be herself. He might be a duke, but he was also a human being, just like her.

"Ah." She forced her voice to smoothness, though her heart was galloping as if it intended to leap straight out of her chest. She prayed he couldn't hear it. "Forgive me for addressing you incorrectly, Your Grace. It won't happen again."

"The fault is mine," he said stiffly, the formality in his tone icing over her attempt to be warm and welcoming, "for not identifying myself immediately upon entering your"—he looked around the tiny space—"er…establishment."

Tilting her head in acknowledgment of his apology, she opened the drawer to her right, produced a folded sheet of paper, and slid it across the desktop to him. "This is my fee schedule and a detailed description of what you might expect from the process, Your Grace."

He took the sheet without opening it and tucked it into his coat pocket without saying a word. Since the aristocracy usually found it vulgar to openly discuss money and payment, this was not surprising. Indeed, Jo had experienced similar behavior before. He would pass it on to the appropriate person, who would then ensure she was paid. He would have nothing to do with it.

Her services were expensive, but nothing a duke would have a problem with, surely. And her customers…well, they had all been quite pleased with their happily ever afters. Not one of them had ever complained about her fees.

She gazed at the Duke of Crestmont. His lips were still flat, his features taut, his eyes seemingly in their natural state as suspicious slits.

Happily ever after might not be so simple with this one.

Still, she was a skilled matchmaker, and he was a *duke*. Her heart gave another excited surge. If she could match a duke, then everyone in London—no, all of England—would want to work with her. She could hire an assistant. Maybe start saving a few shillings here and there for emergencies, or even have some pretty new dresses made for everyone in her household. Talk of her skills would spread like wildfire, clients would be pounding her door down, and she'd have enough money that the giant ice slab of worry she carried around on her shoulders would finally melt.

She scooted forward on her seat and opened her mouth to explain her method, but the duke stood abruptly.

"Very well," he said. "I shall return in two days. I expect you will have a suitable candidate for me at that time."

She rose as well. "I'm sorry, Your Grace. That is absolutely impossible. I cannot wrap a suitable bride up in a bow and hand her over to you."

At the door, he turned to face her, his perpetually narrow eyes even narrower. "Why not?"

"Because your bride must be matched to you as an individual. The Duke of Crestmont would require quite a different bride than, say, the Duke of Edevane, for example."

She waited a moment to allow that to sink in. The Duke of Edevane, unlike the Duke of Crestmont, often headlined the scandal sheets. He was in his sixties and had fathered a half-dozen children by his wife and another dozen by his two mistresses. The man in front of her was thirty years younger and had never—as far as she knew—fathered children. And there had been rumors—that she'd paid little heed to but was grateful now to pull from the cobwebs of her *memories-of-things-that-have-nothing-to-do-with-me*—that the two dukes despised each other. "So I cannot just pluck your future duchess from the pool of eligible young ladies. That simply won't do!"

The duke cocked a skeptical brow at her. "Matched to me as an individual? That seems hardly necessary. I simply require someone who will fulfill her duties as the Duchess of Crestmont. Perfectly, of course."

"If you will allow me to explain to you how the process works—" she began, but he scoffed.

"I am familiar with how it works, madam. You procure me a bride. Legal documents are drafted. I marry her, she produces my heir and my spare, and that, as they say, is that."

Jo fought from reeling back. She struggled not to clutch her hand to her chest in abject horror.

What a poor, pathetic, sterile idea of marriage this man possessed! It was tragic, really. Awful. She'd feel sorry for him if he didn't have that disdainful, haughty look plastered on his snobbish, aristocratic face.

"No," she snapped, "that is *not* that."

Now she could see him checking his own body from reeling back. She doubted anyone ever spoke to him so sternly. Poor duke. So accustomed to people groveling and saying yes to his every pronouncement, no matter how ludicrous.

So *un*accustomed to a person standing her ground.

Well, Crestmont just might have met his match with her. She was not a duke, but she was also no simpering miss who would allow a client to walk all over her. In matters of the heart, she knew her business, and he would do it her way or she'd wish him the best and watch from a distance as he sabotaged his own happiness as well as the happiness of the unfortunate lady he chose for himself.

Of course, her very soul howled at the prospect of letting him go. Lord, but she didn't want to give up all the opportunities he'd bring to her business.

Still, she couldn't sacrifice her standards merely

to find him an expedient wife. Ultimately, he and his duchess would be unhappy, and Jo's reputation would suffer.

No. She needed to keep him, *and* she needed him to see the light.

"*Here* is how it will go," she began, her voice laced with steel. "We will meet several times, during which I will ask you questions that will draw a clear profile of the bride who will be compatible with you. The bride who will make you the happiest man alive, while you have the same effect on her."

He shook his head. "I have no interest in—"

"*Then*," she interrupted him—so rude per the rules of society, but so, *so* gratifying to watch his mouth snap shut—"I will create a list among the batch of eligibles this Season and set up introductions for you through the proper channels at various social functions. You will report back to me on those in whom you see potential—and you will find potential in most, I am sure. Then, you shall choose the one to whom you feel the deepest connection, and commence to court her. Oftentimes, this courtship results in a happy marriage. However, on the rare occasion it does not, we will start the process again, until you find the woman who is your heart's desire."

At the words "heart's desire," the duke's mouth pinched as if he'd just taken a bite of a very sour lemon. When he finally managed to unclamp his lips, he asked, "How long does this 'process' take?"

"My clients have taken from three weeks up to a year to find their ideal matches."

"A *year*?" He made it sound like a millennium.

"It shan't take near that long for me. Three weeks, at most."

She raised a brow. She'd only known the man for a few minutes, but she doubted it would be easy to find a perfect bride for someone as haughty and stubborn as the Duke of Crestmont. It might even take longer than a year. "Three weeks is no time at all."

"My minutes are valuable," the duke said. "Three weeks full of them adds up to a great amount indeed. I will take no longer than necessary to locate a suitable duchess."

Duchess, not wife. "I see."

The man was approaching this very much like a pesky errand. He clearly did not consider love as part of the equation. Yet in order to preserve her flawless reputation as a matchmaker, Jo would have to find a way to make him see how necessary love was.

Actually, it would be wonderful to see this cold, austere man find true love for himself. It would be her most gratifying challenge yet.

"Therefore," he continued, "it shall not take long. Find me someone suitable, and I will be satisfied. I intend to be married by the middle of July, at the latest."

"Why July?"

"I always leave London directly after Parliament adjourns. Afterwards, I shall be relocating to my country house. My bride will join me there."

She understood. He didn't want his duchess inconveniencing him by altering his perfectly scheduled summer. Heaven forbid.

"That is quite a rapid courtship and engagement," she said flatly.

"I wish for someone properly prepared to be the mistress of a great household. It seems to me that every chit of the *beau monde* is raised from birth to be such a lady. Hence, she should be quite easy to find and then propose to, etcetera. I demand nothing further..." His voice trailed off. It seemed he had something to add, but he clamped his mouth shut and threw another hard, meant-to-be-intimidating glare her way.

She prompted him anyhow. "But?"

His jaw flexed. "But nothing. That is all. I merely require someone who will make a perfect duchess."

They might as well begin with this. But she would need to puncture that hard surface shell and discover what he truly wanted—no, *needed* in a bride. She'd better not push for it now. It would come later.

Hopefully.

"All right, then, Your Grace," she said patiently, drawing out a blank sheet of paper and uncorking her inkpot. "Tell me all about the perfect Duchess of Crestmont."

CHAPTER THREE

Matthew felt the insane urge to loosen his cravat. Instead, he removed his hat, and when Mrs.—Miss?—Porter gestured to the green velvet monstrosity of a chair again, he sat.

Sir Harry had gushed so profusely about the wonderful Mrs. Porter, Matthew had developed an image of her in his mind—a matron of perhaps fifty or sixty, quite short, white-haired, and thick around the middle. In his imagination, she was motherly and doting and would offer him sweetcakes and tea while assuring him she'd find him the most perfect duchess in all the land.

This…this strangely businesslike young woman, with her clear voice and her simple blue dress covering her ample feminine curves, her smooth pink cheeks, dark-blond hair highlighted with streaks of shiny gold, gray eyes…

Dragging his own eyes away from her, he pulled in a breath. *Well*. She was not at all what he'd anticipated.

She'd been looking at him expectantly, and he scrambled to remember what she'd asked him. Oh, right. He was supposed to tell her about the perfect Duchess of Crestmont.

"Well," he said, straining to think of something. "She'll be a duchess. She'll need to be…duchess-like."

"What, exactly, does 'duchess-like' mean?" she queried.

Hell if he knew. Wasn't this *her* job?

"It means, *like a duchess*," he drawled.

Her pretty brows arched. "And what's a duchess like?"

This was the oddest encounter he'd ever had. Aside from his closest male friends, people rarely, if ever, questioned him. Young, unattached women never *dared* question him. And generally speaking, if one were to meet a woman in a dark room in this part of London, it would be for an entirely different purpose.

And yet, here this young lady was, flouting propriety, attempting to interrogate him about his future wife. She was a woman he didn't even know yet, asking him about things—private things—that men like him never discussed.

"A woman who possesses the qualities of a duchess," he answered.

She gave him a patient look, something akin to how a governess might regard a headstrong child. "I certainly do have an idea of what a duchess is like, but I am positive my image doesn't match yours. What I want to know is, in your mind, what are the characteristics of a duchess—a *perfect* duchess, to be specific?"

He ground his back teeth together, not liking how this Mrs./Miss Porter made him feel so off-balance, like she was attempting to tear apart, board by board, the rigid tower of guidelines by which he lived. As if she was enjoying every moment of it.

He remembered how, when he'd told Sir Harry that he intended to seek out the matchmaker, the man had slapped him on the back. "Just go along with whatever she demands of you, Crest," Harry had said. "She doesn't make matches by the book, exactly, but she'll get you the results you're looking for. I promise."

Then, he'd winked. That bastard.

Harry hadn't warned him that she was so lovely.

Wait…had his mind truly conjured *that* adjective to describe her? Of all the others available, like presumptuous, impudent, brazen, bewildering…

He was addled. Maybe it was the heat.

Yet it was a cool day outside.

Matthew blinked, then hesitated. He stood at a crossroads. He could stand up and leave this tiny space and pursue the task of bride-finding alone. Or he could stay and see what happened.

He'd already spent the better part of the Season attempting to procure a wife. The whole process had been…well, it had been *hell*, for lack of a better word. The parties, the balls, the dancing. Half of the ladies and their female relatives squawking at him, the other half fawning over him. A few of them, to be sure, had appeared to be adequate at first glance. But when he'd attempted to converse with them in order to see if they would measure up to his expectations, they'd all fallen flat. They were all ambitious for his title, a fact that overwhelmed every other aspect of their personalities and caused a sour taste to well in the back of his throat.

There could be no harm in staying and seeing what Mrs./Miss Porter had to offer, he decided. What did he have to lose? If this was a waste of time, he'd simply go back to attending various dreadful events of the Season in a desperate attempt to find a proper bride.

"The characteristics of a duchess," he said slowly, "are...many."

"Excellent," Mrs./Miss Porter said. "I shall make a list." She dipped her pen in the inkpot and rolled her other hand in a "proceed" gesture.

He'd start with an obvious one. "Well, she must be able to work closely with my housekeepers to keep my houses in order."

"Your houses?"

"Right. My townhouse in London, Crestmont Manor in Northumberland, and Hanford Castle in Nottinghamshire."

"Ah, that's right," she murmured, "Hanford Castle is yours."

"It is," he said. That historic pile was his favorite of the three homes, the oldest, mustiest, and most drafty, too. Likely his wife would hate it—women always hated drafts—but the future duchess would have to suffer living there for a third of the year. Unless he went alone. He supposed that could be arranged if she preferred one of the other homes. She could stay in one of his other homes while he resided at Hanford.

Draft problem, solved.

"I love those old castles," Mrs./Miss Porter said with a wistful sigh. "So much history within their walls."

"Indeed. Have you ever visited my castle?" The staff did conduct tours on occasion when he wasn't in residence.

"I haven't," she said. "But my family is from Nottingham—my father was the rector of St.

Nicholas Church—so I'm familiar with it."

He considered her name—had he ever known a Porter family? He didn't think so. Probably because they never entered his exclusive circle.

"We drove past Hanford Castle a few times when I was young," Mrs./Miss Porter continued. "I have never been inside, though I always dreamed of exploring the place."

He huffed a sigh. "What shall I call you?"

Her head cocked to the side.

"I mean, shall I call you Mrs. Porter or Miss Porter? Mrs. seems, well, it seems *incorrect*, and for some reason…" He frowned. "Miss seems somewhat…forward."

"Not at all." She smiled. Damn that thing. It was too pretty by half and made his insides feel rather soft. "Please, call me Miss Porter. If we are to ever encounter each other in public, that is the name you will know me by."

"Very well."

"So," Miss Porter said as she wrote, "the duchess should be able to efficiently manage your three houses and communicate well with your housekeepers."

"Yes," he said. "That will be extremely important."

"*Extremely* important," she repeated softly, jotting that down and re-dipping her pen into the inkpot before looking back up at him, her gray eyes twinkling with a silver glint.

He shifted uncomfortably in the uncomfortable chair.

"What else?" she asked.

"She must be an excellent hostess," he said. "I often entertain prominent guests, and I have started a tradition of having a house party every autumn as my father once did."

"An excellent hostess," she said. "How do you mean?"

Did she not understand the term "excellent hostess"? Honestly? "Someone who hosts guests," he said drily. "Excellently."

She not only smiled at him this time, she outright laughed. "Oh, Your Grace. I think you're being purposely obtuse. I'm certain you know what I'm asking. I should like to know the specific characteristics of a person you would consider an excellent hostess."

This was excruciating. Once again resisting the urge to loosen his cravat, he sighed. "She would be welcoming, of course. She'd make our guests feel at home in my house. She'd be witty and interesting in conversation. She'd have the menus and events planned to perfection to ensure everyone's entertainment throughout their visit. She'd coordinate with the servants and hire temporary help to ensure everyone had every possible need met."

"I see," she said. "The usual excellent-hostess-type behavior."

Was she teasing him? "Exactly," he said flatly.

"Menu planning and servant coordination aside," she said, "let us go a little deeper into what you mean by 'witty and interesting in conversation.' Do you consider this a valuable trait in a bride outside of moments she is hosting your guests?"

"I suppose it would be valuable if she were witty

and interesting at other social functions as well," he conceded.

"But what about with you?"

"With me?" He gazed at her dispassionately. "I've told you before, Miss Porter, I require someone who will fulfill her duties as the Duchess of Crestmont. I've no desire to *converse* with the woman."

"But she will be your wife. You will be required to speak with her from time to time."

"Of course I will. As long as she has the most basic of communication skills, it will be acceptable. It will be beneficial to have the ability to discuss household matters, and our various schedule requirements, etcetera."

She stared at him, mouth slightly agape.

He knew what she was doing. Trying to coax him into admitting that he wanted some deep and meaningful connection with his bride-to-be. Someone he could chat with for so long, he wouldn't notice they'd talked all night until the dawn sun peeked over the horizon.

Someone he loved.

By all that was holy, he did *not* want that. He'd tried traveling down that road once, and there was no way he'd make that mistake again. He just wanted a duchess, for God's sake, not any of that other nonsense that some people believed marriage should entail.

"Aside from your aversion to having a spouse you can converse with, what about your wife's feelings on the matter? Would you care if she were to be unhappy?"

That made his hackles rise. "Of course I'd care. I'd want her to be happy. She shall not be in want of anything, ever."

"Except love," Miss Porter mumbled.

He pretended not to hear. "What was that?"

"Nothing." Her steely eyes met his, and this time, there was something stubborn in them.

"I do not believe in love," he said stiffly.

"Then why marry at all?"

He pasted a bored expression on his face. "To procure an heir, of course. It is time." Past time. He'd delayed the inevitable long enough.

She looked intensely disappointed in him.

"I suppose," he said, trying to throw her a bone, if only the tiniest of tiny herringbones, "if you wish me to describe a single character trait of my ideal duchess beyond her capability to perform her role, it would be *amiable*."

"Amiable," Miss Porter repeated as if the word tasted rancid.

"Yes, yes." He gestured impatiently at her list. "Write it down, if you please. A-m-i-a-b-l-e."

With her lips pursed, she did as she was told, though her demeanor was stiff and annoyed—not amiable at all. When she finished writing the word, she asked, "Are there any additional features of your perfect duchess you'd like to share?"

He thought about it a moment. "Yes, perhaps one more."

"What is it?"

"Well, while she must be a wonderful hostess, she must be cognizant of her elevated social status."

She eyed him critically, and he had the sudden

urge to defend his statement. "You must understand, there are those who, given any opportunity, will take advantage of a duke's—and a duchess's—power and wealth."

"Oh, of that there is no question," she said airily, scribbling down his latest requirement. When she finished, she looked up at him with glittering eyes. "You'd best be careful. I am liable to pick your pocket at any moment."

Her incessant impertinence kept startling him, but also…he found his lips twitching with the desire to smile at her. A desire he quickly quelled. "I have become quite skilled at assessing signs of danger, and I assure you, you are—"

"—not dangerous." She sighed. "You are so perceptive, Your Grace. Most people find me terrifying at first glance."

A laugh bubbled up in him—he quelled that, too. "I rather doubt that," he said stiffly. "In any case, women are more vulnerable to such things, and she will be new to the role she shall be required to play."

"Of course. I, myself, am vulnerable to the schemes of the lower classes daily, and I imagine it would be *so* much more of a problem if I were a duchess."

Sarcasm. Another trait he rarely saw in women and never saw in the ladies parading themselves on the marriage mart. He supposed most men found sarcasm in women unappealing. Maybe he would as well, in his wife. But not in Miss Porter. In her, he found it interesting. Attractive.

She laid her pen down and drew a watch from a pocket in her frock. "Ah," she said. "It is four o'clock.

I apologize, but I must cut this meeting short. I'm late for another engagement."

She stood, and he did as well, clapping his hat back on. "I understand."

"Yes, you see, I always have tea with my house-keeper and maid this time of day. I know they are of a lower class than I, but I wouldn't miss it for anything. I adore them. My maid is one of my best friends in the world."

She looked him straight in the eye, and he understood perfectly. She was sending away a duke to go to her servants. And she wanted him to know it.

"But," she continued, "we have only just begun our exploration into finding your perfect match. Shall we meet again? Saturday, at, say, one o'clock?"

He was due at the boathouse Saturday afternoon at two, but meeting with Miss Porter felt important, and in any case, that should be enough time for Miss Porter and him to take care of their business for the day. "Right," he said. "One o'clock."

"See you then." She nodded at him in a curt gesture he'd make to one of his own servants.

He'd been dismissed.

CHAPTER FOUR

Jo had rushed in late to tea yet again, this time vexed and flustered thanks to the didn't-deserve-to-be-as-handsome-as-he-was Duke of Crestmont. Now that she had gulped back one cup of tea and poured another, she settled back in her chair, running a finger over the lip of her teacup. "If it works out, this new match will be my most illustrious one yet."

Though she was still pale and heartbroken, Lilly was rallying. She'd started by reopening her notebooks—she had dozens of them filled with architectural designs—not only for homes, but for churches and theaters, too. Her designs were classic but also original, appealing to the senses and sparking the imagination.

Jo's father, who had been a trained architect, had mentored Lilly in architecture when she was a child, but from the age of fifteen, she had been self-taught. She had no living mentors and was unknown in the field, but her talent shone off the pages of her notebooks. For the past two days, Lilly had been working on a brand-new design—a grand palace that drew inspiration from the architecture of the Far East and India. Jo's mouth had dropped when she'd first seen the sketches—the design was intricate and striking, but nothing like anything Jo had ever seen, from Lilly or anyone else.

Today, she was joining the household for tea and finally engaging in conversation about something other than the loss of her beloved. But that fact did not soften Jo's desire to meet face-to-face with Charles and give him a stern dressing-down.

"Who *is* your new client?" Lilly asked now.

Jo looked at each of the women one by one, heightening their anticipation. They were going to love this. "The Duke of Crestmont."

There was a moment of dead silence in the room. Then, all four women spoke at once.

"What?" Lilly gasped.

"A duke?" Mrs. Ferguson's blue eyes went round as she pressed a hand to her bosom.

"Oh my goodness!" Bess exclaimed.

"That horrid man?" Mama asked. "Impossible!"

Jo turned to her mother, smile slipping. "Did you say horrid?"

"I certainly did."

"Why? What did he do?" Frankly, Jo could easily conjure a few reasons why someone might call the Duke of Crestmont horrid. He was a pompous prig. But her mother, like most of society, was generally forgiving of those annoying traits that so many men of the aristocracy possessed.

"He abandoned Fanny Fleming at the altar."

Lilly frowned. "Who is Fanny Fleming?"

Jo recalled Fanny, if not very well. The young woman had been older than her, and she had left Nottinghamshire before Lilly had joined the Porter household. "She and her family were members of Papa's parish."

Jo remembered Fanny as haughty and condescending—even worse than the duke she'd met today, though Fanny had no title to defend her behavior as he did. She was the daughter of a wealthy country gentleman, and she had not only been quite lovely, but she also radiated ambition.

"When I was eleven years old," Jo continued, "Fanny married into an outlandish amount of wealth, and we never heard from her again."

"That is true," Mama said. "She married a copper magnate and relocated to Cornwall. But prior to that, the young Duke of Crestmont had been courting her."

"Really? I never heard about that."

"It was the talk of the aughts, my dear, but far too scandalous for your innocent young ears. The duke and Miss Fleming were both quite young—only seventeen or eighteen years of age, I believe, and Crestmont had only recently come into his title. All of a sudden, and to everyone's surprise, they rushed off to Scotland to be married. Everyone throughout the county was chattering about it. But days later, Fanny returned from Scotland alone, ruined and brokenhearted, because just as they were about to repeat their wedding vows, the duke changed his mind and simply rode off."

"My heavens," Bess breathed.

"But she did marry," Lilly said, "and you said she married well. It seems the scandal didn't run that deep."

"She went from nearly marrying a duke to marrying a man of little consequence in society," Mama said.

"Yet she married into one of the richest families in England," Jo said.

"Some might say that's a poor tradeoff for a title."

"Some might believe that," Jo said. "*I* am not one of them." She well knew the value of money. It kept food on their table and clothes on their backs. Those things were much more valuable than that feeling of superiority a title afforded. She didn't need to feel superior to anyone. She just wanted her family— these women surrounding her—to thrive and be happy and fulfilled.

Lilly nodded. "I don't believe it, either. Money is far more important than social status."

"I agree," Bess chimed in.

Mama turned to Jo, frowning. "Will you be able to work with such a scoundrel?"

"I believe I can. He is quite…ah…*pompous*, but I can endure that. Of course, if he proves to be as horrid as you say, or is impolite, improper, or inconstant with any of the ladies I present to him, I shall part ways with him at once and demand he apologize to the lady in question."

"I wonder why he's searching for a wife now," Mama mused.

"I'd say it's the proper time for it, most like," Mrs. Ferguson asked. "He's probably in his early thirties, which is the age when a lord might start to understand he is not invincible and begins thinking about producing an heir."

Jo sighed. What Mrs. Ferguson was saying was true, but Jo would have preferred people to think of it differently. Like, "He's reached the age when most men start understanding the value of an enduring passion."

But she was well aware that most people didn't have her faith in love. And the duke himself definitely wouldn't agree with her, though she was still determined to prove him wrong.

"So, tell us what he's like." Lilly leaned forward and waggled her eyebrows. "*Physically.*"

A bit of levity from her brokenhearted friend. That was a good sign.

"Hmm…" Jo tapped her fingers on the edge of her cup. "He's tall, dark, and handsome. I suppose."

Bess cocked a brow. "You *suppose*?"

Jo straightened. "As he is my client, I must observe him in a dispassionate fashion. I must recognize what others will see in him. I must work with him to enhance his best and most appealing features."

"And what are those?" Bess asked.

"Dispassionately speaking, of course," Lilly added with a grin.

"Well, he's quite tall, as I previously mentioned. I think he must be near a half foot taller than me."

"Ooh, that's quite tall indeed," Mrs. Ferguson murmured. Mrs. Ferguson and Bess were nearly a half foot shorter than Jo. "He sounds like a strapping young man."

Strapping was not the term Jo would have used, but then she thought of the muscles she'd seen rippling under his coat, and she supposed it was accurate.

"He dresses"—she quelled a tiny butterfly in her belly as she thought of how his clothing had hugged his body—"quite…well. He clearly has an excellent"—and expensive—"tailor."

"Tight breeches, eh?" Lilly said with a salacious wink.

"Lilly!" Mama exclaimed. But she was smiling, too.

"He wasn't wearing *breeches* as daytime attire, Lilly. That is so 1799."

"I know. But I long for breeches to return to fashion as everyday wear." Lilly pouted. "Now all men wear about town are trousers, which are either loose and dull or so ridiculously tight and high a man cannot bend his legs properly even to walk, and pantaloons, which…" She grimaced, clearly thinking of the various bumps and bulges that the pantaloons displayed so clearly—and sometimes scandalously. "…are not at all complimentary to a man's form."

Jo considered the duke's buff pantaloons, which had been *very* complimentary to his form. The thick muscles in his thighs had strained beneath the linen, and the fabric had disappeared beneath his knees under the supple black leather of his Hessian boots.

"What color are his hair and eyes?" Lilly demanded.

"He has dark hair that brushes over his shoulders," Jo said. "It looks quite soft. Dark, serious brows over eyes that are a light brown, almost amber. Or perhaps it is just flecks of amber I see in them—I am not entirely sure. His features fit together finely on his face, but his lips…he is so serious that he makes them look so stern and uncompromising, but when you catch him unawares, they are so soft and full-looking. I should like to see him smile—"

Realizing the room had gone quiet, she cut herself off, looking up from her teacup to see all four women gaping at her. "What?"

"You forgot we were in the room for a moment there, Jo," her mother said.

"You sounded so dreamy," Bess said on a sigh.

Jo set her teacup onto its saucer with a clatter. "Nonsense. I was merely describing his features, that's all."

"Mmm," Lilly murmured, looking down into her tea. "And so *dispassionately*, too."

• • •

"You're going, Crest," Viscount Coleton told Matthew, handing him a soft cloth. "You will not talk your way out of it this time. You owe me."

Groaning, Matthew passed the back of his hand over the sweat that beaded his forehead, then turned to buff the red-painted boat, which was aptly named *Red*. It certainly wasn't warm out today, but the five-mile row up and down the Thames had not only heated him through, it had also turned his arms into jelly.

"I'll go to the next one," he said to Cole.

Rubbing down the front end of the boat, Oliver Jameson smirked. "You told him that last time."

Matthew scowled at his friend.

"And," Jameson continued, "you also told me we would win today. So now you're two lies deep."

From the other side of the boathouse, the Earl of Winthrop snorted as he sanded a rough spot on one of *Blue*'s seats. "I think he's gone a little soft."

"Aye," agreed Jameson, "in the body as well as the head."

"It is this boat, I tell you," Matthew muttered.

"Something is wrong with it."

"There is nothing wrong with it," Cole said, his eyes alight with mischief. "As you know well, we built both of these at the same time with the same plan and same material."

"They're exactly the same," Jameson agreed.

"And yet, *Red* is slower more often than not," Matthew argued.

"Only because you're in *Red* more often than not," Winthrop said.

Muttering under his breath, Matthew turned away and went back to his work.

Jameson patted him sympathetically on the shoulder. "It's natural, old man. We all deteriorate with age."

Matthew cocked a brow. "You are a mere three months younger than I am."

"Three months makes all the difference." Jameson grinned. "Just think of it this way—I will forevermore be filled with more youthful vigor than you."

"Excellent," Matthew said drily. Then he held up a hand to Cole and Winthrop. "I don't want to hear it from you," he told them. Both men were two years younger—when Matthew and Jameson had started their rowing club at Eton, The Lions and the Lilies, Cole and Winthrop had been smaller boys who'd looked up to them like older brothers.

"I won't say a word," Cole promised, "if you agree to accompany me to my sister's soiree."

"Why wouldn't you go?" Jameson asked Matthew. "Cole said there will be a bevy of unmarried females there. I thought you were on the hunt for one of that species."

Matthew hesitated, but only for about half a second. If he told them about his visit to "Mrs." Porter, they'd torment him to eternity. Usually, he was amenable to a bit of teasing from his friends— the friendships between the four of them had been lighthearted from the beginning, though they were all the first to jump to one another's aid when one of them encountered any kind of difficulty.

But this...*no*. Aside from Sir Harry Acheson, who had referred him to the woman and therefore knew about Matthew employing her, he had no intention of telling anyone else.

"I believe I might give it up," he said casually instead.

"What?" Winthrop said. "Why?"

Matthew shrugged. "Society is..." He searched for the right word.

"Obnoxious?" Jameson supplied. Jameson knew him well.

"Yes, that," Matthew said. "And—"

"Superficial?" Cole asked.

"Absolutely. And—"

"A groveling crush, thanks to your lofty title?" Winthrop supplied.

"You know what that's like," Matthew agreed. Winthrop was an earl, after all.

"I do," Winthrop said.

Jameson rolled his eyes. "Oh, you poor, poor lads. Those blasted titles. Making your lives unbearable with the prettiest ladies in London dogging your steps, fluttering their eyelashes at you, soaking up your every word, drowning you in compliments—"

"Trust me," Cole said, "it's worse than it sounds."

"It doesn't sound bad to me," Jameson said.

Jameson had been a scholarship student at Eton. From an impoverished London family, he'd been plunked right in the middle of the lives of the wealthy and privileged, but he had never tried to insinuate himself into the good graces of another student for access to their favors. That had probably been what had drawn Matthew to him in the first place.

"The bad part of it," Cole explained, "is that you have to endure their flirting and flattery, and then you can't do a deuced thing about it."

"True," Winthrop agreed. "Asking one of them for a kiss is equivalent to asking one of them to clasp a shackle 'round your ankle."

"Dangerous, is what it is," Cole said. "Merely touching a well-bred lady—beyond the gloved fingertip brushes of a country dance—could mean a lifetime of misery, if it turns out you're ill-matched. Which you usually are."

Matthew thought of the ladies whose hands and waists he'd so lightly touched at so many dances, balls, and celebrations this Season. The young, fresh faces who'd gazed at him so adoringly. But those ladies didn't adore him. They couldn't. They didn't even *know* him. They did know about his title and his fortune, however, and they all wanted those.

He sighed. "That is exactly why I'm considering abandoning the quest. Those ladies aren't the slightest bit interested in me—they are interested in who I am and what I can give them. I think it might be impossible to find anyone who isn't instantly enthralled by the title."

Except yesterday, Miss Porter hadn't seemed enthralled at all.

Hopefully he'd find someone like her.

Well, not *like* her, of course. Miss Porter could never be an appropriate duchess. Just…someone who met his conditions but who also wasn't so damned besotted with the title.

Jameson began to rinse his buffing cloth, and the rest of the men threw theirs into the bucket as well. The sweat from the earlier row was making Matthew's shirt cling to his body, the spring chill in the air seeping through to his skin. He took his coat from the peg near the open door of the boathouse and shrugged it on.

"There's someone out there for you, Crest," Winthrop said. "I know it. You should attend Cole's sister's rout with him tonight."

"Why?" Matthew demanded. "So you will enjoy my tales of torture next time we meet?"

"Not at all," Winthrop said. "But you won't find The One if you never meet anyone new."

"'The One'?" Jameson made a choking noise. "I think we're losing him, lads. Evan Locke, the Earl of Winthrop, has succumbed to the romantic notions of our generation."

Winthrop shrugged. "The man desires a bride. He might as well hope to find an amiable one."

Amiable indeed, Matthew thought.

A-m-i-a-b-l-e.

CHAPTER FIVE

At first, Lilly had refused to attend Mr. and Mrs. Dickerson's soiree, though she and Jo had planned to go for weeks and both had been looking forward to it.

Jo understood her friend's hesitance—Charles Cherrington was going to be there.

"Please, give them our regrets," Lilly had begged yesterday. The three young women had been gathered in Jo's bedroom. Lilly was sitting on the bed, one of her notebooks open in her lap, Jo was mending the hem of one of her dresses, and Bess was folding linens and returning them to the wardrobe.

"That's rude, though," Jo said. "They might never invite us to one of their events again." Jo had developed a warm relationship with Beatrice and Harold Dickerson after having matched them two years ago. She and Beatrice shared an interest in reading novels as well, and they met monthly to discuss their latest reads.

"Then *you* go," Lilly said, then sniffed. "Tell them I have come down with a cold."

"Lilly, you know that's impossible. I cannot attend by myself. It would be…" She'd shaken her head, unable to imagine it. A young woman attending a party on her own. An utter embarrassment was what it would be. A scandal, even.

Last week, she'd merely *wanted* to go to the Dickerson soiree. But now, she *needed* to. It would be her only opportunity to draw Charles aside and make sense of the wedge he'd driven between himself and Lilly.

Jo couldn't mend it unless she understood it.

Bess, who had been folding and putting away linens in the wardrobe, turned to them. "I think you should go, Miss Lilly. You need to show him that you won't cower. That you're strong and won't let him break you."

Lilly had absorbed that, thought about it, then slowly nodded.

"That's true. If I don't go and he does, he'll feel like he won." She'd straightened, a new determination lighting her eyes. "You're right, Bess. I must be strong. I *am* strong. He has broken off our courtship without even giving me the courtesy of explaining why, which means he's a…" Her face twisted in consternation. "Well, he's a horrid *boor*, that's what he is."

It was probably the worst name Lilly had called anyone in her entire life.

"He certainly is," Jo had agreed.

"I shall go to the Dickersons' soiree," Lilly had pronounced, twisting her lips in a ghastly representation of a smile. "And I will laugh and smile and have the merriest time *ever*."

Now, the party was well underway, with a great deal more guests than Jo had anticipated. A crush of prominent members of the *beau monde* crowded into the Dickersons' comparatively modest London ballroom, many of whom Jo knew, if only by name, from her meticulous study of the eligibles of the Season.

Unfortunately, Lilly was neither laughing,

smiling, nor having the merriest time ever. She'd seen Charles at a distance and nearly choked in her attempt to stop herself from bursting into tears. She and Jo had escaped to the ladies' retiring room, and it had taken the better part of an hour for Lilly to compose herself. Now, they were back, standing like the proverbial flowers crushed against the wall while a good portion of the attendees were whirling around to the final strains of a lively country dance.

Jo glanced at Lilly, who took a sip of punch. Jo didn't know how, but after that long and painful cry, the chandeliers gave Lilly's face a fresh, young look and made her eyes shine.

Just as she was thinking that, Beatrice approached with a handsome man in tow. Seeing the similarities in their auburn hair and lively bright blue eyes, Jo had only one guess as to who the man was.

"I'd like to introduce you to my brother Henry, Viscount Coleton," Beatrice said, proving Jo's guess to be spot-on. "Cole, this is my good friend, Miss Joanna Porter, and her companion, Miss Lillian Appleby."

Jo and Lilly bobbed curtsies, and Lord Coleton bowed then turned to Lilly. "May I have the honor of dancing the next dance with you, Miss Appleby?"

Lilly gave the man a radiant smile. If Jo didn't know better, she would think she was thrilled at the prospect of dancing with Lord Coleton. "I'd love to, my lord."

A few minutes later, they left, arm in arm, and Beatrice leaned toward Jo. "He saw Miss Appleby when you first arrived and told me he wouldn't go home tonight until he danced with her."

Jo smiled. Lilly's rare beauty always caught gentlemen's eyes.

"Now tell me true," Beatrice said. "Are you enjoying yourself?"

"I am," she assured her host. It was the truth regardless of the time she'd spent consoling Lilly. Even to be a wallflower at a party like this was exciting—a rare chance to, quite literally, brush elbows with the elite. "Thank you so much for inviting—"

Just then, someone pushed past her roughly, nearly knocking her down. She stumbled to the side. "Oh!"

A firm hand grasped her upper arm, pulling her back upright. Another hand gripped her other arm, steadying her on her feet.

"Pardon me, Miss—" The hands suddenly released her as if she were on fire, just as she turned to see the Duke of Crestmont, who'd gone ashen, his mouth agape as he gazed at her wide-eyed, arms now hanging limply at his sides.

She understood. Mrs. Porter the matchmaker was out of context in such a glamorous setting.

She, however, was accustomed to encounters with clients in the "outside world," and she immediately dropped into a curtsy. "Your Grace. It's lovely to see you again."

He snapped his mouth shut and swallowed, but when he didn't immediately respond, Beatrice cut in. "Oh! You two know each other?"

The duke cleared his throat. "Uhh…"

"Yes," Jo cut in. Of course, for discretion's sake, she could not say that she met him in the same place she'd met Beatrice—in her office. Instead, she said, "We met briefly, long ago."

"In Nottinghamshire," the duke supplied, instantly in accord with her little lie.

"Oh, how lovely." Beatrice smiled fondly at the duke and told Jo, "His Grace has been Cole's good friend since we were children. I remember many summers spent in the country with them tormenting me." Her grin belied her words—if they'd truly been tormenting her, Beatrice had long since forgiven them.

The duke stiffened. It was truly amazing he could do that since he was so stiff to begin with. "I do apologize for any—"

"Oh," Beatrice said with a lighthearted wave, "do not apologize. I am just teasing you, Your Grace. And I think you know that." Her gaze caught on something beyond the duke's shoulder. "I believe my husband's parents have finally arrived. I must greet them. I'll speak with you later, Miss Porter." She gave the duke's forearm a sisterly squeeze. "I'm thrilled to see you, Crest. I'm so glad you came tonight."

With that, she swept around them, and they both turned to watch as she warmly greeted the older couple who'd just entered the ballroom.

Jo really did like Beatrice. Her father was a marquess, and, as such, she associated with the most influential members of London society. But she had married a commoner and had never treated Jo as if she were "lesser."

The duke standing beside her was another matter, however. He radiated so much coldness she had to fend off a shiver. With an inner sigh, she turned back to the man.

"Are you having a good evening, Your Grace?"

"Tolerable," he responded succinctly.

"So, you are a friend of Viscount Coleton?"

"Yes."

Jo hid another sigh. Such an engaging conversationalist, this one. "The same Viscount Coleton who's dancing with my friend at this moment?"

They both observed the dancers sweeping around the tightly packed ballroom, skirts swinging just inches from her and the duke's bodies. "Is that your friend in the pink?"

"It is."

"Then, yes."

They watched the dancing for a few moments more—well, the duke was watching the dancing. Jo was *pretending* to watch the dancing while surreptitiously observing the man standing beside her. He was very handsome in profile—straight, sloping nose, strong jaw, thick, wavy hair brushing the back of his collar, his black tailcoat and breeches accentuating his masculine form.

But he was so stern. So unapproachable.

She smiled up at him. "Have you danced tonight?"

He started, as if he'd forgotten she was standing beside him. "Me? No."

"This party is brimming with eligible ladies. Perhaps you should ask one of them to dance. Who knows, one of them might be The One."

His jaw flexed as he ground his teeth. "All this talk of The One," he muttered.

"Isn't that what you're searching for? I assume you don't intend to engage in polygamy."

"Of course not," he huffed, looking offended she'd dare to utter so vulgar a word.

"Then there is only to be one bride for you, and therefore talk of The One shouldn't be so offensive."

"I suppose not," he said tightly. "But must you capitalize it?"

"What do you mean?"

"By your tone. I can tell you capitalize The One in your mind as you are speaking it."

"Even if I am, what's so wrong with that?"

He shook his head, exasperated, then turned back to the dancers. "You want me to dance? Very well. I'll dance. Whom shall I ask, o' esteemed matchmaker?"

Me.

Jo blinked, disconcerted by the thought. Her? Dance with the Duke of Crestmont at a party attended by the most respected members of the *ton*? Ridiculous.

She doggedly scanned the crowd from one end of the ballroom to the other, but about halfway through, her gaze snagged on someone. It was that horrible heartbreaker, Charles Cherrington, dancing with a dazzling young woman wearing diamonds.

Jo's fists clenched and unclenched at her sides. "Her." She gestured subtly to the diamond dazzler, who smiled up at Charles, the chandelier light making the gems in her ears sparkle. "Dance with her."

The duke frowned. "She is very…slender."

"Oh, come now. You didn't tell me you required a

woman of physical substance. Would you turn down someone merely because they possessed a form that society considers ideal?"

He raised an imperious brow. "I suppose not. As long as it is within the bounds of acceptable size in society's eyes."

This man was far too rigid when it came to the aristocracy and what it considered proper. It was quite annoying, actually.

"Dance with her, then," she ground out.

"Very well. I will ask."

"She won't say no."

He sighed and said in a glum voice, "I know."

Because he was a duke. No one would say no to a dance with a duke. Even Jo. Even though he might be the most vexing man she'd ever met, she still wouldn't hesitate if he asked her to dance.

Yet…she didn't think she'd jump to dance with him merely because he was a duke. There were other reasons, like how their verbal sparring made her heart race. Not to mention that dark hair, the muscles in his upper arms pushing against the fabric of that tight-fitting coat—

Focus, Jo!

She needed to stop filling her head with thoughts of the Duke of Crestmont. He was a client, and she wasn't here for him tonight. She was here to speak with Charles Cherrington. *For Lilly.*

She and the duke stood in silence—except for the constant stream of admirers who approached Crestmont, giggling and fluttering their lashes at him while he responded in monosyllables and gave bows that looked like they made his bones creak—until the dance ended.

As soon as the couples began to move off the dance floor, Crestmont strode toward the diamond-clad woman with purpose and presumably asked her to dance, his face and body as stiff as if they had been coated with shellac. The sparkling young lady nodded eagerly and took his arm. *Of course* she hadn't said no.

Lilly had been making her way toward Jo but was intercepted by another man—this one a young officer she had danced with at an assembly last month and who, earlier in the evening, had asked Lilly to partner with him for the quadrille. Lilly took the man's arm, and they walked back out onto the dance floor to line up next to the duke and the diamond dazzler.

But where had Charles Cherrington gone? He wasn't in the row of dancers lining up in the center of the room. Jo turned to scan the room and found him pouring himself some punch at the refreshments table. She marched toward him, reaching him just as he guzzled down his drink. When he looked up from it and met her eyes, his eyes widened, and he gulped.

Good. She smiled sweetly, hoping he spit up all that punch right over the snow-white of his cravat.

He managed to keep it all down—unfortunately—then produced a tight smile. "Good evening, Miss Porter."

"Is it?" she asked with forced pleasantry. Her fingers quivered with the urge to punch him in the jaw.

"Uh…er…" He swallowed again, his eyes flicking around as if hoping someone would magically appear to rescue him from her. No one did.

"I should like to have a word, if you would be so kind, Mr. Cherrington."

He looked surreptitiously this way and that, the panic in his eyes as palpable as if she'd touched the point of a sword to his neck. She supposed she had, metaphorically speaking. "Um…all right."

"Follow me."

She spun on her heel and walked toward the doors leading out onto the terrace, glancing back once to ensure he was following. She'd checked the terrace earlier. It was abandoned, perhaps due to the chill in the night air. It was a lovely area overlooking a pretty courtyard, and if it were a more temperate evening, it would be crowded with revelers. But the weather was cooperating with her tonight, offering her a private-though-not-scandalous place for her to have a brief chat with Charles Cherrington.

She pushed open the French doors and walked outside. Lamps blazed at the railing corners, so if she and Charles were caught conversing out here no one would give it a second thought. They were in plain sight of the ballroom, after all.

Jo walked straight out to the far edge of the railing and put her hands on it, looking out over the courtyard. A frigid breeze whipped the loose strands of curls that framed her face. She'd be cold if not for the hot stream of anger coursing through her.

Charles stopped a few feet behind her.

Jo closed her eyes, listening to the lively strains of the music behind the glass doors, the sounds of laughter and conversation. Finally, she took a deep breath. "Why?" She turned toward him.

He stood there looking hopeless, shoulders slumped. "I'm...sorry."

"Why?" she repeated.

"Because..." His dark curls bobbed to his shoulders as he looked down, scuffing his highly polished shoe over the tile like a repentant schoolboy.

Jo remembered the first time she and Lilly had met Charles. Jo and Lilly had been outside the British Museum, and Lilly had been discussing the remodeling and expansion that needed to be completed since Britain had been acquiring so many pieces of historical and artistic significance from all over the world.

Charles, who'd been accompanying his sister Martha to the museum, had joined the conversation, claiming an interest in architecture that, Jo shortly realized, was more of an interest in hearing *Lilly* talk about architecture.

The four of them had spent the afternoon together, first Lilly describing how she'd personally expand the British Museum, then Martha taking them to a basement office nearby to view Egyptian artifacts she had been cataloguing for the renowned antiquarian, Mr. de Havilland.

Sparks had crackled between Lilly and Charles from the moment they'd met, and by the end of the afternoon, Lilly had shared every design in the notebook she'd brought with her, and Charles had promised to call at their house to see the rest. The way Charles had watched her all afternoon, the way they'd talked together...the attraction had been so instant and so strong, it had been nearly palpable.

"Because I must marry someone else," Charles said now.

Jo took a measured breath, her hands clenching into fists so tight, her nails dug into the skin of her palms. "That. Is not. An answer."

He shook his head helplessly. "I love her. I do."

Jo scoffed. "Someone who loved Lilly would never treat her like this. She is the loveliest, kindest, most pure-hearted girl, and you have broken her heart."

He blanched.

"Tell me *why*, Mr. Cherrington. I won't stop pestering you until you do. Did you meet someone else? Are you inconstant?" She leaned forward. "A liar? A *cheat*?"

He squeezed his eyes shut. "No! I— Well…yes. I suppose I am all those things. Maybe… I don't know. I'm sorry. So sorry."

"Explain," Jo demanded.

He opened his eyes. Swallowed again. "Believe me when I say I want nothing more than to marry Miss Appleby. Please tell her that as well, because it is true. Seeing her here tonight… Her eyes. I know she has been weeping." He shuddered, his own eyes glistening. "I love her. Nothing I've ever said has been truer."

"And yet, you led her on. Deceived her. Courted her under false pretenses. Gave her false hope."

"I didn't mean to! I was… I was carried away. We both were."

Jo narrowed her eyes. "How do you mean?"

"It was so perfect, being with her, I didn't think—"

"Think about what?"

"How marrying her would be impossible."

"Why?"

"Because…" He pressed his lips together and looked away, his face crumpling in shame.

"What is it?"

"It's… It's just that… I have five younger sisters."

"I know that. What does that have to do with anything?"

"None of them are married, and I am the head of the household."

She knew that, too. His father, the third son of an earl, had died a few years ago. "And?"

He folded his arms over his chest in a defensive gesture. "My father inherited a decent living from my grandfather, the Earl of Wydwick. But he lost it all in drink and gambling before he died. Nearly every penny. Now we are…" He drew in a shaky breath. "Now, we are quite… We are *quite…*" He closed his eyes and whispered, "Impoverished."

And, just like that, clarity rushed in. Jo's fists opened, her fingers relaxing at her sides.

Lilly was impoverished, too. She had nothing. No dowry, no income. She had nothing to bring to a marriage but her spirited, lovely, brilliant self.

Lilly was the daughter of a Nottingham linen merchant who had been a part of Jo's father's flock at St. Nicholas Church. Papa had seen a spark of something in Lilly when she was about nine years old and had invited her into their house to be educated alongside Jo.

When Papa had introduced her to his great passion, architecture, there had been no turning back for Lilly. She had become enamored of the elements of design and form. She studied Greek and Roman architecture, all the contemporary architects as well as any book on architecture she could find, and constantly worked on new designs in her notebooks.

Lovely, educated, and talented, Lilly was now a lady in every respect—except the one that mattered to the *ton*. She was the daughter of commoners, her place cemented on a low rung of society's ladder.

Jo had thought Charles better than that. He had known exactly who Lilly was, but he'd loved her anyway.

Yet if it were true that he had no fortune, he would need to marry someone who brought not only pedigree into the marriage, but a handsome dowry.

"Oh no," she murmured.

"Thanks to my many debts and my inability to repay them, my family is on the verge of being cast out from society." He made a choking noise. "I can't—I won't—allow that to happen to my sisters."

Hence, Charles Cherrington dancing with that dazzling lady in diamonds. He needed to marry into money. He needed to do it to ensure his family's future. With his bloodline as the grandson of an earl, his charm, and good looks, he would easily find someone suitable.

"I need to save my family," Charles whispered.

This was not something Jo could fault. She'd do the same for her own family. She'd done everything she could, aside from selling her body and soul, to keep them out of the poorhouse.

"I must marry someone with a dowry." Charles

looked green about the gills, his voice raspy and dry, and paper-thin. "An heiress, or a daughter of a great house, or someone who will be able to help me dig my sisters and myself out of the shambles my father made of our family."

"Oh, Charles," Jo murmured. "I'm so sorry."

The young man stepped forward and leaned heavily on the balustrade beside her. "As am I," he mumbled.

"But you should have told Lilly sooner," Jo added. "Before…"

Before they'd taken it as far as they had.

"I know." He groaned. "I was stupid. I was a fool in love. I wasn't thinking. And now I've hurt"—he took a shaky breath—"the person most important to me in the world. And I must marry someone I shall never love."

Every part of Jo rebelled at this. This couldn't happen. It was appalling. Wrong. There had to be a way out of this.

She'd always believed love could conquer all. But in this case, how could it?

CHAPTER SIX

Matthew couldn't decide if the anxious anticipation he felt before his Saturday afternoon meeting with Miss Porter was due to dread or excitement. He gazed out the carriage window as the horses clomped down Duke Street, trying not to think about it. Trying to quell that strange sensation stirring in his gut.

His experience at the Dickersons' soiree had confirmed one thing: He needed the matchmaker's help. He'd danced with three young women. He might not consider himself particular when it came to finding a bride, but those three had entirely missed the mark.

The first one had been a literal diamond heiress who had simpered and fawned, as if she thought of herself as nothing more than an ant beneath his toes. The mere thought of spending an entirety of a marriage trying to convince her otherwise exhausted him.

The second had been a young widow who'd been so self-conscious and shy that you'd have thought she'd neither met nor touched a man before. Her face had been beet-red throughout the entire dance, and she and Matthew had said less than ten words to each other, most of them including the words, "Would you like to dance?" and "Yes, thank you."

He had a difficult time believing the lady had ever been married.

The third had been the worst. She'd stroked his shoulder and commented on the lovely wool of his coat. Then she'd asked about the size of his house in London, how many carriages he owned and whether one of them was a phaeton—"I've always wanted to ride in one!"—and whether his castle boasted a turret, because she'd "always imagined I'd have a turret in my future."

His castle boasted more than one turret, and he did own a phaeton, in fact, but he'd be damned if he'd marry a woman who wanted him either for his wheeled conveyances or for a musty tower.

The carriage stopped in the mews behind Miss Porter's Beaumont Street townhouse, and Matthew grabbed his walking stick and stepped onto the short garden path that led to the house. "Thank you, Ted," he said to his driver through the mist of rain. "You may return in a half hour to take me to the boat-house."

Surely half an hour would be all he needed.

Ted frowned dubiously. "Doesn't seem like much of a day for a row on the Thames, Your Grace."

Matthew glanced at the sky. It would clear in the next hour or so. "It will be fine."

Ted knew better than to question him further. He tipped his cap. "Aye, sir."

Turning away from his coachman, Matthew stepped onto the stoop of what once had been the door to a scullery or a larder at the back of a relatively modest townhouse tucked on a street in the parish of St. Marylebone. The small room had been converted at some point and now served as the office of Miss Joanna Porter.

He knocked on the door, and, like last time, it was answered promptly by the lady herself, wearing the same day dress in pale blue she'd been wearing the last time he came to her office—a color that suited her and brought out the color in her cheeks. Her thick, lustrous hair was piled into a roll at her nape, and the only jewelry she wore was a pair of simple pearl earrings.

She was very pretty, though not in the traditional sense. She was older than society considered respectable for an unmarried lady—he had learned that she was seven-and-twenty, though he'd believed her much younger when she'd first informed him that she was "Mrs." Porter. Her hair was light brown streaked with gold, her eyes a stormy gray, and her body—well, it had curves in all the right places. Luscious curves he could fill his hands with—

"Good afternoon, Your Grace," she said brightly, then moved aside. "Come in. This rain is wretched, isn't it?"

"It will depart from the area shortly," he said automatically, trying to banish the carnal images. They weren't the first he'd had of her. They'd intruded the last time he'd come here, though he'd been quicker to shove them aside that day. Then, they'd returned in full force at that blasted rout, where she'd been wearing a white, low-cut dress that revealed the creamy tops of her full breasts, and soft curls had framed her lovely face while her plump cheeks glowed pink in the flickering lights of the chandeliers. Matthew had had to forcibly scour his brain of thoughts of her even as he'd danced with three other, very different women.

"Do you think so?" She gave a hopeful sigh as she shut the door, closing them into the tiny room furnished with only the desk, her simple desk chair, the green monstrosity of an armchair, and a pair of wall sconces. At least there was a fair-sized square-paned window beside the door that let in some light, even on this gray afternoon.

"Although the rain isn't all bad," she said. "It will keep the grass green and the flowers in bloom. There's nothing better than London in the springtime, don't you think?"

He could think of many better things than London anytime of the year, but he didn't say so. Instead, he muttered a noncommittal answer.

"Do sit down," she said, gesturing to that awful green chair.

He removed his hat, laid it near the edge of her desk, and propped his cane against the rigid back of the chair before sitting. Right on top of a particularly lumpy area of the stuffing. He shifted uncomfortably. "What do you require of me today, Miss Porter?"

They needed to get this over and done with quickly. He hoped a sweat-inducing, muscle-mashing row up the Thames would stop these annoying, inappropriate thoughts.

At least he'd come prepared today. Tucked in his coat pocket was a list of everything anyone could ever wish to know about his future bride.

She took her seat on the other side of the desk. "I have several questions I'd like to ask you today. I'll use the answers to help me find a compatible match for you."

"Several questions, you say?"

"Yes."

"How many is that?"

She looked surprised. "I haven't counted them."

"I see." Wonderful—more than she'd bothered to count. It was a good thing that he'd taken the time to pen all the answers in advance.

"Shall we get started, then?" She smiled at him, and it lit up her gray eyes until they shone the color of the moon. Her smile was genuine and kind, but it also sparkled with intelligence and mischief at the same time. A complex smile for a complicated woman, he supposed.

"If you like."

"Very well. I shall listen, and, on occasion, take notes, but most of all, I like to think of this as a conversation between friends."

He raised a brow. "Yet, you are not my friend."

"Well, Your Grace, I would certainly like to be."

Matthew had few friends. None of them were women. In fact, he'd never had a female friend, and the idea of having a friendship with a woman struck him as highly irregular. He pressed his lips together so as not to give a sarcastic "we'll see about that" kind of retort. She didn't deserve his sarcasm, after all. Neither did her pretty smile.

Her face remained friendly and open, but that didn't mean that she wasn't thinking, at this very moment, what a complete snobbish ass he was. And she'd be justified in thinking it.

He gritted his teeth, forced a smile that he was certain emerged more like a grimace, and drew the list from his pocket. "Fortunately, I won't need to take up your entire afternoon with this. I am prepared." He slid the paper across the desk toward her. "I've already answered every possible question you might ask."

Miss Porter took the sheet, and he watched myriad expressions play over her face as her gaze scanned over it. "Thank you, Your Grace. This will be helpful, I'm sure, but I wanted to start with something else today."

"What else could there possibly be? I described my requirements in very specific detail."

She lowered the page. "And, while knowing that 'any hair color is acceptable, though I'd prefer my bride neither to be balding nor entirely bald,' is quite helpful indeed, I was interested to hear about your experience at the Dickersons' soiree on Wednesday evening. I saw you danced a few times. Tell me about it. What did you think of those ladies? They were quite different from one another but all very lovely in their own right."

He stiffened. "Unfortunately, none were acceptable."

"And yet…all had full heads of hair, and were…" She looked down at the paper. "…shorter than you, younger than you, well-dressed, in possession of figures deemed acceptable by society, polite—"

"I disagree," Matthew interrupted. "They were not *all* polite. The first two were. The third was…" He trailed off because the lady hadn't exactly been *im*polite. He'd just found her insufferable.

Miss Porter raised her brows. "She was what?"

"She…" He frowned, trying to put it into words. Words more polite than *she was a parasitic leech*. "She seemed to be more interested in my phaeton than in me," he finally managed. "I found that quite rude."

Miss Porter's brows climbed higher. "That *is* rather rude. I don't blame you for thinking so. Though I daresay some gentlemen would be quite pleased by a lady's interest in their phaeton."

"Not me."

She tapped the top of her pen on her desk. "What about the other two? The first and second?"

"The second was quite shy."

"Ah," Miss Porter said. "I understand immediately. Not an acceptable conversationalist for your house parties?"

"Exactly."

"And the first? The one who wore the diamonds?"

"She was…obsequious."

"Oh? I thought you were looking for someone just like that."

He scowled. What kind of man did she think he was? "What gave you that idea?"

She opened her mouth, closed it, then shrugged. "Well, I suppose it was your general demeanor on the occasions we previously met. So, allow me to clarify—are you saying you desire a woman who considers herself your equal?"

"Equal? Of course not. Men and women aren't equal."

"Oh?" she said drily. "Really?"

"Generally speaking, no. Women are smaller, have less muscle mass and body hair—"

"I didn't mean your physical equal, Your Grace."

"Then…my equal in status? I assure you, I've put

some thought into this, but in the end, I believe limiting my search to a duke's daughter would be far too limiting. I'd prefer a peer's daughter, of course, but I might be convinced to marry a gentleman's daughter if said gentleman is sufficiently well connected and has a verifiable pedigree."

She smiled at him, shaking her head. "There you go again, Your Grace, falling into the old pattern."

"What pattern is that?"

"The one where men approach looking for a bride as if they're planning to purchase a broodmare."

He'd never heard that one before, but he shrugged. "You must admit, there are some similarities." He ticked the items off on his fingers. "Pedigree is important in a wife and in a broodmare. So is fertility. There's also the cost to consider, whether she is comely and malleable—"

Miss Porter coughed. "The similarities are thin indeed. Cost should be the least of your concerns. You are rich as Croesus and needn't worry yourself with such trivial matters."

She said the last somewhat bitterly, but she was correct. He didn't care what his wife brought to the table in terms of a dowry or income, and if she came to him as a daughter of an impoverished aristocratic family—such families seemed to be on the rise in numbers of late—of course he'd assist them in regaining their financial footing.

Miss Porter continued. "Fertility, alas, is difficult to determine unless you're perhaps searching for a widow already in possession of a brood of children?"

He shook his head. "I wouldn't be averse to

it"—though the thought of a brood of children who weren't his own, or even *were* his own, terrified him—"but I'm not searching for it purposely."

"Comely is subjective," she continued, "and I daresay you aren't overly concerned with it either, as"—she gestured to the sheet of paper he'd given her—"you wrote 'beauty is unimportant,' on your list here."

She was rather beautiful, he thought, sitting there across from him and knocking down his comparisons one by one. But once again, she was right. He wanted a perfect duchess with a flawless pedigree who presented herself properly and was above reproach. He'd seen many a woman do so without possessing much in terms of beauty. Also, what did his personal preferences matter, in the end? He and his future wife weren't meant to love each other, or even to be passionate for each other. They were meant to serve each other's purposes.

"And then…pedigree." She looked up at him, silver eyes snapping in challenge. "Can I ask what difference it makes?"

"Pedigree makes all the difference."

"That is not an answer."

That was because he didn't have one, not really. The one he could think of was ever so important, but it also felt… Well, to be honest, it felt ever so stupid at the moment. For lack of something better, he voiced it anyway, bracing himself for her inevitable sarcastic response. "It makes all the difference in the eyes of the *ton*."

There was a brief silence as they gazed at each other, then her eyes narrowed. "Have you ever wondered why?"

"No."

"I have."

"And have you come up with any conclusion?" he asked her.

"My conclusion is that the elite need to cling to their status because, above all, they are petrified of losing it. If they open the doors to their exclusive club, if they expand it by marrying those of lower status, they also dilute it, and eventually, they will tumble from their position at the top of the social ladder."

He tapped his chin. Her argument had some merit.

She continued. "Aristocrats don't marry daughters of aristocrats because they are more intelligent, more attractive, or better able to bear them heirs. They marry daughters of aristocrats to keep their exclusive club small. To inform the rest of the world that it is not worthy of being elevated to their status."

"What you say might be true," he told her. "But it is not my reasoning for wanting an aristocratic spouse."

"What is your reasoning then, Your Grace?"

"Marrying a woman with an aristocratic lineage will prevent me and my bride from being publicly mocked. My bride will be accepted into society circles without question. It will also bode well for our future as husband and wife."

"How is that?"

"I told you earlier that I desire a perfect duchess."

The edges of her lips canted up. "You certainly did."

"Someone who was born into the aristocratic life will experience a smoother transition to the life I lead. She will find it easier to perform her various duties as the Duchess of Crestmont. Do you not agree?"

"I don't disagree. But I'm also certain that many a commoner would adapt, and more quickly than you'd think." She waved her hand dismissively, and beyond it, he saw that a pink flush had begun to crawl up her chest above the line of her bodice. "But I don't wish to argue with you about it, Your Grace. You want a wife with aristocratic roots, so never fear, I shall find you a wife with aristocratic roots. The pedigree of your broodmare—I mean, better half—will be intact."

There it was…her sarcasm. It made his heart beat faster. It made him want to—

Damn. He cut off the thought before his mind could form it into words.

"Well, then"—she straightened, the businesslike tone back in her voice—"now that we've established why none of the ladies at the Dickersons' soiree are good matches for you, I have a few more questions."

"More questions beyond those I already answered?"

"Yes, indeed. Several of them."

Meeting with this woman was exhausting. She argued with every damn thing he said. It was a miracle she'd ever managed to make any successful matches at all.

He sighed dramatically, letting her know the

extent of his impatience. He'd been more than forthcoming. What else could she possibly want to know? "Fine," he said. "Proceed."

She looked up at him with narrowed eyes, then her gaze caught on something beyond his shoulder. Her lips parted, and then she shook her head, frowning. "Well, look at that. The sun's come out, Your Grace. You were right." Then she turned back to him with an expression that looked like an odd cross between suspicion and admiration. "How did you know?"

CHAPTER SEVEN

Jo had stayed up for hours after she and Lilly had come home from the soiree, trying to conjure up a way for Lilly and Charles to be together. But she had nothing. When she'd finally fallen asleep early that morning, her dreams had been of all her clients coming back to her and telling her they had to separate. They were all miserable and brokenhearted. They should have married someone else. Someone perfect. Someone with money.

"Why?" Beatrice had sobbed to Jo in her dream. "*Why* did you introduce me to Harold? He has left me for a diamond heiress. You are a terrible matchmaker. You have caused me nothing but pain and heartbreak. I shall never be happy again. Never!"

The day after the soiree, Jo had gone to visit Beatrice in the guise of thanking her friend for the lovely evening and sharing a bit of gossip about the attendees—excluding the Duke of Crestmont, of course—but really to ascertain that Beatrice and Harold were still happily married.

They were, thank goodness. And Beatrice had confided that she thought she was with child, though she hadn't told Harold yet, because she wanted to be certain first. Then, she'd loaned Jo her copy of the latest novel by the anonymous author of *Waverley*, and they scheduled a time next month to discuss it.

Beatrice and Harold were still happy. It was such

a relief. It eased Jo's worries about her other clients, and about any part of her awful dream coming true.

It didn't help with the Charles-and-Lilly problem, though.

What could she do for them? How could she unbreak Lilly's heart?

Even with all her worry about Lilly, thoughts of the Duke of Crestmont had constantly insinuated themselves into her mind for the past two days. She kept thinking of him, and not in the "who will make the perfect bride for him?" kind of way like she should be. She thought more of the way he looked at her, how he stood so tall and proud. How stiff and uncomfortable he seemed to be in his own skin. And why on earth he'd left Fanny Fleming at the altar.

When he'd first come into her office and brought that ridiculous list with answers to "all the questions" she might ask, she'd nearly laughed in his face. He truly believed that knowing he would prefer not to have a woman who was older than him, bald, or taller than him—few women in London would stand taller than him, given that he must be an inch or so over six feet—truly helped her in determining his perfect match. But she'd managed to contain herself. Well, she'd contained herself until that broodmare nonsense came up. And then the nonsense about pedigrees.

Now, she sensed, from his tight lips and narrow eyes, that he was becoming as irritated with her as she was with him. Above all, she didn't want him to leave. As pompous and annoying as he was, he was a challenge.

To be sure, Jo had been known to walk away

from challenges—when she deemed them a waste of time or concluded that the risk was not worth the reward. But she was determined not to walk away from this one because the reward would be worth her time, and her risk. Her future depended on making him a match.

So did his, for that matter.

Needing to change the tone of the conversation, she rose from her chair and looked outside, where the sky had turned blue, the clouds white and puffy, the sun reflecting over the wet cobbles and walls of the buildings across the mews.

How had he known?

He rose and came to stand beside her. "I am proficient at predicting the weather."

"Are you?" What an odd skill.

"I am."

"How do you do it?"

"I use various scientific instruments, compare current conditions with my past data, and analyze the sky."

"My mother studies the sky sometimes, too. She says if the color of the sky darkens from pale blue to a deep blue, then the rain will stop."

He smiled. Was that a first? Had she actually made him smile? With such a simple and short anecdote about herself and her family?

"The color of the patches of blue in the sky can influence my predictions, as well."

"My mother believes there's something to it."

"She is correct. There are also wind patterns, seasons, temperature, hygrometer and barometer readings—"

"Do you keep track of all those things?"

"I do. I keep detailed charts."

"That's fascinating." Heat rose to her cheeks. "I mean...I suppose most people don't find weather interesting. It's always considered to be the most common topic to start a mundane conversation, but I actually love the weather. I love all four seasons. I love storms and rain and snow and lovely, perfect days. I love when the weather changes with each season."

His smile grew natural, relaxed, and she felt the tension begin to drain from his body. "So do I."

"I would very much like to see your charts sometime."

"I will bring the most recent ones next time I see you." His smile faltered. "Er, assuming there is to be a next time."

"Usually, I see my clients about once a week so we can go over the potential matches they've met. So there will be," she assured him.

Her eyes dropped to her arm, where the sleeve of his waistcoat brushed against it. He seemed to notice at the exact same time and jerked away. Then he took a big step back.

"Excellent," he said.

They stood there for a too-long moment, staring at each other.

Jo swallowed hard. "I suppose we should get back to the questions."

"Yes," he said. "I'd like to get it over with. I have an appointment on the Thames this afternoon."

"An appointment on the Thames?"

"Yes," he said shortly, and took his seat, clearly

having no desire to explain what he'd meant.

She strode around the desk and retook her seat. "All right, Your Grace. I'm going to ask you the question that's the first one I usually ask my clients. Though in our case, it's probably the fourth or fifth question."

"Or the hundred and fifth," he muttered. "Are you certain I haven't already answered it?" He gestured to the paper she'd left on her desk.

"You haven't."

"I find that difficult to believe."

She sighed. "The question is, who was your favorite person in the world when you were a boy?"

"How does that have anything to do with finding me a bride?"

"It has everything to do with it. It tells me about the kind of person you are, the kind of people you admire, and the kind of woman to whom you might be attracted."

He opened his mouth. Shut it. Stared at her. Then shrugged and said, "Well, it wasn't just one person; it was two. My parents, of course."

That startled her and made warmth flush through her at the same time. She always loved it when people responded that their parents were their favorite people. It would have been her answer, too, if anyone ever asked it of her. When she was young, Jo's parents had been her world. The three of them had been a unit, loving and caring for each other through thick and thin.

Some clients responded with either their mother or their father, which implied they were close to one parent and not the other. Others gave answers such as a sibling, governess, grandparent, or friend. Each answer led to more questions that ultimately showed something of their character and characteristics of others that appealed to them.

But when clients answered that their parents were their favorite people, it meant something different. It meant that family was important to them. It meant that they would most likely be excellent parents themselves.

From an aloof man like the duke, she'd expect him to say a close friend or a young uncle, perhaps his nurse. He'd surprised her.

"Why is that?" she asked him.

He frowned. "Because they were my parents."

Ah, here it was. They were clearly back to the "give the matchmaker the most obvious answer then treat her like she's an imbecile" part of the program.

"What about them did you love?"

Grief washed through his eyes, but then it was gone as soon as it had arrived, leaving his face strangely expressionless. A corresponding empathy clenched Jo's chest. She'd known his father was gone, because he was the duke, but she hadn't known about his mother.

"They were good parents. Both of them. They..." He swallowed hard and looked down at his lap. "They loved each other—and me—deeply. I was their only child. They took me everywhere with them. The three of us were quite close."

Just like her own family.

"What happened to them?" she asked softly.

"They were in a curricle at night," he said. "My father loved his curricle, and he loved driving my mother all over the countryside. When I was at home, the three of us would bundle up and go on evening drives throughout the county. But that night, I was away at school. There had been a bit of a drought across the midlands, and it decided to rain for the first time in months. The heavens opened up over them, and as they rushed home, a flash flood broke their axle and swept them off the road. They…" He closed his eyes. "They died together, at least. They would have wanted that."

This was another surprise. The Duke of Crestmont was not looking for a love match, and yet it was clear his own parents had had one. What had soured him to the idea? Could it have been Fanny Fleming?

"How old were you when they passed away?" she asked.

"Seventeen."

"I'm so sorry, Your Grace."

He shrugged, then looked back to her, his expression flat. "They were my favorite people. When I was younger. That is what you asked, correct?"

"Correct." She swallowed back her sympathy. He didn't want it right now, and that she understood, as well. "What about when you were older? Who was your favorite person after your parents?"

"I haven't had one," he said.

She opened her mouth to argue, then decided to allow him this. "Perhaps that will be your wife."

His eyes went narrow again, and she knew she'd made a mistake. "That's not necessary."

But it should be, Your Grace. You deserve to have a favorite person again. You deserve to be someone's favorite person.

Jo bit her tongue.

"I would appreciate it if you didn't look at me like that," he said.

"Like what?" she asked. But she knew.

"Like you pity me. Don't. I am not alone in this world. There are several people in this world I care deeply for. I have friends."

She managed a smile. "Well, that's a relief," she said lightly.

After a moment of silence, he asked, "Do you have more questions? I really think we're almost—"

"I have a few more," she said. "Please bear with me."

"Very well." He sat stone-still, as if bracing himself for a punch.

Goodness, she hoped he didn't feel like she'd been metaphorically punching him.

"What do you do in your life that brings you joy?" she asked him.

He looked at her blankly.

"Do you have a favorite pursuit? Like…" What did aristocrats do for fun these days? "Um…cards, perhaps. Cricket? Horse racing? Hunting?" *Women?* She didn't say that out loud, but she always wished she could. It would tell her so much about her aspiring grooms. "Star-gazing? Meteorology?"

"Meteorology, as you already know."

"A fascinating pursuit, to be sure."

"And I row."

"You row? Like…a waterman?"

"Something like that."

She leaned forward, rapt. "Will you tell me more?"

For a long moment, he kept his lips stubbornly pursed. Then, he huffed out a sigh. "Very well. When I was a boy at Eton, some friends and I found an abandoned old rowboat. We restored it and began the Lions and the Lilies, a rowing club whose name we derived from the school's coat of arms." For the first time, he seemed to relax a little, settling back in the chair. His lips quirked at a memory as he continued. "Though at first, we called ourselves the Lion, singular, and the Lilies, as only one lion appears on the crest, but that resulted in quite a few—rather violent—disagreements. Obviously, *I* was the lion, as the founding member and the eldest, but none of the other lads understood basic logic."

She smiled. Finally. *Finally*, they were getting somewhere.

"So eventually, I decided to make the lion plural and generously allowed all the other club members to be lions as well, and we thought of all those slow boats we passed on the river as lilies. In any case, by the time I left Eton, we had four boats, two of which were quite fast boats we'd built on our own. I continued rowing after that, and now I own a boathouse on the Thames, where I build boats with the same group of friends and we race them against each other."

"Ah," Jo said, understanding dawning. "Your appointment on the Thames this afternoon?"

"Exactly."

"You've been building and racing boats for many years, then."

"Over twenty."

"What do you enjoy about it?"

He thought about it for a moment. "Well, it's complicated. You're out there, nothing between you and the murky depths but a plank of wood, and you're going as fast as humanly possible, every single muscle in your body straining toward the goal. You know that one wrong movement will destroy your momentum, but you don't destroy it—you're in harmony with the water and with your boat, and if you're rowing as a team, your crew. You're working in perfect unison. You're a machine." He sighed wistfully. "And then, when it's over, every muscle in your body strained to its limit, you are exhilarated. You've done your best work, and you've gone as fast and as far as you possibly could ever go."

Jo didn't know much about rowing, but she'd never imagined it was such hard physical labor. It made sense considering the tight fit of his coat across his broad shoulders, his slender waist, his flat stomach, how his thighs bulged beneath the fabric of his trousers.

"It sounds wonderful. I should like to try it sometime." He laughed, and her spine straightened. "Do you think I am jesting?"

He shook his head. "Women don't row."

"Why not?"

"Because it can be cold, wet, exhausting work. Women despise being cold, wet, and exhausted."

"Take me to your boathouse, and you will learn otherwise."

Oh, good Lord. What had she said? She'd brashly invited herself to his boathouse. What was *wrong* with her? Did she have a fever?

She brushed the back of her hand over her forehead. Cool as a spring breeze.

"I have half a mind to do just that," he said quietly, a smile still playing around the edges of his lips. "I daresay you would set foot on the premises, then spin on your heel and leave straightaway."

"Why is that?"

"It smells like the Thames...multiplied by... around ten, I'd say."

She grimaced. "Really? That does sound rather intolerable."

"There's some level of grime, I've found, associated with anything to do with large bodies of water, and the Thames ranks as one of the worst, in my experience."

"The Thames," she said, "highly ranked in rankness."

"The rankings rank it *quite* highly in rankness."

She laughed. She wanted to tell him that she'd still like to go. She'd still like to sit in one of his boats and draw an oar through the river water, rank though it may be, and experience the boat beneath her slip through the water. But Jo had been forward enough for one day, and she held her tongue.

"Well," she finally said, "your pursuit is quite an original one. I've never had a client who fancied himself a rower before."

"I'd wager you'll have more in your future. The club we started at Eton sparked off a schoolwide one that has five times the members now as it did when I was there. And Oxford has started racing eights on the Isis in the summertime."

"Eights?"

"Eights are boats with eight rowers and a coxswain."

"Well," she said, impressed at the image of a boat full of nine men speeding down a river, "I should like to see that sometime."

"Maybe—" He cut himself off abruptly, then shrugged. There was another awkward silence, then he said, "Are there any more questions?"

Right. Questions. She searched around her mind and remembered one…one that might lead to the true question she wanted to ask him—what happened with Fanny Fleming?—but couldn't bring herself to blurt out. She had to go about it in a more roundabout way.

"I asked you before about your favorite people in your life. Now, I'd like to ask about your least favorite people."

His dark brows arched. "Would you, now?"

"I would."

"That's something I'm not likely to share with my closest friends. Why would I tell you? Who knows what you might do with that kind of information?"

"You will tell me because I've no wish to waste either of our time with someone who has the qualities of your least favorite people."

She saw right away that her answer was an effective one. He'd made it clear, more than once, that he didn't like wasting his time.

"And," she continued, "I will do nothing with that information except use it to help you find your match. As I told you before, you can expect absolute discretion from me."

He pressed his lips together, giving her that

suspicious, narrow-eyed gaze that she found equally annoying and stimulating.

Finally, he said, "Very well. You must know already about my longstanding feud with the Duke of Edevane, since you mentioned him at our last meeting when you were trying to make your point about finding me a match specific to my tastes."

Her lips twisted. "I see my point worked."

"I admit...it did."

"What is it you disagree with His Grace about?"

"Everything," he said shortly.

"What do you disagree with him most passionately about?"

"His morals. His politics."

"What about them?"

"Everything."

"An example might help," she said patiently.

The duke's voice grew dark, and his eyes narrowed. "He was one of the lords to vote against the bill abolishing the slave trade."

"I see."

"He doesn't seem to care that people are dying of disease and starvation every day because men like him are so busy stuffing wealth into their own coffers."

Hmm. Perhaps she ought to stop grouping all the dukes and royals of England into the selfish bowl of inhumanity she'd shoved them into.

"All right, who else?"

"My father's brother."

Ooh, intriguing. "Why do you dislike him?"

"He's an ass."

She blinked. "I see."

"He's also my heir."

Slowly, she nodded. "So your dislike of him has prompted your matrimonial pursuits?"

"It has."

"How, may I ask, is he an ass?"

This time, he blinked at her. It was true, she didn't use the word "ass" often, especially when referring to people and not donkeys, and certainly not in the company of dukes.

But he'd used it first.

"Well, for one, he covets my title. I used to believe he wouldn't hesitate to poison my food, but now I think he's too cowardly to do it. He's just hoping I catch some deadly disease or drown in the Thames so he can inherit. He's got two sons, too, so if he perishes before me, then they're next in line."

"What are your cousins like?"

"They are children. But by all accounts, he is raising them to be as vicious as he is."

She winced. "I'm sorry to hear it."

"Anyhow," he continued without prompting, "my father never admired him. He advised me to avoid him, but then when he died and it felt like my existence had shattered"—Crestmont swallowed hard—"he was my only family left. I felt I had no one else to turn to."

Jo leaned forward. "What happened?"

"He came to live with me at Hanford Castle. I was young and grieving, and it took many months for me to realize that he was undermining everything I did. Within the year, he'd taken control of most of my unentailed holdings and a large portion of my father's fortune."

Jo sucked in a breath. "That's horrible."

"As I said…he's an ass."

"That seems a mild word for what he is," she grumbled.

He shrugged. Despite talking about his awful uncle, at this moment, the duke was relaxed and easy, and it struck Jo that this was her opening.

"I lived in Nottinghamshire as a child," she began, "and while I knew naught of your uncle, there was some other—different—gossip being spread about you at the time."

He stiffened. "You are several years younger than me. You were a child."

"Nevertheless, my family was acquainted with the Fleming family. Will you tell me about what happened between you and Fanny Fleming?"

The air in the room turned frigid, as if the season had just snapped to midwinter and a blizzard was raging outside.

His expression icy, he stood abruptly. "I am late. My coachman has been waiting for some time. I must go."

"Your Grace!" She rose, too, and hurried around her desk. "I am so sorry—I didn't mean to—"

He slapped his hat on and grabbed his cane. "Good day, Miss Porter."

Swinging open the door, he strode out and shut it firmly behind him.

Jo slumped against the door with a groan. It had been going so well, but then she'd bungled it, badly.

Now, she might have lost him for good.

CHAPTER EIGHT

Jameson was waiting when Matthew arrived at the boathouse. Arms crossed over his chest, he scowled at Matthew as he stepped down from the carriage.

"Don't." Matthew brushed past him to go inside. "I am not in the mood."

"You're late," he said anyway.

"True." Usually, he'd apologize. Not today.

Jameson's frown deepened. "What happened?"

Matthew stopped. Then, gripping one of the supports that held the boats off the floor, he turned. "I need to marry."

Jameson stared at him. "Uh…all right. I thought you'd given up on your matrimonial pursuits."

"I lied."

Jameson raised a brow.

"But I assure you, I have hated every moment."

"That much has been obvious," Jameson said. "Come on. Let's get the boat down."

They hefted *Red* off the stand and flipped it. Then, they walked it outside and carried it over wet, trampled weeds and mud down to the floating dock's edge.

As he fitted a scull into position, Matthew said, "All these frivolous society events are killing me with fake smiles, shrill platitudes, and over-perfumed bosoms."

Jameson gave him a crooked smile. "Pass some of the over-perfumed bosoms my way. I'd make good use of them."

Matthew scowled. "No."

Jameson gave a long-suffering sigh. "And I thought we were friends."

They climbed into the boat and Matthew pushed off with one of his sculls, then fitted it in the oarlock. He glanced over his shoulder at Jameson. "I have engaged the services of a matchmaker."

Jameson's brows rose. "Really?"

"Yes. She's…" Matthew gazed over the gray water, sifting through the words that came to mind to describe Joanna Porter.

Pretty. No.

Intelligent. No.

Understanding. No.

Interesting. No.

Fascinating. No.

Someone I'd like to take to bed… No, no, no.

"Nosy," he muttered.

"What was that?" Jameson said behind him as they turned the boat to prepare to begin rowing.

"Her name is Mrs. Porter… Well, that's her professional name, in any case. She's not married, and she's quite young, but by all accounts, she is the best matchmaker in London."

"Well, then…" Jameson's voice trailed off as if he didn't quite know what to make of this new information.

Matthew twisted his upper body to look at his friend. "She asked me about Fanny," he said darkly.

All lightness left Jameson's face. "Damn."

Damn indeed. No one talked to him about Fanny Fleming. Even Jameson, who knew everything about him and was more comfortable in his presence than anyone else in this world, knew better.

"Let's row," he growled. And he turned his focus to dragging his oars through the rancid waters of the Thames.

• • •

Jo felt horrid about her meeting with the duke. She'd been doing well—he'd actually been lowering some of his guards, and she'd been learning more about him, surprised to find there were parts of him she truly liked, and then she'd pushed him. Too far, too fast.

She was furious with herself.

After the duke had walked out, she'd gone upstairs and found Lilly back in bed, her eyes puffy from crying. Jo had spent the remainder of the afternoon tending to Lilly until her head pounded with an ache born of frustration and defeat.

After night fell, the household shared a simple dinner of broth, bread, and cheese at the table in the kitchen. Just as Jo and Bess were clearing the dishes, a knock sounded. Not on the front door—on the door leading to the mews. The door to Jo's office.

She glanced over at Bess, brows raised.

"Should I answer it?" Bess asked.

"No, that's all right. Finish up here. I'll see who it is." Jo grabbed the rest of the loaf of bread—it might be a beggar asking for scraps from their dinner. She couldn't spare much, but she could certainly spare a bit of bread.

Picking up the lantern, she went through the

narrow door of the kitchen then down the two steps that led to the onetime scullery that she now used as her office. She set the lantern on her desk so that she could crack open the door.

"Yes?" she said, peering through the small opening.

It wasn't a beggar—it was a liveried servant. "I've a message for Mrs. Porter," the young man said.

"Oh." She opened the door wider, then realized she was still clutching half a loaf of bread. She smiled ruefully down at it. "Sorry. I thought you were someone else."

The man's eyes flicked down to the bread, then back to her, his face carefully devoid of expression. Obviously, he was quite a well-trained servant. He held out a folded letter with a very proper-looking seal of stamped wax. "Mrs. Porter?"

"Yes. Thank you." She took the letter, he bowed, and she closed the door. She wandered back to her desk to look more closely at the letter under the lamplight. The seal belonged to the Duke of Crestmont.

She closed her eyes, clutching the letter briefly to her chest. He was probably dismissing her.

It would be a fitting cap to a perfectly wretched day.

She pushed her thumb under the seal and read the missive in the flickering light.

Mrs. Porter,
Forgive my abrupt departure earlier this afternoon. As I mentioned earlier, I had an urgent appointment on the Thames.

I should like to meet with you later this week to discuss your list of potentials. If Friday afternoon at two o'clock is not a convenient time for you, please advise.

Respectfully,
Crestmont

Jo blew out a relieved breath.

Thank goodness. He'd decided to give her a chance. And though she hadn't asked him all the questions she usually asked of her clients, she knew him well enough to start the hunt for his bride.

She thought she did, anyhow.

The Duke of Crestmont. Stern and stiff, but with a sense of honor. A man who didn't know he needed—or wanted—love. A man who'd mourned his loving parents, suffered the treachery of an uncle, then had something even worse happen to him. Something he wouldn't—perhaps felt he *couldn't*—speak of.

He thought he wanted a perfect duchess. Jo could easily find him that—it was the rest of it that would be the challenge. His wife would need to be someone strong and humble, someone with the ability to understand his complex layers, to penetrate his thick outer shell…someone who could stand up to him yet give him room to breathe when he needed it.

Jo gathered the lantern and the bread and made her way back into the now-quiet kitchen. She wrapped the bread and put it into the cabinet, then went into the parlor, where her mother sat in her favorite chair under the glow of a lamp, reading.

Mama smiled up at her, closed her book, and set

it to the side. "How was your matchmaking today? You met with the Duke of Crestmont, didn't you?"

"I did…and, you know, he's not horrid—not really. I think there might be more to the Fanny Fleming situation than meets the eye."

Mama looked intrigued. "Really? Did you ask him about it?"

"I did." Jo flopped on the sofa and leaned back to stare at the plain white of the ceiling. "He became angry and walked out of my office."

She could almost hear her mother's resulting cringe. "Oh dear."

Jo sighed. "I just wanted to know what happened. So I can ensure a successful match for him."

Her mother was quiet for a moment. Then, "Are you sure your curiosity doesn't run deeper?"

Suddenly, Jo's throat felt thick. Was she that transparent? Was it obvious to everyone how deeply Crestmont intrigued her? She swallowed hard. "Well, as you said, it was a famous scandal. And I'm a matchmaker. I make a study of matches that fall apart so I can be the best at what I do and it never happens with any of the matches I make."

"Of course."

Jo straightened and narrowed her eyes at her mother. "What are you thinking?"

"I'm thinking," Mama said patiently, "that I have noticed in the past week or so how you come to life whenever the Duke of Crestmont is mentioned. You become animated and passionate. I am starting to think that you might be developing a bit of a tendre for him."

"Mama!"

The older woman shrugged. "Perhaps I am only imagining it."

"You most certainly are," Jo said, trying to be convincing, but half convinced she was completely failing. "I am a professional matchmaker. I do *not* develop tendres for clients. Heaven forbid."

"Mmm, yes," Mama murmured. "Heaven forbid, indeed. The Duke of Crestmont would never be appropriate for you, Jo. But perhaps a different client will walk in one day... What about Mr. Pellegrini?"

She thought of Mr. Pellegrini and laughed. "Mr. Pellegrini is lovely, but he is three-and-forty and two inches shorter than me. And...well..." The truth was, while she did like him very much, she wasn't attracted to him in the least.

Not like she was attracted to the Duke of Crestmont.

"Well, maybe it is only my old heart wishing for you to find someone to fill yours."

That was easy to respond to, because this was a response she'd been giving since she was twenty and realized that to the majority of the gentlemen browsing in the marriage mart, she was too plain, too plump, and too poor. Seven years ago, she'd begun to come to terms with her fate—that she was doomed to be a wallflower and a spinster for the rest of her life.

It was then that she began to understand that she could not and would not base her future happiness on her ability to find a husband. She refused to doom herself to feelings of inadequacy for things that were out of her control. She had determined that she'd find happiness in other pursuits. And she had.

"But my clients fill my heart, Mama. And so do you and Lilly, Bess, and Mrs. Ferguson. Between all of you, my heart is filled to the brim." It was true. She loved her clients, and she loved her family. Her heart *was* full.

Except when it wasn't. There were some moments, those times that mostly came at night, when the fullness drained away and a heavy blanket of loneliness covered her like a shroud.

But it was a shroud she thrust away. She rejected it, kicked it off like a restless sleeper on a hot night.

"Oh, my dear child. You have clearly never been in love."

"I don't need to be in love to lead a full life."

Her mother patted her hand and made a noncommittal humming noise in her throat.

"In any case," Jo said, trying to redirect the conversation to its original subject, "I stepped out of bounds with the duke, and I thought he would most certainly dismiss me. But I just received a note from him. He is asking for a list of potential brides on Friday."

"That's only a few days away. Will you have enough time?"

"I think I might be able to come up with a few options by Friday." Jo handed her mother her book. "I'm just glad he's coming back."

If he'd been truly angry with her, he wouldn't be coming back. But he was, and that made her unaccountably happy. Smiling, she wished her mother good night and headed upstairs.

"Jo." Lilly laid a sheet of paper on her lap as Jo opened the door and peeked inside.

Jo fervently hoped she wasn't reading that awful letter from Charles for the thousandth time. "How are you?"

Lilly shrugged and waved her hand listlessly. "Oh, you know…"

"Wretched?"

"Well, yes. But I've been thinking of how Mrs. Ferguson told me I needed to be strong. She's right, you know."

"I do know."

"I'm young," Lilly continued. "I shall find someone else to love."

"Of course you will."

Pressing her lips together, Lilly pressed a hand to her stomach. "Though it makes me sick to think about loving anyone else in this world besides Charles."

Jo sat on the bed beside her friend. "I know it feels that way, but that feeling will fade, I'm sure of it."

She actually wasn't so sure, but she didn't tell Lilly that. She believed there was one true love for a person in their life, and she'd always thought Charles was that person for Lilly. Perhaps she was wrong.

She glanced down at the letter in Lilly's lap. "What were you reading?"

"It's a letter from Martha."

"Charles's sister?"

"Yes. His sisters are so lovely and kind. I felt like…" Lilly swallowed hard. "Like they'd already invited me into their family."

"Oh, Lil—"

"Anyhow," Lilly said. "Martha said she considers me a dear friend and she and her sisters hope to see me soon. They said they'd be happy to receive me at their house—"

"Horrible idea," Jo muttered, imagining Lilly breaking down in Charles's drawing room.

"I know. At least for now. But maybe someday…"

Someday.

At that moment, the seed of an idea materialized, as if by divine intervention, right in the center of Jo's chest. Her heart began to beat hard, and she clenched and unclenched her fist, trying to force herself to stay calm.

It might not work.

Then again, it might.

Oh, good Lord…it might!

She sucked in a shaky breath. *Settle down, Jo.* "Tell me about Charles's other sisters, Lil." She tried to modulate her tone to not reveal her excitement to her friend. It was far too early for that. "He has five of them altogether, doesn't he?"

"Yes." Lilly leaned back. "Well, the eldest is Mary. She is my age—a year younger than Charles. You know Martha, and she has a twin called Frances. They are two-and-twenty, two years younger than Mary. Then there is Harriet, who is one-and-twenty, and the baby, Esther, is eighteen. They are all out in society except for Esther, who wishes she were out, but Charles has told her she must wait another year or two."

"What are they like?"

Lilly sighed. "Oh, Jo, they are all wonderful, just like Charles is. I honestly don't know how all of them turned out so amiable, given that they are motherless, and his father was such a scoundrel."

Amiable. The duke had said he wanted someone amiable.

"How did you know that about his father?" Jo asked.

"Charles told me."

That he'd confided such information to her was further evidence that Charles had truly loved Lilly.

"He spent all his time away from home," Lilly continued. "Gambling and whoring, leaving poor Charles to essentially raise the girls on his own."

"What happened to their mother?"

"She died when Charles was thirteen."

"If your description of them is accurate, then he has done a fine job with them." Her estimation of Charles rose several notches higher.

"He loves them all dearly. They think he is the best brother in the world."

"It sounds like they might be right," Jo admitted.

"They are," Lilly said fervently. "He will make the best father someday."

Jo had told Lilly a bit about the conversation she'd had with Charles at the soiree, specifically about his desperation to find a wife who could help him financially. While that news hadn't mended Lilly's broken heart, it had made her instantly forgive Charles for ending their courtship. He hadn't been inconstant, and he hadn't betrayed her. He was breaking it off due to his loyalty to his family. His need to ensure the safety and security of his sisters.

There was almost nothing else Jo herself would have forgiven, but as unfair and horrible as it all was, she could forgive Charles this. Still, she yearned for Charles and Lilly's happiness. A way to keep his family safe *and* bring them together.

And she might have just discovered it.

Jo had known that the four eldest Cherrington sisters had been out in society for a few years, but aside from Martha, she'd never met them, nor had she interviewed them as they hadn't been potential matches with any of her previous clients. "Have they received any offers?" she asked Lilly. "Are any of them engaged?"

"No."

"But why is that? If they're as lovely as you say they are—"

"I believe there have been a few offers between the four of them, but you know how it is in this town, Jo. They aren't great beauties, and they have nothing significant to offer in terms of their dowries. The *ton* has overlooked them for the most part. *Quite* unfairly, too, if you ask me."

"Is something wrong with their appearance?"

"Not at all! They are quite pretty, all of them. Just…not great beauties."

"You mean, not like you?" Jo teased.

Lilly's mouth fell open. "I didn't say that!"

Dear Lilly. So persistently modest. "But you *are* a great beauty. You know that, don't you?"

Lilly bumped her shoulder against Jo's. "Stop."

Jo grinned at her friend, letting her excitement brim over. It was time to tell Lilly what she was thinking. Jo cupped Lilly's hand between her own and squeezed. "I might have an idea."

Lilly turned to her. "What?"

"I think I might have found the perfect match for one of the Cherrington sisters. It's one of my clients."

Lilly gasped. "Really? Ooh, is it Mr. Pellegrini?"

"No, not Mr. Pellegrini."

"Who then?" But Lilly knew—Jo could see it in the widening of her eyes.

She confirmed it anyway.

"The Duke of Crestmont."

CHAPTER NINE

On the surface, the Cherrington sisters made ideal candidates for the Duke of Crestmont. They were the granddaughters of the previous Earl of Wydwick and nieces to the current earl. The four eldest had been presented at court, and they had all been given ladies' educations. Charles had ensured they were all fully prepared to become wives of the *beau monde*.

The outward criteria were all there. Perfect.

Jo would need to meet with them first, of course, but she'd spent the past day quivering with excitement. If one of them turned out to be a good match for the duke... Well, one of Charles's sisters would be a duchess. That would pull his family straight out of financial ruin and firmly back into society's good graces. All his problems would be solved.

Best of all, he'd be free to marry Lilly.

Maybe Jo was being too optimistic. She tried to temper her excitement, but it was difficult. First, one of the sisters would have to fit into the Duke of Crestmont's definition of a perfect duchess. The morning after Jo had the idea of matching the duke to one of the Cherrington sisters, Lilly had sent a letter to the eldest sister, Mary, and the lady had responded, saying she'd be happy to visit with Jo and Lilly that afternoon.

Now they sat in the parlor, Lilly on the sofa with Mary beside her, her hands clasped demurely in her lap, with Jo on the chair across from them. Bess brought in some tea and biscuits, and Lilly poured while Jo asked Mary about herself.

"I am quite busy," Mary told them. "Aside from keeping the house in order, I spend a great deal of time studying scripture and working with Deacon Robinson in his mission in the orphanages of London. Reverend Robinson is a most honorable man. As the Bible says, 'Pure religion and undefiled before God is this: to visit the fatherless in their affliction.' Reverend Robinson's dedication to God and the betterment of all of humankind humbles me." At that, Mary, who was pretty, if not a beauty like Lilly, blushed, and Jo knew that Mary Cherrington was in love with three things, and three things alone: Reverend Robinson, scripture, and Godly pursuits…in no particular order.

Mary was not the right lady for the Duke of Crestmont. She already belonged to someone else.

It was for the best, Jo thought. Mary did have several sisters, and at least now Jo could be candid about her idea.

"Have you heard of Mrs. Porter?" Jo asked her.

Mary frowned. "Your…mother?"

Lilly laughed. "No, no. Mrs. Porter is a famous matchmaker here in London."

"Maybe not quite famous—" Jo began.

"—and she's sitting right in front of you," Lilly finished, making a flourishing motion with her hand toward Jo.

Mary's mouth rounded to an *O*. "You're…?"

"Yes," Jo said. "I am a professional matchmaker."

"She's made a dozen matches in the past year,"

Lilly said. "Do you know Sir Harry Acheson?"

"Why, yes, I do."

"Jo matched him and his wife."

Heat flushed through Jo's cheeks, as it did whenever Lilly spoke of Jo's skill at her profession with such pride in her voice.

"Oh, Lady Acheson is lovely. She is a patron of the church," Mary said.

"She *is* lovely," Jo agreed. Best of all, Sir Harry thought his wife was the loveliest creature in creation, and that was what was most important.

"And do you know Mr. Harold Dickerson?" Lilly asked.

"Of course—Mr. Dickerson is Charles's good friend." Mary's eyes widened. "Oh! You matched the Dickersons as well?"

"I did."

"All of her matches are successful," Lilly said proudly, "and all have been love matches. Every couple she has matched has been blissfully happy."

Lilly had gushed a little too much. Jo cleared her throat. "I'm looking for a match right now, for a man of discerning taste and principle—"

"He's a duke!" Lilly burst out.

"Lilly!" Jo turned narrowed eyes on her friend.

Lilly clapped a hand to her mouth. "Was I not supposed to say so?"

Jo sighed, then looked back to Mary. "Allow me to move directly to the point, Miss Cherrington. I have a client who is looking for a bride. Your younger sisters are all of marriageable age and as yet unattached, and I would like to interview them to determine if one of them might suit."

Mary's lips parted. "Is your client truly a duke?" she whispered in an awed voice.

Jo nodded. "He is." The title shouldn't make a difference, but she knew it would. A duke would make an extraordinary match for any young lady in the Cherrington family.

"Which duke?" Mary asked.

"The Duke of Crestmont."

"The Duke of Crestmont," Mary repeated in a musing voice. "I have never made his acquaintance, but I have not heard rumors of him being a dissolute or a profligate."

Jo supposed, given her dedication to the Church, it made sense that those were Mary's two most immediate concerns. "He is not," Jo confirmed. "And I believe that if he makes the right match, he will make an excellent husband."

Mary nodded slowly. "He's not over fifty, is he?"

"He is three-and-thirty."

"That seems a reasonable age." Mary gave Jo a slight smile. "And would you say he is kind?"

Jo hesitated. "Kind" would not be her first word to describe the Duke of Crestmont. Instead, "ornery," "stubborn," and "demanding" came to mind. But then…there had been moments when she believed he could be kind, but the kindness was buried under all those other things.

"He is quite kind," she said, hoping she was right.

She *was* right. She shouldn't doubt her instincts. They'd always proven correct in the past.

"I'm sure my sisters would love to meet with you." Mary hesitated. "Well, except, perhaps, for Esther. She is not out in society yet."

"I'd like to meet with her despite that." That could be overlooked, after all.

Mary smiled. "Even she will be intrigued by the possibility of meeting a duke."

"Or the possibility of marrying one?"

"I imagine so. Who wouldn't be intrigued?"

"Indeed." Jo smiled back. She couldn't understand why her heart wasn't in it. She had four potential matches for the Duke of Crestmont. If one of them married him, then Charles Cherrington could marry Lilly. Everything would be right in Jo's world again.

Yet…

Yet nothing. That strange pang in her chest when she considered matching Crestmont to a Cherrington sister…it meant nothing.

. . .

Later that afternoon, Jo met with the youngest Cherrington sister, Esther. Jo knew, almost as quickly as she'd known with Mary, that Esther and the duke wouldn't make a good match. Esther was eighteen, but she was a young and coddled eighteen and possessed neither the maturity nor the poise the duke was looking for in a duchess.

After she finished with Esther, Martha entered her office. "Good afternoon, Miss Porter," the young woman said. "It is good to see you again."

Like all the Cherrington sisters, Martha was slight and petite, with dark, curly hair and dark eyes. They were all pleasantly pretty, though Martha was the prettiest of the three Jo had met until this point.

That should have pleased Jo. Even though the duke said he cared nothing of beauty, he was a man, after all, and Jo had never met a man who was completely immune to the physical charms of the opposite sex. If she could find a lady for him who was beautiful in his eyes, it would bode well for their future.

And yet, seeing this Miss Cherrington, the prettiest Cherrington sister thus far, she wasn't pleased. Instead, a despairing feeling clutched at her.

Jealousy? No. No, it couldn't be.

"Good afternoon, Miss Cherrington. Would you like some tea?"

"Oh, thank you, yes. It is chilly outside." Removing her gloves, Miss Cherrington rubbed her hands together. Her cheeks were pink, too.

"Did you walk here?" Jo asked.

"I did. Your house is only a mile from the museum. I was there this afternoon when Mary sent me a message to come here when I was done with my work."

"Do you still work with Mr. de Havilland?"

"Yes!" Martha's face lit up. "I have become quite a devoted student of Egyptian antiquities. Mr. de Havilland says I am becoming so proficient that he will take me to Egypt to assist him with his next dig!"

It wasn't as outwardly obvious that Martha wasn't a good fit for the duke, but as Jo spoke to her more, she revealed the depth of her passion for antiquities, specifically those from the ancient Egyptian civilization. It consumed her. With a passion like that, she'd never have the time or inclination to perform her duties "amiably" as the Duchess of Crestmont.

When she realized that, Jo should have been frustrated. She should have started to worry that her plan might not work—there were only two more Cherrington sisters, after all: Harriet and Frances.

But frustration wasn't the emotion that struck her. It was *relief*.

It made no sense.

Jo met with Frances the next day. She was identical to Martha in looks but not in personality. While Martha was passionate about Egypt, Frances seemed passionate about...nothing. She was quiet and looked down at her lap instead of looking Jo in the eye as they conversed. Her voice was soft and serious, and she was so bleak, Jo just wanted to hug her and tell her everything would be all right.

"An excellent hostess," Crestmont had decreed. *"Engaging and witty in conversation."*

Sadly, Frances wouldn't do.

That left Harriet, who arrived at Jo's office on Wednesday afternoon.

Jo sucked in a breath upon seeing her. She looked very much like her twin sisters, though she was a little prettier, and she was the tallest of the five sisters, though still a hair shorter than Jo. Her dark brown hair was thick and rich, a few strands of it curling around her cheeks, her skin milky pale but with a blush of health. She was poised and polite, far more composed than Esther, livelier and more energetic than Frances, less devout than Mary, and possessing none of Martha's singular obsession with Egyptology.

When Jo asked her about things she enjoyed, she said, "I play the piano, and sometimes I sing."

"Oh, that's lovely," Jo said. "Do you enjoy playing and singing for others?"

Harriet flushed. "I like to play, but singing… My family says I should sing for others, but seeing people staring at me… Well, it flusters me. When I'm playing the piano, I can gaze down at the keys instead of at people's faces, and that keeps me from losing my nerve."

"I can understand that." Jo couldn't imagine getting up in front of a large group of people and performing anything. And a bit of modest reserve wouldn't hurt in a woman who was to be a duchess someday. Harriet seemed just pleasant and outgoing enough, and not even close to being brash or ostentatious. "What else do you enjoy?" Jo asked her.

"I adore drawing portraits of my family."

"With pencil?"

"Yes, and sometimes I dabble with watercolors."

What a perfectly ladylike occupation.

"And I love parties and other social events," Harriet said. "I adore meeting new people and learning all about them."

They talked more. Harriet and her sisters were all proficient in French, thanks to a French governess their father had employed prior to his plunge into drink and debauchery. During that time, they had also been visited weekly by a dancing master, a drawing master, and a music master, but Harriet was the only one of the sisters who'd taken a liking to, or had a talent for, the two latter pursuits.

Harriet was perfect.

She and Jo shared a pot of tea and a plate of biscuits, chatting throughout, and afterward, Harriet said she'd be amenable to meeting the duke at Lady Campbell's spring ball, which, upon approval from Harriet's brother, Jo would attend as her chaperone.

By the time Harriet left Jo's office, evening was encroaching, and Jo knew she needed to go up to dinner. Instead, she sat in her chair, her mind a whirl.

She should be ecstatic. *Should* be. She'd found the perfect candidate for the duke, in the perfect family that, if successful, would bring Charles and Lilly back together.

Instead, Jo felt hollow. She kept thinking of Crestmont, of his hard eyes and stubborn outlook. His belief that love wasn't an element of a successful marriage.

He could love Harriet, certainly. Goodness, after an afternoon with the beguiling young woman, Jo was nearly in love with her herself.

And it made Jo feel…well, not sad, exactly, but something close to it. She wished she could be Harriet right now, ready to meet with a potential future husband. And not just any potential future husband. With Matthew Leighton, the Duke of Crestmont.

Jo squelched a small shiver, thinking of his proud nose, the press of his lips, his narrowed eyes, and raven black hair. The way his eveningwear had clung to him at the soiree. His pride, his distrust, and how it had softened for a while the last time he'd been sitting across from her here. His rare smile and even rarer laugh not only brought her satisfaction that she'd elicited such a response from him, but also made her want to smile and laugh in return. The light brush of his arm against hers as they stood at the window discussing—of all things—the weather, and the heat that fabric-covered contact sent sparking through her body.

She'd never had these feelings about any of her previous clients. And she needed to stop. Not only would she be a highly improper match for the Duke of Crestmont, but he also wasn't at all interested in her. She rather thought he despised her, trusted her little, if at all, and was using her only because he felt his other options were more distasteful than dealing with her.

Jo sighed and pushed back from her desk. She needed to thrust these silly thoughts away. She *needed* to be ecstatic. She was going to match the Duke of Crestmont with Harriet Cherrington, and not only were they going to live happily ever after, but Charles Cherrington and Lilly would live happily ever after, too.

That should be enough to make Jo happy. She'd been able to will herself to happiness for twenty-seven years, and she'd keep doing it.

So Jo hid away that secret kernel of longing inside her. She locked it up tight and buried the key under all her hopes and dreams for those she loved.

CHAPTER TEN

Matthew had busied himself for the last few days with rowing, Parliament, and contacting experts to help him find a solution to the strange fungus that had been attacking the trees in the apple orchard at Hanford Castle.

Certainly a *fungus* should have been enough to keep his mind off the matchmaker and the list of potential brides she'd provide him with on Friday.

It wasn't.

Actually, it was Miss Porter herself, not her list, keeping his mind occupied. Her final question on Saturday had made long-tamped emotion well up— rage and impotence and those feelings of inadequacy that had plagued him since he was a youth, doubling when his father had died, leaving him an untarnished legacy and shoes too big to ever be filled. His father had been one of the most respected men in England, and Matthew understood exactly why. Compared to the wisdom of his father, he was still, at three-and-thirty, a bumbling, inept, impulsive youth.

That had been made clear to him, a final and undeniable message that he'd never be the man his father was, when, just two months after the duke's death, he'd run away to Scotland with Fanny Fleming.

He'd been rude to Miss Porter by stomping away, but it had been his only option. If he'd stayed, he would have certainly lashed out, and Miss Porter didn't deserve that.

Truthfully, he'd never met a woman who'd annoyed him to such an extent, a woman who was overbearing, nosy, and superior while at the same time intriguing him, and not only physically, though he found her curves erotic as hell. As much as he'd attempted to hold onto his reserve in her presence, she'd drawn him out. The *real* him.

He didn't know how she'd done it, but when he'd been in her office on Monday, he'd felt comfortable. Like he could tell her anything, and she'd look at him with those pretty gray eyes without judgment. Like she respected him for who he was. Not for his title, who he could never be, or even who he *should* be. But just for him.

Matthew left his house on Friday at noon, giving himself a full two hours to walk the mile to Miss Porter's office. Of course, it would not take him that long, but it was a pleasant enough day outside, and he could not stand another moment of prowling around his cavernous townhouse waiting for the time of the meeting to come round.

He took a most circuitous route to Marylebone, first going in an opposite direction to Hyde Park, taking his time to stroll along the paths adjacent to the Serpentine River, studying the young ladies strolling through the park with their chaperones and suitors and wondering if any of them would be on Miss Porter's list.

Then, checking his pocket watch often to determine which twists and turns would get him to Miss Porter's office at two o'clock on the nose, he walked along the edge of Kensington Gardens before striding north and winding through Marylebone. He turned south, passing the enormous, crowded workhouse just a few blocks from Miss Porter's modest townhouse and doubling back to arrive at 18 Beaumont Street at 1:59 in the afternoon.

Clutching his walking stick, Matthew stood gazing at her door. What was she doing beyond the thick slab of wood? Was she finalizing his list? He imagined her writing, looking down at her desk, chewing absently on her plump lower lip as she wrote, those soft strands of hair curling around her chin.

Was she daydreaming about him as he was about her?

Of course she was not. She was professional and businesslike with him—never looked at him like all those ladies he was introduced to and danced with at the society functions. She was practical and focused on the end goal of finding him a bride.

Something he should be focused on as well. Something he *would* be focused on, if he had any sense.

It struck him, standing in front of her door like this, that the thoughts going through his mind were similar to those he'd had when he was seventeen years old. Thoughts he'd had of Fanny Fleming.

And look what disaster those thoughts had led to.

He needed to stop. Immediately. *Feelings*—those pesky things led to disaster. They should be beneath him, but they were not, because he was weak. And he was a damn fool.

"You stupid simpleton."

"You aren't half the man your father was."

"You don't deserve the title of duke."

Matthew sucked in a breath and closed his eyes. He needed to banish thoughts of Miss Porter, once and for all.

When he'd finally gathered himself enough to knock on the door, he was one minute late.

She opened it, and at her kind, welcoming expression, all those feelings he'd just squelched came roaring back.

Deuce it all, he was *happy* to see her. Happy to see her smile, her kind gray eyes, her not-quite-brown hair...*all* of her.

"Your Grace!" she exclaimed. "Please, come in."

He entered, and they went through the ritual of sitting in their respective places. Once they'd done so, he placed a hand on her desk and leaned slightly forward. "Before we begin, Miss Porter, I should like to apologize. I fear I was unforgivably rude last time I was here."

"Oh," she said. "No, no, not at all. It was I who was unforgivably rude."

"I refused to answer your questions," he said, his heart beating fast, "and I know you were simply asking them to better help you choose an ideal bride for me."

She hesitated. "That's true, but it is all right. Truly. I didn't mean to pry."

And yet, she still wanted to know. He could see it in her eyes. Glancing around, he wished this room weren't so tiny. He wanted to pace. Instead, his hand slid off the desk, and he clenched it in his lap. "I..."

He cleared his throat. "Last time we met, you expressed some interest in my weather research, and I... Well, I brought some of my charts."

She clapped her hands together and grinned in delight. "Really? Oh, Your Grace, thank you. Will you show them to me?"

Her interest confused him but at the same time, he found it charming. He pulled out the sheets of paper he'd tucked into his pocket and unfolded them, then pushed them to the center of her desk. "This is a graph of this month's weather, compared to April of last year."

She bent over the sheets, her finger moving over the lines as she studied them. "It is warmer this year."

He showed her his other charts—predictions, barometric trends, and historical readings, including rainfall and snow averages.

She thought it was magnificent. She wasn't faking it because he was a duke, or because he was one of the richest lords in England. No, she was truly impressed. That made his chest swell with something akin but not quite equivalent to pride. It made him feel accomplished. *Satisfied.*

Finally, they finished going over his long-accumulated data and study, and he tucked the papers back into his pocket. For a moment, he stared at her as she smiled back at him.

"About Fanny Fleming," he said suddenly. "I'd like to tell you what happened."

She jerked back, surprised.

He hadn't known he was going to say that. He hadn't planned to tell her a damn thing about Fanny.

But there she went again, opening his mouth like she was the sole person to hold the key to what he kept inside.

"All right," she murmured. Then, she waited patiently as he gathered his courage.

Finally, he started. "The Flemings were acquaintances of my parents, and as such, I'd known Fanny since I was a young boy. We went from despising each other, as young girls and boys tend to do, to developing affection for each other." He laughed ruefully. "At least, I felt affection for her. I believed she did for me, too."

He closed his eyes, opened them, then forced himself to continue. "When my parents died, I rushed home from school to take on the responsibilities that had been suddenly piled upon my shoulders. My uncle George arrived as well, presumably to help me make the transition into my new role. But he…" Swallowing, Matthew shook his head. "He didn't do a very good job of it. He implied my parents had failed at preparing me to take on the role of duke. He made me feel insignificant. Incompetent. Like I'd never live up to my father's legacy."

"You were so young, and in mourning, though," Miss Porter said. "You needed love and support, not to be belittled."

She was right. He *had* needed love and support. He'd needed time to mourn, then he'd needed more time to learn everything about what was expected of him now that he was the Duke of Crestmont. Uncle George had probably known it, but he'd done everything possible to undermine Matthew's sense of self-worth.

He shrugged. "With him consistently, and deliberately, I believe, picking away at my confidence, I began to feel—well, one might say I became rather lonely."

"What a *horrid* man." Miss Porter's features had gone dark with fury. "I should very much like to have been there. I would have given him a piece of my mind."

"What would you have said?"

"I would have told him to leave you alone to grieve. To give you time and space to find your footing as duke. To stop belittling and demeaning you. I would have reminded him that you were young and needed support."

Her words made him realize that, since his parents had died, not many people had stood up for him. Aside from Cole, Winthrop, and Jameson, no one had really cared about him. No one had given a second thought to protecting him; rather, they begged to be protected *by* him.

This woman before him, a near stranger, wanted to stand up for him. He was grateful. More than that.

He wanted to kiss her.

The thought bolted through him, and he jerked to standing from the ugly green chair. Looking away, he sucked in air and strode to the door before turning around and raising his hand to combat the sudden expression of alarm on her face. "Don't worry, I'm not leaving. I just—" How could he explain? He couldn't. So he didn't try. Instead, he merely sighed.

She walked around the desk and came to stand

closer to him, placing her hand on his arm. He wanted to lean into her, but he held himself stiff. "I understand this is difficult. You don't have to—"

"No, no. I'll continue." He swallowed again, looking down into her upturned face. So pretty. The kindness glowing there lent him strength.

"The Flemings asked if they could stay at Hanford Castle a while to 'help me through such a difficult time.' Knowing that Mr. Fleming and my father had been friends, I said yes, and after they arrived, I began to feel human again. For the first time, I felt like I could be a duke. A man. Fanny and I grew close, and when she said she loved me, I clung to that, telling myself that I loved her, though now I'm not so certain I actually did. Perhaps I just loved the idea that, after the loss of the people in the world most important to me, there was still someone who cared. I felt like she was all I had in this new world where I felt so alone. I wanted to keep her by my side, so I clung to her. I was determined she would be the one thing I wouldn't lose.

"I knew my uncle would disapprove of the match, because she was a country girl with no family of note, so I did what I believed would be the most romantic thing…" He paused.

"You took her to Scotland."

"I did." He swallowed. "My uncle discovered the scheme a few hours after we left, and he followed us in a mad pursuit to Gretna Green. We'd just arrived and were speaking with the blacksmith when Uncle George's carriage rumbled up and he flew out of it in a rage."

"Oh my goodness," Miss Porter murmured, her

hand still on his arm in a comforting squeeze.

"I told him I was marrying Miss Fleming and there was nothing he could do to stop it." He sucked in a breath, but there wasn't enough air in this tiny room. He gave in and loosened his cravat. "But…I was wrong."

"What did he do?" Miss Porter breathed, her eyes shiny and wide.

Matthew's lips twisted. "He'd found a letter Fanny had written to one of her school friends. In it…" His voice dwindled, and he took a moment to find it again. "In it, she talked about how she'd duped me. She said she didn't love me, but she was willing to do anything to be the next Duchess of Crestmont, including falsifying a personal interest in me, who she found dull, insipid, and morbidly overwrought by the loss of my parents."

"Oh, Your Grace," Miss Porter breathed. "I am so sorry."

"Perhaps she was right," Matthew said. "I learned the importance of keeping a stiff upper lip from birth, but when my parents died, I…I just *couldn't*. It was the biggest blow of my life, and it was difficult for me to face an existence without them in it. They were so healthy. I'd always believed they had many happy years in front of them."

"Of course you did."

He smiled down at her. "You're very kind, Miss Porter."

"No, not really."

"Compassionate, then."

"It's difficult not to be. In the matter of a few months, you were dealt so many blows a boy of your age should never have had to face."

He gave a self-deprecating shrug. "It was years ago. I should not have reacted as I did when you mentioned Fanny. But I never speak of it, or of that time at all, and it brought it all back so quickly, I—"

"I understand," she said quietly. "And I really am sorry for forcing you to relive all those awful memories."

"Don't be." He meant it. He felt better having poured it all out to her. Like the contents of a heavy sack of flour had blown off, bit by bit, from his shoulders.

The way she looked up at him, lips slightly parted, eyes shining... She did care, he had no doubt about it. And she was so lovely, so engaged. They were together, complete in sharing a memory that had, until this point, belonged solely to him.

He couldn't help himself. He leaned closer. Closer still.

Reaching up, he stroked a single finger over her cheek. The silky softness of her skin was a balm to his soul. She tilted her head up to his, her eyes so wide and clear and honest.

He brushed his mouth against hers, feeling her gasping intake of air rush against his lips, feeling her body tense a hairsbreadth away from his. Her lips were warm, pillowy soft, and delicious. He slipped his arm behind her back and tugged her closer.

She gave in. He knew the moment she did, her hand, still holding his arm, tightening, her lips moving in tentative exploration against his own.

She tasted sweet and sensual and innocent, and he wondered if anyone had ever kissed her before. If not, she was a quick learner—her movements grew bolder, more erotic by the second.

He deepened the kiss, his hand sliding up and over the buttons running down her back, tugging her closer and closer still, until his fingers were submerged in the soft hair at her nape and both their breaths were harsh. Touching his tongue to hers, he moved his hand back down, flicking open the top button of her dress.

She froze, lips still pressed against his, and he stopped breathing. Slowly, he drew back.

God, what was he doing? What did he think, that he was going to bed her right here, right now? When she was about to procure her list of his potential brides? What was wrong with him?

He dropped his hand, realizing her dress was gaping just below her neck where he'd released the button. She released his arm, her own hand slipping down his forearm until it dropped limply to her side. She was gazing straight ahead, her eyes seeming to bore holes into his clavicle. He pulled all the way back.

"I'm so sorry," he rasped out.

For the first time since he'd met the woman, she seemed utterly speechless. Her gaze jerked upward until she stared at him, eyes glassy, cheeks a dark pink, and lips shining from their kiss.

Her lips parted, and she murmured a breathy, "Oh."

He blinked hard. "Forgive me. I just…" He shook his head. "Forgot myself. My apologies. Please…" He moved around behind her. "Allow me to…uh… remedy this situation."

His heart was still pounding furiously. With fumbling hands much less smooth than they'd been while beginning to undress her, he rebuttoned her dress as she stood there as if she'd just laid eyes on Medusa. When he was done, he placed his hands on her shoulders and turned her to face him.

"Miss Porter?" he asked, as once again she turned her eyes to his. "Please...say something."

CHAPTER ELEVEN

Finally, Jo was able to push out some words, though they emerged in a whispering rasp. "I... May I sit down?"

He led her on legs that felt as insubstantial as raw dough to the green armchair, which he angled away from her desk, and she sank into it, not taking her eyes from his. He looked handsome, as always, as he knelt in front of her. But beyond that, his eyes and lips were pinched in concern. She'd never seen that expression from him before.

He gathered her hands in his. "Are you all right, Miss Porter?"

"Jo," she murmured. "Please. Call me Jo." He might as well at this point.

He took a moment, allowing this to sink in. Then said, "Are you all right, Jo?"

No. Trembles had overtaken her body, and she felt weak, and her heart was beating so hard she feared it might decide to give up and stop altogether.

"Yes," she said. "I've never... I've never been kissed before. I thought I never would be."

This man kneeling before her—he'd kissed her. And it wasn't a fleeting, brushing, cool pass of his lips. It was hot and deep and real, and his strong hands had traveled possessively over her body, and it had weakened her knees and made heat bloom low in her belly as she'd kissed him back, tasting the bergamot and citrus flavor of him. It was the most wonderful thing. She'd never imagined it would be like that—a delirious cloud of pleasure surrounding her, overwhelming her.

"I...didn't think I'd like it so much," she told him, her voice raw with honesty.

His eyes widened.

But then, he'd unbuttoned her dress, and she'd come crashing back down to earth, her body growing tense all over and her mind freezing into a sudden state of shock.

"It took me by surprise, that's all. I had no idea..." Her voice dwindled, and heat washed up her neck. She knew if she looked in a mirror, her chest would be covered with unsightly blotches of pink.

Slowly, his concern vanished, replaced by another expression she'd never seen on his face before as he took a shallow breath. What was it?

But she knew, and her body responded in kind. *Desire.*

They stared at each other. *Oh.* Heat pulsed between them. Carnal desire. She wanted him with a need that radiated from within her. She wanted to wrap herself around him, find her pleasure in him, and pleasure him in return. She leaned forward, breathing in his sweet and tart essence. She wanted everything from this tall, powerful man, this duke. This *client.*

She drew back, snapping out of the haze of lust in an instant. He stared at her, then with a subtle shake of his head, he drew back, too, banking the fire between them.

"I'm so sorry," she murmured.

"No," he said gruffly. "It is I who must apologize.

Forgive me."

Forgive him? She rather felt like *thanking* him. The last few moments had been the most exciting of her life.

But alas, he was her client, and she was in the process of finding him a proper wife. She'd *found* him the proper wife. Accomplished and amiable Harriet Cherrington, who'd be an excellent conversationalist at his fancy house parties and make him a perfect duchess.

Jo was doing this not only because it was her job to do so, but because matching him would be the greatest coup of her career. And for Lilly. Dear Lilly, whom she loved beyond measure and wanted with all her heart and soul to find her happily ever after.

She rose, and he instantly came to his feet to stand before her. "We should…proceed," she said. She'd meant the words to come out firm and businesslike, but instead they emerged with an airy tremble.

The duke cleared his throat. "Of course."

She walked woodenly around her desk to resume her seat behind it. She looked down at the list she'd created for the duke, then back up at him. The wariness was back in his eyes.

He had no idea what she'd do next. She had to put him at ease, but she had no idea how.

She must say something. They both needed to move past this.

She took a deep breath. "I want to…to thank you, Your Grace."

He stared at her.

"It was…um…quite…" She scrambled for a word

that was true. "Wonderful."

They gazed at each other until she wrenched her eyes away. "However, it was a momentary lapse of judgment on my part, and—"

"No, not at all," he interrupted. "It was a lapse of judgment on mine."

She forced a smile, though she feared it looked more like a gruesome twist of her lips. They were in agreement, then. It was a lapse of judgment on both their parts. "It shouldn't happen again, however."

"I agree," he said.

Excellent. Perfect. They were in agreement on that as well. Where was the relief she ought to be feeling? She dug around for it, but it was nowhere to be found.

"Right, then." She cleared her throat.

His stiff demeanor had returned, settling over him like armor. She should be grateful for it.

She wasn't.

She ground her teeth together so hard, it was a miracle they didn't crack. She'd force herself to be relieved that they were in agreement, that the duke had returned to his closed-off self. That was how it should be. That was how she *wanted* it to be.

Even if she didn't want it, she'd *make* herself want it.

There. Better now.

She rotated the paper on her desk and pushed it toward him.

"Here is a list of five young ladies, all of whom would make excellent duchesses for you."

She'd curated the list carefully. Harriet Cherrington was by far the preferred candidate, and she was certain that the duke would agree. The other four were in their first or second Seasons this year. They weren't necessarily improper, but she'd chosen them deliberately to highlight Harriet as the most ideal candidate.

She'd never done that before—create a list for a client with a favorite in mind for him. She hoped it worked.

It will *work, Jo. It has to.*

He shifted uncomfortably in his seat. It must be because of the awkward moment they'd just shared, because sitting on her green armchair was like floating on a cloud.

The urge to squirm overwhelmed her, and she shifted in her seat as well. This was ridiculous. Unable to bear a second longer in this tiny, stifling room, she rose suddenly. Ever the gentleman—except, apparently, when he kissed her—the duke rose an instant after her. "It's a lovely day outside," she said, then looked sharply at him. "I trust it will remain so?"

"It will," he said warily.

"Then I propose we go for a walk."

He raised a brow. Of course, it wouldn't be proper for her, an unmarried woman, to walk with someone such as him out in the open, but Bess could chaperone them. She'd served that purpose before with Jo and her clients. "Don't worry," she said. "My maid will accompany us, of course."

"Your good friend, the maid."

"Exactly." She shot him a saucy look, her mouth curved up at one corner. "My *dear* friend."

He shrugged, stolid mask firmly in place. "Very well."

"The fresh air will do us some good, I daresay," she said, "and as we walk, I can tell you more about the potentials on my list and about our plans for the next step. I'll go fetch Bess."

She hurried inside, finding Bess in the parlor patching an old coat. The younger woman was more than happy for the opportunity to spend some time outdoors. She quickly pulled on her pelisse, while Jo donned her black velvet bonnet and matching spencer. Arm in arm, they walked back into the office, where the duke was waiting, cravat retied— though somewhat less meticulously—hat and gloves on, walking stick in hand. After Jo introduced him to Bess, the younger woman dipped into a curtsy. "Good afternoon, Your Grace."

The duke took a moment to study Bess, then opened the door, and the three of them stepped outside. Jo and Crestmont pulled slightly ahead as they left the mews and turned southwest toward Mayfair—the location of the duke's London residence. She knew better than to parade them through Hyde Park, where they'd be seen—and gossiped about—rather keeping them to busy streets where people were too busy with their own troubles to pay them much heed.

The duke allowed her to lead the way, seemingly uncaring of the route, which she appreciated. Many of her clients questioned her when they walked together. "Don't you think we'll avoid the mud if we take Park Lane instead?" etcetera. Whereupon, she'd have to patiently explain that she'd perfected routes through London that would keep them out of the keen observations of the rumormongers.

As they walked, she told him the details of the ladies she'd chosen for him to meet. There was Miss Islington, second cousin of the Earl of Derby and granddaughter of the Marquess of Winterhaven, who was in her second Season and had already turned down three marriage proposals. She was poised and well-bred, but a bit haughty and not as pretty as Harriet.

Miss Gainsborough was the second daughter of Viscount Gainsborough, the patriarch of an influential and highly respected family of the *haute ton*. She was rather young, in her first Season, and prone to fits of the giggles.

Then, there was Harriet. "I do think you'll like Miss Cherrington," Jo told the duke as they walked along the edge of Cavendish Square. The sun blazed overhead, the white clouds like cheerful puffs of cotton. "She is one-and-twenty, in her second Season, and she is an accomplished artist and pianist."

"Her pedigree?"

"Perhaps you'll recall our conversation about broodmares?" she said archly.

He narrowed his eyes at her but rephrased. "Have you any knowledge of her lineage?"

"She is a niece of the Earl of Wydwick and the granddaughter of the previous earl."

He nodded, satisfied, and Jo went on. "Miss Cherrington is quite pretty, and she is lively and entertaining in conversation."

The duke took this in, his walking stick tapping along the cobbles, his back straight, his expression a cool mask. They walked close to each other, and Jo had not been able to stop her breath from catching each time his coat sleeve brushed the velvet sleeve of her spencer. She also hadn't been able to stop from watching how his black-gloved fingers curled over the top of his walking stick, remembering his fingers bare and open, pulling her toward him, sinking into the hair at her nape…

"All of these ladies sound perfectly acceptable," the duke said when she'd finished describing all of them. "But I will have to meet them."

"Of course. I have already made plans for you to meet Miss Cherrington and Miss Islington at Lady Campbell's ball on Monday."

The duke's lips pursed. "You know how I feel about balls."

"I do," Jo said sympathetically. "But the balls, soirees, and assemblies—"

"*All* of which I dislike," the duke interrupted.

"All of which you dislike," Jo agreed, "are the easiest and most accepted ways for a titled gentleman like yourself to meet a potential match in London."

The duke let out a sigh. "Very well. I will attend Lady Campbell's ball. I believe I have an invitation."

"I am certain you do."

"What about the rest of them?" the duke asked.

"The other three ladies will be in attendance at Almack's Assembly Rooms on Wednesday. You will attend and meet them then."

Almack's was the premier "public" ballroom of London, presenting balls every Wednesday night. Though the venue wasn't particularly grand and the food so bland and meager as to be a joke, admittance was regulated by a group of society ladies who doled out vouchers based on very strict criteria. A spotless reputation was crucial. Wealth on its own was not enough. A title helped but still wasn't a guarantee. The patronesses searched for some unmeasurable quantity of all three.

"Will you be in attendance at either gathering?" the duke asked.

"I will be at the ball chaperoning Miss Cherrington. Unfortunately, I do not have a voucher to allow me entry to Almack's."

"Why not?"

She smiled. Sometimes he was refreshing. "Because I do not meet the patronesses' strict criteria for entrance. But do not worry," she added graciously, "you will. You must apply post haste."

He scowled. "I should speak with the patronesses regarding your admittance. Lady Jersey is one of them, isn't she? Who else?"

She waved her hand. "Nonsense, Your Grace."

"I would like you to be there," he grumbled.

Those ladies of Almack's Assembly Rooms were nothing less than dragons who guarded their lair with sharp claws and breath of fire. Penniless, titleless spinster that she was, Jo was fairly certain that a hundred dukes wouldn't have the ability to win her entry into the place, but she kept that to herself. His words sent a flush of happiness through her, nonetheless. "I needn't be present for every meeting you have. You will manage well enough on your own. You will dance with each of the young ladies, and then you will report your opinions of each back to me on Thursday at one o'clock." Seeing the skeptical look on his face, she added, "Easy."

"It doesn't sound easy."

She raised her hand to touch him, thought better of it, and dropped her hand back to her side. "It will be."

Sidestepping a steaming pile of horse manure on the side of the road, they turned toward Berkeley Square. Jo would need to be sure to keep her distance from him now—this was an elite area of London. People would recognize the Duke of Crestmont here.

They moved on to other topics—his new method of making a rain gauge and how he and Oliver Jameson had raced yesterday in the boat they called *Red* and had failed to beat their friends yet again. He asked about her family, and Jo told him about Mama and Lilly, about how her father had seen something in Lilly and brought her into the rectory to be tutored alongside Jo.

"She absorbed knowledge like a sponge, and when my father began to share his passion in architecture with her, something in her latched on to it. She's absolutely brilliant. Her designs are pure genius."

"I should like to see them sometime," the duke said.

"I am sure she would love to show them to you."

They walked on, crossing the square and turning into Hill Street, the location of the duke's London townhouse. As they approached, the duke's step faltered. Seeming to suddenly realize where they were, he turned to her, his mask temporarily forgotten.

"We are close to my house."

She smiled at him. "I thought I'd walk you home."

"That is the opposite of how it should be," he said.

"How do you mean?"

"The gentleman should be escorting the lady to her front door."

"Well, that wouldn't have been a very pleasant walk, would it?" she asked. "Given the fact that we were just a step from my front door when we commenced walking."

"I suppose not. Still, I feel as if I should walk you back."

"Nonsense. Bess is with me," she said. "Besides, I've some shopping to do on the way home." That was a lie, but their business was done, and Jo needed space from the Duke of Crestmont. After all that had happened today, she had to reorient herself. Remember and solidify her priorities.

Crestmont turned to Bess, nodded at her, and gave her a small, surprising smile before moving his gaze back to Jo. "Very well." He bowed stiffly. "Good day, Miss Porter."

She curtsied. "I will see you at Lady Campbell's ball on Monday."

His nod was sharp. "Monday."

CHAPTER TWELVE

Matthew spent the next two days in a state of anxiety. The minutes seemed to drag on. Even rowing didn't make the time pass any faster.

He couldn't wait for this business to be over. The more he thought about meeting his future duchess, the more the weight of a ton of bricks seemed to press on his chest.

Once it was all over, he'd retire to Northumberland, where the air was not so heavy with coal smoke nor the streets so crowded with people. Where he could breathe and be out in the open and be free.

Where he'd have to do his duty and bed his wife until he impregnated her.

God.

He couldn't think of bedding any of the ladies on that list Miss Porter had given him. He couldn't think of bedding anyone.

Except her.

Joanna Porter. Jo—he'd heard her friend address her by that little nickname at the Dickersons' soiree. It was a tiny name that packed a mighty punch. Sweet Jo, sharp-tongued and brightly innocent. That curved body and those beautiful, intelligent gray eyes that saw through the steel barrier of his title.

Yes, he could think of bedding her. And he did, often, the thoughts of her naked beneath him so raw and decadent, he had no choice but to slake his lust with his hand.

His hand was nothing compared to how her soft body would feel under him.

Those names on that list would be nothing compared to her.

No, he couldn't think that. He would make one of those five women his duchess. He would make it work. Jo had said that if none of them were suitable, they'd try again, but he couldn't do that. He didn't have the time. Worse, it might just kill him, having to go through this again with her. Having to talk about the appeal of other women while thinking no other woman could hold a candle to her.

And so his thoughts went on Saturday as he rowed with Jameson on the Thames and then discussed the plan for a new boat over ale at a tavern, Sunday when he appeared at church and only just managed to refrain from falling asleep during the rector's extra-long sermon, and Monday as he paced his study trying to focus on correspondence from his country estates, then sat through a droning session at Parliament, when all he could think about was seeing Jo that night.

What would she be wearing? It was true that at the last dance she'd attended, she'd been simply dressed compared to some of the other ladies there. But her body was made of sin, and the modest clothes only piqued his curiosity about what lay beneath the layers of fabric.

The hours dragged on until it was time to prepare for the ball. His valet, Timothy, stood by, towel at the ready, as Matthew shaved, and once he'd donned his stockings, knee breeches, shirt, waistcoat, and tailcoat, Timothy carefully tied his freshly starched cravat. When that was done, the valet turned around with a jar of pomade, but Matthew waved him off.

"I'm done with pomade. If society decides to shun me because I refuse to smear my hair with that nasty-smelling stuff, then I will happily be banished."

"This pomade is infused with mint, Your Grace," Timothy said.

"Yet you can still smell the stench of the suet beneath it." No matter how heavily it was perfumed, pomade still smelled rank to him.

"As you wish, Your Grace." Impassively, Timothy returned the pomade to its shelf.

An hour later, Lady Campbell was greeting him. He'd known her father, Lord Norsey, who was a stern sort of man who'd raised his two daughters under an iron hand, but Lady Campbell was energetic and vivacious as she introduced Matthew to her husband, the Scottish war hero, Sir Robert Campbell. Obviously, the two were smitten with each other. Matthew wondered what it would be like when he and his wife—who might be in this very room at this very moment—greeted people at their own parties. Would they look at each other like the Campbells did? With unadulterated affection in their eyes? And would they touch each other so companionably, with such fondness? Doubtful.

Matthew strode into the horde of people, many of whom stopped to greet him. Since he'd avoided social events until this year, he'd known few of these people at the beginning of the Season, but that was changing now. The faces were growing more familiar, but finally he saw a pair more familiar than the rest—Lord Winthrop and Lord Coleton, who both grinned widely as he walked up.

Winthrop slapped him on the back. "You came."

"Despite your aversion to these things," Cole added.

"Indeed."

Cole turned in a slow circle. "Damned hot in here, isn't it? Where is the refreshments room? I require punch."

"*I* require a dance partner," Winthrop said.

They split up, Matthew deciding finding refreshment was a better choice than finding a dance partner. As they entered a room filled with tables laden with hors d'oeuvres, cakes, tarts, and biscuits, Matthew saw Joanna Porter standing off to the side. She wore a simple gown of pale yellow that revealed her voluptuous curves—the dip of her waist, the roundness of her bottom, the creamy swells of her breasts. God, she was lovely. After taking a glass of punch, Matthew excused himself from Cole and walked over to her.

"Miss Porter."

She startled, and her punch sloshed over the lip of the glass. "Oh dear!"

"Sorry." Taking out his handkerchief, he knelt and mopped up the tiny amount that had spilled onto the floor. When he rose, she was smiling at him, which softened his own tight lips enough to turn upward.

"Well, good evening, Your Grace."

"It's good to see you," he said, and he wasn't lying. Seeing her had loosened something in him.

Her eyes flicked back to the dance floor, and they

stood for a few moments in companionable silence. Then, she said, "Are you ready to meet Miss Cherrington and Miss Islington?"

"I suppose." He supposed he didn't have much of a choice.

"They are both dancing, but when she is finished, Miss Cherrington will return to me, so you will be meeting her first. I'd suggest you ask her for the next dance. If you enjoy yourself, you should ask her for a second dance in approximately one hour."

"You have this all planned out, don't you?"

"It is my job, isn't it?"

Her job. Right. He took a healthy sip of punch.

The music wound down, and the tension in Matthew's belly wound up. Harriet Cherrington would be approaching him soon. Would she be the one? *The one* in lowercase, of course. Not in uppercase—he wasn't looking for that, as much as Jo would like him to think he was.

His eyes scanned the ballroom as the dancers separated from their partners. There were many, many young women here tonight, some attractive, some plain, some tall and some short, some fair and some dark. He'd no idea which one was Harriet.

Until she was practically on top of him.

"Your Grace, I'd like you to meet Miss Harriet Cherrington. Miss Cherrington, this is the Duke of Crestmont."

Harriet Cherrington was passably pretty, which was neither here nor there, he supposed. Her hair was dark, her stature average, her jewelry and dress appropriate for the occasion.

"Your Grace," Miss Cherrington said as she

bobbed a curtsy.

He bowed. "Miss Cherrington. I am pleased to meet you." They chatted about the fine weather for a few minutes, Matthew forbidding himself to delve too deeply into the topic, and when he asked her if she'd care to dance, she said, "Why, thank you. I'd love to."

Her response to him, he had to admit, was perfect. Not overly unctuous and gushing, but neither was she disinterested. She was pleasant and unassuming. He held out his arm. "Shall we?"

Miss Cherrington glanced over to Jo, but Matthew forced himself to keep his gaze firmly fixed on the dark-haired young woman. She took his arm, and he led her onto the dance floor.

He bowed, she curtsied, and the dance began.

She was a good dancer, and that boded well for their future, he supposed. And she smiled graciously and appeared as though she was enjoying herself.

She wasn't all fiery curves under his hands like Jo had been. But that was of no consequence.

He supposed he should attempt conversation. "Where is your family from, Miss Cherrington?"

"Cumbria. Have you ever visited the area, Your Grace?"

Only once. On his way to Gretna Green with Fanny Fleming. He swallowed hard as he completed a figure and they were face-to-face once again. "Never, but I hear it's a lovely part of England."

"Oh, it is. I haven't been there since my father died—"

"I'm so sorry for your loss," he said automatically.

"Thank you." They separated into another figure.

When they were back together, she said, "It has been many years, and my brother Charles sold the house a decade ago. But I would like to return to Cumbria one day. My happiest days were spent up there. My sisters and I spent so many summer afternoons by the lakeshore, our nurse feared we'd cook ourselves to leather under the sun."

"Her fear seems to have been unfounded." Her skin was perfectly adequate. Not leathery at all.

"Thank goodness," she murmured.

Her skirts swished around his lower legs as they executed a turning figure with another couple. "How many sisters do you have?" he asked her.

"Four. And one brother, Charles. He is the oldest of the six of us—and he is a wonderful brother. Actually, we are all quite close."

He continued to ask her questions, and she answered readily, telling him about her passion for drawing and playing the piano, and her more secretive love of singing. She talked more about her family, and about her many friends among the fashionable set in town.

He could find absolutely nothing wrong with her, though he was trying his damnedest to find something.

This lady might make an acceptable duchess. In a few weeks, he just might make her his bride. He gazed down at her in a rare moment of silence between them. It seemed odd, to think of this stranger as someone with whom he might spend the rest of his life.

He remembered his parents, who'd not only been husband and wife, but they'd been best friends as well, with true respect and admiration for each other. How many times had his father told him his mother was the most beautiful and intelligent woman in the world? And how many times had his mother told him his father was the most handsome and wise man in the world? Countless. Until he was seventeen and realized that they were, in fact, mortal, he'd been close to believing his parents could walk on water if they ever wished to. And if they did, they'd do it together.

He was quite sure he could never see Harriet the way that his father had seen his mother. But that was all right. It was to be expected. His parents were a rare jewel of a couple. That type of love was as uncommon as an egg-sized diamond, and it wasn't for him.

It was safer to guard his heart because he knew what was likely to happen when he didn't. He'd given himself fully to one person only once, and he wouldn't be stupid enough to do it again. It was better to protect oneself against love, to never allow it to penetrate your armor, than to allow it to take hold and destroy you.

He gripped Harriet Cherrington's hand, thinking these thoughts, girding himself, and as he looked down at her, she offered him a gentle smile that made him feel safe. Safe from being mocked, made a fool of, taunted, and all the things he'd endured after his parents had died. Especially heartbreak.

She could be the one.

Lowercase.

CHAPTER THIRTEEN

The evening was going swimmingly. The duke had danced twice with Harriet and was at this moment dancing his second dance with Miss Islington, who seemed smitten with him. Still, Jo felt that the duke had been more receptive during his dances with Harriet.

She hoped.

Harriet had been popular tonight. Her dark hair contrasted with the shiny white of her elegant satin ball dress overlaid with tulle, and she looked quite fetching. Now, she was sitting in a chair next to Jo, fanning herself demurely while sipping at a glass of punch. In a few minutes, she'd be dancing again with yet another gentleman who'd asked her earlier in the evening.

No one had asked Jo to dance. Not that she'd expected anyone to, but she couldn't help the little worm of sadness that wound its way through her. Five years ago, when she attended balls, one or two gentlemen might ask her to dance, but now...no one. It was like she'd climbed the hill then toppled over it to land firmly on the shelf, where she'd be glued forevermore.

Jo the spinster. Jo the old maid. Jo the ape-leader.

She closed her eyes in a long blink. *Stop it.* She was not prone to melancholy and wouldn't start now. She was seven-and-twenty, with a long life ahead of her. When Charles and Lilly married and had children, she'd be the best godmother in the world. She'd spoil and coddle their children, and when they were old enough, she'd find each of them their one true love.

That thought made her smile. See? There it was. Contentment. Happiness. She didn't need men asking her to dance to feel it. She refused to be denigrated by those whispers of "impoverished spinster" and "pathetic old maid." She refused to succumb to the idea that unmarried women of a certain age were worthless. She was neither useless nor was she lacking in providing anything of value to society. On the contrary, she facilitated the most important thing society could ever desire—love.

The dance ended, and Miss Islington and the duke made their way toward Jo and Harriet. Without a word, Harriet rose as they approached.

"Thank you so much for the lovely dance, Your Grace," Miss Islington said.

"It was my pleasure," the duke said. Was that warmth in his voice? *Warmth?* The man was chilly to his core.

At least, with Jo he had been. Until…

She pressed her lips together.

The four of them stood for a few minutes, talking about the heat of the ballroom compared to the relative coolness of the air outside, but then, Harriet's and Miss Islington's dance partners approached and drew them away, leaving Jo standing alone with the Duke of Crestmont for the second time that evening.

"How are you faring, Your Grace?" she asked. Then in a lower voice, "Tolerating this event, I hope."

In fact, it rather looked like he was having as good a time as any of the other gentlemen here.

He nodded at her, a faint smile on his lips. His soft, delicious lips—

"I am tolerating it," he said. "However, this talk of fresh air has me craving it. Would you like to take a turn around the grounds?"

She glanced at the dance floor, where the couples were starting a quadrille. "I can't abandon my charge."

"Nonsense. Your charge is busy dancing with John Gifford. This is the longest set of the evening. It'll go on for three-quarters of an hour, at least."

She hesitated for a moment, glancing over at Harriet, whose attention was completely focused on the young man dancing with her, her smile wide and pretty as she laughed at something he said.

"Do you know Mr. Gifford?"

"I do. He is a respectable man. Even if the dance were to end early, he would ensure she was safe."

She watched Harriet and Mr. Gifford for a moment longer. They seemed truly enchanted by each other, and an arrow of worry shot through her. Had Harriet looked so enthralled when she'd danced with the duke? Had the duke appeared as enamored as Mr. Gifford did?

She brushed off the worry. Harriet might not have looked so enthralled, but she had certainly been engaged. And the duke was a reserved man. He was simply not as expressive as young Mr. Gifford was.

Everything was fine.

He leaned toward her, and his essence wafted

over her, reminding her of his touch, his kiss. Prickles ran down her arms. "Fear not," the duke said in a low voice. "I'll have you back by the end of this dance. I promise."

After an additional moment's hesitation, Jo nodded. After all, she was curious if she'd judged the duke's reactions to Harriet and Miss Islington properly.

At least, that was the excuse she gave herself for going outside with him.

Side by side, they slipped into Lady Campbell's garden, which was softly lit with overhead lanterns and peppered with people enjoying the cooler night air. Instantly, Jo was glad they'd stepped outside—it felt like she could draw in a clean breath for the first time in hours. Awareness of the man beside her radiated through her, but she steadfastly ignored it.

When they were in a private enough corner of the garden, she murmured, "Well?"

He frowned at her. "Well, what?"

She grinned. There he was, her obtuse duke. Well, not *her* duke, but… She hummed low in her throat. "What do you think of Miss Cherrington and Miss Islington?"

"They are appropriate."

It was her turn to raise a brow. Perhaps it was her turn to be obtuse, but what did he mean by that? "Appropriate?"

"Yes."

"Explain," she commanded.

He sighed. "It appears as though they might make adequate duchesses."

"All right." She paused. "But what do *you* think of them?"

His frown deepened. "I just told you what I thought."

"I know that, Your Grace. I just…" She hesitated, deciding to take a different tack. "Did you like one of them over the other?"

He gestured to a stone bench tucked in between two hedges, and she nodded. When they sat, close beside each other because the bench was small but taking pains not to touch, he shrugged. "I suppose if someone held a knife to my throat and forced me to choose, I'd select Miss Cherrington."

Well, that was a relief. Or…it should be. She could not understand the tangle of reactions inside her when her true reaction to his choice should be perfectly obvious. She wanted him to choose Harriet—she *needed* him to choose her. So far, he had. Excellent.

"That's wonderful," she said, modulating her tone very carefully so he wouldn't realize Harriet was her preference, as well.

It struck her that she was being dishonest with him, but she brushed that away. The fact was, Harriet would make him a wonderful bride. She really would. All Jo had to do was ensure that he fell in love with her.

Even if a part of her didn't want him to.

But, if he loved Harriet, then Jo would have nothing to be ashamed of. She would have made yet another brilliant match, and that was something she should be proud of, not guilty about. There would just be the wonderful additional perk of another happily ever after when Lilly was able to marry Charles Cherrington as well.

"Miss Cherrington meets all your criteria. She is lovely." She turned her head to gauge his reaction, but he seemed not to have heard her. He was staring at her. Staring, specifically, at her mouth.

The mouth that instantly watered as her own gaze settled on his lips. He had quite lovely lips— especially when they were slightly parted, as they were right now.

What she wouldn't give to have them on her again. And this time, not only on her mouth but on other parts of her body—

She sucked in a sharp breath, jerking her gaze away. A couple walked by on the adjacent path, arm in arm, laughing and paying no attention to them whatsoever.

"Jo," he said softly. The way he said her name made shivers skitter up her spine. Then he touched her, his finger crooked beneath her chin, pulling her gaze back to him. "I can't stop thinking about kissing you," he murmured, his dark gaze roaming over her face.

She swallowed. "I..." She closed her eyes. *Harriet. Harriet, Lilly, Charles. HARRIET!*

The back of his gloved hand stroked her cheek, and she shuddered as he gently pushed a wisp of hair behind her ear, his fingers brushing the sensitive skin of the shell.

"Come here." He grasped her hand and pulled her up off the bench, and as if drugged, she let him lead her beyond the bench, behind the hedge there and beneath the boughs of a crabapple tree, its branches heavy with pink blooms.

He stopped beside the trunk, then, without taking his eyes from her, he bent lower, lower still until all her senses filled with him.

"May I kiss you, Jo?"

She should hesitate—no, she *shouldn't* hesitate. She should say no.

But why? She couldn't think of a single reason to say no when her whole body was screaming yes.

"Yes," she whispered.

His lips were soft, and she sank into the kiss, wrapping her arms around his hard, masculine body, then pushing upward until her fingers dug into the dark curls at the base of his scalp. Not weighed down and made greasy by the pomade most of the men wore, but soft and thick and natural.

His hands grazed over the dip in her waist, then back up, one arm wrapping around her, pulling her flush against him and the other moving to the front of her body, cupping her breast through all the layers of her dress and petticoat and stays and shift. The feel of him grazing her nipple, even through all that fabric, made her gasp as heat rushed through her, then pooled in her center.

His sex pressed against her stomach, hard, rigid, and…good Lord…*huge*. Perhaps it should scare her, but it only made her ache more for him, knowing that his body ached for her.

His thumb brushed roughly over the tip of her breast, and his lips moved from her mouth to her jaw, lower, until he was kissing her neck, the bristles of his evening beard scraping her sensitive skin and making her limbs shudder and quake.

She pushed herself more tightly against him, trapping his hand between their bodies, running her fingers through his hair and over the tight cords of his neck, then down, over the muscles of his shoulders, his arms, his back that tapered to a narrow waist.

She didn't know how long they kissed—minutes or hours. She was carried away on a tide of pleasure, the only annoyance all the clothes and her gloves preventing her from *really* touching him in all the places she wanted to explore—everywhere. It was a mixture of desire and curiosity and the knowledge that she was so close to learning something she'd never thought she'd be privy to—the true form of a naked man.

Still, she did the best she could, grazing her lips over his neck, his chest, his arm, while she explored him, fingers traveling up and down his back, then slipping one hand to his front, where she cupped the heavy length of him through the front panel of his breeches, then moved up and down, squeezing gently.

He pressed his forehead to her shoulder. "God, Jo," he whispered. "Do that again."

She did, and this time he growled softly. Then, he grabbed her bottom in his palms and lifted her slightly, pushing her back against the tree.

"Again," he rasped against her lips.

She did it again, loving how he gasped and bucked against her. Then, he stilled. "Stop."

Instantly, she pulled her hand away. "You don't like—?"

He silenced her with a kiss, then murmured, "I

love it. Too much. If you keep doing that, I'm going to forget myself and take you under this tree, to hell with whoever might see us."

No one had ever said anything so erotic to her, and she trembled against his hard body, her eyes closing with the promise of it, of the idea of him taking her right here, against this tree trunk.

"But I promised I'd return you to the ball before the dance ended. We need to stop." Gently, regretfully, he lowered her legs until they were firmly planted on the ground. She came back to earth, in more ways than one. She looked frantically around.

"Don't worry," he said. "No one saw."

She looked up at him, wanting to thank him for kissing her again, for touching her, for allowing her to explore what the hard body of a man felt like under her hands... But she bit back the words. She'd sound silly, wouldn't she? And awkward, and probably needy, too.

He gazed down at her, then shook his head as if in awe. "You are a spitfire, Joanna Porter."

"I am?"

He gave her a brilliant smile, and she melted a little inside. She loved making him smile. "You didn't know that?"

"No," she admitted. "Not really."

He touched her cheek reverently. "A lovely, sensual spitfire. Do you know what I'd love?"

"What?" she whispered as he bent down until his lips brushed over her ear.

"I'd love to see you come. To make you scream my name. To watch your face while I give you pleasure."

"Oh." She swallowed hard. Then she added, "I'd...I'd like the same from you."

He sucked in a breath, but he didn't pull back. Instead, he bit down gently on her ear, and her knees went so weak, she clutched his arm to steady herself.

"Next time." He finally pulled back, and his eyes went soft for a minute as he tucked away strands of her hair that had fallen out of her chignon. He straightened her dress, and she reached up and smoothed the wrinkles in his cravat. Then, she brushed her fingers through his ridiculously soft hair to tame it.

When they'd finished helping each other look presentable, they stared at each other, hands at their sides. Then, the duke glanced back toward the house. "The music will end soon," he said. "It is time to go back."

Side by side, they returned to the ballroom, Jo wondering if she'd ever feel the same about anything ever again.

CHAPTER FOURTEEN

"I find it unfair," Matthew said to Jameson, "that you refuse all invitations to those routs, and yet you expect *me* to attend them."

In the two days since Lady Campbell's ball, Jo had consumed Matthew's thoughts. He'd come to the boathouse today to divert his mind to other matters, but it wasn't doing much good—thoughts of her smiling lips, her soft skin, and her intelligent gray eyes pushed in at every opportunity. He knew he had to stop, but she was like a decadent dessert he couldn't stop craving. Delicious and addictive.

"I am a free man." Sawing a plank of wood, Jameson looked over his shoulder at Matthew and added pointedly, "You are not."

Matthew scowled at the other man from his spot on his knees, where he was measuring another plank. "I'm free as you are."

Jameson snorted. "Come on, man. You know that isn't true. I have no need to ingratiate myself to society. You do. I have no need of a wife. You do. I have no bloodline I need to preserve. *You* do. And I care not one whit about producing an heir." He finished sawing, and the small piece he'd cut off dropped to the sawdust-covered floor of the boathouse. "Alas," he said, picking up the piece and depositing it onto the small pile of discards they might be able to use later, "you do."

Jameson wasn't wrong. Matthew scowled down at

the measuring rod and marked the next spot to be cut with his pencil.

"I still think you should attend some of them with me." Jameson would not qualify for a voucher for Almack's—since he'd received his own, Matthew had learned that only the cream of the *bon ton* were granted one—but there were a number of events to which he had been invited. Jameson was popular among the members of the aristocracy. He'd led a charmed life since those first years at Eton, where he'd been bullied mercilessly as a penniless commoner who'd relied on scholarship funds to attend. Now, he was richer than most of those poor titled fools who'd whittled away their fortunes on gambling, drink, and women, and many of them owed him either money or favors. Matthew had the utmost respect for his friend—the way he'd fought to rise out of poverty, and how he'd done so with careful scruples, never stepping on others' coattails but relying on his own intelligence and hard work.

"What?" Jameson asked, taking the plank Matthew was holding out to him. "You wish I would hold your hand, lad?"

"Something like that," Matthew admitted. "You cannot understand how degrading and miserable those events are."

"Degrading?" Jameson scoffed, hefting the saw again. "How is that? I'm certain that it's the opposite. Those people want nothing more than to fall to their knees and lick your boots."

Matthew shook his head but didn't respond. Even though Jameson was right once again, it didn't change the fact that Matthew found all that highly degrading. All those boot-lickers didn't see him as a person. Rather, they objectified him, and it disgusted him. Made him feel cheap.

He knew he shouldn't complain. Matthew was well aware he had been born into immense privilege and would continue to live with that privilege for his entire life. Unlike Jameson, who only in the past few years had been able to reap the benefits of his hard work.

Matthew and Jameson continued to work, their outward focus on cutting, planing, and creating the intricate angles of the boat they were building. Jameson had designed this latest project: a fours boat he claimed would be the fastest in the world. After watching his friend, first at Eton and then the years of building and racing with him afterward, Matthew had no doubt Jameson's creation would destroy the competition, and he couldn't wait to row it.

But as they worked, thoughts of Joanna Porter circulated through his mind, first about how she'd been so interested in his antics on the Thames, then how she'd said she'd like to learn to row. He'd bring her here someday, show her the boats he and his friends had built, take her out and teach her to row. Afterward, she'd be flushed, flashing that playful smile at him, and he'd kiss her. Maybe draw her to the floor right here on the sawdust. He imagined the softness of her body beneath him, her breathy sighs, the way she touched him.

Those thoughts were making him hard. Rather inappropriate while kneeling on the boathouse floor next to Oliver Jameson.

Teeth gritted, he thrust thoughts of Jo to the back of his mind.

He'd see her tomorrow. He couldn't wait.

First, though…Almack's.

• • •

By midnight, Matthew was finished with Almack's. There had been much of the metaphorical boot-kissing on the parts of the attendees, especially the patroness on duty for this evening who'd introduced him with relish to several young ladies, including the three Jo had on her list: Miss Gainsborough, Miss Buckman, and Lady Janet Astley.

He'd seen enough of them, to be honest. They were all perfectly adequate. Appropriate. They would all make acceptable duchesses. Unfortunately, he'd already promised another dance to each of them, and he was honor bound to remain here till the bitter end.

In any case, he knew Jo would ask him if any of them could be perfect. He damned himself for using that word on their first meeting, because he was beginning to doubt there was anyone in the whole of England who would really be a perfect duchess for him. He was no longer exactly sure what that even meant.

Did Miss Gainsborough have the ability to be a perfect duchess? Did Lady Janet or Miss Buckman? Or even Miss Cherrington or Miss Islington?

Yes? No? *Maybe?* Hell if he knew. All he knew was that it was rather a miracle that he remembered their names. They all seemed to flow into each other, their looks and personalities overlapping and merging together.

Well, except Miss Cherrington. She stood out somewhat, he supposed. She seemed to align with the rules he'd established in his mind, and that he'd given Jo on paper, most closely. Also, she was rather pretty, which, as much as he'd argued to Jo that looks didn't matter, was a positive.

She wasn't as pretty as Jo, though.

He shook his head as if to fling that thought away. He shouldn't compare his potential matches to the matchmaker. That was just… Well, it was *wrong*.

No one could compare to Jo. Jo was one of a kind.

He pressed his handkerchief to his temple before tucking it back in his pocket. It was damn hot in here, and crowded. For the life of him, he couldn't imagine why it was considered such a coup to gain entry into this place. They didn't even serve decent refreshments—in his brief foray into the refreshments room, Matthew had only found a plate of stale, thin-sliced bread and butter, and the lemonade was barely palatable.

"Your Grace."

He turned toward the feminine voice to see a young lady curtsying before him. A blonde. Which of the two of tonight's blondes was she? Damned if he knew. Beside her stood a glowering older woman, also blond, and it was only then that he remembered. This was Miss Buckman, a granddaughter of Queen Charlotte's Keeper of the Robes, with her rather terrifying mother, a broad matron of German descent who looked as though she might be hiding a dagger in those voluminous skirts. A dagger that she wouldn't hesitate to impale him with should he dare glance askance at her daughter.

It was refreshing, actually. This was the one woman here who probably wouldn't kiss his boots if he asked her to.

He bowed. "Mrs. Buckman. Miss Buckman." He held out his arm, realizing the music had been stopped for a few minutes, and people were starting to line up again. It was time for their dance.

"Shall we?"

"Thank you, Your Grace," Miss Buckman said.

He led her to the dance floor, feeling her mother's gaze skewer him the entire way. They took their places, and Matthew smiled at his young partner, though his back teeth were clenched hard. Just a few more hours. And tomorrow, he'd see Jo.

It was that thought that kept him going.

CHAPTER FIFTEEN

The day had not gone well. Jo had had no money to put meat on the table this week, and they were running out of tea. Late this morning, she'd received a note from Mr. Pellegrini. The woman he had decided to pursue had declined his offer of courtship. That had never happened to any of her clients before, and it was a blow. Poor Mr. Pellegrini. How had Jo recommended someone to him who would turn him down? It was a lapse of judgment on her part. She was furious with herself.

The truth was, she'd let the Duke of Crestmont distract her. She'd been so caught up, between his kisses and matching him with Miss Cherrington, that she'd failed Mr. Pellegrini.

"How is Lilly?" Mama asked that afternoon as she and Jo mended old stockings in the parlor. "When she sits with me, she is all smiles and her usual buoyant self, but I know she has been hurting."

Neither Jo nor Lilly had shared the scheme regarding Harriet Cherrington with anyone. Jo had sworn Lilly to secrecy. She knew as well as anyone that secrets had a way of spreading. Keeping it between the two of them was the one way to keep it safe.

"She's better," Jo said reassuringly. "Slowly returning to herself."

"Shame on that boy for breaking her heart," Mama said. "She must have really loved him."

"She did." *She still does*, Jo thought.

Mama smiled softly. "Like I loved your father."

Jo's heart squeezed as Mama's eyes brimmed with tears. "Papa loved you, too."

She remembered sitting in church and listening to her father's sermons, which had often been about the Christian ideals of love, compassion, and community. One of his sermons had been about matrimony, how it was a perfect communion between like-minded people who respected, admired, and most of all *loved* each other deeply.

She'd been about eight years old when he'd first given that sermon. She was fairly certain that it had sowed the seeds of her future profession. She'd spent the rest of her formative years dreaming of love. While she dreamed, she also studied as many marriages as she could, those that contained that kind of love and those that didn't, and analyzed what made marriages fail and what made them succeed.

How she missed her father.

"I'll go check on her before my appointment."

"With the duke?" her mother asked.

"Yes."

Mama pressed her lips together. "Do be careful with him, Jo."

"Yes, Mama." With her cheeks heating at the thought of how *un*-careful she'd been with him at Lady Campbell's ball, Jo set her darning down and headed upstairs. When she leaned into Lilly's open doorway, Lilly looked up from her desk with a soft smile on her face.

"What are you doing?" Jo asked her.

"Writing a letter."

"To whom?"

"Charles." Seeing Jo's eyes widen in alarm, she quickly added, "Don't worry! I won't send it. I have decided to write him a little every day until we are together again, and then I shall give him the letters all at once."

Her expression glittered with optimism. She was truly convinced that Jo was going to make this work.

Lilly's glitter scattered over Jo and fizzled away like sparks colliding with ice.

Oh no. She dropped heavily onto the edge of the bed as the realization struck her like a sledgehammer.

Her heart didn't want to make this work.

She was developing affectionate feelings for the Duke of Crestmont.

Which was stupid.

And useless.

It could go nowhere.

It would risk her losing everything. Her livelihood, her career, her ability to care for her family, her desire for Lilly's happiness.

Her mind knew better. But her heart, stubborn thing that it was, was attempting to clamor over logic. It was attempting to undermine her expertise at matchmaking. It would, if it could, destroy everything she'd worked so hard for.

"What?" Lilly asked, the brightness fading from her face. "What's wrong?"

Jo swallowed hard. Throughout their lives, Lilly and Bess had been her closest friends and confidantes. But they'd been so caught up in Lilly's drama of late that neither of them had noticed anything was amiss with Jo.

For the past several years, there had been only one thing Jo had hidden—and she thought she'd hidden it well—from the women who surrounded her. It was the loneliness she tried to conceal with the secondhand happiness she received from the women she lived with, and with the satisfaction she felt when she made a perfect match.

"Nothing's wrong, really," she reassured her friend, even as the familiar feelings welled up within her. Her heart was lying to her, telling her it was forming some kind of bond with the Duke of Crestmont. "I just had a moment of worry, that's all. But it was silly."

"Worry? What about?"

"That it might not work out between the duke and Harriet."

Lilly gasped. "Did something happen?"

"No, no." She proceeded to tell Lilly about Mr. Pellegrini's failed courtship. "It's shaken my confidence a bit, that's all."

Lilly chewed on her lip, tapping her pen on the desk. "It's the first time that has happened, and it was bound to happen at some point. Mathematically speaking, it's probably impossible for every single match you make to end in utter bliss."

"But they all have so far," Jo said.

"But this one—this one between Harriet and the Duke of Crestmont—it won't. Harriet is absolutely *perfect*. Haven't you noticed?"

"I have, actually," Jo said. That word again. Perfect. She tamped down a shudder.

"Any man would be lucky to have her, prince or pauper."

"True."

"Then it will be easy," Lilly said confidently. "Anyone in Harriet's presence cannot help but note how wonderful she is. All you have to do is make the duke see it."

• • •

Jo's heart sang when she opened the door and beheld the handsome countenance of the Duke of Crestmont, but she immediately threw a wet blanket over it, drowning out its ballad of joy.

"Your Grace," she said with what she hoped was a polite, businesslike smile. She opened the door wider to allow him entry.

He smiled back, making her heart punch at that wet blanket. "Jo."

She loved it so much when he said her name. But she needed it to stop. She needed them to move backward, spool back through their last few meetings and return to that perfunctory dislike they'd felt for each other upon encountering each other for the first—and second—time.

"You must call me Matthew."

Yes! her heart screamed.

"No," she murmured. "I cannot."

She shut the door, and immediately he crowded her against it. Her body melted.

Lord. This was going to be more difficult than she'd anticipated. His lips were close to hers, her body enveloped in his citrus and bergamot essence. Her mouth already watered in anticipation of receiving another one of his knee-melting kisses.

She gripped his arm. It was so hard, so solid and masculine beneath her fingers. "What are you doing to me?" she whispered.

"Hmmm," he murmured, his lips brushing her temple. "Seducing you, I hope."

She went stiff. Thank God he'd said that. It had knocked sense right back into her head. It had also knocked the breath from her lungs.

Using the hand already gripping him, she shoved him back. "No."

He blinked at her, wiping away the haze of lust that had sheened his gaze the moment before.

"Your Grace, I am here to find you a bride, not to…to…" She swallowed and shook her head, unable to find a word that fit. Or, rather, one she could bring herself to say aloud.

"Jo. I like you."

She closed her eyes. "I like you, too. That's the problem."

"How?"

"I cannot 'like' you and do my job properly. I can't separate the two adequately. If I have romantic feelings for you…it makes me…" She blew out a frustrated breath. "It feels wrong encouraging romantic feelings between you and someone else."

His jaw dropped slightly as realization dawned. "You're…jealous?"

She jerked her face away. "Please, Your Grace. I don't wish to speak of it anymore. I just… I can't do this."

Holding her chin, he forced her to face him again. "Are you jealous?"

It appeared the question was genuine. True

curiosity shone on his face.

"I don't know if that's the right word for it," she said honestly.

"Then what is the right word?"

"I don't know. What I do know is that if I develop a strong…'liking' for you, our relationship will end once you marry, and that will…that will hurt."

He stood still. She pulled back from him and then moved to put the desk between them like a shield before facing him again.

"Am I correct? You wouldn't stray on your wife, would you?" She sent up a quick prayer that he'd say, "Of course I would never do such a thing," because it would break her heart if he ended up being one of those libertines who would tup anything in a skirt, whether he was married or not.

He gasped. "Of course not. I would never do such a thing," he said, which, coming on the heels of her prayer, and in nearly the exact same words, jolted her. "What kind of a man do you think I am?"

"I don't know," she pushed out. "Because I don't know what your intentions are with me."

He stared at her, jaw ticking.

"I mean…did you mean to bed me, then discard me? I'm sorry, Your Grace, but I am worth more than that. I am not someone who will allow myself to be used like a—"

He was behind the desk in a single lunge, his hands gripping her waist. "No, Jo. No. That wasn't my intent. I would never intentionally hurt you."

Even now, the feel of his hands on her made her tremble with need.

"But that's what would happen, don't you see?"

she whispered. "Whether it is your intention or not. You would make me 'like' you…maybe even more than that, and then you'd leave to marry your perfect duchess."

He cringed.

She continued, "And my heart…it would be shattered."

He closed his eyes.

"My heart is a valuable thing, Your Grace. At least it is to me. I cannot—I *won't*—allow you to break it."

His hands slipped from her waist. "I find your heart is valuable to me as well."

The devastated look on his face gutted her, but she clenched her hands into fists and tried not to show it.

"You're right," he said softly. "I'm sorry. Forgive me. I wasn't thinking."

She suddenly felt weak. She leaned heavily against her desk.

"I was living in the moment, so happy to see you, and I wanted…" He jerked his gaze away. "I wanted *you*. But you're right. I wasn't thinking of the repercussions of that, to either of us. It was unfair of me."

She had expected him not to listen to her. To continue to try to seduce her. Or maybe simply to be angry with her for refusing him. She hadn't expected this.

It made her love him a little bit. A little bit more. No. *No, no, no.*

"I was…greedy."

Greedy was how she'd felt as well, at Lady

Campbell's ball when her hands had been all over him.

He blew out a shaky breath. "I find it impossible to be near you and not want you."

"Your Grace—"

"But I am not a green boy. I am a man, and I can control myself." He gave her a wobbly smile. "Just know, Jo…I find you beautiful."

She stared at him, her jaw dropping. Beautiful? *Her?*

He continued. "I find you intelligent and intriguing, and I miss you when I'm not near you and think of you constantly. When I am with you, I can be myself. I can be true *to* myself, and I can tell you the truth. It's been a very, very long time since I've felt that way with anyone." He gazed at her, his expression full of wonder. "I've never encountered anyone like you."

He could not know how deeply his words touched her. No one had ever spoken to her like this. No one had ever called her beautiful. And he wasn't lying to her—she could see it in his face. He truly thought her beautiful. And he thought her all those other wonderful things as well.

She shook her head slowly. "I've never encountered anyone like you, either," she whispered.

He leaned closer, closer, until the space between them crackled. She held herself still, fighting it so hard, struggling against the connection between them, the desire, the intense longing. But how could one conquer electricity? It bolted through whatever it desired, and the power of no man could thrust it aside.

But then he pulled back, forcing the connection to fizzle away. They gazed at each other for a long moment. Jo took the time to catalog every part of him, remembering how they felt under her hands and lips. She would never forget that first kiss, nor those moments in Lady Campbell's garden. She would hold the memories close late at night. Use them as comfort when she felt like the loneliness might be too much to bear.

She closed her eyes in a long blink then opened them. It was time to move on. She'd done the right thing—the proper thing. She'd maintained her self-worth. Even if a part of her had wanted to give him everything. It wanted her to sink to her knees and beg him to do whatever he wanted to her, as long as he kept his promise to make her come.

She pressed her lips together and resettled her businesslike demeanor over her like a cloak. "You still wish to marry, don't you?"

"I don't want to," he said, shaking his head. "I *need* to."

"And I *need* to find a proper bride for you. That is what you have employed me to do."

He nodded, lips tight. Good. Those thinned lips were definitely a step in the right direction.

She took her seat. "Please sit down, Your Grace."

"Very well, Miss Porter," he murmured, enunciating the more formal version of her name. Even if it was awkward and stilted, they both were doing what needed to be done.

"Tell me…how was Almack's?"

"It was fine," he said tightly. "I commend you for your choices for me. All of them were quite appropriate. But I have chosen a favorite."

She sucked in a breath. This was it—the moment that would decide Lilly's future. "Who was it?"

"Miss Harriet Cherrington."

CHAPTER SIXTEEN

A butler opened the door to the Cherrington townhouse. "Good afternoon, sir."

Matthew handed him his calling card and said he was here to see Miss Harriet Cherrington. He was taken to the drawing room, where he waited only a few moments before Harriet and two other ladies entered the room.

"Your Grace." Harriet smiled brightly. "It is wonderful to see you again. I'd like you to meet my sisters, Mary and Frances."

They exchanged bows and pleasantries, sat on the assorted furniture, and Harriet rang for tea. When it arrived, she poured it with a steady hand, not spilling a drop, and then added the perfect amount of cream for his taste, all the while keeping up a lively conversation about the differences between Cumbria and London, of which there were many. She had been to Northumberland and knew the area near his country house, but she was interested in learning more about Nottinghamshire. He told her about the county and about Hanford Castle, and she said that Crestmont Manor sounded far more comfortable and modern. Not surprising. Then, she'd smiled and asked him if he knew the Sheriff of Nottingham.

"I do," he said, "but I can assure you, he's nothing like the sheriff of lore."

"That's a relief," she said with a smile.

"However, there are no Robin Hoods nearby

stealing from the rich, either. I couldn't tell you what the sheriff might do if there were."

"Prosecute them, of course!" Mary exclaimed.

"Why?" asked Harriet.

"The Lord commands that thou shall not steal. Corinthians tells us, 'nor thieves, nor covetous, nor drunkards, nor revilers, nor extortioners shall inherit the kingdom of God.' So of course he should prosecute. To the fullest extent of the law." Mary sniffed.

"Even if they are just stealing back what has already been stolen?" Harriet asked.

"Stealing is stealing," Mary said primly.

Harriet and Matthew exchanged a small smile, then he turned it to Mary and said mildly, "Indeed."

Miss Harriet Cherrington was much more lively and interesting than her sisters. Frances barely spoke and looked at everything and everyone in the room as if it possessed a particularly putrid odor. By contrast, Mary *did* speak, but her interjections were most often religious in nature—it seemed she had a quote from the Bible for every situation. Matthew couldn't ascertain if she had any interests apart from scripture.

The conversation moved to music, and Matthew admitted he liked listening to it though he had no talent in creating it. Then, having noted the piano in the corner, he wondered aloud if Harriet would like to play.

She did, and wonderfully. He stood beside the piano as she played, and her fingers were captivating as they moved with confident precision over the keys. When she finished, she beamed up at him, and he clapped with feeling that wasn't faked.

She would make a fine duchess.

Perfect, though?

Ugh. Then and there, he decided to eliminate that obnoxious word from his vocabulary. There was no such thing as a perfect duchess. He was a fool.

At the end of the call, the Cherrington sisters thanked him for his visit, and he promised to return, hoping that wasn't against protocol. He didn't quite know how Jo expected him to end such encounters.

In any case, he had another meeting with her tomorrow to tell her about it. She'd likely recommend he visit the Cherringtons again, and probably attend another party, soiree, or ball where Harriet would be in attendance.

He was looking forward to his meeting with Jo tomorrow. Beyond that, he wasn't looking forward to any of it.

• • •

The following day, the duke swept into Jo's office without knocking.

"Miss Porter," he announced. "Please don your pelisse. I am taking you somewhere."

She blinked up at him in confusion. "What do you mean?"

"It is too fine a day to be trapped within this tiny room. So we shall conduct our business elsewhere."

"It's fine?" She frowned. "Earlier it looked like it was going to rain."

"Exactly! It will be ideal."

"But…where do you wish to go?"

He smiled—and, of course, she melted. "You'll know soon enough."

Why, oh why, did he keep melting her? She was made of butter. Next time she encountered the duke, she'd need to fortify herself with steel.

"Shall I bring Bess?" she asked.

"That won't be necessary. No one will see us."

A cold sweat broke out on the back of her neck. No one would see them doing what? She swallowed hard. "Your Grace, I already told you that I cannot…"

He cocked his head at her, one brow raised. "You cannot what?"

"I cannot be *intimate* with you. We discussed the reasons why."

His lips curved in a slow smile, so seductive she nearly reached back and undid her buttons for him so he wouldn't have to bother.

"You misunderstand, Miss Porter. This meeting is business, nothing more. I merely wish to conduct it elsewhere."

"Oh," she said, disappointment flushing through her. She battled it back. "Of course, Your Grace. Forgive me."

He lifted her pelisse off its peg and held it open so she could push her arms through the sleeves. When she was working on fastening the buttons, he leaned down and whispered in her ear, "Trust me, Jo."

Slowly, she turned around.

He gazed at her solemnly. "Do you trust me?"

She considered this for a long moment, trying to pose an internal argument to the answer that had instantly come to mind. But she couldn't pose any argument whatsoever. She trusted him down to her marrow. He was, above all, an honorable man.

"Yes," she said, "I do trust you."

"Good. I shall have you back by your tea time."

Outside, he helped her into his elegant black-lacquered carriage with the gilded ducal crest on its door, then tapped his walking stick on the roof, and they were off. A few minutes later, she peeked out the window from the edge of the curtain and frowned at him. "We are heading north? Out of London?"

"We are taking a short trip to Tottenham Green, where I'd like to introduce you to a friend of mine. In the meantime, I shall update you on my visit to the Cherrington house."

"Very well."

"I visited Harriet Cherrington. Her sisters, Miss Mary Cherrington and Miss Frances Cherrington, were in attendance. The setting and the tea were adequate."

"And Miss Cherrington?"

"Also adequate."

"Really, Your Grace. Adequate? That is a terrible word to use to describe a lady."

He frowned at her. "What other word should I use?"

"There are many to choose from. Lovely and talented, for example. Amiable." *A-m-i-a-b-l-e*, she thought. "Perfect."

"Very well. She was lovely and talented. She plays the pianoforte well. She was also quite amiable."

She noted that he didn't go so far as to say she was perfect.

"I will meet with her again," he continued. "If our next few meetings go well, I shall propose."

Jo shouldn't have been surprised by this, given the duke's timeline, but it still felt like a punch straight to her heart.

Pushing the curtain aside a little more, she gazed out the window and watched the fields rumble by.

"We spoke at length about my houses," the duke said after a long silence. "She thinks she would prefer Crestmont Manor, as Hanford Castle sounds drafty."

"Is it?" she asked.

"Of course."

She smiled, and they spoke of his castle for a bit longer, which led them into a discussion about the great old houses of England.

"I think the finest house in England must be Leeds Castle," she said.

"Hanford Castle might be smaller than Leeds Castle," Matthew said. "But it is wound up in just as much history. Inside, you can take the exact steps of a half dozen kings. Sleep in the same beds they slept in, eat at the same table, stand in a courtyard that held tournaments where knights jousted for their ladies, and where minstrels sang into the night."

Jo sighed dreamily. "I should very much like to see it the next time I'm in Nottinghamshire."

"If it's not open for visitors," he said, "I'll have it opened just for you."

Not that she'd ever have the funds, or the time, to visit Nottinghamshire. As the house where she had spent her childhood had been given to the new rector when her father had died, there was nothing left for Jo and Mama in Nottinghamshire. Only a few of her distant cousins remained in the area, but they had offered succinct condolences when Papa had died, then turned their backs on their two near-penniless female relatives.

In any case, the duke's sentiment was kind. Maybe someday she *would* have the opportunity to tour Hanford Castle. A girl could dream.

She felt a brush of warmth and looked down. Their hands were both flat on the bench seat, Matthew's little finger touching hers in the barest of caresses.

The heat rushed through her until she felt the flush blooming in her core. Gritting her teeth, she pulled away and clasped her hands together tightly in her lap.

Sometime later, they arrived in Tottenham Green just as it began to rain. "Excellent!" Matthew exclaimed, looking up to the sky as he knocked on the door of an unimposing green-painted house.

A plainly dressed older couple opened the door, and the pair and Matthew greeted each other warmly. Matthew turned to Jo. "Miss Porter, may I present my friends, Mr. and Mrs. Howard. Mr. Howard is a highly respected chemist and meteorologist."

"I am a chemist by trade," Mr. Howard clarified, "but my passion is meteorology, though I still consider myself an amateur on the topic." Stepping back, he gestured them inside his home. "I hear that thou art a budding meteorologist, Miss Porter."

These people were Quakers, Jo realized. She

hadn't met many Quakers in her life, and though the church had named them as dissenters, Jo had always admired their philosophies. They put into practice what other religions preached.

"I wouldn't go so far as to call myself a meteorologist," Jo said, "but I do have—shall we call it—a fondness for the weather and its patterns."

He laughed cheerfully. "Well, I daresay thou hast just defined a budding meteorologist most accurately. Go on, go on. I hear you haven't much time."

He gestured up a flight of stairs, and Matthew took her hand and tugged her up alongside him. "I cannot wait to show you Mr. Howard's treasures."

They walked up two flights of stairs, eventually leading to a single large room on the top floor of the house. Matthew opened the door and gestured her inside with a flourish.

"Oh my," Jo breathed.

It was a meteorologist's heaven, from the charts on the walls, to the bookshelves filled with scientific tomes, to the four tables in the center of the room that boasted various instruments. Gripping her hand, Matthew led her over to them, pointing each one out and explaining how it worked: several thermometers, hygrometers, barometers, various insulated rods that measured electricity in the atmosphere, and a cyanometer, which Matthew explained measured the blueness of the sky.

She ran her finger reverently over the deepening shades of blue on the circular device. "How beautiful."

Matthew grinned. "It is, isn't it?"

He took her to the wall opposite, where several

drawings of different kinds of clouds were arranged in rows. "Mr. Howard has studied and classified the different kinds of clouds," he told her. "I use his work extensively in my own weather predictions."

She looked at the odd labels under the pictures. They were words she'd never seen before: *cirrus, nimbus, stratus, cumulus*.

Beside the clouds were rows of charts, including dates, temperatures, barometer and hygrometer readings, and visual observations. After she and Matthew spent several minutes studying the charts, he gestured at the adjacent rolltop desk. The top was open, and several neat stacks of paper lay upon it.

"He is working on a book detailing the climate of London—an ambitious project, but one that he is most qualified to write about given the amount of data he has acquired over the years."

"I look forward to reading it," Jo said, hardly able to imagine how Mr. Howard could possibly clarify the tangle of contradictions that was London weather.

He squeezed her hand. "I shall send you a copy of it as soon as it is published."

They returned downstairs, where Matthew led her through a back door. They paused under a small awning to gaze out into the downpour. Matthew handed her an umbrella. "As I said—absolutely ideal."

"Why?" she asked him, though his innate joy about all that he was showing her sparked through her.

"It is best to see everything during a rainfall."

Outside, there were more of the instruments

they'd seen upstairs, a brass wind vane, and several ingenious devices that measured rain and evaporation. Matthew showed her how to check the rainfall level.

"My goodness!" She glanced up at him. "It's already rained a quarter of an inch!"

It was only just then, as he helped her back to her feet, that she realized she was soaking wet. So was he. The umbrella leaned uselessly against the wind vane, forgotten.

A drop of rain had formed on his nose, and she gently brushed it away, realizing they were grinning at each other like giddy children.

At that moment, there were no walls between them. No constraints. No rules. They were just two like-minded people taking pleasure in the magnificent world around them on a rainy afternoon.

If only it could always be this way.

Slowly, their grins slipped away as the awareness between them grew. Their hands tightened in each other's. Jo didn't want to let him go. Ever.

But she would have to. As always, the real world encroached. Inside the house, dishes clattered. A door creaked as it opened.

Matthew dropped her hands, and they both turned toward the sound.

"Why, you are both soaked to the bone!" Mrs. Howard exclaimed from beneath the awning. "Come inside. I've made a nice pot of tea."

"Thank you," Jo murmured.

They went inside, wrapped themselves up in the toweling Mrs. Howard offered, and sat down for tea, Jo gushing about all that she'd learned and Mr.

Howard and Matthew delving into the intricacies of the new, more accurate rain gauge Matthew was building. A half hour later, they were back in the carriage and headed south, both of them tucked under a warm blanket.

"That was fascinating," Jo said. "Thank you so much for taking me there."

Matthew smiled. She'd lost count of how many times he'd smiled today, but she treasured each one. "We English do enjoy discussing the weather. But I know no one who has analyzed it with more dedication than Mr. Howard."

The afternoon had been… Well, it was wonderful, if Jo was to be blunt about it. Talking to the Duke of Crestmont had become easy—easier than even speaking to Lilly or Bess.

When she looked at him, the tiniest things set off sparks of heat deep inside her: the brush of his dark lashes as he blinked, his clean, blunt-cut fingernails, the flex of a muscle under his sleeve when he raised his arm. She doggedly ignored those sparks but still caught herself no fewer than four times staring at his lips. She had dragged her gaze away instantly each time.

And while she struggled to keep her insides from melting, a constant thrum of awareness twisted around them in the carriage, a low-grade current of electricity that Mr. Howard could probably detect on one of his fancy instruments. Jo thought Matthew felt it, too, in the way their gazes would snag together, or the way they'd inadvertently touch in the close confines of the carriage cabin, then forcibly pull away as if against the draw of a strong magnet.

When they stopped at the door to her office, Matthew helped her out, walked her to her door under cover of his umbrella, then politely said goodbye.

Jo beat back the urge to ask him to stay a while longer. Instead, she walked into her quiet, lonely office. She was still damp from their outdoor adventure, but she didn't care. She was warm to her core.

But as soon as her door closed, she sank back against it and pressed her palms over her eyes. "Stop this," she whispered. "Stop it right now, you wicked thing."

She was talking to her heart, ordering it to cease and desist. Because, despite all her best efforts, it was heading in the one direction she couldn't let it go.

It was falling in love.

CHAPTER SEVENTEEN

The following afternoon, Jo sat at her desk, scrawling on a rather dear sheet of stationery she really shouldn't be wasting. She was a dreadful artist, and her drawings confirmed it. There was a series of rather misshapen hearts scrawled across the page, overlapping and inconsistent, some fat, some thin, some tall and some squat, some large and others tiny. Jo laid her pen down and capped her inkpot. This page would make for some expensive fuel for the fire later on.

Harriet was a good artist, though. Actually, she might be bordering on excellent. One of the many attributes that Matthew—goodness, she'd truly sunk into the habit of calling him that, but she *must* stop doing it, even in her mind—one of the many attributes that the *Duke of Crestmont* was looking for in a duchess.

She finally rose, then went to tell Lilly that she was going to call on Harriet.

"May I join you?" Lilly exclaimed, her book falling unheeded to the floor as she jumped up from her spot on the sofa. Jo bent down to retrieve it, closed it carefully, and laid it on the side table. To destroy a sheet of paper was one thing, but the abuse of an innocent book was quite another. "You may come, but if we see Charles there—"

"I know," Lilly interrupted. "I won't say a word to him."

"No, you mustn't give him the cut direct in his own house," Jo said. "You must be polite but distant."

"It will be difficult," Lilly admitted. "I'd prefer to throw my arms around him and tell him our problems are soon to be solved."

Jo narrowed her eyes. "You will not."

"I know, I know. I won't do it," Lilly promised. "As difficult as it will be, I shall keep my hands to myself and all my excitement bottled inside until the duke proposes to Harriet."

"Which won't be for at least another fortnight."

"That long?" Lilly asked mournfully as they both donned their pelisses.

"Yes," Jo said firmly. "*At least* that long."

They ventured into the cool, cloudy day. Jo fancied she could smell the threat of more rain in the air and thought of how Matthew had looked at her yesterday, his black eyelashes damp, a drop of water on the tip of his nose, that toe-curlingly handsome grin on his face.

Unlike yesterday, rain today wouldn't be ideal. If it rained, she and Lilly would have to shoulder through it on the walk back, as she couldn't spare the coin for a hackney right now.

Fortunately, the sky remained dry on the twenty-minute walk to the Cherrington residence, and when they arrived, they were ushered in by the butler to encounter all five of the Cherrington sisters in the drawing room. Harriet looked up from where she was playing the pianoforte to greet them. The others all chimed in, giving special attention to Lilly, who they hadn't seen in a while.

"Oh, Lilly!" Esther exclaimed, beaming. "We missed you so!"

As Lilly hugged each of the sisters in turn, Jo wondered when Lilly had become such good friends with them—but then it struck her. She was so often holed up in her office that Lilly had started living a life of her own, separate from Jo. She had been so busy she hadn't given it much notice.

Crowding around them, the sisters bade them to sit and offered them tea and cakes.

"Oh, look." Martha moved to the window as the rest of them sipped their tea. "The sky is clearing. I think I shall walk to Mr. de Havilland's offices. He is expecting a crate from Africa to arrive today."

"More stolen antiquities?" Frances asked with raised eyebrows.

Martha scowled at her twin. "You are incessantly ungrateful, and unfair. Mr. de Havilland has preserved so many ancient artifacts and shared so much knowledge with the entirety of the civilized world, and you persist in calling him a thief."

Frances shrugged. "That's because he is."

Martha made a sound of disgust. "Fluff and nonsense." Waving off Frances, she turned to the rest of them. "Would anyone like to join me?"

Jo hoped all of them would, except Harriet. She wanted to talk to the young woman in a more private setting.

But to her dismay, Harriet piped up. "I'd be happy to go with you, Martha. I could use the air after being cooped up all day."

Drat.

After only a brief hesitation, Jo volunteered to

accompany them. Then, she cast Lilly a pointed glance.

"Oh, Jo. May I stay a bit longer? I am having such a lovely time."

"Oh, please let her stay!" Esther exclaimed.

Jo sighed, but Mary cut in. "I would love for Lilly to stay. Our carriage is…indisposed, Miss Porter, but I'll ensure she's properly chaperoned for her walk home."

Their carriage was "indisposed"? Had Charles sold it? That was the most likely scenario, Jo thought with a sinking feeling.

She smiled at the ladies, who sat side by side on the sofa, Esther's hand gripping Lilly's tightly. "Very well."

Lilly grinned. "I'll be home before dinner. Thank you, Jo."

Jo, Martha, and Harriet set off, two footmen following at a discreet distance behind them. One would remain with Martha to escort her home later, and the other would accompany Harriet and Jo.

"It's quite a walk," Jo told Harriet.

"It's perfect," Harriet said. "I love nothing more than a long walk in the country."

"This is *not* the country, though," Martha said with a laugh.

"No, but it's second best," Harriet declared.

Chatting companionably, they strolled to the offices of Mr. de Havilland, and Martha showed them the basement room where the boxes of antiquities were categorized and kept. Though the latest crate from Africa had not yet arrived, her face glowed with excitement, which reminded Jo of how

Matthew had glowed yesterday, how he had been almost boyish in his eagerness to show her all the treasures of Mr. Howard's collection.

She really needed to stop thinking about the man.

Sometime later, after Harriet and Jo had left the museum and were walking down the busy street toward Jo's house, she said, "Your sister's passion for antiquities is catching."

"It is, isn't it?" Harriet said.

"It is a fascinating subject."

"I agree, but I shall never be as obsessed with it as she is. It is interesting, but it is the past, after all." Harriet smiled. "I am more interested in the present."

Good, Jo thought; she'd brought the subject directly to the present, and the matter at hand. "I heard the Duke of Crestmont called upon you."

Harriet's smile didn't falter. "He did."

"What did you think of him?"

"He was very polite." Harriet's slender throat moved as she swallowed, and Jo studied her discreetly while maneuvering around the heavy street traffic.

"Anything else?"

"He seems to be quite fond of his castle in Nottinghamshire."

"Really? Was he...bragging about it?" The duke could be considered a braggart. Jo could imagine him talking about his castle in that haughty voice of his, his lips thin, looking down the long slope of his nose.

But he wasn't a braggart. Jo knew that now.

Harriet seemed to consider this. "I don't believe he was bragging. He said it is a cold, unwelcoming place. He seemed to imply that I wouldn't like it." She gave a small shudder. "And he's right—I probably wouldn't. Drafty places chill me to my bones. But he has a modern country house, Crestmont Manor, and it sounds quite agreeable."

Jo murmured her acknowledgment of this, and Harriet went on. "He said the gardens are stunning, with flowers blooming with abundant color throughout the summertime. And that they would look lovely in watercolor."

Implying, of course, that once they were married this summer, Matthew would take Harriet to Northumberland, where she could paint the gardens.

And he could get her with child.

Jo stumbled over a cobble that seemed to rise up directly in front of her toes. Harriet grabbed her arm. "Oh, dear! Are you all right, Miss Porter?"

Damn her foolish heart. Through sheer force of will, Jo made herself recover her wits. She would not falter. She could not.

"Of course." She patted Harriet's hand, which still grasped her arm. "Just not paying attention to where I'm walking."

They forged onward, until Jo gathered enough strength to ask softly, "Would you like to paint the gardens at Crestmont Manor someday, Miss Cherrington?"

Harriet kept her eyes straight ahead. "Of course," she murmured. "I love to paint beautiful gardens."

The answer was, Jo thought, decidedly noncommittal. It was not the answer she would have expected from a besotted young lady.

And that worried her.

• • •

Matthew leaned back against the wall in Joanna Porter's office, his arms crossed over his chest.

He'd danced with Miss Cherrington twice at two private balls. He'd called upon her after each event. Each encounter had further proven how adequate a duchess she'd make.

He had decided to go through with it. Get this charade over with, get himself shackled, set his wife up at Crestmont Manor, and move on with his life.

He was here to tell Jo. Honestly, he didn't know if the words would thrill her or hurt her. She'd been friendly yet distant this past week. Engaging yet cool. He had been the same. They had both been protecting themselves, but on Matthew's part it had nearly killed him.

He still looked forward to their meetings. He still thought about her when they weren't together. And his thoughts weren't only carnal—though those thoughts had made him thoroughly wild with desire for her. He thought about her when he recorded his daily observations of the weather, or when he checked his rain gauge. He and Jameson would be discussing the new boat, and he'd think, "Jo would find this fascinating." Or he and Jameson would have a good run on the water, almost beating Cole and Winthrop, and Matthew would daydream about telling her how exhilarating it had been.

Jo sat at her desk, her hands clasped so tightly on

the desktop he could see the whites of her knuckles.

God, he wanted her.

He took a deep breath, fortifying himself, then finally spoke. "I intend to speak with Miss Cherrington's brother next week."

She stared at him for a long moment, then slowly shook her head. "I do not think that is a good idea."

He gaped at her. "What do you mean? Why?"

"You're not ready. Neither is she."

"What?"

"I think you heard me, Your Grace," she said drily.

He ran a frustrated hand through his hair. "I did, but you make no sense. Don't you *want* me to marry her?"

"Of course, but…" She shook her head, then squeezed the top of her nose between two fingers. "You're not *ready*."

He scoffed. "Of course I am."

"I just…" She threw her hands in the air. "I have concerns."

"What concerns? She's perfectly adequate—"

"She's more than adequate, and you know it!"

He growled in frustration, pushing his body off the door. "You've done your duty, matchmaker. You've found me an acceptable match. Now I shall marry the chit and be done with it."

He knew he sounded bitter and hard, but hell if he cared.

She made a small sound of dismay and rose from her chair. Hands on hips, she paced her tiny office— three steps from one wall to the other and back.

"This isn't right," she said on a frustrated breath.

"I can't let you do this. I can't."

"Why the hell not?" he snapped.

She reeled to a stop in front of him, her pretty face screwed up in a scowl. Behind the scowl, though, lurked something else.

"Because you"—she poked a finger at his chest—"don't love her."

"Good God, Jo." How could she expect him to love Harriet Cherrington? *Jesus.* "Of course I don't love her."

She looked up at him, shaking her head, her lips in a flat line. "Then *of course* I can't let you do it."

He narrowed his eyes at her, staring her down. "Do you want me to love her? Really? Do you want my heart to ache and my palms to sweat and my body to grow hard whenever I think of her? Do you want me to have pretty daydreams about her while men are screaming politics all around me at Parliament?" He had had such thoughts, but they sure as hell weren't about Harriet Cherrington. "Do you want me to feel like I'm going to die if I can't touch her…have her under me…be *inside her* for another moment?"

His words were like lashes, and he could see how they struck. Deeply and painfully, and he instantly regretted them.

The blood drained from her face, and her hands—hands that had been all over him not that long ago—clenched at her sides. "Yes," she said from between clenched teeth. "Yes, yes, and yes!"

He stepped forward. "Is that so?" he rasped down at her.

She closed her eyes. "Yes." But this time it was an

unconvincing whisper.

"Liar."

"Yes. *No*." She opened her eyes and looked up at him. "You need to love her," she whispered. "You *must*."

Had she forgotten? "I told you. I don't believe in love."

They stared at each other. Finally, she reached up, touching her cool, bare fingers to his cheek. "You deserve love, Matthew," she whispered, her voice shaking with certainty. "You deserve to love and be loved."

Their gazes held, the connection between them like a lit fuse of explosives, rushing toward something neither of them was capable of stopping.

And then he snapped. He dragged her against him and kissed her with hot, desperate, open-mouthed kisses. She kissed him back, equally hot, equally desperate, making little whimpering noises in the back of her throat that sent shudders of lust through him.

Love? That was what *she* deserved. He would love her thoroughly. Right now.

He turned them both and pressed her against the wall, keeping his lips locked to hers. He moved his fingertips down, his lips following over her cheek and then her jaw, her neck, her collarbone. He tugged her bodice down until her nipple appeared, soft and pink, and he closed his mouth over it. She groaned wantonly. She was so perfect. So soft, so sweet. His hands shook as he rucked up her dress. His whole body shook.

"Matthew," she moaned, her fingers threading

through his hair. "Matthew."

His name on her tongue drove him out of his mind.

He finally managed to slip his hand under her hem, then he was stroking her stockinged thigh, then tucking his fingers beneath the ribbons of her garters to caress the smooth flesh beneath.

Then his hand found her center, cupping it gently. Her body jerked at the contact, and she cried out.

"Shh," he murmured against her breast. He licked her nipple. "I'm going to make you feel good, Jo. So good. Let me."

"Yes." She bucked against him, and he laughed softly. His spitfire.

Using his fingers, he spread her and felt the wet heat waiting there for him. He groaned, kissing back up the smooth, silky skin of her neck. "You're so hot, love. So wet."

"Is…is that…um…correct?"

"Quite correct. Better than correct," he breathed against her lips before taking them right as he found her opening and slipped one finger inside. She gasped into his mouth, her body quaking against him. He slid one arm around her and cupped her bottom, dragging her against him, unable to stop himself from pressing his needy cock against her stomach.

But this was about Jo. Her pleasure. He began to move his finger, stroking her, pressing his palm against her until he discovered the spot that made her pant and squirm. When he pressed his thumb against it, he absorbed her cry with his mouth.

He rubbed, his eyes nearly rolling back in his

head at the burning heat of her slickness coating his fingers. He whispered encouragement into her ear. "Let go, Jo, love. Feel it. You're so beautiful. So sweet. I want to taste you. Fill you. I want to hear you come. Scream my name."

Pleasure shot through him as she squirmed more desperately, shuddered more violently, panted more heavily. She loved his wicked words. He loved her reaction to them even more.

He slipped a finger inside her once more, then curved it up, pressing his palm to her. Her knees buckled, but he held her up, kneading her soft bottom with his other hand.

"Come for me, sweetheart," he murmured, kissing the shell of her ear.

And, on his next press, she did. As her body gave a violent tremor, her channel clenched and pulsed around him, growing even wetter, even hotter, though he hadn't thought that was possible. He held her closely, tucked against him, knowing she was probably unaware that he was supporting her weight entirely as she came, her voice an erotic keen that made him so hard he nearly came himself.

Her body undulated in his arms, a pulsing bundle of ecstasy. When it finally subsided, she laid her head on his shoulder, completely spent. He slipped his finger out of her and pulled his hand away, her skirts falling back down to hide her stockinged legs. He tugged up her bodice gently, then took her in his arms and carried her to that awful chair. He wished there were a bed, or even a sofa, where he could lie beside her and hold her awhile, but all that was available was that uncomfortable lumpy monstrosity.

He sat, then positioned her on his lap, gratified when she settled in against him, slipping her arms around his waist.

"Mmm," she said, blinking up at him sleepily as he tugged her closer. He couldn't stop touching her. "You were right."

"I was?"

"Yes. So good."

He stroked a finger down her smiling cheek, loving the feel of her soft, warm flesh. "I'm glad."

She tilted her head. "Now what?" Her eyes cut to the floor, then back to him. "Will you not ravage me in a fit of passion?"

He nearly choked, because…well, *yes*. He would love to do that. Ravage her. Sink inside her, feel her wrapped around him, squeezing him…

Instead, he said, trying to keep his voice smooth, "I said before that I can control myself. I'm a man, not a randy youth." He leaned a little closer, murmuring into her hair. "Today was for you, sweetheart. Not for me."

"Are you trying to prove that you are unselfish?"

He considered that. "Perhaps." He chucked her chin. "Or perhaps I was just eager to see that look on your face."

"What look?"

"This one." He brushed his thumb over her lower lip, which was plump and pink, slightly swollen from his kisses. "The look of a woman relaxed, happy, and well satisfied."

"Oh? Is that how I look?" She seemed truly curious, but her voice and body were still slow and languid.

"It is."

Laughing softly, she laid her head on his shoulder. "Didn't we say this wasn't going to happen?"

"Do you regret it?" he asked her.

She opened her eyes and looked up at him with her most piercing gray gaze. "How could I possibly?"

He breathed out in relief.

"We have been dishonest, though," she said quietly. "To each other and to ourselves. We have made false promises."

She was right. He gathered her hand up in his, bringing it to his mouth and brushing his lips over the smooth skin. "I generally keep my promises, Jo. I want you to know that."

"So do I," she murmured, closing her eyes again and tucking her body closer against him.

"My honor is one of the few things I can pride myself on."

She sighed. "I know."

But this…whatever it was that was between them made them so mad for each other, made them set aside such things as vows and promises and honor. With a sinking feeling, he realized that once he committed to marrying Harriet Cherrington, he could no longer see Jo. At all. Unlike all her other clients, who were friendly with her, corresponded with her, and invited her to their social events, he couldn't risk getting near her again.

That was a depressing thought.

But a necessary one. While he couldn't expect to have a loving marriage like his parents, he sure as hell wasn't going to be an adulterer like his uncle.

He would have to talk to her about proposing to

Miss Cherrington. But he didn't want to do that right now. He wanted to spend the afternoon with her, if not making love, then at least holding her close and, perhaps, talking about the weather.

So, that's what he did.

CHAPTER EIGHTEEN

"They're inviting us to meet them at the opening of the Vauxhall Pleasure Gardens tonight!" Lilly exclaimed.

Jo looked up from the book she was reading. "Who's inviting us?"

Lilly waved the letter she'd just received. "The Cherrington sisters. Please, can we go?"

Jo sighed. "Can't we wait until later in the summer when the crowds have thinned?"

"We could, but I'm *dying* to get out of this house. I have been so cooped up, I feel like an anxious chicken. All I do is work on my design." Lilly gestured to her pile of notebooks.

"How is your design going?" Jo asked her.

Lilly smiled. "It would be so marvelous if it were ever built, Jo."

"Show me," Jo said.

She sat beside Lilly as her friend opened her most recently completed notebook to her latest vision. The palace boasted not only towers, but also domes and minarets, and was unlike any palace—or, in fact, any building—Jo had ever seen.

"It is stunning," Jo breathed. "You should show it to someone."

"I'm showing it to you right now."

"I mean someone who could actually do something with it."

Lilly raised her brows. "I know nobody who'd

deign to look at this design. And even if they did, they'd probably laugh. It is such a departure from our staid British ideals of symmetry and balance." She sighed. "I know I've been wasting my time. I should work on redesigning our garden—something that could actually be put to use. My mind refuses, though. Instead, it continues conjuring ideas on such a grand scale as to be laughable."

"Not laughable," Jo argued. "Your ideas are wonderful."

"Even if they are wonderful, it is unrealistic to ever think that they might one day become reality." Lilly closed her notebook. "It is fine. I enjoy dreaming of what will never be. That, at least, brings me joy."

Jo sympathized with her friend. Finding a perfect love match brought her joy, yet it still left a part of her feeling as if she was missing something important. She squeezed Lilly's hand.

"Vauxhall Gardens tonight?" Lilly asked hopefully.

It occurred to Jo that it was a good idea—a distraction from both their passions, and both their feelings of unfulfillment.

"Harriet will be there," Lilly added.

Jo *would* like to speak with Harriet again. And it was true that Lilly had hardly been out of the house since receiving Charles's letter. She'd only gone to the soiree, then to visit the Cherringtons. She needed an evening away from this house and all her notebooks.

Jo could afford it right now, too. Just yesterday, she'd received full payment from a client who'd married last month, as well as an advance on the duke's fees.

The duke. It had been over a week since the afternoon he'd touched her so intimately in her office. Jo repressed a shudder of longing.

In any case, it had been three years since she and Lilly had visited the Vauxhall Pleasure Gardens across the Thames, a place where everyone was welcome as long as they could afford the entry fee. Vauxhall was entertaining, too, with many nighttime amusements to stimulate all the senses. They had recently added a rope-dancer to complement the midnight fireworks, and Jo had heard her feats were magnificent to behold.

"Very well," she began, but before she could continue, Lilly threw her arms around her.

"Thank you, dear Jo. I know it is expensive. I promise I will eat and drink very well before we leave and shall not spend a penny once we are there."

"I appreciate that, but we will only be able to go once this year. We might as well enjoy ourselves."

Lilly squeezed her tighter then smacked a kiss on her cheek. "Thank you!"

"Of course." Jo stared down at her book, but the print danced in front of her eyes.

What would she say to Harriet when she saw her?

Jo had been utterly confused since her last meeting with the duke, her heart a mess of emotion. She still wanted Crestmont to marry Harriet—of course she did. She still *needed* him to marry Harriet, too. Her business depended on it. *Lilly* depended on it.

The way he made her feel, though… Lord, it was going to be difficult to hand that to another woman. The affection she had developed for him was beyond what she'd ever thought she'd feel for any man.

But it was an absolutely impossible affection. So much as to be silly.

First, she would never agree to be mistress to a married man — and considering his disgusted reaction when she'd mentioned adultery, he would never allow that, either.

Second, Crestmont would never consider marrying anyone as imperfect as her. She could never be a perfect duchess. She'd make a duchess of the sort that other ladies whispered about behind their fans. "An impoverished country girl, can you believe it?" they'd say. "A conniving, ambitious woman. Clearly she schemed to marry above her station," they'd gossip. "Not a drop of aristocratic blood to be found anywhere within ten feet of her," they'd sneer.

And if they discovered her profession, which was extremely likely — once the *ton* was interested enough in a person and wanted information on that person, they had noses like hounds — that would add a whole new layer of ugly mockery and contempt.

But all those thoughts showed how far Jo had gone ahead of herself. Before all that happened, the duke would need to consider her worthy of marriage. Something he'd never do.

She was plain, humble Joanna Porter. And she *worked* for a living. Though she did something she adored, something she never wanted to give up, the aristocracy disdained those who worked. Considered them inferior.

So...what to do? All her clients married for love, but could she really survive it if Harriet and the Duke of Crestmont fell madly in love?

Maybe she shouldn't push for love between Harriet and the duke. She knew well enough there were some marriages—not the ones she encouraged, of course—that succeeded without passionate ardor.

Even if she did work her considerable powers on them, Harriet and the duke might not actually fall in love. The Duke of Crestmont was far more determined and stubborn than any of her other clients had been regarding matters of the heart.

The Duke of Crestmont was a *duke*, after all. Dukes—good ones, at least—were known for doing their duty. For marrying well and siring heirs. They weren't known for loving their spouses to the ends of the earth.

Maybe the duke would be happiest if he *wasn't* in love with his wife.

No.

That was a selfish, horrible thought. One Jo needed to remove from her consciousness permanently. The faces of her clients passed through her mind's eye. That look they had when they realized they were in love, when they told her of an accepted proposal, or when she encountered the couples afterward, holding hands, gazing at each other with such devotion it made her own heart overflow.

If there was one thing she had to do, it was follow her heart. She sold her services through her clients who'd fallen in love, and every one of them had. How would she explain her matchmaking services in the future if she let Crestmont marry someone he considered merely "adequate"?

"Ah, yes, sir, my clients do fall in love on occasion. I guarantee you might be happy. Or not. It is rather hard to tell."

The reality was if the duke *was* going to fall in love with Harriet Cherrington, he likely would have done so by now. They'd met several times, and while their conversations had been perfectly pleasant, they didn't love each other. Jo could tell.

Surely she could find Crestmont someone else. Someone who truly *was* perfect.

But that would ruin Lilly's dreams.

Was the future of two young people who wanted each other beyond measure but were forced apart thanks to the grim realities of their situations less important than finding the Duke of Crestmont a duchess he was madly in love with?

She rubbed her temple as the answer came to her. Slowly. Painfully.

No.

Because the Duke of Crestmont didn't want love. He didn't believe it, didn't care about it. He'd told her as much, more than once. And while it would sadden her to never have the opportunity to prove to him that love truly did exist, he'd specifically requested a match for himself that had absolutely nothing to do with love. Matching him with someone who fit his specifications in all ways wouldn't hurt her business, because she would have given him exactly what he claimed to want: Harriet

Cherrington, perfect duchess.

She couldn't rip true love away from a young couple who believed in it and wanted it with all their hearts, only to bestow it on a man who neither believed in it nor wanted it.

Jo believed in love. She *wanted* to stand by it, but in this case, she couldn't. She had no choice. She would have to sacrifice one potential love match for another that was already true and real.

"I'm sorry, Matthew," she whispered under her breath.

She couldn't account for the way tears stung her eyes.

• • •

"Come on, man," Cole said. "It'll be amusing."

Matthew's lip curled. "Really?"

It was a warm day, and all four men were stripped down to trousers and shirtsleeves, their shirts spotted with sweat. It had been an excellent row, though Matthew had been so overheated, he had been tempted to splash river water over the back of his neck. He didn't, though—the stuff would have cooled him off, but it was full of excrement and every other foul thing imaginable, and on warm days like today smelled particularly disgusting.

Bending over a bucket of clean water to scrub hands that were covered in grease from rifling around the tool shelf, Matthew sighed. "Well, the weather will bé fine, for once." The Vauxhall Pleasure Gardens had the reputation of bringing torrents of rain whenever it was opened. "And Miss

Cherrington mentioned going there tonight, as well. Perhaps I should propose at Vauxhall."

He grabbed a cloth and wiped at the area between his fingers. How the hell had grease found its way there?

After scrubbing his hands thoroughly, he realized that none of the men had spoken for several moments. He glanced up to find them all gaping at him. "What?"

"Who the hell is Miss Cherrington?" Jameson snapped.

"Propose? What the devil are you talking about?" Winthrop asked at the same time.

Cole just stared at him openmouthed.

Damn, he thought the entire *country* knew that he'd been courting Miss Cherrington. He'd just found it rather odd that none of his friends had asked him about her. He figured they had simply been allowing him his privacy—which the rest of London, it seemed, had no problem invading. "Don't you ever read the gossip columns?"

"No!" all three men answered in unison.

"The society papers? The broadsheets?"

They shook their heads.

"Are you completely deaf to the rumor mill?"

"We try to be," Cole said.

"Do you talk to anyone? Anyone at all?" For God's sake, Matthew had been bombarded with information and speculation about his courtship of Harriet Cherrington from all sides.

"Just you lads," Jameson said.

"I have been busy," Winthrop said. "I have no time for gossip."

"I talk to everyone in London." Cole scratched his head, his eyes narrowed as if he was digging deep for some sort of recollection. "I may have heard something about you expressing vague interest in some society chit. But a proposal? No. I've heard no such thing."

Shaking out his dripping fingers, Matthew took a rag from the shelf and wiped his hands. "Well, I'm proposing." He shrugged. "Maybe tonight."

Jameson raised his hands in the universal gesture to stop. "Pause a moment, there, Crest. First of all, *who* is Miss Cherrington?"

Winthrop narrowed his eyes. "Second, why are you proposing?"

"Miss Cherrington is the niece of the Earl of Wydwick. I'm proposing because I wish to marry her."

"Cherrington," Cole mused. "I know a nephew of the earl—Charles Cherrington—he's a friend of my brother-in-law. I hear he has an assortment of sisters. Are you referring to one of them?"

"Yes."

"But *why*?" Winthrop asked.

"Why does anyone propose?" Matthew asked.

That seemed to stump Cole and Jameson, who looked as repulsed by the act of proposing as they would be by kissing a rabid wolf.

But Winthrop didn't hesitate. "Because you love her beyond measure."

The man was starting to sound like the matchmaker. Matthew cast his eyes heavenward.

"And I find it impossible to believe you love this woman beyond measure," Winthrop continued, "since you've never spoken a word of her to us until two minutes ago."

Matthew refused to take Winthrop's bait. "I assumed you knew all about it," he said, moving over to throw the rag into a bin. Soiled cloths brimmed over the top—he'd have to take them home for washing. "All of London is muttering about it behind their cheroots and fluttering fans."

"Wait…shouldn't you ask her father first?" Cole asked.

"Her father is dead."

"Well, her guardian, then. Don't be obtuse, Crest. You know what I mean."

"That would be her brother. I thought I'd ask him once I asked her, since he won't say no."

It wasn't false confidence that made him say it. It was absolute fact. The Cherringtons belonged to the impoverished side of the Earl of Wydwick's family. Hell would freeze over with pineapple ices from Gunter's before Charles Cherrington would refuse the Duke of Crestmont, along with the title and the massive fortune, for his sister.

"True. You're the most eligible bachelor in England. Some distant ancestor of an earl wouldn't dare refuse you," Jameson said.

"Not a distant ancestor," Matthew said pointedly. "A niece."

"Still," Jameson said.

"A proposal," Cole griped. "A goddamn proposal. You're falling—*willingly*, no less—straight into the parson's mousetrap."

Matthew looked at his friends who were still frozen to the spots where they'd been standing when he'd dropped the P-word. Then he looked around the boathouse. The boats needed to be rinsed, the floor needed to be cleaned, the items scattered over the floor needed to be returned to their proper places. "Well, at this rate, we'll be here all night. If you lot want to go to Vauxhall Gardens tonight, let's get to it, shall we?"

Cole shook his head morosely. "It's just…we… We're going to lose you."

"Don't be dramatic. You won't lose me."

"But you won't be the same."

"Cole's right," Jameson groused. "Something about wives. They get under a man's skin. Change him." His face went dark. "I don't like it."

Winthrop clapped him on the shoulder. "You should marry, too, then, Jameson. God knows you could use a change. Maybe it would wipe that glower from your face."

"Doubtful." Jameson spun away from all of them, stomped to the corner, and took the broom from its peg.

As he stacked the clean towels he'd brought from home into their cabinet, Matthew remembered a time when they'd all been young and at Eton. He'd been twelve or thirteen when the four of them had agreed that girls were tender, tedious creatures. All they did was sit primly in their frills and lace, usually indoors, and prattle on about ribbons and bows. And if they got a little scratch on their arms or a bruise on their knee, they'd weep for hours. Matthew, Jameson, Cole, and Winthrop had each vowed never to speak to a girl, much less marry one.

Now, Matthew was on the cusp of doing just that—again.

As they cleaned, Cole asked him, "What is she like?"

Determined, *stubborn*, and *strong* were the first words to pop into his mind. Many others followed, like *beautiful*, *sensual*, and *sweet*.

Wait. Cole had meant "she," as in Harriet Cherrington, not Jo.

"She's accomplished, engaging, and polite," he told them.

"What does she think about this?" Cole gestured to one of the boats with the oar he'd been rinsing.

She's interested in trying it herself, Matthew thought.

"We haven't discussed it," Matthew said.

Jameson raised a brow as he swept the dust outside but didn't say a word.

"And what of your obsession with meteorology?" Winthrop asked.

She's fascinated by it as well, Matthew thought.

"We have discussed the weather often," Matthew said.

Of course he and Miss Cherrington had discussed the weather often. All Londoners did. But when he'd started talking about some of his climate prediction factors, she'd smiled and nodded politely, but he had been able to tell by the glazed look in her eyes that she wasn't interested.

"Hm," Winthrop said.

"What is that supposed to mean?"

"Nothing at all." Winthrop turned away.

Correct. There was nothing wrong with Matthew not discussing his interests with his future bride. Nothing at all.

CHAPTER NINETEEN

Vauxhall Gardens was more enchanting than ever. It was a perfect night, and though one rarely saw stars through London's coal-blackened sky, the air was somewhat fresher here on the south side of the Thames. At least, it felt clean thanks to the fresh late-spring breeze.

Jo and Lilly paid the penny toll and traversed the new Vauxhall Bridge across the Thames for the first time—for previous visits, they'd had to take a boat. After Jo doled out seven shillings for their entry, she and Lilly linked arms and stepped into the world of wonder that was Vauxhall Gardens.

A little man dressed in old-fashioned breeches with black tights, black pumps embellished with large black bows, a black tailcoat, and carrying a tasseled cane whisked his high beaver hat off his head and drew a low bow in their direction. "Welcome to the royal properties, my ladies!"

Lilly literally jumped back, then turned to Jo in alarm. After all, neither of them had been properly introduced to this man.

But Jo knew who it was. She remembered him coming to their supper box on one of their previous visits. Mr. Simpson had been a staple here since before the turn of the century, and was known to almost all Londoners as the voice and face of Vauxhall Gardens—also as a silly, unctuous man who was widely known to treat lampposts and the prince regent with equal deference.

She smiled at Lilly. "My dear Lilly, surely you recall Mr. Simpson, the Master of Ceremonies." She dropped a curtsy in his direction. "Good evening, sir."

Simpson looked shocked. He clutched his hat to his chest. "My humblest and sincere thanks for deigning to wish me a good evening, my fair lady. I shall be, from this point and forevermore, your devoted servant." With his hat-holding hand, he made a grand flourish toward the interior of the park. "With my deepest respect and sincerity, I wish you and your dear Lilly a marvelous evening."

He swept his hat back to his chest and bowed low, not rising again until Lilly and Jo were several steps away from him. Lilly giggled as Jo glanced back and saw him bowing again and saying the exact same words to a pair of older ladies entering the grounds behind them.

Jo and Lilly spent the remainder of the afternoon touring their favorite places in the gardens before returning to the front of the park as Vauxhall's star singer, Mrs. Bland, was walking to the balcony of the octagonal orchestra building to begin her set. There, the scents of savory roasting meat and fresh bread wafted from behind the wide arc of the surrounding supper boxes.

A quarter of an hour later everyone in the crowd had gone still and silent, their senses filled by the delicious smells and the dulcet ballads sung by Mrs. Bland. Well, everyone was still but Lilly. She was anxious, glancing furtively around and shifting restlessly on her feet. Jo and Lilly had been at the gardens for nearly three hours, and they'd seen no sign of the Cherrington sisters.

The song ended to much applause, then Mr. Dignum came to join Mrs. Bland on the balcony, and they began to sing a duet.

"Ooh! I see them!" Lilly exclaimed, then dragged Jo to where the Cherringtons had gathered on a small mound of the lawn between two tall trees.

As soon as she saw them, Jo knew why Lilly had begged so fervently to come tonight. Like a raven among swans, Charles Cherrington looked sleek in his black hat, tailcoat, pantaloons, and boots, surrounded by his five feminine and fashionable sisters, all dressed in white.

Jo cut Lilly a stern look and murmured, "You did not tell me Mr. Cherrington would be here."

"I didn't?" Lilly grinned. "So sorry."

She didn't sound the slightest bit sorry. Jo shook her head but didn't say anything more as they approached the Cherringtons, who all smiled broadly at them save Frances—though even she had a faint upturn to her lips.

After everyone greeted everyone else, Charles suggested in a low voice that after the concert, they should go see the cascade, then find a supper box where they'd enjoy some refreshments while awaiting the midnight appearance of the rope-dancer and the fireworks. Then, they all turned back toward the orchestra and listened as Mr. Dignum belted his heart out.

When the concert ended about an hour later, a bell rang to signal the demonstration of the cascade. Their party rushed, along with about a thousand others, under the vaulted colonnade of the Grand Walk until they reached the location of the waterworks. They gathered before a curtain that rose to a scene of bucolic delight: rolling green hills in the background bracketing a wide, mechanical waterfall, the "water" crashing down in a roar into a stream, where it frothed and bubbled under the rotating wheel of a watermill.

Mechanical moving figures populated each side of the stream, and a bridge spanned it. A mail coach rattled along, horses' legs jerking up and down, until it stopped on the bridge, its driver lowering his gun to point at the back of a fleeing robber, a sack of mail strung over his back. The gun went off with a great *bang!*, and the man jerked and tumbled behind a hedge.

On the opposite side of the stream, a man sat, ostensibly ignoring the hubbub of the mail coach drama and rocking in his chair as smoke curled up from the pipe he sucked on. All the people had an authentic quality about them, though by their lurching movements, they were clearly as mechanical as the stream.

It was a miracle, thought Jo, even though hundreds of people crowded her and she could only catch peeks of the scene between the many bodies blocking her view. In all of her visits to Vauxhall, this display never ceased to delight her. The water looked real, but it wasn't water — it was tin, its movement facilitated by mechanical devices beneath the scene, its shimmering surface made to look like sunlight shining on the stream by the myriad lanterns glowing overhead.

To her side, Charles Cherrington lifted Lilly by the waist so she could sneak a better view. Jo's protective-chaperone instincts roared to life, and she almost yanked Lilly down—someone might see Charles with his hands on her! But she forced the thought away. They would, if all went as planned, marry soon. And, as she glanced around at the crowd, she noticed that no one paid any heed to what Charles and Lilly were doing. They were all singularly focused on the cascade and all the antics happening around it.

In any case, Vauxhall was famous for liaisons of a sort far more scandalous than the one happening beside her. Jo resolved to let Charles and Lilly enjoy this moment.

From behind the man on the rocking chair, a mad ox appeared, at first sauntering closer, then stopping as if noticing the man for the first time, blowing steam from its broad nostrils. With a bellow the crowd heard but the mechanical pipe-smoking man did not, the massive beast lowered its horns and charged straight at the oblivious man's backside. The ox struck its target, and the man tumbled forward and out of the chair, his torn trousers exposing his bare, hairy rump. The audience roared with laughter. Charles lowered Lilly and playfully covered her eyes. Laughing, she pushed his hands away and smiled up at him as he returned her smile, looking more a besotted fool than a young gentleman of the *ton*.

With a selfish pang in her chest, Jo wished someone would smile at her that way. She wished she had someone of her own who could lift her high above the crowd, so she could take in every single detail of the scene before her.

But that was never to be. The best she could hope for was to someday come to Vauxhall alone and sneak here during the concert and be at the very front of the crowd when the display began so she could soak in every incredible detail.

It was a lonely thought, the resulting ache inside her a familiar one.

The spectacle lasted a few minutes longer as the ox chased the mail coach over the bridge. Once the curtain was finally drawn, the satisfied crowd drifted off in every direction, chattering about what they'd seen.

Considering the density of the crowd in attendance tonight, Jo, Lilly, and the Cherringtons were lucky to find a supper box close to the orchestra, and Charles ordered them a spread of the foods Vauxhall was most famous for: miniature whole chickens and dishes of ham sliced into paper-thin sheets, an assortment of cakes and tarts, and fresh bread, as well as a pitcher of arrack punch.

Before the food arrived, a whistle was blown, and not one moment later, it seemed as if all of Vauxhall Gardens' twelve thousand lanterns came to life at once. Multicolored hanging lanterns lit the rose-scented paths in rainbows of soft light, and the pavilion, orchestra area, and supper boxes twinkled with star-lights.

It did not surprise Jo that Charles had chosen a seat next to Lilly at the top end of the U-shaped table. He was downright jovial tonight, a complete reversal from his demeanor at the Dickersons' soiree. Unless he'd been buried in a hole for the last two weeks, he certainly knew that the Duke of Crestmont was courting his sister—talk of it was all over London. Perhaps the idea that the duke might marry his sister was giving him hope of having Lilly back in his arms. Still, he should be at least a little cautious—there was no marriage yet, not even a proposal.

Jo herself wasn't confident everything would work out as she'd planned. In fact, she was more nervous about this match than she'd been about any of the dozens she'd made before, even Mr. Pellegrini's, and she probably should have been nervous about that one.

Jo sat at the other end of the table from Charles and Lilly, deliberately sliding between Martha and Harriet, who sat at the end of the bench. Suddenly in high demand, thanks to the attention she'd been receiving from the Duke of Crestmont, Harriet had been managing her newfound popularity with aplomb. No less than a dozen lords and ladies paraded past their box to greet her before the food even arrived. Harriet was unperturbed by all the attention, unfailingly gracious and charming.

Matthew would approve. He would think she was *perfect*, Jo thought, the word crashing like a stone through the window of her heart.

The Cherringtons were generous and very welcoming. Charles was devoted to his sisters, and they doted on him in return. The fact that he had brought his sisters here instead of carousing with other young bucks like most gentlemen his age were wont to do increased Jo's respect for him.

As the meal drew on and Lilly leaned against Martha, both of their shoulders shaking with laughter, it struck Jo that Lilly had already been accepted as a member of their family.

Jo was—and always would be—the outsider of this group. If Lilly married Charles, she would have five sisters to confide in. She'd live in their house and see them every day.

Jo would be left alone in Beaumont Street.

She ground her teeth. Why did her thoughts keep veering into self-pity and melancholy? *You must stop this, Jo*, she commanded herself. *At once.*

She *wouldn't* be alone. Mama and Bess and Mrs. Ferguson were in the house in Beaumont Street. She would miss Lilly, but she adored the three other women in her life, too.

When there was a lull in the conversation, Jo leaned over and, speaking directly into Harriet's ear so she could be heard above the crowd and the music, asked her, "How are things progressing with the Duke of Crestmont?"

Pink suffused Harriet's cheeks. She patted her delicate handkerchief to her lips, then said, "They are progressing very well, I think."

"That's good to hear." She hesitated. She might as well be out with it. "Do you like him, Miss Cherrington?"

"Oh, yes, I do. Immensely. He is very courteous."

Jo thought of his hands on her…between her legs. She could think of many words to describe the Duke of Crestmont. *Courteous* was not one of them.

There were so many other words that fit him so much better.

Jo picked at the deliciously salty ham, wishing she and Harriet were alone in a quiet room, but it could not be helped. This—here in the middle of Vauxhall Gardens surrounded by thousands of people—would have to do.

She laid down her fork and turned to fully face Harriet. "I believe the duke is considering a proposal."

At first, Harriet didn't react at all. She continued chewing on her slice of buttered bread and then chased it with a ladylike sip of punch before pursing her lips—the stuff had a sharp tang of lemon. After the tartness passed, she turned to Jo, smiling. "That would be wonderful."

Would it, though?

Harriet was an enigma—so hard to read, and Jo usually had a talent for deciphering what her clients truly thought of one another. But her whole being was deep in the forest of this situation, caught in such a briar-filled tangle, she had lost her way through.

"Do you *wish* to marry him?" she managed.

Harriet circumvented her question. "He is a wonderful man, and I am so honored by his attention. My family will benefit greatly if I were to marry him."

Jo nodded. That part was a given.

"Charles will be absolutely delighted." Harriet gestured down the table to her brother. "Look at him. He was struggling under the weight of our family's…situation, and now, renewed hope has allowed him to push his worries aside."

If Harriet loved the duke, she'd be talking about

how happy she was about a potential proposal, not about how happy her *brother* would be. Jo finally understood exactly how this would go. For her family, Harriet would marry the duke with a smile on her face. She'd hold her head high and be his perfect duchess.

But she didn't love him.

Still, Jo had to be sure that the disaster of what had happened with Mr. Pellegrini would not happen again. "If he offered for you, would you accept?"

She held her breath, but Harriet didn't take long to answer. She gave a gracious smile. "Of course. I would be honored to accept a proposal. But I dare not expect such an outcome."

Jo studied her closely. On most highborn ladies of the *ton*, such modesty was an affect—fake and insincere. But on Harriet, it seemed to be real.

And it was right then that the Duke of Crestmont appeared, materializing in front of them like an apparition, tall and handsome in his dark evening clothes. Now, rather than finding it irritating, Jo found that his stern expression set her blood on fire.

"Good evening, Miss Cherrington," he said with a bow before turning to the rest of the assembly. He greeted Jo and the rest of the sisters in turn, and then Mary introduced him first to Charles, then Lilly.

"Your Grace," Charles exclaimed, looking rather flustered. Jo couldn't really blame him. He was several years younger than the duke and grasped a lower rung of the social ladder, after all. "Please, sit with us. We've plenty of room. Over there!" He gestured toward Harriet. "Make some room, will you, Harriet?"

"Of course." Harriet scooted closer to Jo to make space on the bench seat.

"Thank you." Matthew slid onto the bench beside Harriet while keeping his gaze on Charles. Both Harriet and Matthew sat stiffly, taking pains to ensure no part of their bodies touched the other's, even though Harriet pressed the other side of her body into Jo's.

The rigid display must be for propriety's sake, Jo decided. Both Harriet and the duke were determined to be models of respectability.

Of course, that thought led to a memory of the duke's *im*propriety in her office, his decadent and sinful kisses, and how she'd come apart in his arms, crying out and descending into pleasure so absolute, propriety had not even been a word she could comprehend.

"I can't stay long," Matthew said. "I came with friends, and they will miss me."

"I daresay none of us will stay long," Martha said. "I believe the rope-dancing is to begin soon, and I want to have a good view of it."

"So do I," Esther agreed. "Better than we had of the cascade. I could hardly see a thing!"

Lilly clasped her hands at her chest. "I have never seen a rope-walker. It is unbelievable that a human body is capable of performing such feats."

"Let's go soon, then, so we will have an ideal view," Charles agreed.

They sat a few minutes longer, chatting about the fine weather and finishing the last of the punch. Jo only drank a single small cup of it, but it had sent a pleasant tingle through her veins.

When they finally all stood, preparing to walk to the other end of the park to find an ideal viewing spot for the rope-dancing and fireworks, Matthew turned to Harriet and bowed. "Miss Cherrington. I hope to see you later."

She gave him one of her soft smiles, and they gazed at each other for a moment.

A perfect picture. A handsome duke and his lovely future duchess sharing a look of respect and admiration with the twinkling backdrop of the lanterns of Vauxhall Gardens. It would make a beautiful portrait to hang on his castle wall one day.

Jealousy roared through Jo with a ferocity that poured bitterness through her marrow.

She despised this. It was torture.

After Harriet moved away from the duke, his gaze turned to Jo and caught her watching. The gentleness infusing his eyes was like a long, sweet drink of chocolate. A balm. He understood how this made her feel, that much was clear. When he walked past her, his gloved fingers skimmed the back of her hand.

Her breath caught, and she glanced back at her party. Already skipping along beneath the arches toward the opposite end of the gardens, they hadn't seen her and the duke's brief interaction.

Jo hurried after them but not before casting one longing glance back at the man who was breaking her heart.

CHAPTER TWENTY

A thick mass of humanity drew Matthew, Jameson, Cole, and Winthrop along the path that led to the fireworks and rope-dancing demonstration.

They walked under the iron arches, the path lit with hundreds of lanterns, some of them bunched up to look like bouquets of flowers, with long green globe lights to represent the stems, then bunches of clustered round lights in pinks and oranges and purples to make up the bouquets.

Loath to press into the densest crush of people that crowded the rope slung hundreds of feet from a thatch of greenery to the tip of a mast placed atop the fireworks platform, Matthew and his friends hung back. They were all annoyed with him for not introducing them to Miss Cherrington, but Matthew had been annoyed with himself, for it was not Harriet Cherrington he'd wanted to introduce to them. It was Jo. He thought they'd like her.

Jameson scowled at him. "What are you smiling about?"

He scowled back. "Nothing."

"Liar," Jameson grumbled.

Matthew shrugged.

Suddenly—Matthew had no idea how it happened—the lights around them went dim, provoking the crowd into immediate silence. Then, a bright burst of blue fire illuminated the rope before dimming to reveal the rope-dancer, her tiny feet balanced upon the rope, her weight causing it to bow slightly.

She was a small, dark-skinned woman, her headdress of enormous and colorful plumes increasing her height by half. Never once losing her balance or seeming the slightest bit concerned that she might fall, she twirled and danced, her spangled gold and silver dress swinging around her. The blue light followed her up and up as she seemed to ascend into the heavens.

Finally, she reached the top, the blue stream of light faded away into darkness, and the crowd burst into enthusiastic cheers, Matthew and his friends included. But then they all were instantly silenced again as fireworks exploded into the sky in a series of *boom*s and an array of dazzling colors, and the rope-dancer danced and twirled, and even tumbled in somersaults, back down the rope. Moments later it was finished, the rope-dancer disappearing into the dark bushes and the dark sky now filled with smoke.

As the lamplighters did their work, the world twinkled into focus again, revealing people scattering in all directions and a pair of Eton men approaching. "Crestmont! Winthrop! Coleton! And Jameson, too! It has been a long time!"

Matthew stood in conversation with them, the six of them reminiscing about the good old days back when they were all youthful scamps, while he surreptitiously searched around the crowd for Harriet. Not for Jo, he told himself—*Harriet*.

It was after midnight, and he hadn't talked to Harriet alone. At this point, he doubted he'd have the chance.

He was grateful for it.

No.

No, goddamn it. He was *not* grateful. Now he'd have to find another way to propose to Miss Cherrington. It would be a damned inconvenience.

Try as he might, he still couldn't muster much disappointment about it.

Then, in the direction of the fireworks tower, he saw a lone feminine figure turning in a slow circle.

He knew instantly that it was Jo. And she was alone.

Filled with sudden concern, he excused himself from his group and hurried toward her, calling, "Miss Porter?"

She whipped around, hand to her chest. "Oh, Your Grace. I think I've misplaced my party. We were watching the show and the crowd was so thick, and I just assumed they were all there, but when the lights came back on"—she closed her gloved hands into fists in front of her then snapped them open—"poof! They had disappeared."

"I'll help you to find them."

"Do you think if I remain in this spot, they'll come back for me?"

"It's possible," Matthew said. "Let's wait here for a few moments and see."

Having finished their conversation with their old schoolmates, his friends approached. "Good evening, Miss Porter," Cole said with a bow.

It was only then that he remembered that Cole and Jo had already met at the Dickersons' soiree.

"Lord Coleton," Jo said politely. "It is nice to see you again."

"Have you met my friends?" When Jo said she hadn't, Cole introduced Winthrop and Jameson, while Matthew stood beside her without saying a word. Even if she hadn't previously been introduced to his other two friends, Matthew had spoken of them often, and he could tell she was enjoying placing the faces with their names, though she didn't give any hint of the confidences they'd shared.

He'd known he could trust her.

Jameson nudged him and whispered in his ear, "Your matchmaker?"

Matthew gave a slight nod, then turned his attention outside their group. He felt strange, as if disconnected from his body, with his friends and Jo in the same setting. The fire that always burned between him and Jo was there, an underlying simmer he was attempting to keep tamped down. He couldn't look at her—if he looked at her for more than a second or two, his friends would know. They weren't stupid. And what he felt for Jo was so hot, it could singe anyone who came too close.

"What is wrong with you, man?" Jameson asked him after they'd exchanged pleasantries for a few moments. "We've been talking about the weather and you haven't interrupted with any clever predictions. What happened, cat got your tongue?"

He narrowed his eyes at Jameson in a warning look. "Miss Porter has been separated from her party. I've been hunting for them in the crowd."

"Well, no need to be so covert about it, Crest," Cole said. "We'll help."

"Of course we will," Winthrop said. "Who is in your party?"

"My friend, Miss Appleby—" Jo began.

"Ah," Cole said, "I didn't know Miss Appleby was here!"

When Jameson arched a brow at him, Cole grinned, keeping his level of wolfishness toned down only because of the woman in their midst. "I danced with her at my sister's soiree," Cole explained, then drawled, "Lovely creature."

Jo stiffened—a defensive posture—then her lip curled. "She is, isn't she?" she drawled right back. "The loveliest."

Cole nodded sagely. "Indeed."

"She is with the five Cherrington sisters and their brother, Mr. Charles Cherrington."

"I see." A note of understanding dawned in Cole's tone.

"So, we are searching for a party of six ladies and one gentleman?" Winthrop said.

"Yes." Jo looked at Matthew. "I suppose if they were going to come back, they would have done so by now."

"You are most likely correct," he said, avoiding meeting her eyes.

"I think we should divide and conquer, as it were," Jameson said. "Crest, you search the Grand Walk and the Hermitage with Miss Porter. Cole, Winthrop, and I will search the South Walk and Druid's Lane."

Matthew's gaze sharpened on his friend, and beside him, he sensed Jo doing the same thing. It was a slight—ever-so-slight—movement, and he wasn't sure whether Jo saw it, but Matthew did. The very edge of Jameson's lip curved up in a knowing smirk.

"Come along, gents," Jameson said to Winthrop and Cole. "We'll meet you back at the orchestra in half an hour." And before Matthew or Jo could respond, the three men strode off.

Jo blew out a breath. "Shall we?"

Matthew nodded, his mind a turmoil. He could feel Jo's eyes on him, though he still couldn't look at her. His chest felt hot as a brand.

They started walking in silence, but as they turned onto the Hermitage, she came to an abrupt halt. Matthew had gone two more steps before his body obeyed his command for it to stop.

He finally turned back to her, managing to raise his brows. "What's wrong? Do you see them?"

But she was gazing straight at him. "Is something wrong, Your Grace?"

I was going to propose. Then I saw you...and I couldn't. That's what is wrong.

He tried to think of Harriet Cherrington. But for the life of him, he couldn't conjure an image of her in his mind. All that occupied it was the beautiful woman standing before him. How he wanted to drag her into his arms and kiss her and touch her until she begged him for more. And then, afterward, he'd hold her close and they'd stare up at the quiet sky and talk and talk until dawn grayed the sky and London came back to life.

It couldn't happen.

"This is more difficult than I thought it would be," he managed.

She frowned. "What is?"

He glanced around. People milled everywhere, pretending like they weren't watching this exchange.

But they were. This crowd recognized him just as they did all over London. Just because Vauxhall felt magical didn't mean it had the magical power of cloaking him from gossiping tongues or protecting Jo from the backlash of being seen in an impassioned conversation with him.

Swallowing hard, he stepped toward her and murmured, "Come home with me."

She gasped. "I can't! Lilly is here with me. The Cherringtons…"

Right. He was an idiot. He closed his eyes. She had people here with her. She couldn't just leave with him. He blew out a breath. "I'm sorry."

"Matthew, what—?"

"Shh." He shook his head. "Don't." Don't call him that, he meant. Not here, in a public place. Not where people might hear and speculate.

He knew he needed to let Joanna Porter go. He just didn't know how he was going to do it.

He would force himself, that's how. Like he might force himself into sawing off his hand or jumping naked into the rancid waters of the Thames in the middle of January.

He yanked his gaze from her and made himself scan the path. "They're not here. Let's keep looking."

He felt her confused gaze on him. He couldn't blame her—he was confusing the hell out of himself.

"Very well."

They kept looking, turning down one walk then another, and finally, as they trudged under the triumphal arches that ran down the grand South Walk, Jo gestured ahead toward the statue of the great composer, Handel, that stood between the rows of trees and supper boxes. "I believe that's Martha."

It was indeed Martha Cherrington. She stood beside the statue with three of her sisters—Frances, Mary, and Esther. Jo and Matthew hurried up to the four women.

Esther looked at them in alarm. "Where are Charles and Harriet and Lilly?"

"I have no idea," Jo said. "I thought they were with you."

"We thought they were with *you*," Martha said.

"When I encountered Miss Porter after the rope-dancing performance, she had been left alone," Matthew said, trying to keep the accusatory tone out of his voice.

"We've been searching for all of you ever since," Jo added.

"Oh, dear!" Mary said, aghast. She turned to Matthew. "Thank the Lord she found a friendly face in the fray."

Thinking of Jo all alone in Vauxhall Gardens after midnight, Matthew shuddered. "I am glad I was there."

"Well," Martha said, "I am sure Charles is looking after Harriet and Lilly. They'll find us eventually, won't they?"

"Certainly," Matthew said.

"Let's go to the orchestra," Jo said. "It's the most central meeting place, so they might even be there now, and the duke is supposed to rejoin his friends soon."

The other ladies agreed, and Matthew accompanied them, merging with the streams of patrons exiting the gardens for the evening. The society crowd usually left this time of night, leaving drunken revelers and those of questionable repute to prowl the grounds into the early hours.

"Look!" Jo motioned toward a group of patrons drunkenly dancing a reel. Near them, on the edge of the dancing area, Matthew's friends stood with Charles Cherrington and Lilly.

As soon as the two groups saw one another, they rushed together.

Then, everyone descended into a panic.

Harriet was still missing.

A young lady alone somewhere in the bowels of Vauxhall at nearly one in the morning? Good God.

Horrible scenarios crowded everyone's minds. The ladies' hands went over their mouths and their eyes filled with tears. The men grew dark and serious, especially Charles Cherrington, who clearly was quite fond of his sister.

After ordering the women to remain together and stay put at their spot near the orchestra, Charles and Matthew described Harriet and the frock she was wearing to the other men. They split in different directions with an agreement to be back to check in after twenty minutes.

Assigned to the quieter northern section of the gardens, Matthew walked, searched, and listened for any noises off the path. He passed a young couple rutting against a tree, the man's bare arse flexing as he thrust inside the woman, her fashionable silk skirts rucked up over her hips, her head thrown back against the trunk, and her intricately feathered hat lying unheeded on the nearby ground. They were so involved in their illicit joy, they didn't notice—or didn't care—that he had seen them.

Matthew walked on, torment twisting through him. What was he doing?

When he'd first gone to Joanna Porter, he'd been so confident in his path. He knew what he wanted, what he needed. He understood exactly how to perform his myriad duties as the Duke of Crestmont.

Now, he didn't know his toe from his arsehole. If he proposed to Harriet Cherrington, he'd get everything he wanted. Why, then, wasn't he satisfied? Why was he more anxious and discontent than ever before?

He *knew* why, of course.

He needed to let Jo go. To remove her from his life and continue to live it as he had planned. But a part of him—very well, a rather *large* part—was flagrantly defying all common sense and screaming *no*. That part of him wouldn't let her go without a fight.

Back on the Dark Walk, the least well-lit path in the gardens, he took his time, listening for any rustle, conversation, or sound of distress that might involve Harriet Cherrington. It was quiet back here tonight, and Matthew glanced up at the dark sky. There was a single star punching its way through London's smoky haze, a bright pinprick of light with a muted silver halo that reminded him of Jo's eyes. He wondered if she was looking up at that star right now, too. Whether they were both wishing upon it together.

"Stop! Thief!"

Jarred from his thoughts, Matthew jumped to

attention. The outraged screech had come from some distance up ahead on the path, and a dark form was reeling around the corner ahead, sprinting straight toward him. Matthew ducked behind the shadow of a tree, then, as the person approached, he lunged out, in a split second determining it was a man and in another, spotting the feminine purse he clutched to his chest.

Matthew leapt at him, and they tumbled to the ground hard, knocking the wind out of both of them. After a stunned moment, Matthew realized he was on top of the fellow, and wrenched the reticule out of the crook of his arm. He jumped up, leaving the man, still gasping for air, on the ground.

A bloody cutpurse.

From above, Matthew could see the man a bit better. Not a man, Matthew realized as he sucked in each breath as if through a very thin straw. A burly, dark-haired youth of fourteen or fifteen years wearing the shabby clothes of a street urchin. He leaned over the lad. "Off with you," he panted, "before I have you thrown on the gallows."

"Please…sir…" the boy choked.

"Go," Matthew ordered. Glancing behind them, he saw a stout couple rounding the corner. *"Now."*

The boy stumbled up and staggered off into the darkness. Matthew leaned against the tree, still trying to catch his breath. Perhaps he'd tackled the boy too violently. They'd gone down *hard*. It was lucky the youth hadn't landed on a rock and cracked his head open.

The couple hurried up to him, and he could now see that they were an older, matching pair, small and rotund. Even their clothes matched, her brown pelisse seemingly made of the same material as her husband's coat.

"Where did that scoundrel go to?" the wife demanded, hands on her wide hips, her face twisted in anger. "Had a knife and sliced my purse straight off my wrist, he did!"

Matthew held out the reticule, which appeared to be of the same brown fabric as the couple's outerwear. "Madam."

"Where is he?" The man scowled into the darkness as if he'd set off in pursuit at any moment, though he hadn't pursued the boy when he actually *had* the item he'd stolen from them.

"He's long gone," Matthew said.

"Well," the woman said, "at least I've got my reticule back." Holding it in front of her, she eyed the cut strap, which hung limply to its side.

The man patted the woman's arm. "Let's go home, dearie." He tipped his hat to Matthew. "I thank you for retrieving it for us, sir."

"My pleasure," Matthew said. The woman clutched the reticule to her chest, and, arm in arm, they rumbled off, muttering about the wicked cutpurse's audacity.

Matthew strode back the way he'd come just to double-check for any sign of Miss Cherrington but found nothing except the couple who'd been tupping against the tree were now seated propped up against it, the man holding the woman tucked in his arms, her pink silk skirts shimmering softly in the dim light of the hazy nighttime sky. They looked to be asleep, and Matthew left them to their rest.

When he arrived back at the orchestra, Winthrop, Jameson, and Cole were returning at the same time, and the sight of Cherringtons and Porters that greeted him made him sigh in relief. Harriet was among them.

"What the hell happened to you?" Jameson muttered in his ear, and Matthew looked down to see that his knees were caked in mud and several wet leaves were plastered to his coat. He brushed the leaves off quickly, but there was nothing to be done about the mud.

"I'll tell you later." Matthew approached the group, and the ladies parted to make way for him, politely ignoring his soiled state. "I found her searching for us in the portrait room," Charles Cherrington explained.

"Praise the Lord she was unharmed," Mary breathed.

Matthew bowed to Harriet, who looked…yes, unharmed, but also pink-cheeked and rather windswept. Which was odd, considering the breeze was quite light—only gusting to six to seven miles per hour from the southwest tonight. "I'm glad you are all right, Miss Cherrington."

Her pink cheeks went darker. "I am fine. Truly, I didn't mean to cause anyone worry. But I…I couldn't find anyone for the longest time."

"We were *terrified*," Esther said dramatically.

Harriet smiled at her sister. "Well, you shouldn't have been. You knew I'd find you, didn't you?"

"No," Esther whispered, wide-eyed. "We thought you'd been abducted. And held for ransom! Or maybe robbed and compromised and left nake—"

"Well," Mary interrupted crisply, "it is an excellent thing none of that happened and you are hale and in one piece."

"A very excellent thing!" Miss Appleby exclaimed.

Charles passed a hand over his sweat-beaded brow. "Now that all the excitement has come to a close, I think we should head home. It's getting quite late." He turned to Matthew and his friends. "Thank you for helping us search for my sister."

"Anything for Miss Harriet," Cole said meaningfully. Matthew shot him a look and said, "Of course. It was our pleasure to help."

The sisters followed with their thanks, along with Lilly and Jo—who he couldn't look in the eye as she murmured goodbye, the word landing in his gut like a brick—leaving Harriet for last.

He hadn't proposed tonight. He'd have to wait until they saw each other again, which would be… "Will I see you at the Houghton House ball on Wednesday, Miss Cherrington?"

"Yes, Your Grace."

"I look forward to it," he said quietly, then bowed and took his leave, vowing to spend every day between now and Wednesday scraping all remnants of Joanna Porter from his mind.

CHAPTER TWENTY-ONE

Clutching the notebook to her chest, Jo looked up at the stately entrance to the Duke of Crestmont's Mayfair home.

What was she thinking? That she'd just walk up and knock on the door? His butler would probably laugh in her face, and if anyone else saw her here…

Glancing furtively this way and that, she saw no one she knew, but that did not mean that people weren't peeking at her from behind curtains.

She'd slipped out to take an afternoon walk—on her own, which was bad enough. Being a spinster came with a few freedoms, but traipsing about London alone was something she'd never done before. She'd told herself to avoid places where anyone might recognize her, especially to avoid the duke's house. Nevertheless, her legs had marched her straight into Mayfair—the center of London society—and to his front door.

When had she become so reckless? When had her logic and practicality vanished under this rush of impulsivity and daring? She was too old to succumb to foolish ideas of romance and passion. And yet, here she was.

This was madness.

She turned on her heel and stalked away from the house, keeping her head down. When she came to the lane that led to the mews, she turned into it. If she went the back way, she'd have less of a chance of being seen.

Finally, she was allowing common sense to prevail.

When she was tucked in the lane behind the row of townhouses, her steps slowed a little, and so did her breaths, which had been coming in short gasps.

It was all right. It was likely no one had been paying any attention to her whatsoever in the busy afternoon. All was well. She'd be perfectly fine.

"Miss Porter?"

Her head whipped up, and when she saw the handsome man a few feet away from her standing adjacent to his familiar, shiny black carriage, her heart leaped so high she thought it might break through the wall of her chest.

She swallowed, trying to regain some moisture into her suddenly dry throat. "Good afternoon, Your Grace."

Lord, he was handsome, standing there with his walking stick and his well-fitted clothes, the sunlight washing his brown eyes with amber as he studied her.

Beautiful, and soulful, and wonderful.

"Are you all right?" Matthew asked her, his eyes going from her face to the notebook she clutched at her chest then back to her face again. She realized she'd been stopped on mews she shouldn't be in, staring at him as if he were one of the antiquities on display at the British Museum.

"No... *Yes*. Yes, of course I am."

He raised a skeptical brow. "Why are you here?"

"Here?" She glanced around as if surprised by the setting. "Oh. I—" She began to panic. "I...uh...

This." She thrust the notebook out to him.

"What's this?"

"It's Lilly's. It contains her most recent creation. You said you were interested in her designs, so…I brought it here. For you."

He raised one brow, then took the book from her. "Wait here a moment." He walked around to the front of the carriage and murmured a few words to the coachman. The man nodded and drove the carriage back into its spot in the stables on the opposite side of the mews.

When the duke returned to her, she asked, "Were you going somewhere, Your Grace?"

"Nowhere of importance."

"I'm so sorry—please don't change your plans on my behalf," she said.

"Jo, I said it wasn't important."

"Very well. But why are *you* in the mews?" she asked. Most gentlemen spent little time in such places. They simply called for their carriages to be brought round, and they'd step out their front doors a few minutes later and find their conveyance ready to take them wherever they wished to go.

"I keep most of my weather instruments in the garden, and I've converted the shed to house some of my tools. I was back here working when it was time to go." He gestured toward a fenced garden area. Jo could see beds filled with various plants, but from this angle, his tools for measuring weather weren't visible.

"Come inside with me, and you can tell me more about Miss Appleby's work," he said.

She swallowed again. No luck. Her throat had as

much moisture as a kettle that had been boiled dry. "Your Grace…I can't. What would…what…?"

He shook his head. "What would people say? Nothing." He looked up and down the mews, which were empty except for a few stable boys and coachmen milling about the stables. "Come."

He took her hand and pulled her past the garden and through a door into a scullery where a maid was washing dishes. She glanced their way. "Good afternoon, Your—" While she might have been accustomed to seeing the duke in the scullery, the girl clearly was not used to seeing him with a woman. She recovered quickly. "—Grace. Ma'am." Pulling her hands out of the dishwater, she bobbed a curtsy.

"Good afternoon, Mildred." Matthew tugged Jo out of the scullery and into a vast, well-stocked kitchen that smelled of the herbs that hung drying in one corner. Two kitchen maids were standing at the center table, one adding what appeared to be flour into a large bowl and the other mixing.

"Your Grace," they said in unison. Then, quicker to recover from the shock of seeing her, they added, "Ma'am," as they dropped identical curtsies.

"Good Lord," Jo muttered, "my reputation will be shredded to tatters."

"Nonsense," he said. "Your reputation will remain in one piece. Don't be dramatic."

"Servants talk," she informed him archly. How naive was he?

"Not mine," he said in a superior tone that made her roll her eyes. "Come."

He took her pelisse and hung it in a closet, then

led her through a grand dining room and up a lovely curving, dark-stained staircase.

"Where are we going?"

"Somewhere we can talk."

At the top of the stairs, he turned down a wide corridor and opened a door at its end. Then he stepped into a library.

Not just a library. It was a *wonderful* library, so wonderful, it made water flood back into Jo's mouth, as if each beautiful, elegant book were a rich delicacy waiting for her to sample it. Just think—all these books, pages filled with timeless words, knowledge, and stories. "Oh," she breathed in awe. "It's...lovely."

Two walls of the large room were covered with volumes tucked into shelves that rose from the floor to the ceiling. On the far wall stood a desk, and behind it, a large-paned window that looked out over Hill Street. To her left was a fireplace with an assortment of chairs gathered round to provide a space for comfortable reading. Of course, the mantel boasted both a barometer and a thermometer.

Matthew stopped and studied the room as if seeing it for the first time. A slow smile curled his lips. "It is, isn't it? It's my favorite room in the house. I spend most of my time here when I'm not sleeping. Please sit down."

She did as he asked, taking the armchair he gestured to—and it *was* just as comfortable as it looked, though nothing could compare to the cloud-soft green chair in her office.

Matthew knelt and got the banked fire going. Then he stood to his full, glorious height and looked down at her, a small smile giving a little curve to his lips. "Would you like some tea?"

"Oh, no. Thank you." She clasped her hands tightly in her lap, feeling entirely uncomfortable while at the same time thrilled that she was inside the Duke of Crestmont's home, sitting in his favorite room. *And*, at the same time, breathless as she always seemed to be when he was so close to her.

"As you wish." He took the chair nearest to her and opened Lilly's notebook. Gazing down at it, he slowly turned the pages, his brow furrowing.

"This is not my expertise," he finally said. "I have some experience in design—of boats—but none of houses...or palaces. This looks quite brilliant, actually."

"I think so, too," Jo said.

"Her detail is amazing. And very imaginative and well planned." He turned another page, then looked from the design notes up to her. "I know someone who might want to see this."

Jo's heart jumped straight into her throat. "Really? I wasn't expecting... I mean—well, Lilly and I don't know any architects."

"I know you weren't expecting anything. I'm certainly not one to say whether she has talent, but these are such original designs, I feel my friend would like to see them. May I keep this for a few days? I'll return it once I show it to him."

"Yes." She grinned, clapping her hands together at her chest. "Lilly will be delighted."

He nodded, then closed the book, set it aside, and leaned toward her, his gaze locking with hers. "Now. We're alone. There are no potential prying eyes or listening ears. Tell me why you were outside my house."

She gestured at the notebook. "Lilly—"

"Jo," he murmured. "It wasn't just that. You could show me those designs anytime. You needn't have come to my house for that."

Oh dear.

She licked her lips, then blurted, "I've been thinking about what happened to you."

"What happened to me?" he repeated with a frown.

"At Vauxhall Gardens."

His frown deepened.

She was beginning to love that look on his face when he was being obtuse. The way he arched his brows while at the same time screwing them together in confusion.

"First, you were behaving somewhat strangely." He'd been neither haughty and stiff, as he generally was when surrounded by people he didn't know well, nor caring and sensual like he had been the past few times he and Jo had been alone together. He had seemed somewhat distraught and rather confused. Quite out of character.

"Then," she continued, "after you returned from your search for Miss Cherrington, you were covered in mud and leaves. Did you fall?"

"Oh." He chuckled. "Right. That. I didn't fall, exactly. I had an encounter with a cutpurse on the Dark Walk."

Her mouth dropped open. She gaped at him, and as the seconds ticked by, she realized the room had gone dead silent except for the occasional crackle of the fire. "Truly?" she finally managed.

"Truly." After another long pause, his expression darkened. "I must insist, if you ever return to that place, you must avoid the Dark Walk. Especially at that hour. And never go there alone. Promise me."

"What happened?" she asked.

"Promise me, Jo."

"Very well, I promise," she said impatiently. "But what happened to *you*?"

"Nothing, really. I was searching for Miss Cherrington when a woman screamed, and the thief came running straight at me."

"Oh, goodness!"

"I tackled him to the ground, retrieved the reticule he'd cut from the poor lady, and then returned it to its rightful owner."

"Matthew," she breathed through the sudden tightness in her chest. "If...if he cut her purse, he had a knife. You could have been stabbed. You could have been *hurt*."

His brows rose as if he hadn't considered this. "Well, perhaps. But I wasn't."

"But you could have been." Jo thought of what would have happened if the cutpurse had stabbed him then run, leaving him lying on the Dark Walk, helpless and bleeding...

She blinked hard to clear the film in her eyes. "You were lucky." Her breath came out shaky. "I—" Squeezing her hands tighter in her lap, she gathered her composure. "If you were hurt..." She swallowed. "I am so thankful you weren't hurt."

He smiled at her—and it was a genuine smile, so honest it made something pang in her chest. "I wasn't hurt, Jo."

She nodded but still took a moment to regain her composure, to wipe away all images of him lying in the dark and bleeding, with her too far away to help him. "And…what about the first part of my question?" she finally asked.

"Which was…?"

She had the impression he remembered exactly what it was.

"When we were alone together after the fireworks, you weren't yourself. Why?"

Blowing out a breath, he looked up at the ceiling, which was inlaid with a large square ropey pattern of plaster, the inside of the square painted the color of cranberries.

"The evening wasn't going as planned," he said.

"How?"

He lowered his head, his gaze piercing her with warmth. "*You* were there."

"Why did that interfere with your plan?"

"You know why." His voice was a low rumble, an erotic stroke up her spine.

She licked her lips, and his focus homed in on her mouth, his eyes darkening. The way he looked at her made her heart pound. Made memories of his fingers inside her pulse through her blood and heat it until a pleasant sensation simmered under her skin.

A slow, wicked smile curved his lips. His eyes bored into her, seeming to look into her soul. "And I know why you're here now."

So did she, even though she'd been denying it to herself.

She wanted him.

She'd hoped for…things. Things she couldn't even imagine, much less articulate. But she did know they included his hands on her bare skin and hers on his. She wanted to explore every part of him and allow him to do the same. She wanted to feel that pleasure again and watch him feel it as well.

He'd drawn her in like the tide. To Mayfair, to his front door, to him. There'd been no stopping it, as much as Jo's practical spinster mind had tried to direct her feet to move in an altogether different direction.

She closed her eyes, unable to look at him for a second longer without lunging at him.

"I tried not to come."

"I know," he murmured.

"But I couldn't stop thinking of you. Of Vauxhall, and how you wanted me to come home with you. And how…how much I wanted to." She pushed out the next words, though it took every bit of her remaining strength. "How much I want you."

"Jo," he whispered. He slipped off his chair and sank to his knees before her, placing his hands over her twisting ones on her lap.

"I thought perhaps…" She swallowed hard, entreating him with her eyes to understand. "I am a spinster, Matthew. One destined to never experience the pleasures of the flesh. But I thought I'd ask you if, just this once, you could let me know what it's like. I promise, I shall be nothing but grateful, no matter what happens after. I just want to experience it. With you. Just once."

Looking straight into her eyes, he nodded, and

she knew he understood.

He squeezed her balled-up fists. Then his hands slid under her, and he scooped her up and carried her out of the wonderful library with its crackling fire.

She draped her arms around his neck, clinging to him, staring into his beautiful eyes, studying the fan of long lashes that shadowed them as he made his way down a long corridor and into a bedchamber. Kicking the door shut behind them, he lowered her gently, until her feet were on the floor and her body was pressed shamelessly against him, her arms still looped around his neck.

She gazed up at him, loving everything about him, how he felt against her, how his lips curved and his lids were low over his narrowed gaze, and how a lock of silky dark hair had fallen over one eye.

Never in her most erotic dreams had she imagined holding a man like him against her, feeling the hardness of his body pressed to hers like this.

"Beautiful Jo." He bent down and kissed her, his lips so warm and soft, they carried her away on a sensual tide. So caught up was she that she noted his hands in her hair like a distant thing, his fingers diving through the strands to pluck out the pins one by one, and the weight of her hair as it finally cascaded over her shoulders.

He pulled slightly away from her, his hands wound in the loose strands. "You have no idea how long I've wanted to do that," he murmured.

"How long?" she asked, smiling.

"Since the day I first saw you, I think. I saw your hair all bound up in the back of your head, just those teasing strands on the sides, and wondered what it would look like down, how it would feel between my fingers."

She sighed as his fingertips grazed her scalp. "Is it what you hoped for?"

"It's better." His lips brushed her cheekbone as he gently turned her head, trailing soft, warm kisses down her hairline to her jaw. "So much better. It's soft. Beautiful. It smells like a warm day in the country."

"What does that smell like?"

"Flowers and heaven."

"Mmm." Nobody but the women she lived with had ever seen her hair unpinned, but her hair had always been one of her best features—thick and wavy, with strands that lightened as the warmer months progressed.

Matthew pulled back, lifting the hair on both sides of her head between his fingers and letting it fall around her face. "So shiny. So many colors. It's like sunshine and autumn leaves."

She gazed up at him, knowing her face was open with all her feelings for this man and, at the moment, not caring at all. She tightened her embrace, but he grasped her forearms and pulled her arms down to her sides before running his fingers up her sleeves to her shoulders, leaving a trail of heat up her skin that made her shudder.

"Turn around, Jo," he said. "I want to see the rest of you."

CHAPTER TWENTY-TWO

Matthew couldn't believe Jo was here, in his bedchamber, pliant as he turned her so her back faced him. He gently moved that thick mass of beautiful hair to the side, revealing the white, cloth-covered buttons of her dress.

She was a dream. So unlike other women he'd bedded, but as soon as the thought of other women entered, it left his head, leaving his mind filled with only Jo, this magnificent woman standing before him, her beauty, her clear gray eyes, her openness and curiosity, her sweet heat and desire, her beguiling mix of innocence and worldly wisdom.

He bent down and kissed her neck, running his lips over the softness of her skin as he unbuttoned her dress. He worked carefully, though in all honesty, he wanted to rip the damn thing open, followed by all the layers beneath.

This might be the only opportunity he'd have to be with Jo. No, it *was* the only opportunity. Hadn't she said that? He was going to draw it out as long as he could, enjoy every single moment, every obstacle he had to struggle through to get to all of her.

So he kissed her as he worked, loving the feel of her dewy skin beneath his lips.

Finally, her dress gaped open, and he turned her around to carefully work the sleeves down her arms. He trailed his hands over her body as he pushed it off her and helped her step out of it.

Now, on to her petticoat. It came off comparatively quickly, only one little tie at the waist. By then, her breaths were coming out in short gasps, and her knees were quivering. He led her to a chair near the fireplace and, after quickly getting the fire going so she'd stay warm, he tugged her onto his knee as he worked the laces of her stays and pulled them from her body, trailing kisses over the back of her pale shoulder and arm.

Finally, he plucked the string at the top of her spine and lifted her shift over her head.

She looked up at him with lips slightly parted, naked except for her stockings, ribbon garters, and half boots.

He could hardly breathe. She was so goddamn beautiful she'd sucked all the air from his lungs. He knew he was the first man who'd ever seen her like this. That she'd bestowed this gift only on him. And he was so honored, so overcome by that and by her loveliness, he could do nothing but stare at her for a long moment.

Shifting uncomfortably, she curled her hands into fists at her sides. She licked her lips again—God, did she know what that did to him?—and then said in a husky voice, "What's wrong?"

Did she really think something was wrong? Everything was so *right*, he could hardly bear it. He shook his head in a jerking motion.

"Nothing, sweetheart. Nothing is wrong. It's just…" He swallowed hard, trying to find his voice. "You are the most perfect thing I have ever seen."

His voice was so raw and honest, she must have known he hadn't lied, or even exaggerated. For the first time since he'd met her, the word *perfect* finally worked. It matched her...perfectly.

He reverently touched her breast, running his fingers over the soft, plump side of it and then over the taut bud of her nipple. She groaned softly but shook her head and pulled back. Her gaze raked over him, up and down, so hot he felt like her eyes had burned the clothes right off his body. "I want to see you first."

Reaching up, she skimmed his cheek with her fingertips, then trailed her touch down the side of his neck and to his cravat.

She took her time untying his cravat, then slipped it off, the fabric sweeping coolly over his neck. She unbuttoned his coat and waistcoat, then pushed both off his shoulders and over his arms. Before she could touch his shirt, he reached behind his head and pulled it off, leaving his chest bare to her heated gaze...and to her touch. Her hands were suddenly all over him, hot and questing, exploring every contour of his chest and his arms, brushing over his nipples and traveling down his belly to where the arrow of dark hair disappeared beneath the waist of his trousers.

He was already close to coming, his cock near bursting against his falls. He shuddered hard, and then his hands were on her body, too, cupping her breasts, then moving lower until he gripped her waist, where he paused as her fingers desperately worked the buttons of his trousers. Finally, they gaped open, and they both stood and pushed them down. Matthew pressed his cock against his lower stomach as the trousers dropped down to his ankles and he awkwardly kicked them off, along with his shoes.

They straightened.

"Move your hand away," she whispered, eyes riveted to his cock.

Swallowing hard, he did as she asked, and it bobbed forward eagerly—and rather uncomfortably. She stared at it, chewing on her lower lip. When she looked back up at him, her eyes wide, she murmured, "It's…huge."

He laughed, though it came out strangled. This woman was going to kill him. "Just what every man wants to hear," he managed.

"Is it truly?"

"It is."

"Honestly, I'm a bit afraid of it."

He pulled her against him, pressing her breasts and his cock between them. "Don't worry," he whispered. "I have one goal, and one goal alone."

"What's that?"

"Your pleasure."

He was trying to keep breathing, to keep going slow, to remember this was all new to her and he needed to be gentle. Above all, he wanted her to love every second of being with him, and to experience pleasure like she had never known. And although every bit of him was screaming to possess her and take her and take his own pleasure from her soft, willing body, he controlled it. It would happen. But only when she was ready for it, too.

"I don't think it will fit."

"It will," he assured her.

"But it might break me in the process."

"It will be uncomfortable at first, but it won't break you." He led her toward his bed.

"Are you certain?"

"I promise." He lifted her and laid her on her back onto his bed, then trailed his hands down her thighs and her stocking-covered calves to remove her boots. Nudging her knees apart, he knelt between them and leaned over her to kiss her, allowing his body to rub over hers, his hardness abrading her softness in the most erotic way possible.

She kissed him eagerly, her hands stroking his back, then pushing at his shoulders as he moved lower, down her neck and to her breasts, whispering sweet endearments and describing how beautiful and soft and delicious she was between kisses.

He kissed and licked the soft, full flesh and her erect little nipples until he lost track of time, his cock raged, and she wiggled and gasped beneath him, panting, "Oh, oh, oh."

He moved his hand between them, and, parting her folds, slipped into her wet heat. Drawing one of her nipples into his mouth, he pushed one finger inside her and grazed her inner walls in a way that made her buck.

He pulled his finger almost all the way out then pushed in again, allowing his palm to graze the sensitive bud above her opening as he flicked his tongue over her nipple.

"Matthew!" Her body arched, and he knew he had her. He intensified his movements, touching and grazing and stroking and thrusting until she cried out, beautifully and loudly. Her entire body clenched, and with an intense shudder, her release roared over her. She came in wave after glorious wave. When she finally went limp, he pulled his hand free of her, nuzzling her breast and then moving up to her lips. Finally, he pulled away and gazed at her. She looked back at him, sultry, her eyes half lidded, her hair fanned out around her face.

"My Jo," he murmured. "So beautiful."

She pulled him down to her for a long, sensuous kiss, licking into his mouth until he was out of his mind, rubbing his cock against her, and she was once again shifting restlessly underneath him.

"I can't," he finally said, jerking away from her. "I can't... I'm going to..."

"I'm ready." She gazed up at him with...was that love in her eyes? He blinked, and it was gone. No, surely it had been lust. Raw, heated lust. She wanted him with a heat he had never seen before. "Now," she whispered.

He heaved in a great, shaking breath and, leaning on one hand, positioned his cock at her entrance. Just the feel of her wet heat against him made him groan. "Oh, God, Jo."

She arched her pelvis up as if to welcome him in, and, trembling violently with restraint, he slowly pushed forward, his eyes rolling nearly all the way back in his head at the sensation of the silky clasp of her body around him.

He felt the moment he breached her virginity. She stiffened, and he went still, shaking with the effort of holding back, a bead of sweat trailing down the side of his face. "Damn it to hell," he gritted out. "Sorry."

Her fists curled on his shoulders, and he felt the scrape of her nails.

"It's...all...right," she panted. "Don't stop."

Her words unlocked his restraint, and with one thrust, he pushed fully inside. She gasped, even as she arched up to meet him.

Just give her a few moments, he told himself, dragging himself out so slowly he was sure it was going to kill him, then pressing inexorably back in. God, she felt so good. So, so damned good.

As he moved, she slowly relaxed under him until her jaw, which had been tightly clenched, released, and her lips parted. She stared up at him as if in awe. Lodged deep inside her, he lowered himself to kiss her lips. "Better now?"

"Yes."

Slowly, he sped his strokes, until her legs rose to wrap around him and she moaned under him—not with pain but with pleasure, and he closed his eyes and let himself be overwhelmed by Joanna Porter. By her clasping body and clutching hands and sweet smell and moans that moved under his skin and became a part of him until he wasn't sure if she was making the low noises or he was.

It didn't take long. He'd known it wouldn't. He'd been ready to come even before he'd pushed inside her. The pressure built at the base of his spine. God, he didn't want to pull out. He continued for as long as he could, savoring the feel of her, thrusting harder, faster, until every muscle in his body strained taut and he yanked out of her, reaching down to work himself as his body undulated in release, spilling his seed over the pale, soft skin of her stomach.

CHAPTER TWENTY-THREE

After he fetched a handkerchief and gently cleaned her off, Matthew lay next to Jo, pulling the bedcovers up over them and cradling her against his still-naked body, her head in the crook of his shoulder, her arm draped across his chest and her leg draped over his thighs.

She hadn't thought ahead about what might happen after he joined with her, but she could imagine nothing more perfect than this.

"Mmm," she murmured, soul-deep contentment suffusing her blood. He was so hard, so solid and warm underneath her, his arm curled protectively around her. Her body felt languid, a not-too-unpleasant ache between her legs a consistent reminder that she was no longer a virginal old maid. No, she was a thoroughly debauched and ruined woman.

She smiled so hard her cheeks hurt.

"What is it?" Matthew looked down at her from where his head was propped on a pillow.

"I'm just thinking about what a wanton I am."

His arm tightened around her. "I wouldn't call you wanton."

"Wouldn't you?" When he shook his head, she asked, "What would you call me?"

He opened his mouth to say something, then seemed to change his mind. His fingertips moved down her back and back up again in a sensual slide.

"Beautiful," he finally said.

He'd said that word in regard to her about a half dozen times today. People had called Jo "pretty" once or twice years ago, but those compliments had vanished when Lilly had started to accompany her to social events. Thereafter, Lilly had been called pretty hundreds of times, while Jo could count the number of times the word had been applied to her on one hand.

No one, though, had ever called her beautiful. Now, he'd said it over and over. She knew the Duke of Crestmont well enough by now to know that he wasn't generous with compliments, nor did he have a tendency to spout pretty words he didn't mean.

No, he meant it. He truly thought she was beautiful. She closed her eyes, her smile slipping from her face, and sank against him. She loved that he had given her the gift of that word. She loved all that he had given her today, and how deliciously wonderful he'd been while doing it.

They lay there in comfortable silence for several minutes—or maybe longer. Jo might have fallen into a light sleep, but she came wide awake when he shifted slightly.

She started to move off him, but his arm tightened. "No. Stay. I didn't mean to wake you."

"I'm just…" She sighed with contentment. "…so *comfortable*."

She felt, rather than saw, his smile. "I am, too."

"I should probably move, though. I need to get home before dinner. Everyone thinks I'm in my office working, but they'll check if I'm late, and if they don't see me there, they'll panic."

"Just a little while longer."

He didn't have to twist her arm to make her stay. She truly didn't want to move. Ever.

"And you," she said. "You'll be extremely late for your appointment, or wherever you were headed, by now."

He shrugged. "It was just to meet Jameson at the boathouse."

"Won't he wonder where you are?"

"Yes, but he'll assume I was waylaid by something important. Which I was."

"Mm," she said, snuggling closer. "Did you just call me important?"

"I believe I did."

There it went—her heart. Melting for him, then handing itself over to him on a platter. Warning bells clanged in the back of her mind. She needed to think about something else, veer to safer territory.

"How is the boat-building going?"

He launched into an explanation of angles beneath the waterline and how they affected the speed of the vessel. His interest in rowing and boats was pure and passionate, and it fascinated her.

"I'd love to take you for a row sometime, though I've never seen a woman row a racing boat before."

"I'd love to be your first."

"As I was yours?" he murmured, and her face went hot. His fingertips stroked down over the swell of her bottom, then his hand flattened and he pushed her more tightly against his thigh. She pulled in a sharp breath at the arousal that shot through her.

He pressed his lips into her hair. "May I be your

second, as well?"

She pulled in another breath, this one shaky. "Yes."

One more time. She couldn't deny him—couldn't deny herself. It would be the last time. It had to be, because her rational mind was telling her that her heart wouldn't be able to endure any more. Her rational mind told her that after today, she'd have to go back to being Joanna Porter, spinster matchmaker, who needed to support her family and make an essential match to ensure her dearest friend's happiness.

But for this moment, for right now, this man could be hers. And she could be his, too.

He paused, though. "Are you sore?"

"Not at all." It was a lie, but only a little one.

"Are you sure? I don't want to hurt you." He hesitated, then added in a soft voice, "Again."

If he thought that he'd bring her any more pain, he'd stop right away. She didn't want him to stop. She'd be all right. "I'm sure."

He grasped her hand and pulled it down until it covered the rigid length between his legs. "Touch me, then."

With his fingers over hers, guiding her, she curved her fingers around him and stroked up and down, marveling at how soft the skin was over such hardness. To think, this part of him had been inside her and would be again, soon.

She shuddered with anticipation as she ran her fingers over his crown and he moaned.

"Are you sensitive there?" she whispered.

"Very," he gritted out.

"Is that why men like it so much? When they are inside?"

"I think that's...definitely...part of it."

"What happens when I do this?" She squeezed as she moved, now pumping him up and down, simulating the movements of him inside her.

"That's...part of it, too," he rumbled. Seemingly unable to stop himself, he thrust his pelvis into her fist with her movement.

He released her hand, leaving her to experiment on her own, and moved to her breast. When his fingers ran over her nipple, the sensation sent a rush of warmth between her legs—oh, Lord...why, oh *why*, did that feel so good?

She stroked him until he grew impossibly harder under her palm, and he stroked her until she was whimpering and trembling and needy.

He had such a strange power over her. The power to wind her up until she was strung so tight, she thought she might burst if he didn't do something to relieve the pressure.

Removing her hand from him, he turned her onto her back and loomed over her, hard and heavy and oh-so male. He gazed down at her with hungry eyes, then lowered himself onto one forearm, tangling his hand into her hair and pressing his body onto hers so his masculine hardness touched her from her feet to her chest without her having to bear the brunt of his weight, his pelvis heavy against her thigh. He lowered his lips and kissed her deeply.

She arched up into him, trying to adjust her body so he lined up with her opening. He kissed her and kissed her, and finally broke it off, his breath washing over her mouth as he lifted slightly away from her. "Guide me in."

Looking into his eyes, she grasped him and moved him to her aching opening. When his tip touched her hot wetness, his eyes closed as if of their own accord, and then he thrust in to the hilt.

Jo cried out as a pleasurable bullet of sensation shot through her core. She squirmed, wanting more, only to realize he'd stopped. She opened her eyes to find him staring down at her, a deep crease dug between his brows.

"Did I hurt you?" he bit out.

"No," she gasped. "No, no, no. Please, Matthew..."

"Please what?" he asked, his expression beginning to change from concern to a need that reflected her own.

"Please...*move*."

He did, pulling out and then thrusting back in, deep. This time, both of them moaned.

"Jo," he murmured. "You feel so good. So damn good."

And then he began to move in earnest, not careful as he'd been throughout their previous encounter, but with long, hard strokes that drove her straight up a peak of pleasure she hadn't known was possible to achieve. And when she'd almost reached the top, it was as if he knew that she was nearly there. He brought his thumb between them to rub at the area right above where they had joined. It took only a moment before she toppled over, bucking beneath him, her nails scratching over his back as she cried out his name and pleasure broke through her in massive, all-consuming waves.

He slowed his movements as the waves receded and her body grew sensitive and languid. He kissed her again, gently this time.

"You are the most beautiful thing I've ever seen," he whispered against her mouth.

There it was—that word again. She thought with satisfaction that she could grow used to this. All of it. His sweet kisses, his loving words, his body lodged so sinfully and decadently inside hers.

He began to move again, starting slowly, and then deeper and harder and faster, until—impossibly—she started to climb to that pinnacle once more.

He brought her over one more time right before he reached his own release, and they shook in each other's arms—him spilling on her thigh this time as her body shuddered against him.

They held each other, a hot, wet, tight unit for several minutes. Matthew's head sank into her hair and her cheek pressed tightly against his chest. Finally, regretfully, she began to pull back. The dull ache between her legs had deepened. Lord, she hoped she would be able to walk normally.

He kissed the top of her head. "Wait. Let me clean you up, sweetheart."

Acquiescing, she lay still while he dampened a towel and wiped her down. "You're bleeding again," he said as he gently wiped between her legs. "Are you all right?"

"Yes, I'm fine." She *was* fine, actually. Terribly sore but the wonderful feeling that suffused her overrode it.

He looked up at her. "Are you telling me the truth?"

She smoothed the line between his brows with her thumb. "Yes."

He finished cleaning her, then pulled on his trousers and guided her up and out of the bed. He helped her dress as if she were a child, tightening her stays and buttoning her up. Then, he combed her hair but declared himself inept when it came to pinning it up.

Jo laughed. "Fortunately, I'm fairly skilled at performing this step myself."

He picked up her pins from the floor as she twisted her hair into the same style she'd worn earlier.

This scene, after an encounter like what Jo and Matthew had just experienced, might, with two different people, feel awkward, but Jo felt comfortable and relaxed, and she could tell Matthew did, too. It was strange exactly *how* comfortable it felt. How natural. How *right*.

She looked into the mirror in Matthew's dressing room. She didn't look too awful, considering what had transpired between them. If she didn't know any better, she wouldn't notice the difference between the Jo of two hours ago and the completely changed—and thoroughly bedded—Jo of right now.

She smiled up at Matthew as he came behind her, his hands slipping around her waist and his chin resting on her shoulder. They stared at their image in the mirror for a moment. They looked like a couple. A very happy one.

But they *weren't* a couple. She sighed, not knowing how to start the conversation she knew they needed to have. Now would be the best time to have it, here, when they were alone and without the risk of anyone overhearing.

She stood, turned around in his embrace, and wrapped her arms around him. "Matthew…"

He stroked one of the strands of hair that framed her face. He really did seem fascinated by her hair. "What is it?"

She drew in a deep and long fortifying beath. "This can't happen again."

He stilled, and when she looked up at him, his eyes were closed. He drew her tighter against him. "Why?"

"You know why."

Another long pause. Then, "I know you're right. I do. But…"

He hesitated again, and all sorts of continuations to that "but" ran through her mind only to be censored immediately.

She held him even tighter, if that was possible. "You said you wanted to be married by the time Parliament recessed for the summer."

"Yes." The word emerged heavy and hard, like it had taken his entire will to push it out.

"I have been a distraction from your goals," she said. And he had definitely been a distraction from hers. "But it is time for you to move on with your life."

He sighed.

"You are on the verge of proposing to…" Lord, she couldn't say Harriet's name out loud right now. "…someone who will make the perfect duchess."

The words "perfect duchess" made him recoil as if she'd punched him. He dropped his arms from her waist, and she dropped her arms from his. Both of them stepped back.

His eyes were open now, his gaze empty. His shoulders straightened. "You are correct, of course. You always are."

Oddly, she felt like apologizing for being correct. But that was not something to apologize for. She'd only spoken truths that they both knew, yet they both needed to be reminded of.

She swallowed through a throat that was suddenly parched. "In fact, it is a mystery why you haven't proposed yet," she said. "You intended to do it last week."

He nodded. "Yes, I did. I will ask her soon. Within the next few days, I'm sure."

She nodded. *Now* things were stilted, with them parroting nods at each other like awkward strangers as he discussed his upcoming proposal to one woman with another woman he'd just taken to his bed.

"I can't do this anymore. My heart can't take it, Matthew." She pressed a palm to her chest as if it could stop that organ from leaking its heartbreak all over his gleaming wood floor. Her voice dropped to a strangled whisper. "It really can't."

She turned to leave, a sudden, blinding urge to escape overwhelming her, but he stopped her by grabbing her forearm.

"Jo…"

She turned back to look at him, to decipher why her name sounded as if it had been wrenched from his chest by a sharp hook.

But the desperation—was it desperation or something else?—faded from his expression as soon as his gaze met hers.

"Don't walk home alone. It's not safe."

She didn't have the energy to argue that she'd walked here alone and had been perfectly safe doing it.

"I'll have my carriage brought round."

She gave a tired sigh. "Very well." While people would see the duke's crest on his carriage, she'd pull the curtain closed. No one would see her, probably not even when she slipped from the carriage and back into her office. "I'll enter it from the mews, though, so no one sees me emerging from your house alone."

He nodded in understanding.

"Thank you."

They returned to the library, and he called for his carriage. While they waited, they talked about the weather, which was growing more summery by the day.

When the footman came to tell them the carriage was ready, they rose, and Matthew walked her downstairs, where he gave his coachman instructions. Then he opened the door for her and bowed formally. "Good afternoon, Miss Porter. I'll see you soon."

She nodded. *Goodbye, Matthew*, she thought as he helped her inside. As the carriage drew away, she watched him through the window, his solitary form growing smaller until they turned and she could no longer see him, and she closed the curtain against curious eyes.

Of course he'd see her soon. Within the next few days, he'd come to her office, bearing the news of his engagement to Miss Harriet Cherrington.

CHAPTER TWENTY-FOUR

Although his body was singing with a kind of satisfaction he hadn't experienced in a long while—perhaps ever—Matthew spent the remainder of the afternoon alone, brooding in his library.

He should have proposed to Miss Cherrington last week at Vauxhall Gardens as he'd intended. Then, this afternoon would never have happened, and he wouldn't have all these deuced *feelings* to contend with.

But if this afternoon had never happened, he never would have experienced Jo raw and open to him. He never would have felt her silky skin or the tight clasp of her body or heard her cries of pleasure.

He would never regret those things. Yet they had burrowed so deep into him that they wouldn't be easy to discount or forget. And now, when he thought of seeing Harriet Cherrington, his stomach twisted with distaste.

Which was definitely *not* how one should feel when considering proposing to their future bride.

The impending task loomed over him, an undesirable chore that he needed to rush through and get over with, not something he anticipated with relish. He should see it as a door opening to a perfect life with his perfect duchess, but it felt more like a door slamming in his face.

And yet, he still wanted it. He could still imagine Harriet Cherrington standing at his side, smiling, welcoming stylishly dressed guests to their spring ball or their summer house party. He could imagine her playing the pianoforte for a large group of the *beau monde*, who loudly applauded with appreciation for her talent. He could imagine them in a more intimate group, her singing for them in her clear, lovely voice.

But the thought of proposing to her? Of spending his days discussing things that were important to him with her? Of spending his nights at her side? God help him. He clutched his roiling stomach.

Late in the afternoon, there was a knock on the library door.

"Yes?"

His butler appeared. "Mr. Jameson is at the door, Your Grace."

Matthew sighed. Jameson was probably here to chastise him for not showing up at the boathouse today. Matthew wasn't in the mood, but he would never turn Jameson away.

"Send him up, Simms," he said tiredly.

A minute later, Jameson strode in. "Why's the fire going in here?" he complained. "It's bloody hot."

"Is it?" Matthew hadn't noticed.

Jameson narrowed his eyes. "Are you ill? Is that why you didn't come today?"

Matthew sighed. "No. I'm not ill." He rose abruptly and went to his desk where he poured himself a healthy tumbler of brandy. He poured a second for Jameson, who still had that suspicious look on his face.

"You aren't one to miss our meetings."

"True," Matthew said shortly.

"What was it, then?"

It was Joanna Porter. Her silky thighs and her sweet kisses and…well, and everything about her. She could take him completely away. She had that power over him, and he'd gladly relinquished it.

Matthew looked over at his friend now occupying Jo's seat. Odd, how Jameson had sat there a hundred times before and Jo had sat there twice and how Matthew now considered it *her* seat.

His friend knew something was amiss. Not surprising. You didn't know a man for twenty-five years without being able to read him without words.

Jameson would listen. He might not understand what was going on—well, he certainly wouldn't, as marriage was the last thing on his mind—but he'd listen, and he'd at least *try* to understand. Because he was Matthew's friend, and while Jameson had led Matthew astray more than once, he always gave his honest opinion.

"Are you going to tell me or not?" Jameson asked.

"I'm considering it."

"Stop considering and spit it out." Jameson sounded annoyed, and for some reason, Matthew found that comforting.

He took a long swallow of his brandy and, realizing there wasn't much left in the glass, he finished it. Then, knowing he was procrastinating, he rose to refill his drink. "Another?" he asked Jameson.

Jameson looked pointedly at his still-full glass. "No."

Matthew took his time, pouring carefully before

returning to his seat. Then, he sat in silence, taking care this time to take smaller sips. He didn't want to be three sheets to the wind before sundown.

Finally, he cracked under the weight of Jameson's stare. "I was supposed to propose to Miss Cherrington at Vauxhall Gardens."

"Mmm," Jameson said. "I noted that you didn't."

"It is unlike me to fail to follow through on my plans."

"I'm aware," Jameson said drily. "So, why didn't you?"

Matthew blew out a harsh breath. "I've been trying to understand that myself."

Jameson raised a skeptical brow. "Have you? Because it seems rather obvious to me."

That stopped Matthew short. He frowned at his friend. "Does it?"

"Yes." Jameson nodded sagely. "It's Miss Porter."

Matthew sucked in a breath. "How the hell did you—"

Jameson leaned forward. "You're having a liaison with her, aren't you?"

Matthew blinked. A liaison? Was that what he should be calling it? He'd had those in the past. What he had with Jo didn't *feel* like a liaison.

"So, what is the problem?" Jameson asked. "It is clear you like her more than you like Miss Cherrington. Marry her instead."

"Marry her— *What*?"

"You wish to marry, against all reason," Jameson said. "You might as well marry someone you like."

"But…I can't *marry* Miss Porter," Matthew sputtered.

"Why not?"

Matthew shook his head and stared at Jameson. You'd think, despite his childhood, after spending all these years associating with the *ton*, Jameson would know the rules they lived by.

"Surely you know why not," he said.

"Because she's not an earl's niece?" Jameson's voice was mild, but his jaw had grown hard.

"Well, yes. That, among other things. She's in trade, for one."

Jameson rolled his eyes. "She's not in *trade*, fool. She's a matchmaker."

"She *works* for money," Matthew said stubbornly.

"Good God. Who cares? So do I." Jameson threw back his brandy then rose to fetch himself more. Matthew sat still, feeling sick to his stomach. He truly didn't believe that working for her money made Jo lesser. He didn't even believe that the fact that she had no titles in her family tree made her lesser. But *marriage*?

It just wasn't done.

Before Jameson had mentioned it, it hadn't—not once—crossed Matthew's mind that he might *marry* Joanna Porter. Men like him didn't marry women like her. They just didn't.

"Fine, you idiot. Just marry Miss Cherrington, then," Jameson snapped as he sat back down. "I hear she works, too—at playing the piano and drawing pretty pictures and singing—but she makes no money from those endeavors, of course, so that makes her acceptable for some illogical reason I shall never understand. *And* she's the niece of an earl. Unlike poor, common Miss Porter, she's worthy of your hand. She'll make a perfect duchess." He glowered at Matthew, who stared right back at him, lips pressed tightly together, his stomach churning like an angry sea.

"So stop dithering and just ask the chit." Jameson waved his hand impatiently and took another angry sip of his drink. "I daresay her brother will be ecstatic to welcome a venerated duke into his family."

Jameson's annoyance was no longer comforting. Instead, it grated against Matthew's nerves. He was right, damn him. If Matthew was going to ask Harriet Cherrington, he should do it. Get it over with. Get the wedding over with. Get the procreating over with. *Then* he could get on with his life.

Propose, wed, then bed. Break it down into three steps. He could accomplish those things. That was his plan, and this time, he needed to follow through, as difficult and painful as it might be.

Jo was also right. He had to let her go. He could still admire her as he'd never admired any woman. He would always be able to hold on to the memory of this afternoon. But they both needed to move on. Until he married Harriet Cherrington and she bore him a son, his uncle would continue to be his heir.

"It's not as easy to propose as you might think," he said dully.

"I imagine it's not," Jameson said.

"It's nerve-wracking," he said.

"Especially when you don't love the woman you're about to propose to."

"How many marriages begin with love, do you think?" Matthew challenged.

"Few, in your exalted position," Jameson said.

"One of the many shortcomings of the aristocracy."

Matthew cast his eyes heavenward. "I'm sure you recall what happened the one time I thought I loved a woman."

"Of course," Jameson said. "Disaster."

"Exactly."

"But that was different. You were just a boy. You'd just lost your parents and were vulnerable to that woman's scheming. She took advantage of you. It doesn't mean love doesn't exist for you—just that it didn't work out the first time. That kind of thing won't happen to you again. You're an old man now. Grizzled and wrinkled and older and wiser, etcetera."

"Grizzled and wrinkled?" Matthew scoffed. "I hardly think so."

Staring at Matthew's hairline, Jameson narrowed his eyes. "I think I see a few grays in there, friend."

"Nonsense." Matthew flicked his fingers at the offending and no-doubt invisible strands. "In any case, what I am doing with Miss Cherrington is safer. How could generations of my forebears have it wrong? One finds an appropriate match in order to maintain one's status and continue one's line, not for any frivolous notions of love."

His parents had been a rare exception to the rule. He, clearly, wouldn't be another exception.

Just then, there was a soft knock on the door.

"Come in."

"Forgive me for the interruption, Your Grace," Simms said. "But Lord George Leighton has just arrived."

Matthew frowned. "My uncle?"

"Yes, sir."

Matthew groaned. George did visit once in a while, unannounced and unwelcome, though Matthew always let him stay out of some—perhaps misplaced—sense of familial duty. After all, his uncle and his wife and sons *were* the only family Matthew had. And George was his heir. If some horrific misdeed or terrible accident killed Matthew, George would need to know what to do. Dozens of people lived on Matthew's lands and relied on him for their livelihoods. Their security and happiness depended on him. These were lessons he tried to drum into his uncle each time he saw him, and though he doubted they made a difference, he had to try.

He glanced at Jameson, who gazed back at him with sympathy. Jameson knew all about George and his antics over the years.

"Show him to his room, Simms, and tell him I'll join him in the drawing room presently."

"Yes, Your Grace." The butler closed the door softly behind him.

"Well," Jameson said, rising, "that would be my cue to leave."

Uncle George had met Jameson once before, a meeting that had entailed George first turning his nose up at Jameson, then overtly ignoring him, having deemed him a lesser being. Since then, Jameson avoided the man at all costs. Matthew only wished he himself had that luxury.

Matthew rose to see Jameson out. As he turned to go, his friend clasped his shoulder. "Put yourself out of your misery, Matthew. Propose."

"I will," Matthew said. "Tomorrow."

And he would. Tomorrow, both he and Miss Cherrington were to attend the annual Houghton House outdoor ball sponsored by the Duke of Trent. The event drew at least a thousand revelers every year. Matthew would find a time to draw Miss Cherrington aside and ask her to marry him. After he proposed to Miss Cherrington, he'd speak with Charles Cherrington, who'd also be in attendance. And it would be done. He'd kill the proverbial two birds with one stone.

He wouldn't fail this time.

CHAPTER TWENTY-FIVE

When Jo returned home after spending the afternoon with Matthew, she claimed a headache to avoid dinner and their usual gathering in the parlor afterward.

She *did* have an ache. More than one, but none of them was in her head. There was the physical ache, the echo of him between her legs, her tender tissues and sore muscles. Then there was the ache in her heart, cracked straight through to its core.

For she'd realized, as his carriage rumbled away from his house, that her heart had been deaf to her commands. She was in love with the Duke of Crestmont. Madly, irrevocably in love with a man who thought of her neither as a potential duchess nor as his equal. It would never cross his mind that she could be either thing to him.

Only, she knew she could. She knew she would make a good partner to him. She knew she could be his friend and his lover. She knew she could stand beside him through the good times and the difficult ones. She *knew* they could be happy together.

But he didn't know any of that. To him, a duchess meant something else. Something Jo wasn't and never could be. And that ideal had been ingrained in him his entire life, reinforced by his experiences with Fanny Fleming, and nailed painfully into him by his Uncle George.

How could Jo undo a lifetime of conditioning?

She couldn't. And if she tried and somehow magically succeeded, he would question whether she'd manipulated him. Whether he would have been happier with a younger woman with the proper breeding who could sing and draw and play the piano and smile graciously at his guests.

Jo couldn't blame him—he was who he was meant to be, who he'd been trained to be since birth, and who society demanded he be. She could only blame herself for falling in love with a man who could never value her the way she deserved to be valued.

And then there was Lilly. If, through some miracle, the duke decided he loved Jo and wanted to marry her, Lilly would lose Charles Cherrington once and for all.

So that night, lying in her bed with a cool cloth laid uselessly over her forehead for her "headache," Jo decided the only thing she could do was ensure the Duke of Crestmont and Harriet Cherrington married. Jealousy of Harriet snaked through her, and when she thought of Harriet and Matthew doing the things Jo and Matthew had done in his bed, tears streamed down her cheeks and the cracks in her heart deepened to painful, sharp crags.

None of that was poor Harriet's fault. Jo couldn't wish ill on Harriet out of her own jealousy or pain.

So, in the end, Jo must endure both the jealousy and the pain. She *did* want Harriet and Matthew happy, not only because she cared for Matthew and liked Harriet, but for her own selfish reasons. Theirs would be another match well made. She would have found the perfect duchess for a duke of the realm. It would be excellent for her career.

And, beyond all that, Lilly's happiness would be secured.

Yes, there were so many reasons, *good* reasons, for the duke to marry Harriet Cherrington. It had to happen.

It *would* happen.

. . .

The next night, at the Duke of Trent's ball at Houghton House, Jo stood by herself watching the dancers glittering under the clusters of lights strung from tree to tree.

Flicking open her fan, she watched over it as Mr. Pellegrini danced with Sarah Fineman, a pretty young widow. From the way they smiled at each other, she had high hopes that Mrs. Fineman might prove a good match for him. She *had* to find him someone special.

Lilly had accompanied Jo, and she'd secured a partner for every single dance, the fawning young men clearly ignorant to the fact that her heart belonged to Charles Cherrington, who had already partnered with Lilly twice.

Jo's own card was not full, though Charles had asked her to dance with him—certainly out of pity— and she had accepted out of politeness.

She'd heard that the Duke of Crestmont was also here, though she hadn't seen him in the crush. Harriet was not in attendance tonight, however. The poor girl had remained at home with a cold. Martha had assured Jo that she was already on the mend and would certainly recover within the next day or two.

Feeling a familiar presence beside her, Jo stiffened, then turned slowly, suddenly struggling to inhale a full breath. Matthew was particularly handsome tonight in his formal breeches and tailcoat, his hair looking as soft as she knew it was, and his full lips pressed into that endearing stern line.

"Good evening, Miss Porter."

"Your Grace."

Lord, it felt strange to be so formal after what they'd shared just yesterday. It might as well have been a lifetime ago.

As one, they turned back to face the dancers. Erotic images flitted through Jo's mind—his talented fingers pressing into her flesh, the muscles on his body rippling with restraint, the way his eyes had squeezed shut as he'd panted out his release.

Matthew bent toward Jo. "Dance with me."

The next dance was a waltz, and she went rigid to combat the instant longing to leap into his arms and waltz the night away with him. "That wouldn't be appropriate, Your Grace."

"Why not?" he asked.

She shook her head. The answers were too many and too complicated to share with him amid all these people. In any case, he definitely knew exactly why he shouldn't be dancing with her. Certainly his asking was merely rhetorical.

They stood for a few moments in silence, surrounded by music and laughter and chatting but not a part of any of it. His breath moved the loose strand of hair curling around her ear. "Please, Jo. Dance with me."

Lord, but she wanted to. She closed her eyes in a long blink and slid her gaze toward him, knowing her eyes were pleading. Every time he spoke to her, every time he touched her, it made this more difficult.

And yet, she couldn't resist. "All right."

Lilly swept by, laughing gaily, her lively gaze flicking toward Jo in the briefest of acknowledgments before returning to her partner.

"My uncle arrived last night," Matthew murmured.

She turned to him, wide-eyed. "At your house?"

"Yes. He arrives unannounced about once a year."

"And you allow him to stay with you?"

He shrugged. "I do."

She licked her lips, knowing how unwelcome his uncle's presence must be. "How… How is he?"

His chest rose and fell with a breath. "The same."

Ugh. That did not bode well.

A smile flickered over his lips. "Let's put it this way. I was happy to come to this ball tonight, knowing I would have the opportunity to be away from him for a while."

"I'm sorry." It must be quite bad if he preferred attending a ball over spending an evening with his uncle.

"That and…well, I rather meant to speak with Miss Cherrington tonight, but—" He shrugged.

She assumed by "speaking" to Harriet he meant proposing, but Harriet was at home. So, no proposal tonight. Jo couldn't stop the rush of relief that swamped her.

Which was stupid. She *wanted* him to marry her, for God's sake!

The dance ended, and in the brief break between sets, Matthew and Jo talked to Mary and Martha Cherrington, then to a flushed and out-of-breath Lilly, who was filling herself with punch but still chattered on about the pretty lights and flowers and how lovely it was to have a ball outside rather than in a hot and overcrowded ballroom.

Then, finally, Matthew coaxed Jo onto the dance floor. When he clasped her gloved hand with his own and slid his other arm around her waist, she trembled. Looking up, she saw him gazing at her with tender affection in his eyes, and love surged through her, stealing her breath. How she loved this handsome, proud, gentle man.

His arm was firm around her waist, his fingers strong in hers. He radiated virility and masculinity in a way that made her center grow molten and gooseflesh break out over her arms.

The waltz began, and he swept her around the dance floor, turning her in huge, sweeping circles that made her laugh. He smiled and took her on another grand turn around the floor, making her feel once again like she was flying in his arms. She'd never danced like this, with a man holding her so closely, so sensuously, as he gazed down at her. The waltz was fairly new to London, and still scandalous, only danced at private balls like this one, and then usually whispered about for weeks afterward. She wondered if her name would be in the gossip sheets tomorrow: "Seen waltzing at the Houghton House ball with the Duke of Crestmont, the obscure and plain spinster, Joanna Porter. One can only speculate by what means she obtained an invitation to the event..."

Right now, Jo didn't care one bit whether she'd be the subject of gossip. All she cared about was Matthew, how he was looking at her like she was the only woman in the world, how he guided her through the waltz with his firm and confident hand.

It ended too soon. The music stopped, and their feet came to a standstill, his arm slipping from her waist as her hand fell from his shoulder. His hand squeezed hers a bit tighter then released it. They stepped back from each other, stared at each other for a long moment, exchanging a look that felt as if it spoke volumes, then he bowed and she curtsied. Then he escorted her to the edge of the dance floor where they encountered Lord Coleton, who greeted Jo and then gestured toward the sky.

"Rain?" he asked Matthew.

The duke's eyes traveled heavenward, and he studied the sky for a moment, though what he saw up there, Jo would never know. The night was utterly black. Even if there had been stars, they were obscured by the haze of coal smoke. "Yes, in an hour or so." He frowned. "I should have known this earlier."

"Don't worry about it." Lord Coleton clapped Matthew on the back and winked. "You were distracted."

Matthew gave his friend a dark look, but then Lilly came up and pulled Jo away.

An hour later, the rain started falling, and while the Duke of Trent invited everyone to continue the festivities inside, Lilly and Jo decided to go home instead.

It was much later, when she was tucked into bed, that she realized she and Matthew had never said goodbye.

CHAPTER TWENTY-SIX

The following afternoon, Jo and Lilly went to see Harriet, bearing a hearty pot of Mrs. Ferguson's get-well-soon stew. Not only was Mrs. Ferguson's stew delicious, but Bess, Lilly, Mama, and Jo ate it whenever they came down with a cold, and all of them swore it made any illness disappear faster.

Jo had been trying to hide her melancholy all morning, her mind on constant repeat with the reasons why the Duke of Crestmont needed to marry Harriet Cherrington, but she wasn't doing a very good job of it. This morning, Bess had drawn her aside and asked her if she was all right.

"Of course I am," she'd said. "Why do you ask?"

"You look pale. Do you think you might be coming down with something?"

"I don't think so. I feel fine, really."

Bess had given her a doubtful look, and Jo had opened her mouth to tell the truth. Where to begin, though? The truth felt so enormous, it seemed to fill all of her, ready to pour out in an avalanche of tears and gibberish. Still, she should try. She trusted Bess, and Bess was the most sensible person she knew. "I have —"

Just then, Lilly had wandered into her room and said they should go visit poor Harriet and take some get-well-soon stew with them.

Bess and Jo had exchanged a glance in which Jo silently told her friend they'd talk later.

Now, she and Lilly walked down Harley Street, trading the heavy pot between them as their arms grew tired.

"When do you think he'll propose?" Lilly asked Jo.

Jo felt like falling into Matthew's role of being obtuse and asking, "Who?" but she knew very well who. "The duke meant to speak with Harriet at the ball last night, but she wasn't there, of course. I'm sure as soon as she's well enough, he'll pay her a call."

"I hope it's soon," Lilly said. "Charles told me that he will announce our engagement the day after theirs becomes official."

Jo's brows rose. "Has he written to your father?"

"What is the point?" Lilly asked. "He will give us his blessing."

"Of course he will, but it would be nice if he didn't hear about your upcoming nuptials after everyone else in town already read the announcement," Jo said drily.

"Hm." Lilly tapped her chin. "You're right. Should I have Charles send a letter today?"

"Wait until it is official between Harriet and Crestmont, please," Jo said. It would be official—she was going to do everything she could to make it official—but it would still be wise for Charles and Jo to practice a bit of patience. Not to mention discretion.

They arrived at the Cherrington townhouse and knocked on the door. The house wasn't nearly as large or as fine as the one belonging to the Duke of Crestmont, but it was tidy and in a fashionable area as befit an earl's nephew.

The butler led them to the drawing room, where Harriet sat with the twins. Harriet was working on needlepoint—another of her great ladylike talents, Jo thought with rancor.

The thought rattled her so much, she faltered in her step. What was happening to her? This jealousy felt like a poison wending through her, leaving bitterness in its wake.

Even as her mind roiled, she pasted on a smile as Lilly offered greetings and asked after Harriet's health.

"I am all better. It was just a little cold, but I didn't want to attend the ball with even a slight possibility that my nose might run all over my dance partner!" Harriet said. "But thank you so much for the lovely stew. I shall have it for my dinner, and I'm certain it'll banish any remaining symptoms forevermore."

Tea was called for, and they sat around the table and began to chat about all the frivolous things ladies chatted about when in a group, the Houghton House ball being the first order of business.

"I'm so sorry I missed it," Harriet said with a sigh. "But," she added, "it wasn't so bad being ill, and it has made our drawing room smell wonderful." She gestured to the two large bouquets of flowers—one on the side table and one as a centerpiece on the round table. The smaller bouquet was a pretty splash of color—lilies, daisies, and wildflowers. The larger one was an almost garish mass of red roses— perhaps fifty of them.

"That one"—Martha pointed to the smaller

one—"came from the Duke of Crestmont, and that one"—she gestured at the enormous one—"is from Mr. Gifford."

Lilly gazed at it, wide-eyed. "My goodness. That is quite a dramatic bouquet. Who is Mr. Gifford? I have not met him."

Everyone looked at Harriet, who glanced down modestly. As if on cue, her cheeks turned a dainty pink.

Harriet even flushed perfectly. When Jo blushed, her skin from chest to cheeks colored with mottled splotches of varying shades of red.

"I was introduced to him at Lady Campbell's ball—the same ball where I met the duke. He has been out of London in the foreign service for several years and has only recently returned."

Jo and Lilly exchanged a glance. Jo remembered Harriet dancing with the man, but she wanted to know more—everything—about Mr. Gifford, because the massive bouquet practically screamed his interest in Harriet. Jo didn't know how to politely ask, however. Harriet's expression was a perfectly smooth mask. She couldn't read it at all. Should that worry her? Harriet's demeanor was always serene, it seemed, no matter the situation.

"It was very kind of him to send you such a lovely bouquet," Jo finally said.

Harriet smiled. "It was quite kind. And it included a lovely note with his wishes that I enjoy a quick recovery. As did the duke's." She turned her smile to the smaller bouquet.

Jo wanted to growl. She should have told Matthew to send her the largest bouquet possible.

Maybe a wagon full of flowers. Something that didn't look so simple and diminutive in the shadow of all those obnoxious roses.

Yet, she hadn't known that Harriet had another suitor, let alone one who preferred to make grand gestures. Come to think of it, Jo hadn't reminded Matthew to send a note or flowers at all, and he'd thoughtfully done it anyway. And, if one removed the ostentatious roses out of the scene, then his bouquet would have been lovely on its own.

Lilly, who had taken the seat on the sofa beside Harriet, turned to Harriet with a sly smile. "So, tell me. Do you think the duke is prepared to propose?"

Jo tried her best to make herself appear unconcerned, though she felt poised on the edge of a cliff waiting to hear what Harriet might say.

"She does have some news." Martha hid her grin behind a cup of tea. "Tell them, Harriet."

Harriet clasped her hands tightly in her lap. "Well, in the note that came with the flowers the duke sent, he said that if I was feeling well enough, he would come to visit Friday and that he had something important he wished to discuss with me."

Jo sucked in a breath. Lilly clapped her hands together in delight. "Friday is tomorrow! Oh, just think, Harriet, tomorrow we...*you* will be affianced!"

"I confess I am rather nervous about it," Harriet said.

"I'm sure all ladies are nervous about being proposed to," Frances said. "I know I would be."

"Not me," Lilly declared. "I would feel nothing but excitement and anticipation if I were you, dear

Harriet. Just think…you shall soon be a duchess. Can you imagine it?"

Jo couldn't speak. She couldn't be a part of this conversation. If she opened her mouth—if she so much as *moved*—right now, she'd lose her composure. She'd cry. She'd scream. She'd sink to the floor in a puddle of despair.

So she just sat, forcing her lips into a smile she hoped didn't look grotesque, clutching her teacup so hard she was amazed it didn't crack and spill tea all over her only serviceable walking dress.

• • •

After meeting his friend, the architect John Nash, at his club that afternoon and handing over Lilly Appleby's notebook full of designs, Matthew returned home. As he dressed for dinner, he thought of the previous evening's ball and how he had been relieved when he learned that Harriet Cherrington wasn't in attendance. Then he'd been frustrated by his relief. He'd wanted to finally propose, but his goal had yet again been thwarted. Yet, instead of disappointment, a sense of lightness had overtaken him when he'd discovered that she wasn't there.

The reason behind his relief had become crystal clear when he saw Joanna Porter in a simple but lovely silver and white evening gown, the lustrous blond streaks in her hair shining under the light of the chandelier as she stood by herself at the edge of the dance floor, her fan blocking the lower half of her face. His heart beating hard in his chest, he'd walked over to her. He'd asked her to dance.

He'd forgotten about Harriet Cherrington for the rest of the night.

Downstairs, Matthew entered the dining room to find his uncle already seated. He was, of course, situated at Matthew's position at the head of the table. His uncle often did these things to elicit some kind of reaction from him that he'd add to his arsenal to use against Matthew later on. Today, Matthew wouldn't give him the pleasure.

"Good evening, Uncle," he said mildly.

George looked at him over his spectacles—a new addition since his previous visit. His hair was a good deal thinner and a good deal grayer than it had been last summer, as well. "Matty, dear boy. I've hardly seen you all day."

Matthew fought his flinch. Only his mother had ever called him Matty. "I've been working," he said.

"Do you have plans for this evening?" George continued.

"Yes."

Cole had invited him to a gaming hell, and Matthew had told his friend no—evenings at gaming hells ranked just below balls, soirees, and musicales on Matthew's list of top ten unappealing things to do in London, but every item on that list was still better than spending an evening with his uncle George.

Come to think of it, he mused as he took up a spoonful of spring soup, he might have to drop balls from the list. Balls where Joanna Porter was in attendance, that was. Before it had begun to rain, he'd had a somewhat pleasant time last night at the Houghton House ball. Especially during the waltz when his arm had been wrapped around the loveliest woman under the stars and he had held her hand tightly within his own, spinning her around the outdoor ballroom as her gray eyes sparkled and her joyful smile and tinkling laughter warmed him through.

George chewed thoughtfully on a forkful of sweetbreads. "What are you smiling about?"

"Nothing," Matthew said automatically. No way in hell would he ever tell George about Jo.

"I see," George said. "So you've acquired a mistress."

Matthew looked up at him in confusion. "What?"

"You're seeing your mistress tonight." George said it as if it were a fact. "I'd recognize that smile anywhere. It's all well and good, lad, as I'm sure your appetites are robust, as mine are, and like all healthy men such as ourselves, you require an outlet for them."

"I assure you—"

George cut him off. "But take some advice from me, Matty." He pointed his fork at Matthew. "Never allow the woman to have any control over you whatsoever. Keep her on a tight and short leash and jerk it hard whenever necessary. It is best she is given little doubt that you will withdraw your support the moment she displeases you—"

For God's sake. Enough of this nonsense. "My evening plans do not involve a woman."

"Oh?"

"I do not have a mistress, Uncle."

"Well." George huffed. "Why on earth not?"

Even if Matthew did have a mistress, he'd walk into the fires of hell before discussing her with

Uncle George.

"I don't *want* a mistress," he said, annoyance creeping in despite his attempt to mask it.

At this, George's eyes narrowed. "Why?"

"Well, for one, I intend to marry within the month." As soon as the words emerged, Matthew wished he could haul them back. He looked down at his bowl, all appetite vanished.

Of course, George bore down on this like a dog with a rabbit in its maw, and Matthew knew he wouldn't let it go until he'd wrung every bit of life out of it.

"Marry! Really? I am so happy for you!" His uncle's voice was warm, but Matthew knew it was an act. George never wanted him to marry or sire an heir and had been quite content as year after year went by with Matthew giving no hint he was interested in marriage. George wanted to become the next Duke of Crestmont, and, failing that, he wanted one of his sons to inherit the title.

"Who will be the lucky bride?" his uncle continued jovially. His eyes, though, never changed. They were dark like Matthew's own, but small and cold. As much as George tried to convey warmth, that emotion never reached his eyes.

"I haven't proposed yet."

"But if it's to be within the month, surely you intend to propose shortly."

"I do."

"Who is she?"

"You don't know her, Uncle." *Thank God.*

A skeptical gray brow rose. "A worthy candidate, I hope."

"She is."

"And she is young, pretty, and accomplished, I assume," George said with a salacious wink. "With good childbearing hips."

"All of the above, of course." Matthew's words were as cold as the lump in his chest.

"Good." George gave him a hard look. "I do hope you will be levelheaded about it. Unlike last time." He took another mouthful of food, then he shook his head sadly, no doubt remembering what had happened. How stupid Matthew had been.

The expression on his uncle's face drove Matthew into memories of clutching hard onto Fanny, believing she was the one and only thing that could draw him out of his grief and loneliness. During the long journey up to Gretna Green, emotion had overwhelmed him. He'd told Fanny he'd make her the happiest girl alive, that he'd bestow riches on her, dresses, jewels, whatever she wanted. He told her he loved her, again and again. He'd knelt at her feet on the carriage floor and proclaimed himself her servant. He'd lavished coin, kisses, and compliments on her.

When Uncle George had interrupted the wedding, he'd dragged Matthew into his own carriage to show him the letter. Fanny had never sent it, likely deeming its contents too damning to share with anyone, even her closest friend.

By the time Matthew finished reading it, he'd been frozen in confusion. He was enclosed in a carriage, with an uncle beside him who was slashing down his dreams of having a loving marriage like his parents', with the girl who'd manipulated him outside pounding on the locked carriage door and calling his name again and again with increasing shrillness in her tone.

Knowing Fanny was safe, as her father's carriage had arrived minutes after George's, Matthew had told his uncle to get him the hell out of there. George had rapped on the ceiling, and Matthew sat, still as a statue as the carriage rumbled farther and farther away from Gretna Green.

Alone in the barren room of an inn that evening, he'd let himself break down. He'd wept—for his parents, for his lost love that had never existed in the first place, and for himself. He'd never felt so utterly alone.

Then, his uncle had barged into the room and seen him there on the floor, knees drawn up to his chest, and had finally lost his temper. "You stupid simpleton!" he'd railed. "You weak little fool. You are a dishonor to your title. You will never be as good, nor as smart, nor as beloved as your father was. Do you know why? Because you aren't half the man he was. You have always been a simpering, pathetic weakling, undeserving of the title of duke. You will *never* live up to his name."

Matthew's tears had dried that night, and he had never cried again. Instead, he had returned to Nottinghamshire with his uncle, then gone on to London, where he'd stayed with Winthrop for the better part of a year. Winthrop, Cole, and Jameson had finally helped him climb out of the pit of misery he'd fallen so deeply into.

After that, he'd poured himself into becoming the best Duke of Crestmont he could be.

He had succeeded. His estates were thriving, and the people on them were happy and healthy, their bellies and hearts full.

He had proven his uncle wrong. So why then did he still believe what the man had said to him all those years ago?

Matthew pushed his plate of food away. "I am expected elsewhere. Have a pleasant evening, Uncle."

He rose and strode out of the room, but he didn't leave the house. Not yet. Upstairs in the library, he lit the lamp, then opened his desk drawer and unlocked the panel in the back before drawing out an old, crumpled piece of stationery.

It was Fanny's letter.

CHAPTER TWENTY-SEVEN

A sane man would have burned the thing, but Matthew had kept the letter all these years as a reminder. As a warning.

He pressed it flat over the shiny mahogany desktop.

My dear Ann,
You would not believe what has happened!

By chance, my father earned the favor of the Duke of Crestmont, whose son is just a year younger than I. A few months ago, the old duke and duchess were killed in an unfortunate (though not unfortunate for me, I must say!) carriage accident, and his heir, at only seventeen years of age, has inherited the title.

The new duke was bereft, and what better to cure a young man of his grief than the modest and heartfelt attentions of a lady? My parents and I rushed to lend our support right away, and thence we became the new Duke of Crestmont's house guests for the summer.

My dear Ann, this duke is passably handsome, but the best part is that he is rather like a gullible mouse, trusting and malleable. I, on the other hand, am like the cat. I carefully stalked my prey, prowling quietly, feigning innocence, pretending surprise when I artfully crafted encounters with him.

I fluttered my eyelashes at him and told him I'd never been kissed. I coddled him and petted him when he moaned and pouted about the old duke and duchess dropping dead.

It still hurt, how someone—anyone—could be so cruel and callous about his parents' deaths and his grief. Matthew turned the page over and continued reading.

And, a fortnight ago, I pounced.

Finally, he kissed me. You might recall that R.B. gave me lessons in kissing two years ago, so I performed exactly as required so the duke would instantly be besotted. And he was!

I then displayed utter horror that he'd compromised my purity with such a lascivious thrusting of tongues, and he was so apologetic, I had to cover my laughter. The simple boy immediately decided we were in love. Within a week, he suggested we take his carriage to Scotland so we might marry right away. Of course, I agreed! Tomorrow, we will be on our way, me and my dimwitted duke.

I have officially ensnared a duke of my very own. The next time we meet, dear Ann, I shall be a duchess.

Fanny (soon-to-be) Leighton, (soon-to-be) the Duchess of Crestmont

Matthew smoothed his hand over the crinkled stationery. He'd read the letter often over the years, lecturing himself never to get caught up in a woman again, never to fall in love. This letter reminded him that falling in love was folly, something only ignorant, childish boys did. Falling in love meant that one wasn't thinking straight, had lost all sense of rationality and logic. Falling in love meant that you were the weakling, the prey. The mouse.

In the years since, he'd allowed this letter—and his uncle's lashing words—to define the rules by which he'd lived.

His rules were rubbish.

He'd observed plenty of happy, fulfilling marriages. He'd known loving couples who weren't weak, nor were they irrational or stupid or immature. The couples Jo had matched. *His parents.*

His beloved parents, who'd loved each other beyond measure. His father, who'd been so devoted to his mother that his peers looked at him askance, and his mother, who was proud and strong and proclaimed the Duke of Crestmont the best husband in the world. They'd stood stoutly beside each other through thick and thin, giving each other secret smiles as others rolled their eyes and tittered at them behind their backs.

They'd modeled a loving marriage to Matthew, but because he'd failed dramatically on his first impulsive, reckless attempt to have what they'd had, he'd given up on having it at all.

And now, he'd fallen in love once again.

He hadn't connected the word to his feelings for the woman until this moment. Until he stared down at Fanny Fleming's letter declaring him silly and malleable. He might have been those things then, but he wasn't now. He wasn't irrational or ignorant, either. Nor was he weak. In fact, he felt stronger than he had in a very long while—maybe ever.

He adored Joanna Porter.

She was perfect for him. She was beautiful and

kind and intelligent and strong. He *loved* her.

Damn it, he wanted to take her rowing.

Uncle George's arrival had made him remember the reasons he didn't believe in love, but it also made him, for the first time ever after that fateful trip to Gretna Green, reject them.

He thought of Jameson asking, "Why not?" when Matthew had sputtered that he couldn't marry Jo, and how he had thrown out two paltry excuses at his friend. She wasn't an earl's niece. She worked for a living.

How stupid. Was he really, truly ready to sacrifice his one true chance at love because Jo wasn't related to someone with a title? Or because she was a matchmaker? Hell, if she weren't a matchmaker, he never would have met her. If she weren't a matchmaker, he never would have *known* her. Part of what he adored about her was the fact that she *was* a matchmaker.

The truth was, Jo had been tucked in a special compartment in Matthew's heart, while his future marriage had been in a completely sterile, separate compartment that resided in his mind.

What if it was possible to merge those compartments?

Why the hell would he not? Because he was afraid to break the arbitrary rules he'd drawn up after he'd nearly married and lived a miserable life with a heartless, cruel creature who'd only wanted him for his title and fortune? Or because Jo didn't fit into the mold of what society expected of a duchess?

He wasn't here to satisfy the pride of the heartbroken youth he'd once been, and he certainly wasn't here for society's approval.

What about what *he* wanted? What he needed?

He wanted Jo. Hell, he *needed* her. With her, he'd be content. Happy. If he was lucky, he might be able to make her happy and content as well. She loved him, too—she'd never said so, but he knew it. He could see it when she looked at him with those soft gray eyes of hers. He could feel it in her touch and hear it in her words.

He'd been hurting her with his ignorance. With the fact that he'd failed to see what she could be to him. What she *was* to him.

She was THE ONE. With every single letter capitalized.

He never wanted to hurt her again. He would do whatever necessary to wipe that wistful melancholy from her expression. He would devote himself to seeing her eyes shining with happiness and a smile on her face.

Rising, he crumpled Fanny's letter in his fist, walked over to the fireplace, and tossed it into the flames.

As he watched it spark then burst into a little ball of fire, determination suffused him. Anticipation sizzled through his veins.

He *was* going to propose tomorrow. Not to Harriet Cherrington, but to Joanna Porter.

CHAPTER TWENTY-EIGHT

Lord Coleton and Matthew sat on side-by-side leather chairs at the gaming hell, watching the "festivities" from the sidelines. There had been a constant stream of men approaching to converse with them, so Matthew hadn't had a chance to speak with his friend one on one.

Annoyed by the current conversation—which entailed two men, corseted so tightly their cheeks were red and they appeared to struggle to breathe, trading gossip about yet another actress being passed around among the male members of the *ton*—Matthew glanced around. The place was full of cigar smoke, of men sipping dark drinks, and of laughter and groans. Charles Cherrington was here, well into his cups, playing a game of whist at a nearby table and laughing uproariously.

Cole had invited Jameson and Winthrop tonight, as well, but Jameson hated the hells even more than Matthew did, and Winthrop was leaving tomorrow morning to spend the remainder of the summer at Pleasant Hill, his estate in Hertfordshire.

Before heading to the gaming hell, Matthew had stopped by Winthrop's townhouse to say goodbye.

"If spending time with your uncle becomes too intolerable," Winthrop had said, "come out and see me."

Matthew shook his head. "I am doing my best to avoid the man. In any case, I have business in

London. I cannot leave right now."

Then he told Winthrop that he'd finally unraveled his confusion about his forthcoming proposal.

"I have to admit some relief," Winthrop told him. "I wasn't certain about Miss Cherrington."

"Why not?"

Winthrop shrugged. "She seems cheerful enough, but rather aloof at the same time."

"Does she?" Matthew frowned, realizing he hadn't even attempted to *know* her. Then again, she hadn't attempted to know him, either. "Perhaps you're right. And though she outwardly appeared to be perfect duchess material, she wasn't perfect for me."

"No," Winthrop had agreed, "she wasn't. I'm happy for you, Crest. I like Miss Porter. She'll keep you on your toes."

Winthrop was certainly correct about that.

Now, there seemed to be a lull in the line of gentlemen coming to talk to Cole and him about frivolous things. Matthew took a breath that wasn't full of pomade and perfume for the first time in over an hour and said, "You know I only came tonight because my uncle is in town."

Cole laughed. "I know. I don't care, though. Just glad you're here."

"Are you thinking of going out to Pleasant Hill?" As the stink of London grew in proportion to the rise in temperature, people were beginning to leave town in droves.

Cole shrugged. "Maybe later in the summer. For now, I am content to stay here." His smile was suggestive, and Matthew wondered if Cole was pursuing a paramour.

"I see."

Cole took a sip of his brandy. "So, have you proposed yet?"

"You mean to Miss Porter?"

"Noooo." A divot appeared between Cole's brows. "I meant to Miss Cherrington. Did you propose to Miss Porter? What happened to Miss Cherrington?"

Matthew glanced around to see if anyone was nearby. It seemed like they would have an additional moment or two of respite. "I haven't yet proposed to anyone. And nothing 'happened' to Miss Cherrington. I simply decided I was in love with someone else."

Cole blinked, then his lips spread into a wide grin. *Jackass*. "The Duke of Crestmont? In love? God save us all."

Just then, a hard slap came down on Matthew's back. "God might need to save us all, but it's the esteemed Duke of Crestmont who's going to save the Cherringtons. *Especially* me."

Matthew leaned away from the sting of the slap and looked over his shoulder to see Charles Cherrington, his face flushed apple red. He raised his glass. "Thank the Almighty for my future brother-in-law!"

It took a moment for Matthew to decode what had just been said. Clearly, Cherrington hadn't heard the bits earlier on in the conversation that had to do with Jo, and it was no surprise that he was under the impression that Matthew intended to propose to Harriet. It was the next logical step in the game of courtship, after all, and Matthew couldn't fault him for making that assumption. But what did he mean when he said Matthew was going to *save* him?

He frowned at Cherrington, who had staggered into the seat directly across from him and Cole and sunk his body into it, his limbs flopping about as if he were made of straw.

"What do you mean I'm going to save you?" Matthew inquired.

Cherrington rubbed his fingers together, and his eyes glowed with a greedy shine. "With all your prestige. And all your blunt." His lips had made a burbling noise as he'd said "blunt," and, apparently fascinated by it, he said it again. "Blunt. B-b-blunt. Soooo much blunt."

Matthew and Cole exchanged a wary look. Seeing their expressions, Cherrington tried to explain. "Blunt," he repeated yet again. "Money? You understand, but not *just* money." He shook his head vigorously. "No…not money. *Riches*. *Wealth*. Thanks to you, our coffers will finally be filled."

Matthew's brows crept toward his hairline. He had heard of drink loosening men's tongues, but Charles Cherrington must be deeply inebriated indeed. No gentleman would knowingly publicly say such things.

"And that will save you from what, exactly?"

"Heartbreak. Misery. A life lacking in meaning and substance." Matthew must have looked bewildered because Cherrington glanced around, then leaned toward them conspiratorially, his cheeks glowing pink. "You see, once you marry Harriet, then I shall be free."

"Free of what?" Cole asked, seemingly equally as confused as Matthew.

"Not free *of*, dear man, free *to*. Free to be with the woman I adore. My dear, sweet, beloved flower." Seeing their frowns, he enunciated the next word carefully. *"Lilly."*

Cole's eyes widened as Matthew's narrowed. Cole pressed his hand to his chest. "Why... Could you mean the lovely Miss Lillian Appleby?"

"She is the loveliest of all the lovelies, is she not?"

"Indeed," Cole said solemnly.

Cherrington's eyes glazed over with excitement. "We will announce our engagement directly after Harriet and Crestmont's betrothal is formalized."

"Well," Cole said carefully. "That's...wonderful."

"Isn't it, though?" Cherrington bounced in his seat. "Her bosom friend, Miss Porter—ooh, she's a wily one—planned it all out."

Matthew's blood went cold.

Cole cocked his head. "Miss Porter? What do you mean?"

"I *couldn't* marry Lilly, you see. She comes with no title, no dowry, and no fortune at all." Cherrington blinked, looking around the hell again as if for the first time, his lip curling. "My father lost the dregs of my family's fortune—right here, in fact—before I came of age. Then he died, leaving me as head of the family and unable to pay off his debts.

"I cannot marry Lilly. It is impossible, unless—" He leaned forward again. "Unless one of my sisters marries someone of great wealth and prestige. Someone such as yourself, Your Grace—thus securing the Cherringtons' victorious re-entry into society!"

Cherrington raised his glass into the air and waved it before bringing it to his lips and guzzling the remainder of the amber liquid. When he came up for air, his eyes were shining with glee. "Miss Porter designed the scheme. You would meet one of my sisters and become enamored of her. You would propose to her, marry her, and when she becomes a duchess, my family will be saved. As sisters-in-law to a duke, my other sisters will be in demand, and I will be free to marry my dear Lilly."

He raised his glass to his lips, realized it was empty, then lowered it once more. "You plan to do it tomorrow, do you not? My sister said you were going to call. I cannot *wait*. What time do you intend to arrive? I will be certain to be at home."

Matthew glanced down and saw Cole's hand on his wrist, applying light pressure. Slowly, as if his head moved through syrup, he looked at his friend.

Cole knew exactly what this meant, and he knew what it meant to Matthew, in particular.

A woman had schemed to marry him for his money and for his title. *Again.*

And this time, it wasn't just one woman who'd been involved. A group had knowingly conspired to manipulate him. Joanna Porter was the architect. Harriet Cherrington was her willing tool. Lilly Appleby and Charles Cherrington provided their support.

Jo was just like Fanny. He'd thought himself in love with them, but they had tricked him. Used him for their own purposes. Fanny for his title and money for herself. Jo for his title and money so Charles Cherrington could marry the woman who was like a sister to her.

She'd made him think he loved her.

He meant nothing to her.

His title and his fortune meant everything. Just like they had for Fanny.

He was pathetic. His uncle had been right.

"Crest," Cole said quietly. "Let's go home."

Cole turned to Cherrington and said something, but Matthew couldn't hear it through the roar in his ears.

Somehow, Matthew rose and stumbled after Cole like the gullible weakling he was.

CHAPTER TWENTY-NINE

Thick emotion had crowded Jo's throat throughout the next morning. Now, it was early afternoon, and she could hardly breathe past it.

Today was the day. Right at this moment, Matthew could be on bended knee, proposing to Harriet.

She dropped her head. *Be strong, Jo. Be strong. Please.*

She'd been telling herself all morning to remain in her office. To get some work done. She needed to write to a few of her old clients to see if they might have any referrals for her. Mr. Pellegrini was due to stop by in an hour to discuss a strategy for proposing to Mrs. Fineman. She should be thinking about that.

But she could focus on nothing but Matthew. Of him asking Harriet Cherrington to be his wife.

She had to stop thinking about him. She needed to think of Lilly.

Yes, Lilly. The happiness that would shine in her eyes on her wedding day. Her bright smile. The way her new husband would shower her with his love, and the way she'd soak it in. Lilly deserved that kind of happiness.

It was all worth it. For Lilly.

Even if she did leap up and run over to Charles Cherrington's house, even if she did run between Harriet and Matthew and try to stop the betrothal… Well, what then? He didn't want Jo. He wanted a perfect duchess.

She'd repeated it to herself a hundred times: *You're not perfect, Jo. You're not what he wants.*

But *he* was what *she* wanted.

It hurt so bad that he'd willingly marry someone else after what they'd shared. But she knew that was what men often did. They murmured sweet nothings into women's ears and then, once they had obtained what they wanted from them, they left without looking back.

She had always known her liaison with Matthew would be temporary. But that tiny kernel of hope within her was too potent to ignore. And the way Matthew had looked at her, the way he'd touched her—it seemed real. It *felt* real. It felt like how she imagined love might feel, if she was ever lucky enough to experience it.

She dashed away the errant tear rolling down her cheek.

She needed to stop this. She was sensible Jo, spinster matchmaker. She'd given too much power to her emotions when it came to the handsome Duke of Crestmont.

The door to the kitchen opened, and Lilly rushed in. "Jo!"

Jo blinked up at her through the haze. Lilly was waving a sheet of parchment at her.

"Oh, Jo, this is going to be the best day of my life, I can feel it."

Oh God. He'd done it. He'd proposed to Harriet. It was all over. Jo couldn't breathe.

"Look!" Lilly set the piece of paper down on Jo's desk and pushed it toward her. "Read it!"

Jo looked down at the neat scrawl.

Dear Miss Appleby,
I have seen your designs, and I am quite impressed, especially with your magnificent vision for a palace. Would you like to discuss this design, and your others, further? If so, I will call upon you on Wednesday at three o'clock.
Regards,
John Nash

Jo blinked at the letter, then read it again. Goodness. Matthew had done what he'd promised and shown Lilly's notebook to a friend. But who was—

"John Nash!" Lilly exclaimed, snatching the letter up and pressing it to her heart. "*The* John Nash! Can you believe it?"

"Who is John Nash?" Jo asked.

Lilly gasped in horror. "He's the most renowned architect in the country. He's the personal architect for the *regent*. The future King of England!"

Jo's eyes widened. "Really?"

"Oh, Jo. It was you, wasn't it?" She grabbed Jo's hand. "How on earth did you do it? You must tell me. Of all the people in the world, I never dreamed John Nash would ever look at my work."

"I...I showed your notebook to the Duke of Crestmont, but I had no idea—"

"You are too good to me. I don't know how I deserve to have a friend like you." With a squeal, Lilly threw her arms around her. Jo hugged her back, blinking, her heart swelling for her friend.

"It's not me, Lil. It's you. You're the talented one."

"But you do so much for me. Thank you. I love you so much, dear Jo."

Lilly stayed for a few minutes longer, gushing her thanks, then bounced out to write a response to Mr. Nash to tell him that Wednesday would be perfect.

When she left, silence rushed into Jo's tiny office. Jo was ecstatic for Lilly and loved Matthew even more for showing Mr. Nash Lilly's designs. But on the heels of that swell of love for Matthew, thoughts of him proposing to Harriet barreled back in.

She should go for a walk. She needed air.

Jo rose, her chair scraping back on the floor. At the door, she tugged down her pelisse from the peg and pulled on her gloves.

Just a few minutes' walk to clear her mind. In a few minutes, she'd return and conjure up some thoughts to share with Mr. Pellegrini.

Taking a deep breath, she opened her office door.

Matthew stood on the threshold, gloves in hand, staring at the space where the door had been a second earlier.

She took a stumbling step back. "Matthew!" she exclaimed, her heart pulsing the way it always did in his presence. But he was probably engaged now. That pulsing needed to stop. She tried to thrust it away, to no avail.

"Did you do it?" she said breathlessly. "Did you p—" Good Lord, it was so difficult to say the word out loud. "Propose?" she pushed out.

"No." The word fell like a rock, solid and hard. It was only then she really looked at him. At the rigid set of his jaw, at the iciness of his expression.

"What is it?" Inexplicable dread crawled up her throat. "What happened?"

He just stared at her, his dark eyes cold, his expression sending a shiver down her spine.

Something was very, very wrong.

She swallowed hard, then stepped aside. "Come in."

He moved woodenly into her office, and, trembling, she closed the door behind them. Suddenly feeling weak, she propped her body against the door.

"Matthew— Um…sorry." She pressed a hand to her forehead and corrected, "Your Grace…what is it?"

He turned around slowly and studied her, his eyes seeming to strip her bare in a way that made ice harden her bones. "I should offer you congratulations. You almost got away with it."

"Away?" She frowned. "With what?"

"Your plan to use my title and fortune for your own benefit."

She gasped. "What? I never…" Her voice dwindled. Then, she shook her head and asked in a quiet voice, "What are you talking about?"

He spun away from her and stepped over to her desk, smacking it hard with the hand holding his gloves. He hadn't removed his hat.

"I mean your scheme for me to marry Miss Cherrington so her family, and yours, would benefit from my fortune and my title."

Her jaw dropped. She'd never thought of it that way. She'd felt somewhat guilty at first for steering him toward Harriet, but Harriet had been perfect for him.

Or had that just been her rationalizing what she'd done?

"It wasn't like that!"

He sneered. "Oh, really?"

"Really! It wasn't."

"What was it like, then?"

"I…" She swallowed hard, unsure how to explain it in a way he'd understand. "I knew the Cherrington sisters needed to marry well."

"Exactly. So Lillian Appleby could marry their brother."

"It is true that is how I originally learned of their dilemma. But many young ladies, and gentlemen as well, are obligated to marry for financial reasons. There is nothing new to that in our world, Your Grace." Her words emerged more firmly as they crystallized in her mind. "And you knew enough of the Cherringtons' situation to understand that your marrying Harriet would put them in a far superior financial position."

He twisted his gloves in both of his hands and took a step toward her. "You manipulated me. You gave me a list of women who wouldn't suit, and you knew it. You knew the only one who'd come close was Miss Cherrington. You knew I'd choose her because I didn't have the patience to waste my time meeting a second group. You engineered the match from the beginning."

She looked down at her hands. She couldn't deny what he said was true. She had done all those things. He was right—it had been for the Cherringtons' benefit, but her motivation had mostly been for herself. So she could ensure her beloved friend's happiness.

"I'm sorry," she whispered. She'd known it was wrong. She'd tried to ignore the pinpricks of guilt at the beginning, and then, when she'd fallen in love with Matthew, the guilt had faded into the background, and she'd all but forgotten she'd been the one who'd manipulated the situation from the beginning.

"I thought you were better than that." He shook his head in disgust. "And I sat here telling you of what happened to me in the past. Do you remember that, Jo?"

"I—" Her chest constricted at the expression on his face. The raw pain resident there, the anguish. She'd put that look there.

"You knew what that experience with Fanny did to me, and yet you repeated it," he said, his cold voice raking over her skin. "Knowing how I might feel if it happened again."

"No," she said in a ragged whisper. "That's not true. That's not fair."

"Isn't it?"

"You thought yourself to be in love with Fanny, and that's why her betrayal affected you so deeply. That wasn't so this time. You said you no longer believed in love. You shielded yourself from ever experiencing that kind of pain again. You never suggested that you might have fallen in love with Harriet."

His mouth twisted, and his eyes went glassy. He blinked hard.

Oh God. Oh no. Jo pressed a hand to her chest.

"Matthew?" she said in a strangled voice. It occurred to her that her heart might actually stop beating, once and for all. "Did you... Did you fall in *love* with Harriet Cherrington?"

He stared at her, unmoving.

"I'm sorry. So sorry. I thought... I *wanted* you to love her. I wanted her to love you. I wanted you to be happy together. My other professional matches have all been love matches. But this one... Well, you insisted you didn't believe in love. I almost gave up, but I always wished that you might rediscover that emotion when you married. That you might feel that happiness that a person feels when they have met their perfect match." She buried her face in her hands and groaned out, "Please. If you love her, understand that she is an innocent party to all this. She understands she needs to marry someone of means, of course she does. But she didn't manipulate you, and I... I truly believe that...that one day, she might love you back. Perhaps she does already. Please, Your Grace. It's all right if you despise me for what I have done, but please don't blame Harriet. I want... I wish nothing more than for the two of you to be happy together."

Those last several words drained the final vestiges of her strength. Her legs went weak, and she slid down the back of the door. She stared up at him, feeling no more substantial than a husk, dry and light, ready to blow away in the wind.

He loved Harriet. Why wouldn't he? Harriet was perfect. And now, he'd discovered Jo's manipulation and was so angry it seemed impossible that he'd agree to marry Harriet now.

Good Lord, she'd ruined everything. "I'm so sorry," she whispered.

His laugh was as sharp as a knife, and it pierced all the way through her. "Oh, no, Miss Porter. You have it all wrong. I did not fancy myself in love with Miss Cherrington."

"What?" Her mind was a tangle of confusion, self-reproach, and pain.

"I said, I did not fancy myself in love with Miss Cherrington."

She stared at him, uncomprehending.

His eyes narrowed, and he spat out, "I fancied myself in love with *you*."

Her mouth dropped open, but she couldn't utter a single word. Even if she could have, she would have had no idea what to say.

"I intended to make my intentions clear today," he continued. "Not to Miss Cherrington, but to you. I wanted *you*."

"Oh God, Matthew." Her voice was half a whisper, half a moan. "I—"

But he cut her off with a swipe of his hand. "Fool that I was, I thought you might love me as well. But that's a ruse, isn't it? Like the match was a ruse, like everything has been a ruse. False and deceitful and a lie. Have you ever told me anything that was true, Jo? *Have you?*"

Pain suffused his voice now, but the hard edge of anger pounded behind it.

"Yes," she said. "Yes, I have." So much. Yet, she hadn't told him the biggest truth of all: that she'd fallen in love with him.

He didn't seem to hear her answer, though. He leaned forward, staring down at her with darkened eyes that might as well be daggers. "I thought I made it quite clear that I would not marry someone who desired me only for my title or fortune. Since you— and Harriet Cherrington—clearly look at me and see nothing but a duke and his riches—"

"No." She shook her head hard. "*No*, that's not—"

But he went on. "I will have nothing to do with you. I have no wish to see you—either of you—ever again. Please refrain from seeking out my company in the future. I will be leaving this place, this city, post haste. And since I will never darken the Cherrington doorstep again, please convey this message to Miss Cherrington as well."

Tears pooled in Jo's eyes and began to stream down her face. Her chest heaved as she gasped for air. She couldn't move, couldn't breathe. Her lungs, her limbs, her whole body felt as if it were made of stone.

"Please move away from the door, Miss Porter," the Duke of Crestmont said coldly.

"Please…I—" With great effort, she hauled in a gasp of air. "I love you." She lowered her face into her hands.

So much. She loved him so, so much. This proud, sensitive, beautiful man. She'd wronged him, and it was all her fault, but she *loved* him. Shouldn't that count for something?

"*Move.*"

Evidently, her love didn't matter. Or he didn't believe her. That was more likely. He thought her a liar and a fraud. But she wasn't—not in this.

She didn't move. She couldn't. She had to keep him there until she made him understand, and yet, she had no idea how to make him understand.

He made a low sound that contained his rage and his pain, each emotion struggling for dominance. She tried to unscramble her thoughts, to think of something to say to him that would be real and meaningful, and that he'd understand and forgive her.

Then she heard the slam of the door that led into the kitchen. When she looked up, he was gone.

CHAPTER THIRTY

Matthew tried his damnedest not to slam the door behind him, but it rattled the entire little house anyway. He located a doorway on the opposite wall and charged blindly through the room, some part of his roiling senses determining that it was a small kitchen. He brushed past a female form that gasped and said, "Excuse me, sir!" but he forged on through the doorway, a pantry, and a short corridor beyond, which finally, thankfully, led to the entryway and the front door of the house.

He burst out into the warm July air and set off in a fast clip down the street. He'd walked several blocks before he realized he'd reached a farm. He was outside London and walking in the opposite direction of Mayfair.

He swiveled around and headed home, too angry to think. He kept his head down, loath for anyone to recognize him and stop him in the street.

He needed to get out of here. Away. He couldn't risk seeing Miss Cherrington or Jo again. Parliament wasn't due to adjourn for another fortnight, but it would plod on without him. He had nothing else to tie him to this place, only things pushing him out.

His mind kept going to Jo and the look on her face, how it was twisted with despair. Those tears streaming down her cheeks. Her words: "I love you."

A lie. Just as false as her smiles and sighs, and her compassion and curiosity about him. As false as her assertion that she wanted to learn to row—he should have known that was too good to be true. He'd been so damned naive—no woman wanted to learn to row!

He rubbed his forehead miserably, ignoring the busy London traffic that swept by all around him.

God, one would think he would have learned with Fanny Fleming, but no. He'd gone and fallen all over again, like the damned besotted fool he was.

So goddamned stupid.

Last time, he'd felt sorry for himself, miserable, and lonely. This time…he felt like an open wound that had been rubbed vigorously with salt.

He needed to get away.

Forget marrying. He couldn't do it. Now that he'd convinced himself he should marry Joanna Porter, he couldn't conceive of marrying anyone else. And he certainly wouldn't marry *her*.

Uncle George would continue to be his heir, but George was old. Maybe it wasn't too late for Matthew to attempt a closer connection to his nephews. Perhaps he could still be a positive influence on them. Probably not—both boys were spoiled, entitled, and devious. Nevertheless, one of them, probably Archibald, the eldest, would become the next Duke of Crestmont. Matthew would have to try. Which would also mean he'd have to spend more time with his uncle George. God forbid. A shackle of its own, but marriage would be a tighter, crueler shackle. Matthew would take the former punishment over the latter, any day.

He'd learned his lesson, once and for all. Marriage was not, and would never be, for him.

He strode into his house, encountering Simms in the corridor as he walked up the stairs. He looked down at the butler from over the banister. "I am leaving London. I will be traveling to Lord Winthrop's estate in Hertfordshire. Please have the carriage readied. I will be ready to depart within the hour."

"Yes, Your Grace," Simms said, completely unperturbed by this news. "How long will you be gone?"

"I have no idea," he said. Then added, "Indefinitely."

His butler remained unflappable. "And Lord George?"

"My uncle shall remain in residence for as long as he wishes."

"Very well, Your Grace."

When Matthew reached the top of the stairs, the door to his right swung open, and his chest constricted. Uncle George peered out of his room. There were dark circles under his eyes, and it appeared as if he'd just awakened—his shirt was loose and untucked, and he wasn't wearing a cravat.

Damn it. Matthew was hoping to leave the man a note. He was the last person Matthew wished to see right now.

"Matty," Uncle George said with that fake joviality that made Matthew want to roar. "Are you engaged, then? Shall I offer you my sincerest congratulations?"

"No, thank you," Matthew ground out.

The resident crease between George's brows deepened. "No, you aren't engaged, or no, I shouldn't offer my congratulations?"

"No to both," Matthew snapped.

George's mouth dropped open, but his gaze grew sharper before quickly correcting into one of sympathy. "*What?* Do not tell me she rebuffed you!"

"No, she did not."

"What then? Did you not ask her?"

"I decided not to ask her, after all." George wasn't at all up to date on Matthew's plans. He would have hated everything about Jo, but Matthew hadn't cared about that. It hadn't been up to his uncle.

But none of it mattered now.

"Really?" A gleam appeared in George's eyes, but he schooled it away. Poorly. The gleam was banked, but still glowing.

Matthew shifted on his feet, combating the impulse to run away. Run straight out of this house and never come back. But he wasn't a child any longer. He could face this man.

"Yes, Uncle. Really."

"Why is that?"

He forced his face to impassivity. "I discovered something about the lady that rendered her ineligible."

George nodded. "Ah. That is too bad, my boy. I am sorry."

"Better to discover it now than after the vows are made, I suppose."

"Yes, it is," his uncle said. "Yes, indeed." It looked like the man was fighting a smile.

Matthew needed his uncle. He needed to have a relationship with him. He needed him to retain some hope of preserving his title, of passing on his responsibilities to someone who would find them as precious and important as he did.

He took a deep breath. "I am called away from London, Uncle. I shall be leaving shortly. Please stay here for as long as you wish. I don't know if I'll return before the end of the Season, but I will keep you apprised of my plans."

"Very well, my boy. Very well *indeed*."

• • •

After Matthew left, Jo curled up in a ball on the floor, knees pressed to her chest, tears streaming from her eyes. She heard the door open.

"I'm sorry, I know you don't like to be interrupted at work, but there was a man—" Then there was a breathy "Oh, dear," before Mrs. Ferguson called into the house. "Bess! Miss Lilly! Come quick!"

Another few seconds, and three women were kneeling at her side. Through her haze of tears, she could only see their shapes, not the concern on their faces, though she felt it radiating off all three of them.

"What's wrong?" Lilly gripped Jo's hand. "Jo, dear, what is it? What has happened?"

What could she say to that? How could she answer?

The man I love loved me, too, until he learned of my deception. And now he despises me.

But that would just confuse them. Lilly didn't know that she was in love with Matthew. No one did. There wasn't a soul who knew—except Matthew himself, and he certainly believed she'd been lying.

She couldn't blame him. She wouldn't have believed her, either.

She couldn't tell them all that. She could hardly breathe. Her breaths were coming out in short, painful gasps, her chest heaving with sobs.

The three women weren't going to allow her to stay curled up on the floor weeping. Within a few moments, they had her up, Bess and Lilly supporting her on either side, and were walking her up the stairs. Her mother appeared at the top. "Oh, Jo, my darling. What is the matter?"

Seeing her mother standing on the landing, Jo straightened. She dashed the tears from her face and stopped halfway up the stairs. "I cannot. I need to…" A sob welled but she beat it back down. "I need to go back to my office. I have a meeting with Mr. Pellegrini."

"I'll let him know that you cannot be there today," Lilly said. "I'll say you've come down with a cold."

Jo opened her mouth to agree, then closed it again. She thought of Mr. Pellegrini and how she'd failed him the first time. If she didn't meet with him, something terrible might happen.

Mr. Pellegrini was a lovely man who would make Mrs. Fineman very happy. They both deserved happiness. She wouldn't throw that away like she'd— inadvertently but thoroughly—thrown away Matthew's.

"I must speak with him. It is important."

Mama gave a sharp nod. "There's clean water in my basin," she said. "Wash your face, then, and go back downstairs."

Jo walked the rest of the way upstairs, washed her face, then gazed at herself in her mother's looking glass. Her eyes were red and glassy, but there was nothing to be done about it.

Mama set a comforting hand on her shoulder. "Go, my strong, dear child."

Within seconds of her return to her office, Mr. Pellegrini knocked on the door, and Jo ushered him inside. She was glad she did. His plan had been to—in very dramatic Italian fashion—play the mandolin and sing a love song outside Mrs. Fineman's drawing room window at night. When she opened her window, he'd fall to his knees, proclaim his love, and offer marriage.

Jo convinced him not to do it. Mrs. Fineman would have liked such a gesture, of course, but she was also a proper English lady, and it would embarrass her greatly to be proposed to in such a setting. It would be a spectacle, and all her servants would likely be watching.

Instead, Jo convinced Mr. Pellegrini to propose more quietly, *in* Mrs. Fineman's drawing room. He still insisted he must play the mandolin for her, which Jo agreed would be perfectly appropriate in that situation.

After Mr. Pellegrini left, Jo went straight upstairs to her bedroom, where she kicked off her shoes before getting into bed, fully dressed, and curling up on her side with her knees tucked into her chest.

Moments later, her family gathered around her. Mrs. Ferguson propped her up on pillows. Lilly sat beside her on the bed, rubbing warmth into her cold hands. Mama sat in the armchair that Bess had pulled close to the bed, and Bess made her take sips of Mrs. Ferguson's cheer-me-up tea.

"I tried, Lilly. I really did, but…" Turning to her friend, Jo drew in a great, shuddering breath, and squeezed Lilly's hand in her own. "I'm so sorry." Tears threatened again, and she couldn't stop them. They pooled in her eyes and slipped down her cheeks.

"I knew it." Lilly closed her eyes in a long blink. "While you were with Mr. Pellegrini, I kept thinking what it could be. It's the duke, isn't it?" she asked. "He's not going to marry Harriet, is he?"

"No, Lil. He isn't. I'm so sorry."

Amid the soft groans and *oh no*s of the three other women in the room, Lilly finally opened her eyes. They shone but remained dry. "Why?"

"He found out…" Jo hesitated as it struck her with the force of an anvil—how *had* he found out?

"What do you mean?" Lilly breathed. "What did he find out?"

"That I schemed for him to marry Harriet so the Cherringtons would be financially and socially secure, and so that Charles would be free to marry you."

"What?" Mama asked, her blond brows shooting toward her hairline. "You did?"

"I did." Jo swallowed down the welling tears. "I'm so sorry, Mama. I only wanted Lilly to be happy—"

"Oh, Jo." Mama sighed, and when Jo looked at her, she saw understanding in her mother's blue eyes. She knew more than she was letting on about

Jo's feelings for the duke.

"But it's not too great a sin, is it?" Bess asked, frowning. "If he's fond of Miss Cherrington, then it really shouldn't matter to him."

Jo couldn't look any of them in the eye. "It matters," she said quietly. "He believes we—and the Cherringtons—manipulated him motivated solely by greed."

"If that isn't the motivation of the vast majority of the *ton*, then I don't know what is," Jo's mother said.

"Perhaps, but a woman attempted to ensnare him before. She seduced him, then gloated about how she had won a duke, along with his fortune. They were literally standing at the altar before he learned of it."

"Fanny Fleming," Mama said.

Jo nodded.

Mama pursed her lips. "Well. She was a dishonest and entitled creature." Mama's back straightened, her eyes narrowed, and her jaw went tight. Jo knew the look well—a mother bear, ready to claw out the eyes of anyone who would threaten her cub. "You are nothing like her. You, my dear, are honorable and humble and kind."

"Thank you, Mama. But the Duke of Crestmont doesn't see it that way. And I don't blame him." Blinking hard, she turned to Lilly. "I don't understand how he found out."

Lilly stared at her, all color drained from her face.

"Oh, Lord…" Jo's breaths grew short and sharp. "Please don't tell me you told Charles."

"I did," Lilly said. "I'm so sorry, Jo."

"Lilly! You promised you wouldn't tell a soul."

"And I meant it…but he…he is—*was*—to be my husband. It felt wrong to keep anything from him."

And that made Jo feel even worse. Not only had she lied to and deceived the duke, but she'd also encouraged Lilly to withhold the truth of the situation from her future husband.

Lilly started to cry. "Charles must have told him. I asked him not to, but even if he had, I wouldn't have imagined this to happen." She gathered Jo into her arms. "Don't feel bad, Jo, dear. I know you tried. You did everything you could. It's not your fault."

But it was. The whole scheme was Jo's fault, so it followed that the collapse of it was, too.

And it was so much more than that, but she still couldn't talk about that…about how she'd somehow, despite all her warnings to herself, fallen in love with the Duke of Crestmont. She was so ashamed of herself in so many ways. So sad for Lilly.

So heartbroken and hurt and devastated by that look of betrayal on Matthew's face.

Lilly's heartbreak was enough for all of them, though. They didn't need to be burdened with Jo's as well. Clinging to her friend, Jo buried her face in the counterpane and wept with renewed tears.

This time, Lilly wept with her.

CHAPTER THIRTY-ONE

Early the next afternoon, Jo stood at the Cherringtons' threshold. Lilly hadn't been able to bring herself to come—not that Jo would have asked her. Bess had offered, but this was something Jo needed to do on her own.

Now, she regretted that decision.

She didn't want to do this. She'd far rather be in bed right now, curled up in a ball, feeling sorry for herself, and drinking Mrs. Ferguson's cheer-me-up tea. Jo had drunk two cups of it last night, and she *had* felt better. Unfortunately, however, she'd felt like death when she'd finally awakened today at noon. Though she didn't know if she could attribute that to the rum in the tea, the oversleeping, or her ragged tangle of a heart.

She dragged up her hand and gripped the door knocker, took a deep breath, and knocked.

Moments later, the butler was leading her to the upstairs drawing room, and Jo wondered who she'd be facing today. When she finally stepped inside, one person rose to greet her. Harriet was alone.

Thank God. It was bad enough to have to deliver this news to Harriet, but having to face the entire Cherrington clan just might kill her.

Harriet greeted her, and they went through the pleasantries of conversation per the dictates of society. But Jo could see the crease between Harriet's brows. She'd expected Matthew's proposal yesterday, but he hadn't come. And now, Jo was here to tell her why.

They sat on the sofa, and Harriet ordered some tea to be brought up. As soon as the maid closed the door, Harriet turned to Jo. "You have something to tell me, don't you?"

"I do." She reached for Harriet's hand and held it in her own. "I'm so sorry to tell you this, Harriet, but the Duke of Crestmont has decided he won't be pursuing his suit any longer."

Harriet released a long *whoosh* of a breath. "Oh."

Jo squeezed Harriet's hand. "I'm so very sorry. I know you and your family anticipated that he'd propose soon—yesterday. But he decided... abruptly...that he wasn't going to. Furthermore, he said he's leaving London, so don't worry that he's set another young lady in his sights." She hesitated. "In fact, I doubt he'll marry anyone anytime soon."

She'd also been responsible for that. His renewed suspicion regarding love. Her chest constricted as she thought of this additional unintended side effect. She'd gone into this determined to make him believe in love again. And perhaps she'd succeeded, for a moment. But then he'd learned of her deception and had instantly erected newer, stronger walls around his heart.

It was bad enough to lose him. But knowing that he would never allow himself love, that he'd never be truly happy having a partner with whom he could share his life—that broke her.

She blinked against the film in her eyes. Harriet wasn't crying, and Jo would not, could not, weep in front of her.

Harriet gently pulled her hand away from Jo's. "It is all right, Miss Porter. Truly."

Jo's breath caught. "It…is?"

Harriet nodded. "Yes. Perhaps…perhaps it is a blessing."

"How?"

"Because, while I would have accepted the duke's proposal for my family's sake, I don't love him. I never did." Harriet's expression crumpled, and she looked down at her hands twisting in her lap. "I simply felt obligated to marry him, you see. And I wouldn't have regretted that decision—I promised myself I would never regret it, for he does seem like an honorable man." She hesitated, glanced around as if to ensure no one was listening to them, and leaned toward Jo. "You see, I have…" She swallowed hard and drew so close, her lips nearly brushed Jo's hair, and whispered, "I seem to have fallen in love with someone else."

"Oh," Jo breathed. A tiny spot of happiness for the other woman sparked in her chest. "That's…"

"I felt terrible about it, though, and disloyal to the duke, so I was trying to not allow myself to love him, but now that I can…" A bright smile bloomed on Harriet's face, making her eyes sparkle with joy. She looked prettier at this moment than Jo had ever seen her.

"May I ask the identity of the lucky gentleman?" As thrilled for Harriet as Jo was, she still couldn't summon a smile, as much as she tried.

"Mr. Gifford."

"Ah." Jo turned to the still-fresh, bright red bouquet on the table. Mr. Gifford, who Harriet had met at Lady Campbell's ball and who had sent that monstrous display of roses when he'd learned that Harriet had been ill. "You only met the one time? At Lady Campbell's ball?" She knew many young women could consider themselves in love after a first meeting, but honestly, Harriet didn't seem to be that type of girl.

After a brief hesitation, Harriet said, "No, not exactly. He called upon me twice after the ball, and then we saw each other again at Vauxhall Gardens."

"At Vauxhall…" Jo's voice trailed off. "I see. You were with him when we were separated, weren't you?"

Harriet had the presence of mind to blush. "I am so sorry about that, but yes, I was. We slipped away during the fireworks, planning to return immediately, but…" Her flush deepened. "We lost track of the time."

Being the older woman, the on-the-shelf spinster matchmaker, Jo supposed there were a variety of issues from that night that she should chastise Harriet about. Yet, her innate passion for romance overruled any objections she might have. Harriet had stars in her eyes, and Jo had no desire to wipe them away. The young woman was in love, and as hurt and sad as Jo was, she still believed in love, and Harriet was as deserving as anyone to find her own happily ever after. "I am so happy for you, Harriet."

Harriet sighed. "The duke calling it off is terrible news for both our families, Miss Porter. But I was thinking, maybe Mr. Gifford—if he should propose to me—will relieve my family's burden, at least somewhat? Then, my brother might be able to offer for Lilly, after all?"

Jo patted Harriet's hand. "Perhaps." But she doubted it. Mr. Gifford was no duke, and if he were in possession of even a quarter of a fortune the size of Matthew's, she would have heard far more about him by now. "Has Mr. Gifford initiated a courtship?"

"No." Harriet shook her head. "But then again, he learned soon after Lady Campbell's ball, like the rest of London, that the duke was pursuing me. Now that that courtship is off, I do hope I shall see him again."

"I wish you the very best," Jo said, and she meant it.

The tea arrived and Harriet poured Jo a cup. As they sipped, they spoke of the season's fashions and how, in the two years since the decisive battle at Waterloo, the trim of women's pelisses and jackets often had a military-inspired cut, but that trend might finally be fading.

When she finished her cup of tea, Jo took her leave, not feeling better, per se, but at least not having to bear the additional burden of another woman's heartbreak.

• • •

That night, after Mrs. Ferguson and Mama had gone to bed and Lilly, Bess, and Jo were sitting in the parlor, Bess rounded on Jo.

"All right," she said. "Enough of this. Out with it."

Jo looked up from the book she'd been pretending to read. "What do you mean?"

"Something is wrong," Bess said. "I see it. Lilly

has seen it. You're keeping something from us, something that is making you pale and preventing you from smiling or eating, and we want to know what it is."

Jo glanced at Lilly sitting on the chair across from her. Lilly shrugged. "I understand you feel horrid about the Duke of Crestmont not marrying Harriet and the fact that Charles and I can no longer…" She trailed off, swallowed, and continued. "We know it is more than sympathy for me, Jo. So what is it?"

Jo looked back down at her book, closed it slowly, and gripped its edges. "I've done a terrible thing," she murmured, staring down at the brown cover.

Instantly, both women moved to her side.

"I doubt you are capable of doing a truly terrible thing," Bess said.

"I *know* you're not," Lilly said.

"But I have," Jo whispered.

"Tell us what it is," Bess said gently.

She looked up, at Lilly on her left and Bess on her right, each one of them holding one of her hands. She squeezed their hands tight.

"I fell in love," she confessed. "With the most inappropriate person possible."

"Who?" Lilly breathed.

"The Duke of Crestmont."

• • •

Pleasant Hill, being situated on the crest of a long, low hill, was not Matthew's favorite place, though he had spent many long days here, sultry summer days, crisp winters during school holidays, and the months after the Fanny Fleming disaster when he'd locked himself in the bedchamber assigned to him, too heartsick and miserable to emerge for days at a time.

For, while Pleasant Hill was pleasant enough, it was not near a body of water. Which meant there was no rowing to be had within several miles of the place, and every muscle in Matthew's body ached to pull an oar.

Day and night, he paced the halls of the country estate rebuilt by Winthrop's father after the turn of the century. Matthew was anxious and restless, and he knew he'd need to go back to London soon, if only to take a visit to the boathouse and row until his body ached and his arms felt like they might fall clean away from his body.

But the idea of returning to London made nausea swirl in his gut. Maybe he'd visit Hanford Castle instead. The castle lands bordered the River Trent, where he'd spent many an afternoon sweating in a boat under the milky sunlight of Nottinghamshire.

Yes, he'd do that. He'd go from here straight to Hanford Castle, where he'd take up residence. Maybe he'd become a recluse, never showing his face in London again.

That wasn't feasible, though. He had responsibilities in London, not the least of which was his seat in the House of Lords, that he couldn't shirk forever.

He entered the dining room where Winthrop already sat reading the *Times*.

"Crest!" Winthrop said. "Pierre has made a delicious plum cake. Have some."

Matthew's stomach made a twisting response.

He'd skipped dinner last night. Truth be told, he hadn't much been in the mood to socialize with his host. Winthrop had seemed to understand this and had given him plenty of space to brood.

He hadn't even told the man the real reason for his appearance, though Winthrop, finding Matthew on his threshold last week, had taken one look at him and concluded his marriage proposal had failed. Matthew had neither confirmed nor denied his suspicion.

Matthew went to the sideboard and dutifully took a slice of the plum cake before sitting across from Winthrop, who closed the newspaper and set it beside his plate. "Well. I was thinking of duck hunting for our dinner. Want to come with me, or would you prefer to continue skulking about my house?"

Matthew swallowed a bite of the cake, then pretended to ponder this for a moment. "I'd prefer to continue skulking. Thank you for the kind invitation, though."

Winthrop shrugged. "To each his own."

He handed Matthew some pages of the newspaper, and the two of them read in silence for a few minutes.

As Matthew studied an article about a new kind of turtle discovered in the West Indies, he felt Winthrop's eyes on him. Finally, his friend asked, "Are you ready to tell me what happened?"

"No."

Winthrop sighed. "Very well. I shall go with what I initially thought, then."

Matthew couldn't hide his curiosity, though he

kept his gaze focused on the turtle article. "And what is that?"

"Miss Porter refused you."

Matthew snorted. "No. Worse."

That seemed to stump Winthrop. "What could be worse than the woman a man loves refusing him?"

"A few things, at least," Matthew said.

Winthrop made a growling noise. "For God's sake, man, just tell me."

Matthew slapped the paper down and narrowed his eyes at his friend. "You wish for me to lay out my private business for the sole purpose of allaying your curiosity?"

"Yes, that is exactly what I wish," Winthrop snapped back. "So hurry it up."

"Fine," Matthew said on a snarl. "Joanna Porter proved herself to be no better than Fanny Fleming."

Winthrop reeled back, his surprise shifting rapidly into disbelief. "Nonsense. Miss Porter is nothing like Fanny Fleming."

"You're wrong. She's exactly like her. Only worse, as she seems to have hidden her true nature from even you, who was so quick to warn me about Fanny."

He remembered Winthrop's letter, so long ago, when he'd written to tell him he was in love and planned to marry Fanny Fleming. Winthrop had responded with a plea for him to be cautious, that something about the Fleming family seemed disingenuous to him. Matthew had ignored him, of course.

"Miss Porter isn't like Fanny," Winthrop insisted. "Her character is the opposite of Fanny's."

"You don't even know what happened."

Winthrop smacked his hand on the table. "Then *tell* me, damn it."

So Matthew did. He told Winthrop everything, from the first day he'd met Jo, to him confiding in her about Fanny and how he could never marry a woman with that kind of cold ambition, to him kissing Jo, making love to her, then admitting to himself that he loved her and wanted her to be his duchess.

Then, discovering the truth of how she'd manipulated the match between him and Harriet Cherrington for the Cherringtons' financial gain. He finished with how he'd confronted her in her office.

When he was done, Winthrop shook his head slowly. By then, they'd adjourned to the drawing room and were drinking brandy—it was early in the day for as much brandy as he'd imbibed, but what the hell.

"She made a mistake," Winthrop said. "At the beginning she surely couldn't have known what happened with Fanny and how you'd feel about it."

"Are you defending her?" Matthew snapped.

"Hear me out," Winthrop said.

"She knew about Fanny almost from the beginning," Matthew said. "I told her before I even met Miss Cherrington."

"All right, but still, I don't think her motivation was for financial gain."

Matthew threw his hands up as if to say, "What could it have possibly been, then?"

"She wouldn't have personally gained financially from you marrying Miss Cherrington. Not a penny."

Matthew pressed his lips together. "Perhaps not, but the Cherringtons would have. And Lilly Appleby—"

"—also wouldn't have gained a penny," Winthrop interjected. "She would only have been free to marry the man she loves."

"What are you saying?" Matthew said.

"I'm saying that you're wrong, friend. Fanny Fleming wanted your money and title. Joanna Porter wanted no such thing. She couldn't have anticipated you would fall in love with her, nor ever propose to her, for God's sake. She simply wanted to bring happiness to her beloved friend. That's a far different motivation from Fanny's."

Matthew gazed at the light sparkling through the amber liquid in his glass. He shook his head, knowing he looked damned stubborn. But there was a valid reason behind his feelings. "She still manipulated me. *Lied* to me."

"Yes, she did," Winthrop said quietly. "But I don't think she was lying when she apologized to you about it. And when she said she loved you, Crest, I don't think she was lying at all."

CHAPTER THIRTY-TWO

Cole and Jameson arrived at Pleasant Hill late the next morning. Matthew didn't know whether Winthrop had asked them to come or they had just decided to, but he was grateful for their presence. They didn't speak of the debacle with Jo at all; instead, while they ate a dinner of duck with orange sauce—delicious, thanks to Winthrop's excellent hunting skills and his French cook's mastery in the kitchen—they made plans to go hunting, to ride the countryside, and next week, to ride to the River Lea waterfront for a row.

As they were finishing their meal, the butler entered the dining room. "Pardon me. You have a caller, Your Grace."

"Me?" Matthew looked between his three friends—they were the only people he'd ever expect to call upon him anywhere.

"Yes, sir."

He frowned. "Who is it?"

"Miss Lillian Appleby, Your Grace."

Matthew stiffened. He couldn't imagine what Lilly could possibly have to say to him. He glanced at Winthrop, who shrugged, seemingly just as confused as he was.

"Show her to the drawing room," he said to the butler. "I'll be there presently."

It came out automatically, a result of long-ingrained politeness. He didn't want to see Lilly

Appleby, though. He stared at the door the butler had just closed and wished he'd sent her away. God, what was this about? Was she here to lambaste him for what he'd said to Jo? Was she here to beg him to marry Harriet so she could marry Charles Cherrington?

He wanted to run, suddenly, just like he had run from London. But he couldn't run anymore. He needed to face Lilly Appleby and get on with his life.

He looked at each of his friends in turn, first Cole, who raised his brows, then Jameson, who gave him an encouraging nod, and finally Winthrop, who murmured, "Good luck."

They sat in silence for another few minutes, until Matthew decided he'd made the lady wait long enough. He rose, nodded to his friends, and left the dining room.

He opened the door to the drawing room to find two young women standing there, not one. Lilly had brought Bess Ferguson with her.

"Miss Appleby. Miss Ferguson." He bowed to each of them in turn.

He straightened to find both women gazing at him before remembering themselves and curtsying with curt greetings of, "Your Grace."

They stood looking at one another for a few seconds. Finally, Matthew said, "What can I do for you?"

He didn't miss the wrinkle in Lilly's demeanor as her courage faltered before she rebuilt it. "There are two items of great importance we would like to discuss with you, Your Grace."

He quirked a brow in a look he knew appeared

arrogant. "And what are they?"

Lilly glanced around. "May we sit?"

He gestured gallantly to the cluster of sofa and chairs. "Please."

They took their seats, Lilly and Bess on the sofa and Matthew in the velvety green armchair across from them. The color reminded Matthew of the chair in Jo's office, but this one, of course, was far more comfortable.

After a tense, silent moment, Matthew asked, "Shall I call for tea?"

Lilly raised her hand. "No, thank you." She glanced at Bess, and they shared a nod. "What we have to say won't take long."

Matthew clasped his hands in his lap in a pretense of patience. "Very well."

Lilly cleared her throat. "First of all, thank you."

Now both Matthew's brows rose. "What for?"

"For showing my notebook to Mr. Nash. We met Wednesday last, and it was…" She took a moment, seeming to catch her breath. "It was quite an excellent meeting. He has asked me to send him more of my plans, and to make some adjustments to the palace I conceived. He's going to present the design to the prince regent."

There was no small amount of awe in her voice when she said the words "the prince regent."

"That is excellent news, Miss Appleby. Congratulations."

"Thank you. I will be forever grateful for what you did, Your Grace."

"Think nothing of it. Talent usually finds its way into the appropriate hands."

"Not so easily when you're a simple woman of no rank."

He couldn't argue with that, unfortunately.

Lilly straightened, and a cool mask replaced the grateful softness of her features. "And now for the second thing."

Matthew braced himself.

"I came here because I wanted to let you know that you have broken my friend's heart."

The breath stalled in Matthew's throat. He couldn't speak. And in any case, what could he say to that?

"Jo is more than a friend to me," Lilly continued. "She is a sister. She is the kindest and most generous soul you will ever meet."

Matthew had once thought that of her, too.

"She believes it is her own fault that her heart is broken, because she matched you with Miss Cherrington. Yet, she hated to do so; she hated every moment she attempted to finalize that match because she fell more deeply in love with you each time she saw you. Jo could hardly bear the thought of you with Miss Cherrington, and yet she believed you'd never deign to marry a simple country clergyman's daughter." Lilly sucked in a shaky inhalation, her eyes shining. "She believed you would never consider her to be good enough for you."

Matthew's body was encased in ice. He couldn't move.

After a protracted silence, Lilly continued. "She *suffered*. For weeks."

Matthew hated the thought of Jo suffering. He

had been such a stubborn ass for so long, convincing himself she meant nothing to him, even as he ached to be with her. But he'd never, not once, thought her not good enough for him.

"She told no one," Lilly continued in a raspy voice, "only berated herself for allowing herself to love someone who could never see her as his equal." Lilly's eyes narrowed to slits. "Her only sin was in attempting to help a desperate friend—me."

"I don't think—"

But Lilly Appleby wasn't going to allow him a word in edgewise. "She fought for my happiness, yes," she said accusingly, "but she also fought for Miss Cherrington's, and yours. Little did she know it would leave her so bereft."

She stood suddenly, and Bess rose to stand beside her, clutching her hand. Matthew came to his feet as well, the politeness of the act ingrained in him, though being polite at this moment seemed utterly unimportant.

Lilly took a menacing step toward him. "I'm here to tell you, Your Grace, that Jo is not only good enough for you, but she is *too* good for you. If only I could make her see it. Instead, she will only blame herself, fool that she is. You accused her of being ambitious, of only wanting you for your title and your money. You are quite wrong. Jo didn't care about those things. She only cared about *you*. She would have offered you the most precious gift of all—love—and you chewed her up and spit her out. You are a…a…" She jabbed a finger at him. "A *cad*."

She spat the final word as if it were the strongest curse in existence, then turned to Bess. "Come along,

Bess," she said in a clipped voice. "We're leaving."

She tugged Bess toward the door, but the other woman dug in her heels. She looked straight at Matthew. "Jo is a good person, Your Grace," she said quietly. "And she is in love with you. If you ever loved her, I beg you, don't throw it away. She deserves more."

And after traveling all the way to Hertfordshire to give him a two-minute piece of their minds, they marched out the door, leaving Matthew staring after them.

. . .

A fortnight after the Duke of Crestmont had walked out of her office for the last time, Jo sat at her desk with Mr. Pellegrini sitting across from her. The older man was beaming from ear to ear.

"After I finished the song, I laid down my mandolin. Then, I kissed her hand most graciously," Mr. Pellegrini said, "and I asked her if she'd do me the honor of becoming my bride."

Jo leaned forward and breathed, "What did she say?"

He blinked, his eyes tearing up. "Yes! She said yes! I am so happy!"

Jo's hands flew to her chest. "That's wonderful. I am so thrilled for you." And she smiled—her first smile in days feeling like it glued a piece of her heart back together.

She knew, right then and there, that if she could keep bringing together happy couples, she'd forge onward. She'd be all right. Maybe not blissfully happy, but had she ever been?

Only in Matthew's arms.

She banished that thought instantly and resolutely focused on Mr. Pellegrini's joy. He shook his head. "I rushed into the first courtship," he said. "This one...well...it felt *real*. Do you understand what I mean?"

"I know exactly what you mean," she told him. "Have you set a date yet?"

"We will marry as soon as the banns are read." He smiled shyly. "We would be so thankful if you could stand as our witness."

"I wouldn't miss it for the world," she told him.

A few minutes later, Jo and Mr. Pellegrini stood near the door saying their goodbyes, and Mr. Pellegrini impulsively pulled her into a hug.

"Oomph," she said, as he squeezed her tight.

"Thank you so very much, Miss Porter. You have made me the happiest man alive."

Happy for him, she returned his hug, patting his back when her office door suddenly swung open.

Mr. Pellegrini and Jo jumped back from each other in surprise, the action surely appearing far guiltier than the situation called for.

Jo swung around to the gaping doorway to see none other than the Duke of Crestmont standing there, glowering.

CHAPTER THIRTY-THREE

The duke's eyes were narrow, his lips thinning as Jo and Mr. Pellegrini stared at him. Love surged within Jo—she knew that look on his face well. It was the surest sign of him fortifying all those protective walls he built around himself.

Finally, Matthew cleared his throat. "I must have the wrong address," he muttered, turning away.

Jo lunged forward and grasped his sleeve. "No! I mean, you haven't. I mean, this certainly is the correct address."

She had no idea why on earth he was here. He'd said he was going to leave London, hadn't he? Why come here, of all places, after all he had said? Perhaps he wanted another chance to rail at her, to tell her how badly she'd spoilt everything with him. How she'd hurt him.

Even if that were the case, she still couldn't allow him to leave.

He glanced disdainfully down at her hand on his sleeve, and she let him go. She gestured to Mr. Pellegrini. "Your Grace," she said, "this is Mr. Pellegrini. He is a client of mine, and he has just told me the wonderful news of his engagement."

"Congratulations," the duke muttered.

Jo continued, "Mr. Pellegrini, may I present the Duke of Crestmont."

Mr. Pellegrini bowed with a flourish. "I am pleased to meet you, Your Grace. If you are considering becoming a client of this fine lady, I assure you, you will not be displeased. Mrs. Porter is the best matchmaker in London—no, in the whole of the United Kingdom, if not the whole of this enormous Earth upon which we reside!"

Matthew stared at Jo. "That's quite an endorsement," he said in a flat voice.

"And I offer it with no reservation," Mr. Pellegrini gushed.

Jo barely heard him. She was staring at Matthew, unable to look away.

After an awkward moment of silence, Mr. Pellegrini pressed his hat upon his head, and with a final goodbye, took his leave, promising to send Jo the date and time of the wedding.

When he was gone, Matthew stepped inside, removed his hat and set it on the entry table, then closed the door behind him—still without taking his eyes off Jo.

Jo inched backward, but she didn't break her gaze away, either. She hadn't been sure she'd ever see him again, and just looking at him felt like a marvelous gift, one that she could soak in and hang onto forever.

They stood there for long moments, until Matthew broke the silence. "Jo."

"Yes?" she asked in a rasp.

"I…" He swallowed hard, looked away, then resolutely looked back at her. After a long pause, he said, "I missed you."

She could see the effort it took for him to say that. His fear of offering her these words of vulnerability radiated out from him in the tension around his eyes and mouth. But she wouldn't ruin it. She'd take his vulnerable side and cradle it in her hands like the delicate offering it was. She'd teach him that he didn't need to fortify those rigid walls in her presence. He was safe with her. He always would be.

"I missed you, too," she said. "So very much."

He let out a slow, long breath. "I was wrong. All those things I said to you. I didn't mean them."

"*I* was wrong," she said. "I knew what I did was wrong, and I feel horrid about it, and I am so sorry for it."

He nodded somberly.

"But," she continued, "truth be told, I had forgotten all about my deception. When you reminded me of what I'd done to manipulate the match between you and Harriet—well, it was even worse, because it had completely slipped my mind."

His brows drew together in confusion. "How is that possible? How could you forget about deceiving me? How could you forget how such a deception would destroy me?"

"It's possible because I drowned one sin with another—one I felt was far more terrible."

Renewed fear entered his eyes, and he asked hoarsely, "What else have you done?"

She finally looked away from him, her gaze moving down toward his midriff that blurred behind her misty eyes. "I fell in love. With the most inappropriate person in London. The very person I was attempting to match with someone else." Slowly, she looked up into his face. "You."

The silence felt like it dragged on forever. Finally

he said, "How is that a sin?"

"You were supposed to marry Harriet. You *wanted* to marry Harriet. Loving you was a selfish act, but as much as I tried to stop it, I couldn't. It just kept growing and growing until..." She shook her head. "Until I was certain I couldn't bear to watch you marry her."

"Jo."

She looked up.

"I never wanted to marry Harriet."

"But—"

"I was expected to marry someone like Harriet. I believed it was my *duty* to marry someone like Harriet. It was something I was forcing myself to do because almost everything I've ever known told me it was the only correct way for me to marry. It was not something I wanted."

"What do you want, then?" she asked him breathlessly.

He took a step toward her. "You."

Tears sprang to her eyes. "Don't say that."

"Why?"

"Because I lied to you. I betrayed you. I'm exactly the kind of woman you do *not* want."

"You never lied to me. You withheld the truth from me—someone you didn't know well—to secure the happiness of someone you've known and loved for much of your life."

"An omission of truth is as bad as a lie," she said, then wondered why she was arguing against her own cause.

"No, it isn't." His fingers went under her chin, gently tilting her head up so she was looking at him.

"I was developing feelings for you," he said softly, "deeper than I've ever felt for anyone. But those feelings terrified me. I have always believed what Fanny and my uncle said about me as a boy. I truly thought I didn't deserve love and that there wasn't a soul on earth who would ever really love me. When I heard the truth of why you wanted me to marry Miss Cherrington, I was quick to use your deception to prove my hypothesis. I am not lovable, not really. I will never have a love like my parents did."

"That's not true," Jo breathed. "It never has been."

Matthew rubbed his knuckles over her cheek. "You have always believed that, haven't you?"

"Always."

"It is not as easy for me to believe, though. When Charles Cherrington told me I was to marry Harriet to lift his family up out of poverty and to allow him to marry Lilly, I equated your actions in facilitating the match to Fanny Fleming's treachery. But they weren't the same at all."

"They weren't," she said, her tone pleading. "Truly, they weren't. I meant no harm."

"I know that now," he said.

"From the beginning, I was determined that you and the woman I found for you would find happiness together. That you would have that love match you thought you could never have. The first day we met, I promised myself I'd make it so."

"Even though I told you it would never be so?"

"*Especially* after you said that. And then, I was hoping to make it happen with Harriet, who seemed so perfect for you."

He laughed. "What about now?"

She couldn't breathe. "I still hope—more desperately than ever—that you make a love match." Her eyes fluttered away, but he nudged at her chin, forcing her gaze back to his.

"I hope so, too," he said.

"I vow I will never deceive you again, Matthew. I will never hurt you again. I'm so sorry."

"And I'm sorry, too, sweetheart. For judging you too quickly and too harshly. I vow that I will trust you from now on. Your heart is the sweetest one I've ever known. I will hold onto it and nurture that sweetness for the rest of my life, if you allow me to."

She nodded. "I will. For as long as you will have me."

"For life, then?" When her brows drew together in confusion, he said, "Marry me, Jo."

She lurched back. "What do you mean?"

"Marry me. Make me the happiest man alive. Become my bride."

In an instant, he'd stitched her heart back together, but the stitches were already frayed, beginning to rip apart all over again.

Because what he said was impossible.

"I…can't." It nearly killed her to say it, but it was true. She was a romantic at heart, but she desperately gripped her last shreds of practicality.

"Why?" he gritted out, his expression going from hopeful to dark in an instant.

"I cannot marry you. Society would laugh at me—at both of us. I follow none of your rules of engagement. And…" Her voice trailed off.

"What else?"

"I am a matchmaker. I work for a living, and I adore what I do. Nothing has made me happier than making people happy, until…"

"Until what?"

"Until I met you," she admitted. "But don't you see? I cannot have my cake and eat it too. I cannot be a duchess and a matchmaker at the same time."

"Why the hell not?" he asked so harshly, she recoiled.

"Because it's not…it's simply not *done*."

He laughed humorlessly. "Then we shall be the first to do it."

Staring at him, she shook her head.

"Listen to me, Jo." He gripped her upper arms. "Listen to me. I don't give a damn about what's done and not done. Not anymore. Those rules stifled me, limited me, turned me into nothing more than a hard shell of a man. With you, I am a complete man—a *happy* man—and I care naught about what society thinks is appropriate. I want you to be happy. If you love matchmaking, then by all means, continue to do it for as long as you like. And as to society and its rigid and *stupid* ideals of what is proper, to hell with it. I want *you*. I don't care if people laugh. I don't care if people shun us." He shook her gently. "Don't you see?"

She stared up at him, completely breathless. "I can't play the pianoforte. I can't sing or draw, and I don't know the first thing about being an excellent hostess—"

"I know. I don't care."

"I am nobody. I have no lineage. That's so important to you—"

"No. That's important to my uncle and to society. I don't give a damn about it. You are the woman I want. That trumps everything."

"But you said—"

"No. What I said at the beginning—all my rules— they no longer apply. They never did. I only *thought* they did. I was wrong."

Hope began to bloom in her chest, fortifying the stitches that made her heart whole, thickening them and then hardening them, turning them into bands of iron.

Reaching up, she cupped his jaw in her hand. It was warm, hard, the hint of afternoon bristles pressing into her palm.

"Are you sure?"

"I am."

"I want you to be happy. I don't want you to regret this."

"Never," he vowed.

"I never want you to feel I'm not good enough, that I don't deserve you."

"The only person who isn't good enough is staring down at you."

She frowned. "If you say that again, I shall have to don my armor, heft my sword, and duel for your honor."

A hint of a smile curved his lips. "Then perhaps we are both good enough. Perhaps we do deserve each other."

"Perhaps we deserve to be happy," she said, hope now reaching into every part of her, "together."

"Yes."

"Do you think we can be?" she asked.

"I *know* we will be."

For the first time since he'd entered her office, she allowed herself to smile. It spread across her face, flowed into her eyes, and melted the tension in her body, suffusing it with a warm glow. Gazing up at him, she saw her radiance reflected in him.

"Jo," he murmured. "My Jo."

She linked her hands around his neck and pulled his lips down to hers. He slid his arms around her, and his lips touched hers gently, reverently, before he pulled back. He looked down at her. "Will you marry me?"

"Yes."

"Tomorrow?"

She laughed softly. "I don't think that's possible."

He pulled something from his pocket, unfolded it, and handed it to her. Taking it, she looked down at the paper. It was a special license for them to marry, signed by the Archbishop of Canterbury himself.

"It is possible. I visited the archbishop's office yesterday. We can marry anytime we like."

She grinned at him, because she wanted to marry as quickly as possible as well. "Tomorrow, then."

She pulled him back to her, and this time she kissed him hard, trying to tell him with her lips how much she loved him. He answered her with his own declaration, not in words but in actions. The way he yanked her against him until she was wrapped up in his arms, the way his kiss demanded of her, his tongue claiming her mouth with an erotic thrust.

I love you. Her fingers tangled in the soft hairs at his nape.

I love you. She touched her tongue to his.

I love you. She pressed her body against the hardening ridge against her stomach.

He sucked in a breath, then pulled back again. "I want you, Jo. But if you'd like to wait until after the wedding…"

"No," she breathed, "I don't want to wait. I want you now. Please."

He groaned, then turned her and walked her backward until her back pressed against the wall. Then, his lips collided with hers as he hiked up her skirts in great handfuls. His fingertips brushed over one of her garters, then moved between her legs. She thrust wantonly against him as his fingers dipped into her wet heat.

She gasped, "Matthew!" as he slid over her hot flesh, brushing the part of her that was so sensitive she flexed her hips, wanting more.

He gave her more, one hand passing over her bodice then rubbing hard over her breast so she could feel her nipple straining beneath the layers of fabric. His other fingers slipped over her, then he pushed inside her and moved against that secret spot that made her moan and writhe. He knew her body so well already. The pressure built within her, and he pressed and rubbed her slick flesh, kissing her on her lips and throat and down the edge of her bodice, pinching her breasts, touching that spot again and again.

"Matthew, I'm going to…"

"Yes, Jo, come. Come, my love."

Love. The word made her explode, her world fragmenting into thousands of shards of bliss, and the hand that was at her breast slipped around her bottom, supporting her as spasms of pleasure wracked her body, and his lips closed over hers, muffling the sounds of her cries.

As the waves subsided, his hands slipped away, and she murmured a complaint, vaguely registering that he was working the buttons on his falls. A moment later, he was lifting her.

"Wrap your legs around me, love," he said, and when she did, he positioned himself at her entry and, without hesitation, thrust inside her to the hilt. She cried out at the instant, overwhelming sensation.

He held her there, both of them panting, and pressed his forehead to hers. "Sweet Jo," he murmured gruffly. "Sweet, beautiful Jo."

She pulled him down into another kiss. "You feel so good inside me," she whispered in wonder against his lips.

He gazed at her. "This, right here, is the closest to heaven I've ever come. There's nothing like the feel of you all around me like this." He kissed her again and rasped out, "Nothing."

He started moving, his hands under her thighs, her dress crushed between them, her back pressed against the wall, his thickness stroking against her inner walls again and again, his lips fused to hers. His citrus and bergamot essence surrounded her. His body supported her, his movements quickly taking her once again to the brink of ecstasy.

This beautiful, proud man wanted her. He wanted to *marry* her. He wanted her to be his as much as she wanted him to be hers.

He moved his hand to grip one of her wrists and

guided it through the crushed fabric between them until her hand was at her center.

"Touch yourself," he said.

Her finger brushed over that spot that made her wild. It was more sensitive than ever, and just grazing it made her whole body jerk.

"There," he murmured. "I want to feel you bringing yourself pleasure, Jo. Show me."

He replaced his hand under her thigh to support her, then thrust inside her, deep, pushing her fingertips against her own body. She let out a needy whimper, and he groaned.

"Yes," he gritted out. "Just like that."

He began a rhythm of hard thrusts, pushing her against the wall, rubbing her fingers against her core, driving into her so thoroughly she could feel him everywhere. His breaths came in gusty whooshes of air that seemed as if they were being wrenched out of him.

"Jo," he said over her lips, around her body, inside her. They were together, one, safe and whole in a cocoon of love. Jo's newly patched heart, her mind, her body filled to bursting with it. Every one of her muscles thrummed with pleasure as her fingers trembled over her center.

She opened her eyes and watched her fiancé as he drove into her again and again, his eyes squeezed shut, his jaw tense, a sheen of sweat shimmering on his forehead, the cords of his neck standing out in stark relief. He was beautiful. He was *hers*.

She shattered into a million shards of bright light, her body sparking and glowing and thrashing and completely outside her control. But she did nothing to control it, knowing she was safe in Matthew's arms.

She cried out her joy and pleasure as she came apart, and then she felt him follow, his whole body turning into steel against hers as he grew impossibly big within her and then, with a hoarse gasp, pushed deep, deeper than she'd thought possible. It felt so exquisite, it sent her own body into renewed spasms as he jerked out his release. This time, he came inside her. This time, they were joined.

CHAPTER THIRTY-FOUR

Three hours later, Jo sat in the parlor twisting her hands in her lap as Mrs. Ferguson went to answer the door. Jo knew who it was, but Lilly, Bess, Mama, and Mrs. Ferguson had no idea. Though Jo had been bursting to tell them, and though it had taken a herculean effort not to spill everything, she'd somehow managed to hold her tongue.

A moment later Mrs. Ferguson returned, pale-faced, her eyes darting from Jo to Mama. "The Duke of Crestmont inquires if Mrs. Porter is at home."

Mama glanced at Jo in alarm. "Why?"

Jo couldn't restrain her feelings from her mother this time. She pulled in a shaky breath, tears sprang to her eyes, and she managed a watery smile. One glance at her made Mama's back go straight.

"Send him up," she told Mrs. Ferguson tightly.

Bess jumped out of her chair. "I'll make some tea."

When the Fergusons had left, Lilly demanded, "Jo, what is going on? Why is he here?"

"I am surmising that he is here, given we are lacking in male relatives, to ask me for permission to court Jo," Mama said.

Jo broke out in a clammy sweat, suddenly feeling like a young girl again. "Mmm," she managed. "I think it might be something like that."

Mama arched a brow. "You may be smitten, Jo, but understand, I shall be hesitant to accept, given how he has treated you. I shan't allow someone in my home who will throw around their power to harm anyone that I love in any way, form, or fashion."

There it was again—her mama bear coming out to play. The fact that Matthew was a duke of the realm mattered not—Matthew would have to be at the top of his game to spar with Jo's mother when she was in this state.

"He promised not to break my heart again," she told Mama, hoping to give him a fighting chance.

Mama sniffed. "We'll see about that."

They were all standing when, seconds later, the door opened, and there he was, in his finely tailored dark tailcoat and light trousers, his black shoes polished to a high shine.

"The Duke of Crestmont," Mrs. Ferguson announced.

Holding his hat to his chest, he stepped inside the parlor, and Mrs. Ferguson stepped out, closing the four of them in.

Matthew bowed. "Miss Porter, Miss Appleby." He turned to Mama.

"Your Grace." Jo moved to stand beside him. "I'd like to introduce you to my mother, Mrs. Jane Porter. Mama, this is the Duke of Crestmont."

Matthew bowed again. "Mrs. Porter."

Lilly scowled at Matthew from behind slitted eyes. "So, Your Grace, is it true? Have you come to your senses at last?"

"Lilly!" Jo exclaimed. It wasn't like her to be so flagrantly rude.

Lilly ignored her. "Well, have you?"

"Yes, Miss Appleby," Matthew said. "I *have* come to my senses. Thanks, in no small part, to you and Miss Ferguson."

"Wait," Jo said, turning to him. "What do you mean? What did Lilly and Bess do?"

Lilly waved her hand. "Never mind that."

It was Matthew's turn to ignore Lilly. He smiled at Jo. "They paid me a visit at the Earl of Winthrop's seat in Hertfordshire."

"*What*?" Jo and her mother gasped in unison.

"Last Tuesday. They came to tell me—well, Miss Lilly told me specifically—of the errors of my assumption regarding my previous interactions with you, Miss Porter, and laid out in no uncertain terms how I had so grievously wronged you."

Jo turned on Lilly, aghast. "You told us you and Bess were going to spend the day with Martha Cherrington and her antiquities last Tuesday."

"I lied." Lilly shrugged. "And," she added proudly, "Martha would have corroborated the story, had you bothered to ask her."

Jo threw up her hands. "Of course I didn't ask her! I trusted you!"

"How on earth did you get out there and back home in one day?" Mama demanded.

"We took a stagecoach there. For the return trip, Lord Winthrop very kindly lent us the use of his carriage."

"Oh, for heaven's sake." Mama pressed her palm to her forehead.

Despite Lilly's rudeness and deception, gratitude surged within Jo. Right now, she felt surrounded by love, buoyed by it. For the first time, she knew without a doubt that the people she loved cared for her as thoroughly and deeply as she cared for them. It was a heady knowledge.

Matthew turned to Mama. "If I might have a word in private, Mrs. Porter?"

"Of course, Your Grace," Mama said. "Girls, send Bess in with the tea. I will call for you when we are finished."

As she passed by Matthew, Jo let her fingers skim the fabric of his trousers. At the door, she smiled at him, letting all her feelings for him glow in her eyes. He smiled back, and Mama looked over her shoulder. "Go on, dear."

"Yes, Mama." She stepped out, closing the door softly behind her, then sagging against it a little before Lilly grasped her arm and pulled her downstairs.

As soon as they were in the kitchen, where Mrs. Ferguson and Bess waited for them, Lilly clasped her hands together in excitement. "I think he wants more than just to court you. I think you're going to be a duchess!"

Jo blinked. Lilly was right. She would be a *duchess*. It felt completely unreal. Becoming an actual duchess had been the furthest thing from her mind, and now that she considered it, the prospect was nearly overwhelming. The expectations on her would be immense. Still, with all the support she knew she had, she felt equal to the task.

"Oh, Jo," Lilly said, throwing her arms around Jo, "I think he might *propose*!"

"He already has, Lilly." Closing her eyes, she squeezed her friend tight. "He already has."

• • •

A month later, after witnessing the Pellegrini nuptials and celebrating with the newlyweds in a lovely, intimate gathering, Jo sat in her office awaiting the newest client referred to her by Sir Harry and Lady Acheson.

It had been a whirlwind few weeks. After over an hour's worth of discussion with Matthew, during which Jo, Lilly, Bess, and Mrs. Ferguson sat in the kitchen wringing their hands nervously, Mama had finally given her blessing, but only after making Jo and Matthew promise to wait a week before being married.

They had been married in St. George's Hanover Square on a serene August morning. Matthew's three close friends had been there, along with Jo's mother, Lilly, and the Fergusons. The chapel had been filled with fresh flowers — not roses, but cornflowers, irises, daisies, and lilies. Wild and colorful, which matched Jo's love for her new husband.

Jo and Matthew had decided to remain in town for a month in order for Jo to attend Mr. Pellegrini's wedding, then wrap up her business — which was, after all, busiest in the spring and summer months. In September, they, along with the rest of Jo's family, would travel to Crestmont Manor in Northumberland, exploring England's autumn glory along the way. Once there, they'd host a house party for all their friends. They'd arrive at Hanford Castle in Nottinghamshire in time for Christmas and reside there for the remainder of the winter holidays. In January, Jo and Matthew would return to London so Matthew could return to his duties in Parliament and Jo could find a respectable office in order to reopen her business in time for the commencement of the Season next year.

They'd been married for three weeks now, and it had been the happiest days of Jo's life. They'd spent every moment possible at each other's sides, most of the time in bed, getting to know each other in all the intimate ways two people could.

Happiness—no, bliss—like Jo had never believed could happen to her. Matthew had told her he felt the same way. It was surprising and new and wonderful, and while Jo knew the novelty of having each other, mind, body, and soul, might someday wear off, she knew their love for each other never would.

There was a knock at the door, and when Jo opened it, a young, familiar-looking man stood there. He doffed his hat. "I'm looking for Mrs. Porter."

She smiled up at him, his height reminding her of Matthew's. "Good afternoon, sir. I am Joanna Porter."

"I should like to see *Mrs*. Porter."

"That is I."

He frowned. "Are…are you certain? I am sorry—it is simply that you don't look old enough—"

She raised her hand, effectively stopping him. "I assure you, I am." And now, she actually was a Mrs., though no one would ever call her that. No, it would always be, "Your Grace." How odd that was, and even after a few weeks of being a duchess, the strangeness of her changed circumstances still churned through her every now and then.

All the important people, the people who knew her, especially Matthew, knew that she was the same Jo she always had been. That would never change. But people who didn't know her—oh, my. Their perceptions of her had changed, indeed. *Dramatically*.

So it was a bit refreshing that this young man didn't know her at all. Didn't know she was a clergyman's daughter who'd recently married a duke of the realm and was now a duchess. He simply knew what Sir Harry had told him—that Mrs. Porter was a matchmaker extraordinaire, that she guaranteed love and happiness between the ladies and gentlemen she helped bring together.

"Oh, well, my apologies," the young man said, looking quite unconvinced.

She smiled at him and gestured him inside. "No apologies are necessary. Please, come inside and have a seat." Closing the door behind him, she sat at her desk across from him. "How may I help you this afternoon?"

He took a deep breath and then let it out. "I would like to be married."

"That's wonderful. I have a great deal of experience in finding excellent matches for—"

He cut her off. "I'm sorry, Mrs. Porter, but I don't think you understand. I already know who I desire to marry. You see, I just require…*assistance* in making my dream a reality."

Jo stared at him.

"Do you understand?"

Jo held up her hand. "I think we forgot a crucial

element." He really did look familiar, but for the life of her, she couldn't place him. "May I know your name?"

"Oh. Right." His Adam's apple bobbed as he swallowed. "Forgive me. My name is Thomas Gifford."

Mr. Gifford—who'd danced with Harriet, called upon her twice, whisked her away at Vauxhall, and then sent her a monstrosity of a bouquet of roses. Mr. Gifford—the object of Harriet Cherrington's affection. No wonder he looked familiar. He and Jo had met briefly at Lady Campbell's ball when he'd asked Harriet to dance, but he only had eyes for Harriet, and Jo only had eyes for Matthew.

"Mr. Gifford," Jo breathed. "You say you already know the young lady to whom you wish to be matched?"

"That's right," he said.

"So...why don't you simply ask if you might court her?"

He swallowed again, then looked away. "I've been given the strong impression that I...well, that I am not good enough for her family. They seem to believe that she should marry someone of great power, influence, and wealth. A duke, perhaps."

Oh, Lord. Jo fought a smile.

"And I am simply a gentleman with a moderate fortune, nothing more. I fear they will reject me on that basis alone."

Perhaps not, thought Jo. "Will you tell me the name of this young lady?" she asked.

He gave a jerky nod. "Of course. Her name is Miss Harriet Cherrington." Then, seeing her lips curve, he added worriedly, "Do you know her?"

"I do," she said gently, and when his eyes widened in alarm, she raised her hand. "Don't worry, Mr. Gifford. I will not betray your confidence."

The fact was, Jo knew something that Thomas Gifford didn't. And it was this: The day after Jo and Matthew had married, Lilly had received an official offer from John Nash. He wanted to use her church designs throughout London where the churches were crowded, and more needed to be built. He wished to remodel some of the London theaters and other public spaces and had asked Lilly for assistance with those.

But the biggest project would entail John Nash's use of her whimsical palace design. It turned out that he was redesigning the prince regent's estate in Brighton to something that would represent the modern aesthetic and royal grandeur of the man who would someday be king. He thought that Lilly's design would be perfect. She would be working closely with Mr. Nash and the regent, and as they wanted to use her conceptual idea of the space and employ her in helping to finalize the plans, she had already received a large sum in advance.

Enough to ensure that not only could she marry Charles Cherrington, but she could provide a handsome dowry for each of his sisters, as well.

Which left Harriet—and all the Cherrington sisters, for that matter—free to marry whomever they chose. It seemed Mr. Gifford, who was clearly in love with Harriet, and who was a gentleman who would be able to support her in his own right, would make an excellent choice.

"Listen," she said now, "you needn't hire me for this."

"But—"

"I understand your concern, but trust me when I say that while it might have once been the case that Miss Cherrington needed to marry into a title and position, that is no longer true. She is free to marry the man of her choice. And that man...well, it might just be *you*."

He blinked at her. "Truly?"

"Yes. Truly."

He glanced at the door then back to her, his brows twisted with worry but his eyes alight with hope. "Are you certain, Mrs. Porter?"

"Quite certain. In fact, it is the visiting hour. Might I suggest you go to her straightaway?" She rose, and gentleman that Mr. Gifford was, he popped up off her green chair.

She went to the door and opened it. "I'd wish you luck, but something is telling me you don't truly need it."

He swallowed yet again, and his brows flattened into an expression that looked something like determination. "Thank you, Mrs. Porter. Thank you *so* much."

"There is nothing to thank me for. Nothing at all. Good day, Mr. Gifford."

"Good day, Mrs. Porter." He pressed his hat onto his head, bowed, and practically pranced out of her office.

She closed the door and leaned against it, a huge smile stretching her lips as the door to the kitchen opened, revealing her gorgeous husband in all his tailored glory.

In two strides, he was gathering her against him and holding her close. "I believe that man is going to have an *excellent* afternoon."

She laughed. "Were you listening at the kitchen door?"

He gave her a wicked smile. "Of course I was. And I'm glad for it."

"You're terrible," she said.

"Not at all. Just doing what you gave me permission to do."

"You know, in all the years I've worked here, never once did any of the women I lived with eavesdrop at that door. You're worse than a gossipmonger."

"Ah, well, so be it. I'm a meddlesome biddy." He shrugged with no shame at all. "But I'm happy for him. I'd wager he and Miss Cherrington will be engaged within the week."

"Probably," she agreed.

"Good for them."

"You're not jealous?"

He laughed, a sound she'd been hearing with more frequency as the days progressed. She loved it. "Not at all. Why would I be jealous when I'm holding my heart in my arms this very second?"

The look he gave her was filled with heat, but it was also brimming with admiration and respect. "I love you," he said. "Have I mentioned that recently?"

"Yes. About a dozen times today."

"Then I must work on catching up. I'm aiming for at least fifty by midnight. I love you." He kissed the top of her head. "I love you." He kissed her forehead. "I love you." He kissed the tip of her nose, then paused, brushing his thumb over her lips. "I love you, sweet Jo."

Jo kissed him. Wrapped up within her arms, radiating his own gentle sweetness, heat, and above all, love, Jo knew that against all odds, she'd found it.

Her happily ever after.

EPILOGUE

ONE YEAR LATER

Matthew kissed his three-month-old daughter on her tiny, silky-soft cheek. She seemed to smile in her sleep, cuddling deeper into her swaddle. Matthew tilted his head at Mrs. Ferguson, who nodded from her position knitting in a nearby rocking chair. She would watch Evie this afternoon.

Matthew was taking his wife out.

He was thrilled they'd had a healthy girl, though Jo at first had been worried he'd be disappointed she hadn't given him a son. In fact, he was besotted with his daughter. He only wished that the laws of primogeniture would allow little Evie—named after his mother, Evaline—to be his heir, for he often thought that women might make more thoughtful and fair peers of the realm than men.

But she couldn't be his heir, which meant that he and Jo would have more children. Well, they'd have more children regardless of whether their first had been a son. Matthew used to be terrified of the idea of a brood of children, but he'd happily have a dozen with Jo. Nothing gave him greater pleasure than feeling the completeness of having a real family. He loved watching his tiny little girl grow every day. Evie was beautiful like her mother, with gray eyes and a dusting of blond hair, and she was precious—a symbol of the love shared between her parents.

Leaving the nursery, he descended the stairs to the ground floor, where Jo's new office stood tucked between a confectionery and a milliner's shop. He'd bought this building for her over the winter—for not only was it perfectly situated in Mayfair, but it was near their townhouse, and it had a large upstairs room that they'd remodeled into a nursery for Evie. He opened the door. "Ready, love?"

"Almost." Jo was writing a letter to a new client. Her business had flourished here. She'd had an easier time fitting into London society than either of them would have guessed, thanks mainly to an ancestral connection to the Earls of Winchelsea and Nottingham—of which she'd informed him only *after* their wedding—and the *beau monde* had bestowed upon her a new moniker: "The Mayfair Matchmaker."

Matthew thought that was excellent, especially since it negated all that "Mrs./Miss" nonsense he'd had to contend with when he'd first met her.

He wandered inside, hesitating beside that old green armchair that she'd insisted upon bringing from her old office.

"Have a seat," she murmured, not looking up at him. "Just another minute."

"In this?" he asked drily. "Surely, you jest."

She looked up, her eyes sparkling. "I still contend that something is quite the matter with you. That is *the most* comfortable chair in London."

"You meant to say *the least*, I am sure."

"Honestly." She rolled her eyes. "Very well. Stand, then."

"I will. I promise you, I shall feel far more

comfortable standing."

She huffed out a breath, wrote a few more words, then capped her quill, waving her hand over the paper in a rather insubstantial attempt to dry the ink. "There. I am finished. Is the carriage ready?"

"It is."

She tied on her bonnet, and he helped her into the carriage. As Ted drove them toward the Thames, they passed the time talking about Evie's latest accomplishments, how she could hold her head up now and how she was starting to press her body upward while lying on her stomach. The conversation moved to Charles and Lilly's announcement that they were expecting a baby of their own and how Lilly's ambitious architectural design was coming to fruition—ground had been broken and the reconstruction of the Royal Pavilion at Brighton had begun.

"And I received a letter from Mama today," Jo said. Jo's mother was living full-time at Hanford Castle, close to all her old friends in Nottinghamshire.

Matthew had worried that Jo's family would find Hanford Castle drafty, musty, and miserable, and although he missed the old pile, he had no desire to leave his wife alone—ever—so he had offered to remain with them at the manor until it was time to return to London. But they'd insisted on accompanying him to Nottinghamshire.

It wasn't too much of a surprise that Jo had absolutely adored everything about the castle, drafts and all. Sweeping her fingers reverently over the stone walls, she had gushed about the turrets and towers, the long-since filled-in moat, the dungeon that had been repurposed to be a pantry, the Tudor portraits, and the antique bed where King Richard I and a half dozen other kings had once slept.

What had surprised him, though, was how much his mother-in-law and Bess had loved the place. And when he and Jo had been ready to return to London this past January, the two of them had asked to stay.

Jo and Matthew then chatted about Jo's new client, the forthcoming parliamentary election, and Jo gave an update on the Cherrington sisters.

Three of the five sisters had married this year. Mary and Reverend Robinson had wedded in January, and they had dived into their calling of providing care and education to the orphans of London. Martha had married Mr. de Havilland, the antiquarian, who was twice her age but nobody cared because they were so devoted to each other, and they were planning an excavation in Egypt next year. Of course, Harriet was happily married to Mr. Gifford. Frances was in her third Season and had just received her first marriage proposal. And the youngest, Esther, was enjoying her first Season and the handful of proposals she'd received and subsequently rejected.

In the end, despite all that had happened last year, the Cherringtons were thriving.

As Matthew and Jo pulled up to the boathouse, the conversation had turned, as it inevitably always did, to the weather. Matthew and his wife—whose fascination with meteorology now matched his— were so deep in discussion about how the temperatures promised to be moderate for the next week, with only a slight chance of showers on

Wednesday, that they failed for a moment to realize the carriage had stopped.

Finally, they looked up with a laugh, and Matthew went around to help Jo out of the carriage. She'd been to the boathouse before, of course, and had watched various regattas as well as several races between him and his friends in both the single and double boats. Matthew no longer always came in last place. He actually won sometimes, especially when Jo was watching.

The fastest boat, though, as Matthew had predicted, was the fours boat he and Jameson had built last year: *Matchmaker*. When Matthew, Jameson, Cole, and Winthrop were together in that boat, it was a magnificent, exhilarating thing. They felt like they were sliding above the water. Like they were flying.

Jo hadn't ever gone out on one of the boats, however. Matthew had felt intensely protective of her when she was with child. He'd worried about everything, even as she brushed it off, saying she was fine and ordering him not to hover like an anxious mama.

Needless to say, though, rowing had been out of the question.

He lifted *Red* and carried it out to the dock, adjusted the oars in their oarlocks, then helped Jo into the front seat. "Be careful. It's not as stable as a Thames wherry."

She rocked and wobbled, laughing as she nearly overturned the thing. "How on earth do you keep from tipping over?" she gasped, gripping the edges of the hull.

"Skill," he told her with a grin, deftly climbing onto the seat behind her. She didn't look back at him, no doubt fearing capsizing if she moved a muscle. He gently pushed them off the wooden ledge of the dock, and they were suddenly caught in the slow current of the Thames.

He placed his sculls to properly balance the boat, then leaned forward and put his arms over hers. "Now, take your oars in hand." She did, and he guided her through the proper motion. "You have to submerge the scull just so. Too deep and it will get caught in turbulence. Too shallow, and your drag won't have any effect. And you need to be sure to submerge them equally, or your boat will spin round in circles."

"It sounds complicated."

"It's not, really, because you can feel the water on the scull, so it's easy to tell if you've done it wrong." Matthew guided her through it a few times, then he deliberately moved her through some bad pulls to show her what they felt like. Finally, he sat back. "All right. Now try it on your own."

He placed his own sculls, ready to balance the boat if she did anything that might unbalance them. She didn't, though. She dug the sculls in just below the surface and pulled.

"Perfect," he told her, his voice laced with pride.

She did it again, and again. They rowed a few miles down the Thames, away from the city of London against the current, then back up again. When they finally returned to the dock, he helped her get out.

"Oh, Matthew!" she exclaimed, practically

dancing on the dock, her cheeks flushed a rosy pink, her smile wide. "That was wonderful. I *knew* I'd like it. Now I understand why you love it so much."

With a smile pasted on his face he truly thought might never disappear, he dragged the boat inside and lifted it onto its shelf, then she helped him put away the oars. When they finished, he took hold of her hand and spun her around, gathering her in his arms and grinning down at her.

"You were a natural out there," he told her.

"Really? I felt so awkward at first, but then—"

"You were perfect."

"Do you think if I practiced as much as you did, I might win races?"

"I think you could be the fastest female rower in England." He truly did think that, and not only because there weren't very many women in England who enjoyed rowing. She had taken to it like a fish to water, far better than he, Winthrop, Jameson, and Cole had when they were boys, flipping their boats over so many times that for a few years, they swam better than they rowed.

She bit her lip and looked up at him. "You know, I think I might like to try."

That's my girl. A year ago, he'd been looking for a duchess and had created a list of criteria that was, in every way, the opposite of his sweet Jo. She was none of the things he'd thought she'd be, but Joanna Leighton, the Duchess of Crestmont, his wife and mother of his child, was perfect for him in every way.

Holding her close, he kissed her, nudging his hardness against her body and flicking open the buttons of her bodice. When she was gasping with need, he brought her down onto the clean sawdust.

There, on the floor of the boathouse he'd built with his own hands, he made love to his perfect duchess.

Shakespeare meets Bridgerton *in this witty and lively marriage-of-in*convenience *romance.*

MUCH
ADO
ABOUT
DUKES

USA TODAY BESTSELLING AUTHOR
EVA DEVON

As far as William Easton—the Duke of Blackheath—is concerned, love can go to the devil. Why would a man need passion when he has wealth, a stately home, and work to occupy his mind? But no one warned him that a fiery and frustratingly strong-willed activist like Lady Beatrice Haven could find a way to get under his skin...and that he might enjoy it.

Lady Beatrice is determined to never marry. Ever. She would much rather fight for the rights of women and provoke the darkly handsome Duke of Blackheath, even if he does claim to be forward-thinking. After all, dukes—even gorgeous ones—are the enemy. So why does she feel such enjoyment from their heated exchanges?

But everything changes when Beatrice finds herself suddenly without fortune, a husband, or even a home. Now her future depends on the very man who sets her blood boiling. Because in order to protect his esteemed rival, the Duke of Blackheath has asked for Beatrice's hand, inviting his once-enemy into his home...*and* his bed.

A chance encounter leads to a game of desire in this irresistible romance from USA Today *bestseller Stacy Reid.*

A Matter of Temptation

Miss Wilhelmina "Mina" Crawford is desperate. Having been ruined in the eyes of society years ago for one foolish, starry-eyed mistake, she spends her days secreted away at her family's crumbling estate, helping her brother manage the land but not able to truly live life the way she's always dreamed. When her brother admits to just how dire their finances have gotten, she takes it upon herself to procure employment...but the only one who will even consider the scandalous idea of a female secretary is the brilliant, ruthless, and infuriating Earl of Creswick.

Simon Loughton, the Earl of Creswick, needs help if he wants to finally pass the reform bill he's been championing for years and secure the vote for England's most vulnerable constituents. Too bad help comes in the form of a woman with breathtaking nerve, fiery red hair, and a sense of humor to match.

Now temptation—disguised as a lovely, clever-mouthed devil—lives and works under Simon's very roof. And Mina finally feels as though she's truly living life to her wildest dreams. But even the most incendiary of kisses can't incinerate Mina's past...or the shocking secret that could ruin them both.

Beauty and the Beast *meets* Taming of the Shrew *in this laugh-out-loud Regency romance that* New York Times *bestselling author Sarah MacLean calls "smart and sexy."*

The
Beast
of
Beswick

Amalie Howard

Lord Nathaniel Harte, the disagreeable Duke of Beswick, spends his days smashing porcelain, antagonizing his servants, and snarling at anyone who gets too close. With a ruined face like his, it's hard to like much about the world. *Especially* smart-mouthed harpies—with lips better suited to kissing than speaking—who brave his castle with indecent proposals.

But Lady Astrid Everleigh will stop at nothing to see her younger sister safe from a notorious scoundrel, even if it means offering herself up on a silver platter to the forbidding Beast of Beswick himself. And by offer, she means what no highborn lady of sound and sensible mind would ever dream of—a tender of marriage with *her* as his bride.

AMARA
an imprint of Entangled Publishing LLC